Andrew Lang's Fairy Book Collection

The Blue Fairy Book

The Red Fairy Book

The Blue Poetry Book

The Green Fairy Book

The True Story Book

The Yellow Fairy Book

The Red True Story Book

The Animal Story Book

The Pink Fairy Book

The Arabian Nights' Entertainments

The Red Book of Animal Stories

The Grey Fairy Book

The Violet Fairy Book

The Book of Romance

The Crimson Fairy Book

The Brown Fairy Book

The Red Romance Book

The Orange Fairy Book

The Olive Fairy Book

The Book of Princes and Princesses

The Red Book of Heroes

The Lilac Fairy Book

The All Sorts of Stories Book

The Book of Saints and Heroes

The Strange Story Book

The Red Romance Book

This work is based on The Red Romance Book, by Andrew Lang, which is in the public domain.
No claim of copyright is being made to any aspect of that work.
This work has changed the public domain work by doing the following:

• editing and reformatting the original text •
• deleting unnecessary text, illustrations, footnotes, and captions •
• creating a modern book cover and layout design •

Parts of this book are protected under the copyright laws of the United States of America.
Public domain material within this book may be duplicated and reproduced
for personal use without written permission of the publisher.
Any reproduction or other unauthorized use of the material or artwork herein is prohibited
without the express written permission of the publisher.

Published by Hogue Press
© Johnnie Hogue

First Printing: May 2017
Printed in the United States of America

First Edition: May 2017

ISBN: 978-1-54655-348-9

The Red Romance Book

EDITED BY
ANDREW LANG

✝✝✝✝✝✝✝✝✝✝✝✝✝✝✝✝✝✝✝✝✝✝✝✝✝✝✝✝✝✝✝✝✝✝✝✝✝✝✝

HOGUE PRESS

CONTENTS

HOW WILLIAM OF PALERMO WAS CARRIED OFF BY THE WEREWOLF 1
THE DISENCHANTMENT OF THE WERWOLF 4
THE SLAYING OF HALLGERDA'S HUSBANDS 9
THE DEATH OF GUNNAR 14
NJAL'S BURNING 23
THE LADY OF SOLACE 27
UNA AND THE LION 30
HOW THE RED CROSS KNIGHT SLEW THE DRAGON 34
AMYS AND AMYLE 40
THE TALE OF THE CID 45
THE KNIGHT OF THE SORROWFUL COUNTENANCE 53
THE ADVENTURE OF THE TWO ARMIES WHO TURNED OUT TO BE FLOCKS OF SHEEP 57
THE ADVENTURE OF THE BOBBING LIGHTS 61
THE HELMET OF MAMBRINO 63
HOW DON QUIXOTE WAS ENCHANTED WHILE GUARDING THE CASTLE 66
DON QUIXOTE'S HOME-COMING 68
THE MEETING OF HUON AND OBERON, KING OF THE FAIRIES 70
HOW OBERON SAVED HUON 72
HAVELOK AND GOLDBOROUGH 77
CUPID AND PSYCHE 83
SIR BEVIS THE STRONG 89
OGIER THE DANE 95
HOW THE ASS BECAME A MAN AGAIN 99
GUY OF WARWICK 104
HOW BRADAMANTE CONQUERED THE WIZARD 108
THE RING OF BRADAMANTE 112
THE FULFILLING OF THE PROPHECY 114
THE KNIGHT OF THE SUN 118
HOW THE KNIGHT OF THE SUN RESCUED HIS FATHER 122

HOW WILLIAM OF PALERMO WAS CARRIED OFF BY THE WEREWOLF

Many hundreds of years ago there lived in the beautiful city of Palermo a little prince who was thought, not only by his parents but by everyone who saw him, to be the handsomest child in the whole world. When he was four years old, his mother, the queen, made up her mind that it was time to take him away from his nurses, so she chose out two ladies of the court who had been friends of her own youth, and to them she entrusted her little son. He was to be taught to read and write, and to talk Greek, the language of his mother's country, and Latin, which all princes ought to know, while the Great Chamberlain would see that he learned to ride and shoot, and, when he grew bigger, how to wield a sword.

For a while everything went on as well as the king and queen could wish. Prince William was quick, and, besides, he could not bear to be beaten in anything he tried to do, whether it was making out the sense of a roll of parchment written in strange black letters, which was his reading-book, or mastering a pony which wanted to kick him off. And the people of Palermo looked on, and whispered to each other:

'Ah! what a king he will make!'

But soon a terrible end came to all these hopes!

William's father, king Embrons, had a brother who would have been the heir to the throne but for the little prince. He was a wicked man, and hated his nephew, but when the boy was born he was away at the wars, and did not return till five years later. Then he lost no time in making friends with the two ladies who took care of William, and slowly managed to gain their confidence. By-and-by he worked upon them with his promises and gifts, till they became as wicked as he was, and even agreed to kill not only the child, but the king his father.

Now adjoining the palace at Palermo was a large park, planted with flowering trees and filled with wild beasts. The royal family loved to roam about the park, and often held jousts and sports on the green grass, while William played with his dogs or picked flowers.

One day—it was a festival—the whole court went into the park at noon, after they had finished dining, and the queen and her ladies busied themselves with embroidering a quilt for the royal bed, while the king and his courtiers shot at a mark. Suddenly there leapt from a bush a huge grey wolf with his mouth open and his tongue hanging out. Before anyone had time to recover from his surprise, the great beast had caught up the child, and was bounding with him through the park, and over the wall into the plain by the sea. When the courtiers had regained their senses, both the wolf and boy were out of sight.

Oh! what weeping and wailing burst forth from the king and queen when they understood that their little son was gone from them for ever, only, as they supposed, to die a cruel death! For of course they did not know that one far worse had awaited him at home.

After the first shock, William did not very much mind what was happening to him. The wolf jerked him on to his back, and told him to hold fast by his ears, and the boy sat comfortably among the thick hair, and did not even get his feet wet as they swam across the Straits of Messina. On the other side, not far from Rome, was a forest of tall trees, and as by this time it was getting dark, the wolf placed William on a bed of soft fern, and broke off a branch of delicious fruits, which he gave him for supper. Then he scooped out a deep pit with his paws, and lined it with moss and feathery grasses, and there they both lay down and slept till morning; in spite of missing his mother, in all his life William had never been so happy.

For eight days they stayed in the forest, and it seemed to the boy as if he had never dwelt anywhere else. There was so much to see and to do, and when he was tired of playing the wolf told him stories.

But one morning, before he was properly awake, he felt himself gently shaken by a paw, and he sat up, and looked about him. 'Listen to me,' said the wolf. 'I have to go right over to the other side of the wood, on some business of a friend's, and I shall not be back till sunset. Be careful not to stray out of sight of this pit, for you may easily lose yourself. You will find plenty of fruit and nuts piled up under that cherry tree.'

So the wolf went away, and the child curled himself up for another sleep, and when the sun was high and its beams awakened him, he got up and had his breakfast. While he was eating, birds with blue and green feathers came and hopped on his shoulder and pecked at the fruit he was putting into his mouth, and William made friends with them all, and they suffered him to stroke their heads.

Now there dwelt in the forest an old cowherd, who happened that morning to have work to do not far from the pit where William lived with the wolf. He took with him a big dog, which helped him to collect the cows when they wandered, and to keep off any strange beasts that threatened to attack them. On this particular morning there were no cows, so the dog ran hither and thither as he would, enjoying himself mightily, when suddenly he set up a loud barking, as if he had found a prey, and the noise caused the old man to hasten his steps.

When he reached the spot from which the noise came, the dog was standing at the edge of a pit, out of which came a frightened cry. The old man looked in, and there he saw a child clad in garments that shone like gold, shrinking timidly into the farthest corner.

'Fear nothing, my boy,' said the cowherd; 'he will never hurt you, and even if he wished I would not let him;' and as he spoke he held out his hand. At this William took courage. He was not really a coward, but he felt lonely and it seemed a long time since the wolf had gone away. Would he *really* ever come back? This old man looked kind, and there could be no harm in speaking to him. So he took the outstretched hand and scrambled out of the pit, and the cowherd gathered apples for him, and other fruits that grew on the tops of trees too high for the wolf to reach. And all the day they wandered on and on, till they came to the cowherd's cottage, before which an old woman was standing.

'I have brought you a little boy,' he said, 'whom I found in the forest.'

'Ah, a lucky star was shining when you got up to-day,' answered she. 'And what is your name, my little man? And will you stay and live with me?'

'My name is William, and you look kind like my grandmother, and I will stay with you,' said the boy; and the old people were very glad, and they milked a cow, and gave him warm milk for his supper.

When the wolf returned—he was not a wolf at all, but the son of the king of Spain, who had been enchanted by his stepmother—he was very unhappy at finding the pit empty. Indeed, his first thought was that a lion must have carried off the boy and eaten him, or that an eagle must have pounced on him from the sky, and borne him away to his young ones for supper. But after he had cried till he could cry no more, it occurred to him that before he gave up the boy for dead it would be well to make a search, as perchance there might be some sign of his whereabouts. So he dried his eyes with his tail and jumped up quite cheerfully.

He began by looking to see if the bushes round about were broken and torn as if some great beast had crashed through them. But they were all just as he had left them in the morning, with the creepers still knotting tree to tree. No, it was clear that no lion had been near the spot. Then he examined the ground carefully for a bird's feather or a shred of a child's dress; he did not find these either, but the marks of a man's foot were quite plain, and these he followed.

The track turned and twisted for about two miles, and then stopped at a little cottage with roses climbing up the walls. The wolf did not want to show himself, so he crept quietly round to the back, where there was a hole in the door just big enough for the cats to come in and out of. The wolf peeped through this hole and saw William eating his supper, and chattering away to the old woman as if he had known her all his life, for he was a friendly little boy, and purred like a pussy-cat when he was pleased. And when the wolf saw that all was well with the child, he was glad and went his way.

'William will be safer with them than with me,' he said to himself.

Many years went by, and William had grown a big boy, and was very useful to the cowherd and his wife. He could shoot now with his bow and arrow in a manner which would have pleased his first teacher, and he and his playfellows—the sons of charcoal-burners and woodmen—were wont to keep the pots supplied at home with the game they found in the forest. Besides this, he filled the pails full of water from the stream, and chopped wood for the fire, and, sometimes, was even trusted to cook the dinner. And when *this* happened William was a very proud boy indeed.

One day the emperor planned a great hunt to take place in the forest, and, while following a wild boar, he outstripped all his courtiers and lost his way. Turning first down one path and then the other, he came upon a boy gathering fruit, and so beautiful was he that the emperor thought that he must be of a fairy race.

'What is your name, my child?' asked the emperor; 'and where do you live?'

The boy looked round at the sound of his voice, and, taking off his cap, bowed low.

'I am called William, noble sir,' he answered, 'and I live with a cowherd, my father, in a cottage near by. Other kindred have I none that ever I heard of;' for the gardens of Palermo and the life of the palace had now faded into dreams in the memory of the child.

'Bid your father come hither and speak to me,' said the emperor, but William did not move.

'I fear lest harm should befall him through me,' he answered, 'and that shall never be.' But the emperor smiled as he heard him.

'Not harm, but good,' he said; and William took courage and hastened down the path to the cottage.

'I am the emperor,' said the stranger, when the boy and the cowherd returned together. 'Tell me truly, is this your son?'

Then the cowherd, trembling all over, told the whole story, and when he had finished the emperor said quietly:

'You have done well, but from to-day the boy shall be mine, and shall grow up with my daughter.'

The heart of the cowherd sank as he thought how sorely he and his wife would miss William, but he kept silence. Not so William, who broke into sobs and wails.

'I should have fared ill if this good man and his wife had not taken me and nourished me. I know not whence I came or whither I shall go! None can be so kind as they have been.'

'Cease weeping, fair child,' said the emperor, 'some day you shall be able to reward the good that they have done you;' and then the cowherd spoke and gave him wise counsel how to behave himself at court.

'Be no teller of tales, and let your words be few. Be true to your lord, and fair of speech to all men; and seek to help the poor when you may.'

'Set him on my horse,' said the emperor, and, though William wept still as he bade farewell to the cowherd, and sent a sorrowful greeting to his wife and to his playfellows Hugonet, and Abelot, and Akarin, yet he was pleased to be riding in such royal fashion, and soon dried his tears.

They reached the palace at last, and the emperor led William into the hall, and sent a messenger for Melior, his daughter.

'I have brought home a present for you,' he cried, as she entered; 'and be sure to treat him as you would your brother, for he has come of goodly kindred, though now he does not know where he was born, or who was his father.' And with that he told her the tale of how he had found the boy in the wood.

'I shall care for him willingly,' answered Melior, and she took him away, and saw that supper was set before him, and clothes provided for him, and made him ready for his duties as page to the emperor.

So the boy and girl grew up together, and everyone loved William, who was gentle and pleasant to all, and was skilled in what a gentleman should know. Wise he was too, beyond his years, and the emperor kept him ever at his side, and took counsel with him on many subjects touching his honour and the welfare of his people.

And if the people loved him, how much more Melior, who saw him about the court all day long, and knew the store her father set on him? Yet she remembered with sadness certain whispers she had heard of a match between herself and a foreign prince, and if her father had promised her hand nought would make him break his word.

So she sighed and bewailed herself in secret, till her cousin Alexandrine marked that something was amiss.

'Tell me all your sickness,' said Alexandrine one day, 'and what grieves you so sorely. You know that you can trust me, for I have served you truly, and perhaps I may be able to help you in this strait!'

Then Melior told her, and Alexandrine listened in amaze. From his childhood William and the two girls had played together, and well Alexandrine knew that the emperor had cast his eyes upon another son-in-law. Still, she loved her cousin, and she loved William too, so she said.

'Mourn no longer, madam; I am skilled in magic, and can heal you. So weep no more.' And Melior took heart and was comforted.

That night Alexandrine caused William to dream a dream in which the whole world vanished away, and only he and Melior were left. In a moment he felt that as long as she was there the rest might go, and that she was the princess that was waiting for every prince. But who was he that he should dare to ask for the emperor's daughter? and what chance had he amongst the noble suitors who now began to throng the palace? These thoughts made him very sad, and he went about his duties with a face as long as Melior's was now.

Alexandrine paid no heed to his gloomy looks. She was very wise, and for some days left her magic to work. At last one morning she thought the time had come to heal the wounds she had caused, and planned a meeting between them. After this they had no more need of her, neither did Melior weep any longer.

For a while they were content, and asked nothing more than to see each other every day, as they had always done. But soon a fresh source of grief came. A war broke out, in which William, now a knight, had to follow the emperor, and more than once saved the life of his master. On their return, when the enemy was put to flight, the expected ambassadors from Greece arrived at court, to seek the hand of Melior, which was readily granted by her father. This news made William sick almost unto death, and Melior, who was resolved not to marry the stranger, hastened to Alexandrine in order to implore her help.

But Alexandrine only shook her head.

'It is true,' said she, 'that, unless you manage to escape, you will be forced to wed the prince; but how are you to get away when there are guards before every door of the palace, except by the little gate, and to reach that you will have first to pass by the sentries, who know you?'

'O dear Alexandrine,' cried Melior, clasping her hands in despair. 'Do try to think of some way to save us! I am sure you can; you are always clever, and there is nobody else.'

And Alexandrine did think of a way, but what it was must be told in the next chapter.

THE DISENCHANTMENT OF THE WERWOLF

Everybody will remember that William and Melior trusted to Alexandrine to help them to escape from the palace, before Melior was forced into marriage by her father with the prince of Greece. At first Alexandrine declared that it was quite impossible to get them away unseen, but at length she thought of something which might succeed, though, if it failed, all three would pay a heavy penalty.

And this was her plan, and a very good one too.

She would borrow some boy's clothes, and put them on, hiding her hair under one of those tight caps that kitchen varlets wore covering all their heads; she would then go down into the big kitchens underneath the palace, where the wild beasts shot by the emperor were skinned and made into coats for the winter. Here she would have a chance of slipping out unnoticed with the skins of two white bears, and in these she would sew up William and Melior, and would let them through the little back gate, from which they could easily escape into the forest.

'Oh, I knew you would find a way!' said Melior,

throwing her arms joyfully round her cousin's neck. 'I am quite sure it will all go right, only let us make haste, for my father may find us out, or perhaps I may lose my courage.'

'I will set about it at once,' said Alexandrine, 'and you and William must be ready to-night.'

So she got her boy's clothes, which her maid stole for her out of the room of one of the scullions, and dressed herself in them, smearing her face and hands with walnut-juice, that their whiteness might not betray her. She slipped down by some dark stairs into the kitchen, and joined a company of men who were hard at work on a pile of dead animals. The sun had set, and in the corner of the great hall where the flaying was going on, there was very little light, but Alexandrine marked that close to an open door was a heap of bearskins, and she took up her position as near them as she could. But the girl was careful not to stand too long in one place; she moved about from one group of men to another, lending a hand here and there and passing a merry jest, and as she did so she gave the topmost skins a little shove with her foot, getting them each time closer to the open door, and always watching her chance to pick them up and run off with them.

It came at last. The torch which lighted that end of the hall flared up and went out, leaving the men in darkness. One of them rose to fetch another, and, quick as thought, Alexandrine caught up the bearskins and was outside in the garden. From that it was easy to make her way upstairs unseen.

'See how I have sped!' she said, throwing the skins on the floor. 'But night is coming on apace, and we have no time to lose; I must sew you up in them at once.'

The skins were both so large that Melior and William wore all their own clothes beneath, and did not feel at all hot, as they expected to do.

'Am I not a bold beast?' asked Melior in glee, as she caught sight of herself in a polished shield on the wall. 'Methinks no handsomer bear was ever seen!'

'Yes, verily, madam,' answered her maiden, 'you are indeed a grisly ghost, and no man will dare to come near you. But now stand aside, for it is William's turn.'

'How do you like me, sweetheart?' asked he, when the last stitches had been put in.

'You have so fierce an air, and are so hideous a sight, that I fear to look on you!' said she. And William laughed and begged Alexandrine to guide them through the garden, as they were not yet used to going on all fours, and might stumble.

As they passed through the bushes, galloping madly—for in spite of the danger they felt as though they were children again—a Greek who was walking up to the palace saw them afar, and, seized with dread, took shelter in the nearest hut, where he told his tale. The men who heard it paid but little heed at the time, though they remembered it after; but bears were common in that country, and often came out of the forest at night.

Not knowing what a narrow escape they had had, the two runaways travelled till sunrise, when they hid themselves in a cave on the side of a hill. They had nothing to eat, but were too tired to think of that till they had had a good sleep, though when they woke up they began to wonder how they should get any food.

'Oh, it will be all right!' said Melior; 'there are blackberries in plenty and acorns and hazel-nuts, and there is a stream just below the cave—do you not hear it? It will all be much nicer than anything in the palace.'

But William did not seem to agree with her, and wished to seek out some man who would give him something he liked better than nuts and acorns. This, however, Melior would not hear of; they would certainly be followed and betrayed, she said, and, to please her, William ate the fruit and stayed in the cave, wondering what would happen on the morrow.

Luckily for themselves, they did not have to wait so long before they got a good supper. Their friend the werwolf had spied them from afar, and was ready to come to their rescue. During that day he had hidden himself under a clump of bushes close to the highway, and by-and-by he saw a man approaching, carrying a very fat wallet over his shoulder. The wolf bounded out of his cover, growling fiercely, which so frightened the man that he dropped the wallet and ran into the wood. Then the wolf picked up the wallet, which contained a loaf of bread and some meat ready cooked, and galloped away with it to William.

They felt quite strong and hearty again when they had finished their supper, and quite ready to continue their journey. As it was night, and the country was very lonely, they walked on two feet, but when morning came, or they saw signs that men were about, they speedily dropped on all fours. And all the way the werwolf followed them, and saw that they never lacked for food.

Meanwhile the preparations for Melior's marriage to the prince of Greece were going on blithely in the palace, and none thought of asking for the bride. At last, when everything was finished, the emperor bade the high chamberlain fetch the princess.

'She is not in her room, your Majesty,' said the chamberlain, when he re-entered the hall; but the emperor only thought that his daughter was timid, and answered that he would go and bring her himself.

Like the chamberlain, he found the outer room empty and passed on to the door of the inner one, which was locked. He shook and thumped and yelled with anger, till Alexandrine heard him from her distant turret, and, terrified though she was, hastened to find out what was the matter.

'My daughter! Where is my daughter?' he cried, stammering with rage.

'Asleep, sire,' answered Alexandrine.

'Asleep still!' said the emperor; 'then wake her instantly, for the bridegroom is ready and I am waiting to lead her to him.'

'Alas! sire, Melior has heard that in Greece royal brides pass their lives shut in a tower, and she has sworn that she will never wed one of that race. But, indeed, for my part, I think that is not her true reason, and that she has pledged her faith to another, whom you also know and love.'

'And who may that be?' asked the emperor.

'The man who saved your life in battle, William himself,' answered Alexandrine boldly, though her limbs shook with fear.

At this news the emperor was half beside himself with grief and rage.

'Where is she?' he cried; 'speak, girl, or I will shut you up in the tower.'

'Where is William?' asked Alexandrine. 'If Melior is not here, and William is not here, then of a surety they have gone away together.'

The emperor looked at her in silence for a moment.

'The Greeks will make war on me for this insult,' he said; 'and, as for William, a body of soldiers shall go in search of him this moment, and when he is found I will have his head cut off, and stuck on my palace gate as a warning to traitors.'

But the soldiers could not find him. Perhaps they did not look very carefully, for, like everyone else, they loved William. Party after party was sent out by the emperor, but they all returned without finding a trace of the runaways. Then at last the Greek who had seen the two white bears galloping through the garden came to the high chamberlain and told his tale.

'Send to the kitchen at once and ask if any bearskins are missing,' ordered the chamberlain; and the page returned with the tidings that the skins of two white bears could not be found.

Now the werwolf had been lurking round the palace seeking for news, and as soon as he heard that the emperor had ordered out his dogs to hunt the white bears, he made a plan in his head to save William and Melior. He hid in some bushes that lay in the path of the hounds, and let them get quite near him. As soon as they were close, he sprang out in front of their noses and they gave chase at once. And a fine dance he led them! — over mountains and through swamps, under ferns that were thickly matted together, and past wide lakes. And every step they took brought them further away from the bears, who were lying snugly in their den.

At last even the patience of the emperor was exhausted. He gave up the hunt, and bade his men call off the dogs and go home.

'They have escaped me this time,' said he, 'but I will have them by-and-by. Let a reward be offered, and posted up on the gate of every city. After all, that is the surest way of capturing them.'

And the emperor was right: the shepherds and goatherds were told that if they could bring the two white bears to the gates of the palace they would not need to work for the rest of their lives, and they kept a sharp look-out as they followed their flocks. Once a man actually saw them, and gave notice to one of the royal officials, who brought a company of spearmen and surrounded the cave. Another moment, and they would have been seized, had not the wolf again come to their rescue. He leapt out from behind a rock, and snatched up the officer's son, who had followed his father. The poor man shrieked in horror, and cried out to save the boy, so they all turned and went after the wolf as before.

'We are safer now in our own clothes,' said William; and they hastily stripped off the bearskins, and stole away, but they would not leave the skins behind, for they had learnt to love them.

For a long while they wandered through the forest, the werwolf ever watching over them, and bringing them food. At length the news spread abroad, no one knew how, that William and Melior were running about as bears no more, but in the garments they always wore. So men began to look out for them, and once they were very nearly caught by some charcoal-burners. Then the wolf killed a hart and a hind, and sewed them in their skins and guided them across the Straits of Messina into the kingdom of Sicily.

Very dimly, and one by one, little things that had happened in his childhood began to come back to William; but he wondered greatly how he seemed to know this land, where he had never been before. The king his father had been long dead, but the queen (his mother) and his sister were besieged in the city of Palermo by the king of Spain, who was full of wrath because the princess had refused to marry his son. The queen was in great straits, when one night she dreamed that a wolf and two harts had come to help her, and one bore the face of her son, while both had crowns on their heads.

She could sleep no more that night, so she rose and looked out of the window on the park which lay below, and there, under the trees, were the hart and the hind! Panting for joy, the queen summoned a priest, and told him her dream, and, as she told it, behold the skins cracked, and shining clothes appeared beneath.

'Your dream has been fulfilled,' said the priest. 'The hind is the daughter of the emperor of Rome, who fled away with yonder knight dressed in a hart skin!'

Joyfully the queen made herself ready, and she soon joined the animals, who had wandered off to a part of the park that was full of rocks and caves. She greeted them with fair words, and begged William to take service under her, which he did gladly.

'Sweet sir, what token will you wear on your shield?' asked she; and William answered, 'Good madam, I will have a werwolf on a shield of gold, and let him be made hideous and huge.'

'That shall be done,' said she.

When the shield was painted, William prayed her to give him a horse, and she led him into the stable, and bade him choose one for himself. And he chose one that had been ridden by the late king his father. And the horse knew him, though his mother did not, and it neighed from pure delight. After that William called to the soldiers to rally round him, and there was fought a great battle, and the Spaniards were put to flight, and throughout Palermo the people rejoiced mightily.

When the enemy had retreated far away, and William returned to the palace, where the queen and Melior were awaiting him; suddenly, from the window, they beheld the werwolf go by, and as he passed he held up his foot as if he craved mercy.

'What does he mean by that?' asked the queen.

'It betokens great good to us,' answered William.

'That is well,' said the queen; 'but the sight of that beast causes me much sorrow. For my fair son was stolen away from me by such a one, when he was four years old, and never more have I heard of him.' But in her heart she felt, though she said nothing, that she had found him again.

By-and-by the king of Spain came back with another army, and there was more fighting. In the end the Spanish king was forced to yield up his sword to William, who carried him captor to his mother Felice. The queen received him with great courtesy, and placed him next her at dinner, and the peers who had likewise been taken prisoners sat down to feast.

The next day a council was held in the hall of the palace to consider the terms of peace. The king of Spain and his son were present also, and everyone said in turn what penalty the enemy should pay for having besieged their city and laid waste their cornfields. In the midst of this grave discussion a werwolf entered through the open door, and, trotting up to the Spanish king, he kissed his feet. Then he bowed to the queen and to William, and went away as he came.

The sight of his tail disappearing through the door restored to the guards their courage, which had vanished in the presence of anything so unexpected. They sprang up to pursue him, but like a flash of lightning William flung himself in their path, crying, 'If any man dare to hurt that beast, I will do him to death with my own hands;' and, as they all knew that William meant what he said, they slunk back to their places.

'Tell me, gracious king,' asked William when they were all seated afresh round the council table, 'why did the wolf bow to you more than to other men?'

Then the king made answer that long ago his first wife had died, leaving him with a son, and that in a little while he had married again, and that his second wife had had a son also. One day when he came back from the wars she told him that his eldest son had been drowned, but he found out afterwards that she had changed him into a werwolf, so that her own child might succeed to the crown.

'And I think,' he added, 'that this werwolf may be indeed the son I lost.'

'It may right well be thus,' cried William, 'for he has the mind of a man, and of a wise man too. Often has he succoured me in my great need, and if your wife had skill to turn him into a werwolf her charms can make him a man again. Therefore, sire, neither you nor your people shall go hence out of prison till he has left his beast's shape behind him. So bid your queen come hither, and if she says you nay I will fetch her myself!'

Then the king called one of his great lords, and he bade him haste to Spain and tell the queen what had befallen him, and to bring her with all speed to Palermo. Little as she liked the summons, the Spanish queen dared not refuse, and on her arrival she was led at once into the great hall, which was filled with a vast company, both of Spaniards and Sicilians. When all were assembled William fetched the werwolf from his chamber, where he had lain for nights and days, waiting till his stepmother should come.

Together they entered the hall, but at the sight of the wicked woman who had done him such ill the wolf's bristles stood up on his back, and with a snarl that chilled the blood of all that heard it he sprang towards the dais. But, luckily, William was on the watch, and, flinging his arms round the wolf's neck, he held him back, saying in a whisper:

'My dear, sweet beast, trust to me as truly as to your own brother. I sent for her for your sake, and if she does not undo her evil spells I will have her body burned to coals, and her ashes scattered to the winds.'

The wicked queen knew well what doom awaited her, and that she could resist no longer. Sinking on her knees before the wolf, she confessed the ill she had wrought, and added:

'Sweet Alfonso, soon shall the people see your seemly face, and your body as it would have been but for me!' At that she led the wolf into a private chamber, and, drawing from her wallet a thread of red silk, she bound it round a ring she wore, which no witchcraft could prevail against. This ring she hung round the wolf's neck, and afterwards read him some rhymes out of a book. Then the werwolf looked at his body, and, behold, he was a man again!

There were great rejoicings at the court of Palermo when prince Alfonso came among them once more. He forgave the queen for her wickedness, and rebuked his father for having stirred up such a wanton and bloody war.

'Plague and famine would have preyed upon this land,' he said, 'had not this knight, whose real name is unknown to you, come to your aid. He is the rightful lord of this country, for he is the son of king Embrons and queen Felice, and I am the werwolf who carried him away, to save him from a cruel death that was planned for him by his own uncle!'

So the tale ends and everyone was made happy. The werwolf, now prince Alfonso, married William's sister, and in due time ruled the kingdom of Spain, and William and Melior lived at Palermo till the emperor her father died, when the Romans offered him the crown in his stead.

And if you want to know any more about them, you must read the story for yourselves.

THE SLAYING OF HALLGERDA'S HUSBANDS

If any traveller had visited Iceland nearly a thousand years ago, he would have found the island full of busy, industrious people, who made the most of their short summer, and tilled the ground so well that they generally reaped a golden harvest. Many of the families were akin, and had fled some sixty years earlier from Norway and the islands of the sea because the king, Harald Fairhair, had introduced new laws, which displeased them. They were soon joined, for one reason and another, by dwellers in Orkney and Shetland and the Faroe Islands and the Hebrides, and, being men of one race, they easily adopted the same customs and obeyed the same laws.

Now the Northmen had many good qualities and many very troublesome ones. The father of every household had absolute power over all his children; he fixed the amount of money that should be paid in exchange for his daughter at her marriage, and the sum that was due for the wounded slave or 'thrall' as he was called, or even for his murdered son; or, if he thought better, he could refuse to take any money at all as the price of his injuries, and could then avenge blood by blood.

But once he had declared his purpose he was bound to abide by his word.

Fond though they were of fighting, the Northmen had their own notions of fair dealing. If you had killed a man, you had to confess it; if you slew him at night, or when he was sleeping, you were guilty of murder, and if you refused to throw gravel or sand over his body, thus denying your enemy the rights of burial, you were considered a dastard even by your friends.

Now in the valley or dale of the river Laxa dwelt two brothers, each in his own house. One was named Hauskuld, and the other Hrut. This Hrut was much younger than Hauskuld, and was handsome, brave, and, like so many of the Northmen, very gentle when not engaged in war. Like many of them also, the gift was given him of reading the future.

One day Hauskuld made a feast, and Hrut came with many of his kinsmen, and took his place next his brother Hauskuld. They were all seated in the great hall of the house and near the fire Hauskuld's little daughter, Hallgerda, was playing with some other children. Fair and blue eyed were they all, but Hallgerda was taller and more beautiful than any, and her hair fell in long bright curls far below her waist. 'Come hither,' said Hauskuld, holding out his hand, and, taking her by the chin, he kissed her and bade her go back to her companions. Then, turning to his brother he asked:

'Well, is she not fair to look upon?' but Hrut held his peace. Again Hauskuld would know what was in the thoughts of Hrut concerning the maiden, and this time Hrut made answer:

'Of a truth fair is the maid, and great will be the havoc wrought by her among men. But one thing I would know, which of our race has given her those thief's eyes?'

At that Hauskuld waxed wroth, and bade Hrut begone to his own house.

After this some years went by. Hrut left Iceland and spent some time at the Court of Norway, and then he came back and married, and had much trouble with his wife, Unna. But after they had parted and she had gone back to her father, Hrut was a free man again, and he went to visit his brother Hauskuld, whose daughter Hallgerda had now become a woman. Tall and stately she was, and fair, but sly and greedy of gain, as in the days of her childhood, and more she loved Thiostolf, whose wife had brought her up, than Hauskuld her father, or Hrut her uncle.

When Hallgerda went back to Hauskuld her father, he saw that he must be looking out for a husband for her, as the fame of her beauty would go far. It was indeed not long before one came to her, Thorwald, son of Oswif, who, besides the broad lands which he possessed on the island, owned the Bear Isles out in the sea, where fish were to be had in abundance.

Oswif, Thorwald's father, knew more about the maiden than did Thorwald, who had been on a journey, and he tried to turn his son's thought to some other damsel, but Thorwald only answered, 'Whatever you may say, she is the only woman I will marry;' and Oswif made reply, 'Well, after all, the risk is yours and not mine.'

So they two set out for Hauskuld's house and he bade them welcome heartily. They wasted no time before telling him their business, and Hauskuld answered that for his part he could desire no more honourable match for his daughter, but he would not hide from them that her temper was hard and cruel.

'That shall not stand between us,' said Thorwald, 'so tell me what I shall pay for her.'

And the bargain was made, and Thorwald rode home with his father, but Hallgerda was never asked if she wished to wed Thorwald or not.

When Hauskuld told his daughter that she was to be married to Thorwald, she was not pleased, and said that if her father had loved her as much as he pretended to do he would have consulted her in such a matter. Besides, she did not think that the match was in any way worthy of her.

But, grumble as she might, there was no getting out of it, and, as Hauskuld would listen to nothing, she sought for her foster-father, Thiostolf, who never had been known to say her nay. When she had told her story, he bade her be of good cheer, prophesying that Thorwald should not be her only husband, and that if she was not happy she had only to come to him and he would do her bidding, be it what it might, save as regarded Hauskuld and Hrut.

Then Hallgerda was comforted, and went home to prepare the bridal feast, to which all their friends and kinsfolk were bidden. And when the marriage was over, she rode home with her husband Thorwald, and Thiostolf her foster-father was ever at her side, and she talked more to him than to Thorwald. And there he stayed all the winter.

Now, as time went on, Thorwald began to repent that he had not hearkened to the words of his father. His wife paid him scant attention, and she wasted his goods, and was noted among all the women of the dales for her skill in driving a hard bargain. And, beyond all that, folk whispered that she was not careful to ask whether the things she took were her own or someone else's. This irked Thorwald sore; but worse was to follow. The spring came late that year, and Hallgerda told Thorwald that the storehouse was empty of meat and fish, and he must go out to the Bear Isles and fetch some more. At this Thorwald reproached her, saying that it was her fault if garners were not yet full, and on Hallgerda's taunting him with being a miser, struck her such a blow in the face that blood spouted, and when he left her to row with his men to the islands, Hallgerda sat still, vowing vengeance.

It was not long in coming. Soon after, Thiostolf chanced to pass that way, and, seeing the blood on her face, asked whence it sprang.

'From the hand of my husband Thorwald,' answered she, and reproached Thiostolf for suffering such dealings.

'I knew not of it,' said Thiostolf, 'but I will avenge it speedily;' and he went to the shore, and put off in a boat, taking nothing but a great axe with him. He found Thorwald and his men on the beach of the biggest island, loading his vessel with meat and fish from the storehouses. Then he began to pick a quarrel with Thorwald and spoke words that vexed him more and more, till Thorwald bent forward to seize a knife which lay near him. This was the moment for which the other had been waiting. He lifted his axe and gave a blow at Hallgerda's husband, and, though Thorwald tried to defend himself, a second stroke clove his skull.

'Your axe is bloody,' said Hallgerda, who was standing outside the door.

'Yes; and *this* time you can choose your own husband,' answered Thiostolf; but Hallgerda only asked calmly:

'So Thorwald is dead?' and as Thiostolf nodded she went on: 'You must go northward, to Swan my kinsman; he will hide you from your enemies.'

After that she unlocked her chests and dismissed her maidens with gifts; then she mounted her horse and rode home to her father.

'Where is Thorwald?' asked Hrut, who had heard nothing.

'He is dead,' answered Hallgerda.

'By the hand of Thiostolf?' said her father.

'By his hand, and by that of no other;' and Hallgerda passed by them and entered the house.

As soon as Oswif, Thorwald's father, had heard the tidings, he guessed that Thiostolf must have gone northward to Swan, and calling his men round him they all rode to the Bearfirth. But before they were in sight Swan cried to Thiostolf, 'Oswif is coming, but we need fear nothing, they will never see us,' and he took a goatskin and wrapped it round his head, and said to it: 'Be thou darkness and fog, and fright and wonder, to those who seek us.' And immediately a thick fog and black darkness fell over all things, and Oswif and his men lost their way, and tumbled off their horses and tripped over large stones, till Oswif resolved to give up seeking Thiostolf and Swan, and to go himself to Hauskuld.

Now Hauskuld was abiding at home, and with him was Hrut his brother. Oswif got off his horse, and, throwing its bridle over a stake driven into the ground, he said to Hauskuld: 'I have come to ask atonement for my son's life.'

'It was not I who slew your son,' answered Hauskuld; 'but as he is slain, it is just that you should seek atonement from somebody.'

'You have much need to give him what he asks,' said Hrut, 'for it is not well that evil tongues should be busy with your daughter's name.'

'Then give the judgment yourself,' replied Hauskuld.

'That will I do, in truth,' said Hrut; 'and be sure that I will not spare you, as I know it was Hallgerda wrought his death;' so he offered his hand to Oswif, as a token that his award would be accepted, and that at the Great Council of the nation he would not summon Hauskuld for Thorwald's murder. And Oswif took his hand, and Hauskuld's, and Hrut bade his brother pay down two hundred pounds in silver to Oswif, while he himself gave him a stout cloak. And Oswif went away well pleased with the award.

For some time Hallgerda dwelt in her father's house, and she brought with her a share of Thorwald's goods, and was very rich. But men kept away from her, having heard tales of her evil ways. At length Glum, the youngest son of Olaf the Lame, told his brother that he would go no more trading in strange lands, but would remain at home, and meant to take to himself a wife, if the one on whom he had set his heart would come to him.

So one day a company of the men, with Glum and Thorarin his brother at their head, rode into the Dales to the door of Hauskuld's dwelling. Hauskuld greeted them heartily and begged them to stay all night, sending secretly for Hrut, whose counsel he always asked when any matter of importance was talked over.

'Do you know what they want?' said Hrut next morning, when his brother met him on the road.

'No,' replied Hauskuld, 'they have not spoken to me of any business.'

'Then I will tell you,' answered Hrut. 'They have come to ask Hallgerda in marriage.'

'And what shall I do?' said Hauskuld.

'Tell them you would like the match,' replied Hrut, 'but hide nothing. Let them know all there is of good and evil concerning her.'

They reached the house as he spoke, and the guests came out, and Thorarin opened his business by entreating Hauskuld to give his daughter Hallgerda to Glum his brother. 'You know,' he added, 'that he is rich and strong, and thought well of by all men.'

'Yes, I know that,' answered Hauskuld; 'but once before I chose a husband for my daughter, and matters turned out ill for all of us.'

'That will be no hindrance,' replied Thorarin, 'for the lot of one man is not the lot of all men. And things might have fared better had it not been for the meddling of Thiostolf.'

'You speak truth,' said Hrut, who had listened to their talk in silence; 'and the marriage may yet turn out well if you will do as I tell you. See that you suffer not Thiostolf to ride with her to Glum's house, and that he never sleeps in the house for more than three nights running, without Glum's leave, on pain of outlawry and death by Glum himself. And if Glum will hearken to my counsel, leave to stay he will never give. But it is time to let Hallgerda know of the matter, and she shall say whether Glum is to her mind.'

And Thorarin agreed, and Hauskuld sent to summon his daughter.

Now, though nothing had been said to Hallgerda as to the business which brought all these men to her father's house, perhaps she may have guessed something, for when she appeared she was attended by her two women, and clad in her festal garments. She wore a dress of scarlet, girdled by a silver belt, and over it a mantle of soft dark blue, while her thick yellow hair was unbound, and fell almost to her knees. She smiled and spoke kindly to the visitors, then sat herself down between her father and uncle. After that Glum spoke.

'Your father and Thorarin my brother have had talk about a marriage betwixt you and me, Hallgerda. Is it your will, as it is theirs? Tell me all that is in your heart. For, if you like me not, I will straightway ride back again.'

'The match is to my liking,' answered Hallgerda, 'and better suited to my condition than what my father made for me before. And you are to my liking also, if our tempers do not fall out.'

'Let Hallgerda betroth herself,' said Hrut, when they had told her what terms had been arranged, and that Glum should bring goods or money to an equal value to Hallgerda's, and that they two should divide the whole.

After that the betrothal ceremony took place, and Glum went away, and returned no more till his wedding.

There was a great company in Hauskuld's hall to witness Hallgerda's marriage, and when the feast began Thiostolf might have been seen stalking about holding his axe aloft; but, as the guests pretended not to know he was there, no harm came of it.

For some time Glum and his wife lived happily together, though Hallgerda proved herself the same greedy yet wasteful woman she had been before. At the end of a year a daughter was born to her, whom she named Thorgerda, and the child grew up to be as beautiful as her mother. But by-and-by trouble came to them through Thiostolf, who had been driven away by Hauskuld for beating one of his thralls. Thiostolf vowed vengeance in his heart, and rode south to Glum's house.

Hallgerda was pleased to see him, but when she heard his tale she said she could not give him shelter without the consent of Glum. So when her husband came in she ran quickly to greet him, and, putting her arms round his neck, she asked if he would agree to something she wished very much.

'If it is anything I can do in honour,' answered Glum, 'do it I will of a surety.'

Then she told him how her father had cast out Thiostolf, and that he had come to her for shelter, and she wished him to remain, if it was Glum's will. And Glum answered that, if she wished it greatly, Thiostolf should remain, unless he betook himself to evil courses.

For a while Thiostolf went warily, and no fault did Glum find with him; then he fell to marring everything, as he had done in Thorwald's time, and to no one would he listen save to Hallgerda only. In vain Thorarin warned Glum that things would have an ill ending, but Glum only smiled, and let Hallgerda have her way.

When autumn came, and the days grew short and cold, the men went to bring their flocks home from the pastures where they had been feeding all the summer. It was hard work, for the sheep often strayed far, and, besides, the flocks got mixed up, and needed to be separated one from the other. One day, when the shepherds had brought tidings that many of Glum's sheep were missing, Glum bade Thiostolf go into the hills and see if he could find those that were lost.

But Thiostolf grew angry, and answered rudely:

'I am not your slave, and it is not my work to bring in sheep. If you mean to go yourself, perhaps I will consent to go with you.'

At this Glum was greatly angered, and, seeking Hallgerda, he told her what had happened, adding as he did so:

'I will not have Thiostolf here any longer.'

Then Hallgerda waxed very wrathful, and she upheld Thiostolf in his ill doing.

At last the patience of Glum gave way, and he struck her a blow in the face, and crying, 'Words are wasted on you,' went off to his own business. Hallgerda, who loved him much in spite of her unruly tongue, wept bitterly at the thought of what had happened, and, as evil fate would have it, Thiostolf heard her, and saw the red mark across her cheek.

'It shall not be there again,' he said, but Hallgerda answered:

'It is not for you to come between Glum and me.'

When he heard this, Thiostolf only smiled and said nothing, but got ready to go with Glum and his men, to seek after the sheep. After long searchings they found many of those that were missing, and he sent some of his men one way and some another, till at length by chance he and

Thiostolf were left alone. They soon came upon a flock of wild sheep, and tried to drive them down the steep side of a hill towards Glum's house, but it was of no use, and as fast as the sheep were collected together they all scattered again. Very soon, Glum and Thiostolf grew tired and ill-tempered, and each told the other he was stupid and lazy. At length, Glum taunted Thiostolf with being a thrall, and from that blows quickly followed. Both men drew their axes, but Thiostolf struck so hard at Glum that he rolled dead upon the ground.

At the sight of Glum lying dead at his feet, Thiostolf's wrath cooled somewhat. He stooped and covered Glum's body with stones, and took a gold ring from his finger. After that he took the road back to Varmalek, and found Hallgerda sitting in front of the door. Her eyes fell instantly on the bloody axe, and Thiostolf saw this and said hastily:

'Glum, your husband, is slain.'

'Then it is by your hand,' she answered.

'Yes, it is,' said Thiostolf, and added after a moment's pause: 'What is best to be done now?'

'Go to Hrut, and ask him,' replied Hallgerda, and Thiostolf went.

'Glum is slain' said Thiostolf to Hrut, who had come down to the door in answer to Thiostolf's knock.

'Who slew him?' asked Hrut.

'I slew him,' answered Thiostolf.

'Why did you come here?' asked Hrut again.

'Because Hallgerda sent me,' answered Thiostolf.

'Then Hallgerda had no part in his slaying,' said Hrut, with a sound of relief in his voice; but as he spoke he drew his sword, which Thiostolf saw, and thrust at Hrut with his axe. Hrut, too, saw, and sprang quickly aside, knocking up as he did so the handle of the axe, so that it fell full on the ground. Turning himself swiftly, Hrut dealt Thiostolf a blow which brought him to his knees, and a stab in the heart finished the work.

After that Hrut's house-carles laid stones on Thiostolf's body, while he himself rode away to tell Hauskuld all that had befallen. And soon after Thorarin, Glum's brother, came there too, with eleven men at his back. He asked Hauskuld what atonement he would make for Glum, but Hauskuld answered that it was neither he nor his daughter who had slain Glum, and that Hrut had avenged himself on Thiostolf. To this Thorarin said nothing, but Hrut offered to give him gifts, and so peace lay between them.

Now, Hrut's wife, Unna, was of kin to two brothers, Gunnar and Kolskegg. Both were tall, brave men, but there was not Gunnar's like in all the country round for beauty, and for skill in shooting, jumping, and swimming. And, besides this, he was beautiful and gentle, faithful to the friends he made, but not making them readily. His chief friend was Njal, from whom he ever sought counsel, for Njal was a wise man and could see far into the future.

Having a mind to see something of the world, Gunnar set sail for Norway, where he stayed some time, and had many adventures. It was early in the summer when he and Kolskegg sailed home to Iceland, where men were assembling for the great Council, or Thing.

Gunnar's first act was to ride off to Njal's house, and Gunnar asked if he would be present at the Thing. 'No, truly,' answered Njal; 'stay you at home or bad will come of it.'

And Gunnar! What evil was likely to befall him, who wished to live at peace with everyone? But Njal only shook his head and said slowly:

'I remain in my own house, and if I had my way you should do so also.'

But Gunnar would not listen, and rode straight off to the Thing.

What happened to him when he got there will be told in another story.

THE DEATH OF GUNNAR

Now of all the men gathered together at the Thing of the year 974, no man was handsomer or more splendidly clad than Gunnar. He was arrayed in the scarlet raiment given him by King Harald, and he bore on his arm a gold ring, given him by Hacon the Earl, and the horse he rode had a shining black skin.

A brave figure he made one morning as he left the Hill of Laws and passed out beyond the tents of the men of Mossfell. And as he went there came to meet him a woman whose dress was no less rich than his. She stopped as he drew near, and told him that she was Hallgerda, Hauskuld's daughter, and that she knew well that he was Gunnar the traveller, and she wished to hear some of the wonders of the lands beyond the seas. So he sat down, and they two talked together for long, and they agreed well, and became friends. After a while he asked her if she had a husband.

'No,' she replied; men feared her, for they held that she brought them ill-luck; but at that Gunnar laughed, and said, 'What would you answer if I asked you to marry me?'

'Are you jesting?' said Hallgerda.

'No, of a sooth,' replied Gunnar.

'Then go and see what my father has to say to it,' answered Hallgerda, and Gunnar went.

Hauskuld was inside his booth when Gunnar arrived. Hrut was there likewise, and bade him welcome. For a while the talk ran upon the business of the Thing, and then Gunnar turned and asked what answer Hauskuld would give if he offered to lay down money for Hallgerda.

'What do you say, Hrut?' inquired Hauskuld.

'It ought not to be,' replied Hrut. 'No man has aught but good to say of you; no man has aught but ill to say of her. And this I must not hide from you.'

'I thank you for your plain speech,' said Gunnar; 'but my soul is still set on wedding Hallgerda. And we have spoken together, and are agreed in this matter.'

But though Hrut knew that his words were vain, he told Gunnar all that had happened in respect of Hallgerda and her two husbands. And Gunnar weighed it for a while, and then he said, 'You know the saying, "Forewarned is forearmed." Doubtless it is true, all that you have told of Hallgerda, but I am strong, and have travelled far, and if we can make a bargain, so shall it be.'

So a messenger was sent for Hallgerda, and she betrothed herself, as she had done to Glum, and after that Gunnar rode over to Njal, and told him what things had happened.

'Evil will come of it betwixt you and me,' said Njal sadly.

'No woman, or man either, shall ever work ill between us,' answered Gunnar, who loved Njal more than his own father.

'She works ill wherever she goes,' replied Njal, 'and you will never cease making atonements for her;' but he said no more, for he was a wise man and wasted no words, and when Gunnar asked him to come to the wedding feast he gave his promise that he would be there.

The winter after Gunnar's wedding, he and Hallgerda were bidden to a great feast at Njal's house. Njal and his wife greeted them heartily, and by-and-by Helgi, Njal's son, came, and with him Thorhalla his wife. Then Bergthora, Njal's wife, went up to Hallgerda, and said, 'Give place to Thorhalla,' but Hallgerda would not, and she fell to quarrelling with Bergthora, and at last Bergthora taunted Hallgerda with having plotted to do Thorwald her husband to death. At that Hallgerda turned and said to Gunnar: 'It is nothing to be married to the strongest man in Iceland, if you avenge not these insults, Gunnar.'

But Gunnar cried that he would take no part in women's quarrels, least of all in Njal's house, and bade Hallgerda come home with him.

'We shall meet again, Bergthora,' said Hallgerda as she mounted the sleigh. Then they rode back to Lithend and spent the rest of the winter there.

When the spring came, Gunnar went to the Thing, bidding Hallgerda take heed, and to give no cause of offence to his friends. But she would give no promise, and he set forth with a heavy heart.

By ill-fortune, Njal and Gunnar owned a wood between them, and when Njal and his sons departed to the Thing, Bergthora, Njal's wife, ordered Swart her servant to cut her some branches for kindling fires from this very forest. These tidings reached the ears of Hallgerda, and she muttered with a grim face, 'It is the last time that Swart shall steal my wood,' and bade Kol, her bailiff, start early next morning and seek Swart.

'And when I find him?' asked Kol; but Hallgerda only turned away angrily.

'You, the worst of men, ask that?' said she. 'Why, you shall kill him, of course.'

So Kol took his axe, though he was ill at ease, for he knew that evil would come of it, and he mounted one of Gunnar's horses and fared to the wood.

He soon saw Swart and his men piling up bundles of firewood, so he left his horse in a hollow, and crouched down behind some bushes, till he heard Swart bid the men carry the wood to Njal's house, as he himself had more work to do. He began to look about for a tall straight young stem with which to make himself a bow, when Kol sprang out of the bushes and dealt Swart such a stroke with his axe that he fell dead without a word. After that Kol went back and told Hallgerda.

And Hallgerda spoke cheering words, and said he need have no fear, for that she would protect him; but Kol's heart was heavy.

Now Hallgerda had forced Kol to slay Swart, to bring about a quarrel between her husband and Njal, so she straightway sent a messenger to seek Gunnar at the Thing, and tell him what had befallen Swart. Gunnar listened in silence to the messenger's tale; then he called his men around him, and they all went to Njal's tent, and begged him to come out and speak to Gunnar.

'Swart, your house servant has been killed by Hallgerda and Kol her man,' said Gunnar gravely when Njal stood before him; and he told the tale as he had heard it from the messenger.

'It is for you, Njal, to fix the atonement,' he said at the end.

'You will have work to atone for all Hallgerda's misdoings,' answered Njal, 'and it will take all our old friendship to keep us from quarrelling now. But I have it in mind that at the last you shall win through, but after hard fighting. As to the atonement, as you are my friend and have no hand in this, I will fix it at twelve ounces of silver. And if it should come to be your turn to settle an award, I shall not expect to pay more than that.'

So Gunnar laid down the money and gave it to Bergthora his wife when he came home with his sons from the Thing. And Bergthora was content, but said to her husband that it should not be spent, as it would some day do to make atonement for Kol.

Although Hallgerda met her husband bravely and answered him boldly, in secret she trembled a little at his stern face and sharp words, as he told her that she was to remember that whatever quarrels she might choose to begin, the ending of them would always lie with him. But she pretended not to care, and went out among her neighbours as usual, telling all who would listen the tale of the killing of Swart. At length this reached the ears of Bergthora, and she was sore angered, but bided her time in silence.

When Njal and his sons went up to the pastures to see after the cattle, and the thralls were busy working in the fields, Bergthora the mistress was left alone in the house. On this day a man mounted on a black horse and armed with a spear and a short sword rode up to the door and asked her if she could find something for him to do. He was skilled in many things, he said, but his temper was hot, and had oftentimes been his bane.

'I will give you work,' answered Bergthora, 'but you must do whatever I bid you, even though it should be to slay a man.'

'You have plenty of other men whom you can better trust on such business,' replied the man, as if he repented of his bargain; but Bergthora only told him that she expected her servants to do as they were bid, and sent the man to put his horse in the stable.

During that summer another Thing was held and Njal and his sons went to it, and likewise Gunnar. But Bergthora was left alone in the house with her servants.

Then she called Atli, the new man, and bade him seek out Kol, that he might slay him, so Atli took his horse and his sword and spear and departed.

He found Kol in the place where some men had shown him, and he spoke to Kol civilly, but only received rude tones in answer. So, without more ado, Atli thrust at him, and Kol, though wounded, swung his axe above his head; but his eyes had grown dim, and he could not see to aim, and he fell to the ground and rolled over.

Atli left the body where it was, and rode on till he came to some of Gunnar's men, and bade them go and tell Hallgerda that Kol was dead.

'Did you kill him?' asked the man.

'Well, I don't expect Hallgerda will think that he dealt his own death-blow,' answered Atli; and with that he rode back to Bergthora, who praised him for the swiftness with which he had done her bidding. But Atli did not seem content, and at last he said:

'What will Njal think?'

'Oh, never fear him,' replied Bergthora, 'for he took with him the money of the atonement for the slaying of Swart, and now he can pay it over for Kol. But in spite of the atonement, beware of Hallgerda, who knows nought of promises.'

When Hallgerda heard of Kol's slaying, she bade a messenger ride to Gunnar at the Thing, and Gunnar sent to seek out Njal and Skarphedinn his son. They came to his tent, and he greeted them, and then Njal said that Bergthora his wife had done great wrong in breaking the atonement, and that Gunnar must now fix the award for Kol.

'Let it be the same as that which I paid for Swart,' said Gunnar; and Njal laid down the money and they parted, and no ill blood was between them, though their wives were still resolved to do each other all the ill they could.

Njal was too wise a man not to know that Hallgerda would seek revenge on Atli for the slaying of Kol, and he begged Atli would take service far away to the east, so that Hallgerda might not reach him. But Atli told Njal that he would sooner be slain in his service than live free in the service of another master, and he would gladly stay where he was if Njal would grant him the atonement due to a free man.

This Njal granted, and Atli remained in his house.

Hallgerda soon came to know what had happened, and she sent messengers both to Bergthora and to Gunnar at the Thing to tell them about it.

'Hallgerda my wife has caused Atli to be slain!' said Gunnar to Njal and to Skarphedinn his son. 'What atonement must I make for him?'

'The atonement will be heavy, for he was no thrall, but a freeman, and I fear it may cause strife between us,' replied Njal; but Gunnar stretched out his hand and said that no woman should sow strife betwixt him and Njal. Then Njal fixed a hundred ounces of silver, and Gunnar laid it down before him.

'Hallgerda does not let our servants die of old age,' said Skarphedinn, as they rode home from the Thing.

Now the words came true, that Gunnar had spoken, and 'blow for blow' grew to be the rule between Hallgerda and Bergthora; but for all that there was no quarrel between Njal and Gunnar.

So the years went by, and many Things had been held, and much blood-money had been paid, when one spring there was a great dearth of hay throughout all Iceland, and much cattle died. Gunnar, who was wise as well as rich, had seen what was coming and had laid up stores of both dried meat and of hay. As long as they lasted, he shared them with his neighbours, but when his barns were empty he called Kolskegg his brother and two of his friends, and they all fared to Kirkby, where dwelt Otkell the son of Skarf.

This Otkell owned many flocks and herds and wide pastures, and Gunnar hoped that his barns might yet be full.

'I have come to buy meat and hay, if there is any in your storehouses, for mine are empty!' said Gunnar.

'I have yet many storehouses untouched,' answered Otkell, 'but I will sell you nothing.'

'Will you give me them, then?' asked Gunnar, 'and I will pay you back some time in what you will.'

'I will neither give nor sell,' said Otkell.

'Let us take what we want and leave the money,' said Thrain, who had come with Gunnar, but Gunnar answered: 'I am no robber!' and was turning to go when Otkell stopped him.

'Will you buy a thrall from me? He is a good thrall,' said Otkell, 'but I have no need of him.'

And Gunnar bought the thrall, and they all went home to Lithend together.

When Njal heard that Otkell would not sell to Gunnar, he was very wroth and rode up into the hills with all his sons, and took meat from his storehouses and bound it upon five horses, and hay from his barns and bound it upon ten horses, and they drove them all to Lithend, which was Gunnar's house.

'Never ask another man for aught when you can ask me,' said Njal, and Gunnar answered:

'Your gifts are great, but truly your love is greater.'

In a few weeks the summer began, and, as was his custom, Gunnar rode to the Thing, leaving Hallgerda in the house at Lithend.

The day after he had ridden away with his men Hallgerda sent for Malcolm the thrall, and said to him:

'I have somewhat for you to do! Take with you two horses besides the one you ride, and go to Kirkby and steal meat enough to load the two horses, and butter and cheese as well. But take heed, when all is done, to set the storehouses on fire, so that none can trace that the goods have vanished.'

Malcolm the thrall lifted his head and looked at her.

'I have never been a thief, in spite of all my ill-deeds,' said he.

But Hallgerda only laughed and made sport of him.

'Do you think men have kept silent about your misdeeds?' she asked. 'Hie hence when I bid you, or you shall not see the new moon rise!'

And Malcolm the thrall knew that she spoke no jesting words, and he did her bidding; and none would have known of the thing had he not dropped his knife when he was trying to mend the thong of his shoe, and his belt also.

A few days after that Gunnar and his men returned home, and many guests with him. The table was set by Hallgerda herself, and besides meat there were also great cheeses and jars of butter. Well Gunnar knew that Njal had not sent these, and he asked Hallgerda whence they came.

'It beseems a man to eat what is before him and not to trouble himself further,' answered Hallgerda; but Gunnar cried out:

'I will have no part in food that is ill come by,' and with that he gave her a buffet on the cheek.

'I shall remember that,' said Hallgerda, and she got up and went out.

The next morning, Skamkell, Otkell's friend, was riding to bring in some sheep, when he saw something bright on the side of the path. He got off his horse to see what it was, and found the belt and knife which Malcolm had dropped, and he took them straight to Kirkby.

'Did you ever see these things before?' asked Skamkell.

'Yes, often,' answered Otkell; 'they are the knife and belt of Malcolm the thrall. And they asked many men the same question, and they all knew them likewise. Then they went toward Mord the son of Valgard and took counsel with him, how to charge Gunnar's thrall with the theft and the burning; for they feared Gunnar, the mighty man of war. At last, for three silver marks Mord agreed to give them his help, and bade them follow out his plan.

It was this. That they should send women over the country with goods of housekeeping use, and mark what was given them in exchange. 'Take heed that you note carefully,' said Mord, 'because no man will keep in his house the things that he has stolen, if he has a chance of getting rid of them. Set therefore apart whatever you get from each house, and bring it to me.'

And it was done exactly as Mord commanded, and in fourteen days the women came back, all bearing large bundles.

'Who gave you the most?' asked Mord, and one woman answered:

'Hallgerda, the wife of Gunnar; she gave us a cheese cut into great slices.'

'I will keep that cheese,' said Mord.

When the women had gone, Mord rode away to Otkell's farm, and bade him fetch the cheese-mould of Thorgerda his wife. And when it was brought, Mord took the slices and laid them in it, and they filled up the mould.

After this they all saw that Hallgerda had stolen the cheese, and, now that Mord had found the thief, he went back to his own house.

The tidings soon spread far and wide, and reached the ears of Kolskegg, who rode over to Lithend, so that he might speak with Gunnar.

'Know you that it is said by every man that it was Hallgerda who caused the fire at Kirkby, that she might steal the cheese and butter?' asked he.

'I have thought before that it must be so, but how can I set it right?' answered Gunnar.

'You must make atonement to Otkell, and it is better there should be no delay,' replied Kolskegg.

'I will do your bidding,' said Gunnar; and, mounting his horse, he took eleven with him, beside Thrain and Lambi his friends, and they all fared to Kirkby. There, Otkell came out to greet them, and with him were Skamkell and two other men, Hallkell and Hallbjorm.

'I am here,' said Gunnar, 'to offer atonement for the misdeed of my wife and the thrall you sold me, for it was they who caused the fire and stole the cheeses. And, if it pleases you, let the award be fixed by the best of the men round!'

'That sounds fairer than it is, Gunnar,' put in Skamkell, 'for you are a man of many things, whereas Otkell has few.'

'Well,' said Gunnar, 'then I will offer atonement of twice the value of all that Otkell lost;' but again it was Skamkell and not Otkell who replied:

'Beware, Otkell, of giving him the right of making the award when it belongs to you.'

And Otkell answered: 'I will fix the award myself, Gunnar.'

'Then fix it,' said Gunnar, who was waxing wroth at this delay; but once more Otkell turned to Skamkell, and asked what he should answer.

'Let the award be made by Gizur the white and Geir the priest,' and this saying pleased Otkell.

'Do you as you will,' replied Gunnar, 'but do not think that men will speak well of your refusing the choices that I gave you.'

And after that he rode home with his men.

Then Hallbjorm spoke to Otkell, saying: 'Ill was it to refuse the offers of Gunnar, which were good offers, as you know well. Can it be that you think yourself a match for Gunnar in fight, when he has proved himself better than any man in the island? But go and see Gizur the white and Geir the priest at once, and see if the offers of Gunnar do not seem good to them! For he is a just and gentle-hearted man, and perchance he will still hearken to you, if you accept them.'

So Otkell, who ever listened to the last speaker, bade, them bring out his horse and set forth, Skamkell walking by his side. In a little while, when they had gone a mile or two, Skamkell said: 'You have much to look to at Kirkby, and no one but yourself can see after the men. Get home, therefore, and let me ride to Gizur the white and Geir the priest instead of you.'

'Go, then,' answered Otkell, who was lazy and never took the trouble to think for himself; 'but see you do not tell them lies, as you are wont to do.'

'I will lie no more than I can help, master,' answered Skamkell, jumping on Otkell's horse.

Otkell fared home and found Hallbjorm in front of the house.

'Has anything befallen you that you have returned on foot?' asked he; and Otkell, who feared him, said hurriedly:

'I had many men to look over, and much work to do, so I sent Skamkell in my stead,' But Hallbjorm held his peace and eyed him scornfully.

'He who makes a thrall his friend rues it ever more,' he answered at last. 'And it is ill done when men's lives are at stake to send the biggest liar in Iceland on such an errand.'

'If you are afraid now, what would you be if Gunnar's bill were singing,' asked Otkell, who was always brave when there were none to slay, and whose courage always waxed great when there were none to fight.

Hallbjorm laughed as he heard him.

'Who can tell who will fear most at the sound of that singing? But this you know well, that when the fight has begun Gunnar does not give his bill much time to sing!'

Now when Skamkell reached Mossfell, he told truly to Gizur the white the offers Gunnar had made.

'Why did not Otkell accept them?' asked Gizur, 'they were generous and noble, as Gunnar's offers are.'

'Otkell wished to do you honour,' replied Skamkell; but Gizur for all answer bade Geir the priest be sent for, and next morning, as soon as he arrived, Gizur told him the story, and after he had finished he said:

'Let Skamkell tell it again, for I misdoubt him greatly.'

So Skamkell was called in, but he was wary, and he told his tale the second time as he had done the first, and though Gizur still misdoubted him he could find no fault.

'Mayhap you speak the truth,' he said; 'but I know the wickedness of your deeds, and if you die in your bed your face belies you.'

And after a little more talking Skamkell rode home to Kirkby.

'Gizur and Geir greet you,' said Skamkell, 'and they wish that this matter should have a peaceful ending. They will that Gunnar shall be summoned as having received and eaten the goods, likewise Hallgerda for stealing them!'

So Otkell followed this counsel, and five days before the opening of the Althing he rode with his brother and Skamkell and a great following to Lithend.

When Gunnar heard what errand they were on, he was very wroth, and after Otkell had read the summons, and departed with his men, he went away to seek Njal.

But Njal told him not to trouble, as before the Thing was over he should be held in greater honour than before.

Gizur the white rode to the Thing also, and he spoke to Otkell, and asked why he had summoned Gunnar to the Thing. Otkell listened in amaze and then answered that he had done so because of the counsel that Gizur himself and Geir the priest had told Skamkell.

'He lied, then,' replied Gizur; 'we gave no such counsel;' and Gunnar and his friends were called, and Gizur stood forth and bade Gunnar make his own award. At first Gunnar refused, but at length, after Gizur and Geir the priest swore that what Skamkell had said was false, he agreed to do it.

And his award was this: that atonement in full should be made for the burnt storehouses and for the stolen food. 'But for the thrall,' said Gunnar, 'I will give nothing, for you knew what he was when you sold him to me. Therefore I will restore him to you. On the other hand, the ill-words which you have spoken of me, and the way in which you sought to put me to shame, I count to be worth full as great an atonement as the burning of a few sheds, of the stealing of a few cheeses. So that for money we stand equal. One thing more I would say, Beware lest you seek again to do me evil.'

So spake Gunnar, and no man said him nay. But after a little Gizur asked that Gunnar might forgive the wrongs Otkell had done him, and hold him his friend. At this Gunnar laughed out in scorn and answered:

'Let Skamkell be his friend. It is to him Otkell looks for counsel. They are fitting mates. But one piece of counsel I will give him, and that is to take shelter with his kinsfolk, for if he stays in this country his end will be speedy.'

For a while Gunnar rested in peace at home and there was no more quarrelling. He gathered in his harvest and tended his cattle, ploughed his fields, and so the autumn and winter passed away and the spring came.

One day when the sun was shining Gunnar took his small axe, and a bag of corn, and set out to sow seed. And while he was stooping to do this, Otkell galloped past, on a wild horse that carried him faster than he would, and he did not see Gunnar. As ill-chance would have it, Gunnar raised himself at that moment from stooping over the furrow, and Otkell's spur tore his ear, and he was very wroth.

'You summon me first, and then you ride over me,' he said, and, as was his wont, Skamkell made answer:

'The wound might have been far sorer, but your anger was greater at the Thing, when you judged the atonement and clenched your bill in your fist.'

'When we next meet my bill shall have something to say to you,' said Gunnar, and went on sowing his corn.

The corn was all sown, and Gunnar was beginning to think of other work, when one morning his shepherd came riding fast.

'I passed eight men in Markfleet,' said he; 'their faces were set this way, and Skamkell was with them. He ever speaks ill of you, and I have heard him tell how you shed tears when Otkell rode over you.'

'It does not do to mind words,' answered Gunnar; 'but for the warning you have given me you shall henceforth do the work that pleases you. Now go to sleep.'

So the shepherd slept, and Gunnar took the saddle off his horse, and laid his own saddle on it; he fetched his shield, and buckled on his sword, and then he took his bill, and as his hand touched it it sang loudly. Rannveig his mother heard the sound, and came out from the door to the place where Gunnar was fastening on his helmet.

'Never have I seen you so full of wrath,' said she. But Gunnar answered her nothing and rode quickly away.

Rannveig went back to the sitting-room, where many men were talking, and, looking at them, she said:

'Loud is your talk, but the bill sang louder when Gunnar rode away.'

When Kolskegg heard that, he saddled his horse and hasted after Gunnar.

Gunnar's horse was swift and steady, and he never drew rein till he reached the ford which he knew Otkell's men must pass. There he tied up his horse, and awaited them on foot. When Otkell's men came up, they, too, sprang to the ground, and Hallbjorm strode towards Gunnar.

'Keep back,' said Gunnar, 'I have no quarrel with brave men like you,' but Hallbjorm answered:

'I cannot for shame stand by while you kill my brother;' and he smote with his spear at Gunnar. While they were fighting, Skamkell struck at Gunnar's back with his axe, but Gunnar turned round, and, with his bill caught the axe from beneath, so that it fell out of Skamkell's hands. A second thrust with the bill stretched Skamkell on the ground, and after him Otkell and three others. They slew eight men in all, Kolskegg aiding.

After that they rode home, and as they went Gunnar said: 'I wonder if I am less base than others because I kill men less willingly than they.'

The first thing Gunnar did was to seek counsel of Njal, who bid him take care never to break the peace which was made between him and his foes, and never to slay more than one man of the same race, 'else your life will be but short.'

'Do you know the death you yourself will die?' he asked.

'Yes, I know it,' answered Njal.

'And what is it?' asked Gunnar once more.

'One that none could guess,' replied Njal, and Gunnar went away.

Now at the next Thing there was great dispute over this suit, but in the end it was settled to Gunnar's honour, and Gizur the white and Geir the priest gave pledges that they would keep the peace. But there were other men who thought they had been wronged by Gunnar, and laid plots to anger him, so that he might be outlawed and forced to leave the country.

By ill-fortune the words which Njal had spoken when he bade Gunnar never to slay more than one man of the same race were noised abroad, and his enemies made a plan by which Gunnar should be forced to fight Thorgeir, son of Otkell, so that his doom might come upon him.

Thus matters stood for a while, and then Gunnar rode down to the isles to see what his thralls were doing, and his foes heard of it, and resolved to lie in wait for him at the Rang river.

But when Gunnar returned he was not alone, as they expected he would be, for Kolskegg his brother was at his side, and carried the short sword which some of them knew well, while Gunnar was armed with his sword and his bill.

The two were yet far from the Rang river when the bill which Gunnar bore in his hand sweated with blood, and Kolskegg, who had not yet seen this sight, grew cold with terror.

'This has some dreadful meaning,' said he; and Gunnar nodded.

'It only happens before a great fight,' he answered, 'and they are called "wound drops" in other lands. So beware. Let us not be taken unawares;' and they looked well about them, till they saw some men lying hidden on the banks on the other side of the ford.

Long it were to tell of that fierce fight, and of the

men that were slain by Kolskegg and Gunnar. At last Thorgeir, Otkell's son, forced his way to the front and swung his sword at Gunnar. The blow would have been deadly had it fallen, but, leaping aside, he thrust his bill through Thorgeir's body, and flung him far into the river.

At that the other men turned and fled away.

'Our money-chests will be emptied for atonement for these men,' said Gunnar as they drew near Lithend, and when they told their mother, Rannveig shook her head.

'I fear lest ill should come of it,' said she.

And ill *did* come of it.

Njal's heart was sore when Gunnar told him of the fight by the Rang river, for he said:

'You have gone against my counsel, and have slain two men of the same race. So take heed, if you break the award, your life will pay forfeit. But whatever befalls I am always your friend.'

Soon the Thing was held, and upon the Hill of Laws Gizur the white summoned Gunnar, for manslaughter of Thorgeir, Otkell's son, and demanded that his goods should be forfeited and his body outlawed, and that no man should help or harbour him.

After this there was much talking, but at last the award was given by twelve men.

And this was it.

Money was to be paid down for the men slain, and Gunnar and Kolskegg were to depart from Iceland and not return for three winters. But if Gunnar should break the settlement and stay at home, any man might slay him as he would.

Gunnar promised to keep the award, but he did not hold it a just one.

Then Kolskegg began to inquire of the vessels that were sailing that summer, and he settled that he would go on board the ship of Armfin of the Bay, and Gunnar his brother would go with him.

They sent down to the shore those things that they might need in foreign lands, and then Gunnar bade farewell to Njal and his men, and thanked his friends for the help they had given him.

At the last he took leave of the thralls at Lithend, and of his mother, and told them that, since his own country had outlawed him, he would never return to it. Then he threw his arms round every man, and without looking back sprang into the saddle.

As they rode along the Mark fleet, his horse stumbled, and Gunnar fell to the ground. When he got up he did not mount at once, but stood and looked round him for a while. Suddenly he turned and said to Kolskegg: 'Never has my home seemed to me so fair as now when the corn is ripe and ready for cutting. Come what may, I will not leave it.'

'Do not let your foes triumph over you,' answered Kolskegg. 'For if you should break your atonement, any man may deal with you as he will.'

'I will go no whither,' repeated Gunnar, 'and I would that you would stay with me.'

'I cannot do this thing,' answered Kolskegg; 'but if you go back, tell my mother and my kindred that I bid them farewell for ever, for you will soon be dead, and I shall have naught to bind me to Iceland.'

Hallgerda's heart was filled with joy when Gunnar came under the doorway, but Rannveig said nothing, for her heart was sad.

All that winter Gunnar sat fast at Lithend and would not be prevailed on to leave it, and when the winter had gone and the Thing had met, Gizur the white proclaimed Gunnar an outlaw for having broken his atonement. Then he called together all his foes, and they planned together how that they should ride to Lithend and slay him. But Njal heard what they had been saying, and he warned Gunnar.

'You have always dealt truly and kindly with me,' said Gunnar, when Njal had finished speaking, 'and if ill befall me, take heed, I pray you, of my son and Hogni. As for Grani, he has an evil nature, and there is no turning him from bad deeds.'

It was in the autumn that Mord, the son of Valgard, sent word to Gunnar's foes that the time had come to make the attack upon Lithend, as all his men had gone to the haymaking on the isles of the sea. So they set forth secretly, but stopped first at the farm nearest to Lithend, where they seized the farmer, and warned him that unless he came with them and put to death the hound Sam which had guarded Gunnar ever since Olaf the Peacock had bestowed him as a gift, his own life should be forfeit. Thorkell the farmer was sore at heart when he heard what was required of him, but he took his axe and went with the rest. It was easy to entice Sam the hound into a hollow dell; but when he saw the crowd of men behind Thorkell he knew that evil was afoot, and sprang on Thorkell and tore open his throat. Then Aumond of Witchwood smote him on the head with his axe, and Sam gave a howl which was not the utterance of any mortal dog, and rolled over.

Gunnar, who was sleeping in the narrow space above his great wooden hall, heard the awful sound, and said to himself: 'So they have killed thee, Sam, my fosterling. Well, I will follow thee soon;' and, taking his bill in his hand, he went up into the roof of the hall, where among the beams were little slits for windows. In the winter there were shutters fastened over these little slits, but now they were left open.

From the beam on which he was crouching Gunnar saw a red tunic slipping by the window, and he thrust swiftly out his bill. In a moment a man's body fell upon the ground below.

'Well, is Gunnar at home?' said Gizur, and Thorgrim the Easterling answered: 'Go and see for yourselves; but if Gunnar is not at home, his bill is,' and those were his last words, for the thrust had been mortal.

It hardly seemed possible that one man could keep such a force at bay, but wherever they went Gunnar's arrows followed them. Three times they came on, and three times they fell back, and Gunnar's heart beat high, for he thought that perchance their courage might fail, and that they would return whither they had come.

'One of their own arrows sticks outside the window,' he said, laughing loud in his glee; 'I will send it to kill its master.' But his mother answered: 'It is ill to waken a sleeping dog, my son.'

Her words were wise, but Gunnar would not listen to them. He shot the arrow into the midst of the men gathered beneath him, and knew not that it had dealt a death-blow, or that Gizur the white had been watching its course.

'The arm that drew in that shaft had a ring on it—a gold ring such as Gunnar wears,' said he, 'and if they had not shot away their own arrows they would not be needing ours;' and with that he urged them to make a fresh attack.

'Let us set the house on fire,' said Mord, but Gizur answered him hotly, and bade him find out some other plan.

Now Mord was a man of many thoughts, and great skill in planning, so he looked about him to see if there was aught else he could do. Lying near were some ropes, and as soon as he saw them he cried out, 'If we can twist one end of the ropes round the beams, and the other round this rock, we can twist them tight, and pull the roof off the hall.'

And this was done; and when the roof fell down they beheld Gunnar standing on the beam, shooting arrows at his enemies.

At this Mord cried once more that the house should be burned, but the rest called shame on him, and then Thorbrand crept up on one side and cut Gunnar's bowstring with his axe. But before he could reach the ground again Gunnar had seized his bill, and driven it through his body.

Then, without looking round, Gunnar said swiftly to Hallgerda his wife: 'Let you and my mother cut off two locks of hair from your heads, and twist them into my bowstring, so that I may shoot at them once more.'

'Does aught depend on it?' she asked. 'My life,' he said; and Hallgerda made answer: 'Do you remember that time when you struck me in the face?' said she; 'well, now you shall die for it.'

For many a day men sang of the fight which Gunnar made for his life and the numbers that he slew before he himself was struck down and slain.

'We have laid low a great chief,' said Gizur, 'and many hearts will be sore because of his slaying. But, though his body is dead, his name shall live for ever.'

NJAL'S BURNING

Now, Valgard the Cunning was dying. And he sent for his son Mord and bade him stir up strife between Njal's sons and their brother Hauskuld the priest, for he ever hated Njal, and longed to be avenged on him. So Mord fared to Hauskuld, and told him tales of what his brothers had said of him, but Hauskuld bade him begone, for he would listen to none of his stories. Then Mord left Hauskuld the priest, and had ready a long tale, how that Hauskuld had meant to burn them while they sat at a feast in Whiteness, had not Hogni, Gunnar's son, come by. And as this plan had failed, he set about gathering his men together to slay his brothers as they rode home, but neither Grani, son of Gunnar, nor Gunnar, son of Lambi, had the heart to do it.

At first, neither Njal's sons, nor Kari, who had married their sister, would give ear to Mord's false words, but in spite of themselves ill-feelings began to spring up in their breasts towards Hauskuld.

Thus things went on for many months, and whenever Mord met one of Njal's sons, or Kari, who had married their sister, he had new stories to tell them, till at length their hearts grew hot, and they determined that they would slay Hauskuld, lest perchance he might first slay them.

Hauskuld was sowing his corn when his brothers, and with them Mord, Valgard's son, came up to kill him. Skarphedinn, Njal's son, was their leader, and had bidden the rest each to give Hauskuld a wound. But the first blow dealt by Skarphedinn brought him on his knees, and he died praying that they might be forgiven for the ill they had brought on him, guiltless.

When he was dead they went home and told Njal what they had done.

'It had been well if two of you had died and Hauskuld had lived,' said Njal after he had heard the tidings, 'for I know better than you what will be the end of this.'

'And what will be the end?' asked Skarphedinn.

'My death, and yours, and your mother's,' answered Njal.

'Shall I die also?' he asked; but Njal shook his head.

'Good fortune will ever be with you!' he answered, and turned away and wept.

Now all men knew that at the next Thing a suit would be brought for the slaying of Hauskuld, and Njal and his sons made ready to fare to it, and to hear the award which should be given. But first sundry of Njal's friends came to see him and offered to stand by him, and to set up their tents beside his, and among them were Gizur the white and Asgrim. And at the Thing an award was made, but was made void by a quarrel between Flosi, the friend of Hauskuld the slain, and Skarphedinn, and Njal and his sons returned home, and Njal's heart was heavy.

'Are you riding back to your wife?' asked he of Kari, his son-in-law; and Kari made answer, 'Whatever happens to you, happens to me!' and they all stayed at Bergthorasknoll.

In the house dwelt an old, old woman, so old that she had nursed Bergthora, Njal's wife, and she was wise and could see into the future. Njal's sons laughed at her warnings, and took no heed to them, but for all that they knew well that it was often the truth she told them. One day Skarphedinn was standing outside the door, and the old woman came out with a stick in her hand, and she passed silently by him, and walked up the path to where a pile of dried shrubs lay above the house.

'May a curse be upon you!' she cried, shaking her stick over it; and Skarphedinn, who had followed after her, asked wherefore she was wroth with the pile.

'Because with the fire lighted from this pile there will be a great burning,' said she. 'And Njal and his sons will be burnt, and Bergthora, my foster-child. So carry it away and scatter it in the water, or else set fire to it before your enemies can get here!'

'What is the use of doing anything?' answered Skarphedinn, 'for if it is written that we should be burned, our foes will find some other fuel, though I were to scatter this stack to the four winds;' and he went away laughing.

All through the summer the old nurse was ever begging Njal to do away with the stack of vetch, but the harvest was plentiful in the pastures and the men never came home save to sleep.

'We can bring in that vetch stack any time,' they said.

The harvest was stored in the barns, and a good harvest it was. There had been none such since the day that Gunnar had fared from Lithend with Kolskegg, and had returned to his ruin. One day, when Grim and Helgi, Njal's sons, had ridden away to Holar to see their children, who were at nurse there, they heard strange tidings from some poor woman, that the country side was stirring and that bands of men were gathering together, and were seen riding along the same road.

At this news Grim and Helgi looked at each other.

'Let us go home to Bergthorasknoll,' said they.

Now they had told their mother they would sleep that night at Holar, with their children, so she gave no thought to them; but in the evening, when the hour had come to prepare supper, Bergthora bade every man choose whatever dish he liked best, 'for,' said she, 'this is the last food you will eat in this house!'

'Of a truth you must be ill to speak such words,' cried they.

'They are true words,' she said again; 'and that you may know them to be true, I will give you a sign. Before the meat that is on the board to-night is eaten, Grim and Helgi will be in the house!' and she held her peace and went out.

When the food was prepared, Bergthora called to them, and all sat down but Njal, who lingered in the doorway.

'What hinders you eating with the rest?' asked Bergthora; and Njal, as he answered, put his hand before his eyes.

'A vision has come to me,' he said slowly—'the wall is thrown down, and the board is wet with blood.'

At this the men's faces grew pale, and a strange look came into their eyes, but Skarphedinn bade them be of good cheer, and to remember that, whatever might befall, all men would look to them to bear themselves bravely.

Then Grim and Helgi entered with their tidings, and every one had in his mind what Bergthora had said, and knew that ill was in store.

'Let no man sleep to-night,' said Njal, 'but take heed to his arms.'

The band of Njal's foes, headed by Flosi, had ridden to a valley behind the house, and had fastened their horses there. After that they walked slowly up the path, to the front of the house, where Njal and his sons, and Kari, his-son-in-law, and his thralls, thirty in all, stood up to meet them.

Then both sides halted and spoke together. Flosi's counsel was to fall on them where they stood, though he knew that few would there be left to tell the tale to their children.

Njal, for his part, desired that his men might return inside the hall, for the house was strong; 'and if Gunnar alone could keep them at bay they will never prevail against us,' he said.

'Ah, but these chiefs are not of the kind that slew Gunnar,' answered Skarphedinn, 'for they turned a deaf ear to Mord's evil counsel to set fire to Lithend, so that Gunnar and his wife and mother should be burnt up in it. But this band care nothing for what is fair and honourable, so long as we leave our bones behind us.'

Then Helgi spoke:

'Let us do as our father wills. He knows best,' and Skarphedinn said:

'If he wishes us to enter the hall, and all to be burnt together, I am ready to do it. I care little what death I shall die, and if the time of my doom is come, it matters nothing that we try to escape.' And so saying he turned to Kari, and bade him stand by his side.

'They are all mad,' cried Flosi, as he saw Njal and his sons and Kari, his son-in-law, take their place on the inside of the door. 'Surely none of them can escape us now;' and the fight began with a spear which was thrown at Skarphedinn.

But victory was not so near as Flosi thought. Man after man fell back wounded or dead, yet Skarphedinn and his brethren remained without a wound.

'We shall never put them to flight with our spears,' said Flosi, 'and there are only two ways open. Either we give up our vengeance, and await the death that will surely befall us at their hands;

or else we must set fire to the house, and burn them in it. And I know not what else we can do; yet that is a mean and cowardly deed, which will lie heavily on our souls.'

So they gathered wood and made a great stack before the door, and Skarphedinn laughed, and asked if they were turning cooks.

It was Grani, the son of Gunnar, whose soul was black like his mother Hallgerda's, who answered him.

'You will not wish better cooking when *you* are put on the spit;' but he had better have left Skarphedinn alone, for the men around heard his reply, and looked curiously on Grani.

'Your deeds become your mother's son,' said Skarphedinn. 'It was I who avenged your father, therefore it is natural to one of your kind that you should wish to slay me,' and he stepped back to pick up some fresh arrows.

In spite of Grani's boastful words, the pile of wood was slow in catching, for the women threw whey and water upon it from the little windows in the roof, so that the flames were quenched as fast as they sprang up. The men grew angry and impatient, and at last Kol, Thorstein's son, said to Flosi:

'It avails nought to kindle the fire here; but there is a pile of dry vetch at the back, just above the house, and we can light it, and put the burning wood on the beams under the roof.'

So he crept round unseen, and did as he had said, and the other men heaped up wood before the doors of the house, so that none could escape, and those within the hall knew nothing that was doing, till a great light filled the place, and they saw that the roof was burning.

Then horrible dread overwhelmed the souls of the women, and they broke forth into weeping and wailing, till Njal spoke words of comfort to them, and bade them keep up their hearts, for God would not suffer them to burn both in this world and in the next. And when he had stilled their fears he went near the door, and asked:

'Is Flosi nigh at hand?'

'Yes,' answered Flosi.

'Will you suffer my sons to atone?' asked Njal once more, 'or let them leave the house?' but Flosi said:

'The women and children and thralls may go out, but, as for your sons, the time for atonement is past, and I will not leave this spot as long as one of them remains alive.'

When Njal heard that, he went back into the house and called the women and children and thralls round him, and bade Thorhalla, the wife of Helgi, go out first, for she was a brave woman. And Thorhalla went, after bidding farewell to Helgi her husband.

But Astrid whispered softly to Helgi:

'I will tie a woman's kerchief about your head, and wrap you in a cloak, and the women folk will stand about you, and none shall know that you are not a woman also.'

Helgi did not like this plan, for he thought it shame to steal away in his sister's garments; but they prayed him not to be stiff-necked, and at length he suffered the cloak to be put round him.

Now the children of Njal were all tall, but Helgi was tallest of all, except his brother Skarphedinn. And Flosi marked him, and said to his men:

'I like not the height of the woman who went yonder, nor the breadth of her shoulders. Seize her and hold her fast.'

As soon as Helgi heard that he threw his cloak aside and thrust at a man with his sword, and cut off his leg. But Flosi was close behind, and stretched Helgi dead in front of him.

After that he went back to the house, and offered Njal that he should come outside, but Njal answered that he was too old to avenge his sons, and that he would not outlive them, for that would be a shame and disgrace to him.

'Come out, then, Bergthora,' said Flosi, 'for I will not suffer you to burn inside.'

But Bergthora made answer:

'Long years from my youth have I lived with Njal, and I vowed on the day of betrothal that his death should be mine;' and without more words they went into the house.

'I am weary,' said Njal to his wife, 'let us lay down on our bed and rest;' and Bergthora bowed her head, and spoke to the boy Thord, the son of Kari:

'Come to the door with me and go forth with your kinsmen. I will not have you stay here to burn.' But the boy shook off the hand she had laid on his shoulder.

'You promised me when I was little, grandmother, that I should never go from you till I wished it of myself. And I would rather die with you than live after you.'

Bergthora was silent, but she led the boy to the bed, and he climbed in, and laid himself down. Then Njal said to his head man:

'Bring hither the oxhide and put it on the bed, and watch how we lay ourselves down, so that you may know where to find our bones. For not one inch will we stir, whatever befall.'

And he laid himself down, and bade the boy lie between himself and Bergthora.

So they waited.

At the doors and in the windows of the roof Skarphedinn and Grim were casting away burning brands, and hurling spears as if they had had twenty hands instead of two. At last Flosi called to his men to let be, till the fire had its way, for many had been killed and wounded already.

And now a beam which held up the oak fell in, and then another and another. 'Surely my father must be dead,' said Skarphedinn, 'that he makes no sound,' and, followed by Grim and Kari, he went to the end of the hall where a cross beam had fallen.

'The smoke is thick here,' said Kari, 'thick enough to hide a man; let us leap out one by one, and we shall be away before they have seen us. Skarphedinn, you jump first!'

'No!' answered Skarphedinn, 'you go first and I will follow; or, if I follow not, you will avenge me.'

'I have a chance of my life,' said Kari, 'and I will take it. We must each do as seems best to him, but I fear me that we see each other no more;' and catching up a huge blazing beam, he threw it over the edge of the roof, among the men who were gathered below.

They scattered at once like leaves in a storm, and at that instant Kari, with his tunic and hair already burning, leaped from the roof and crept away in the smoke. The man who stood nearest on the ground thought he saw something dark moving, and he asked his neighbour:

'Think you that was one of them jumping from the beam?' but the man answered: 'Nay, but it may have been Skarphedinn hurling a firebrand;' and then they went to their own work, and paid no more heed to the figure on the roof.

So Kari was left free to escape, and he put out the fire that was burning him, and rested in a safe place till he could seek shelter with his friends.

Thrice Skarphedinn tried to leap after Kari, and thrice the beam broke under his weight, and he was forced to climb back again. Then part of the wall fell in, and Skarphedinn fell down with it on to the floor of the hall.

In a moment the face of Gunnar, son of Lambi, was seen on top of the wall, and he cried out, 'Are those tears on your cheeks, Skarphedinn?' and Skarphedinn made answer:

'Now am I finding out in truth how smoke can force tears from one's eyes. But methinks I see laughter in yours, Gunnar.'

'Of a surety,' said Gunnar, 'never have I laughed so much since the day you slew Thrain in Markfleet.'

'Here is a remembrance of that day for you,' said Skarphedinn, and he took from his pouch Thrain's tooth, and flung it at Gunnar. And it knocked out Gunnar's eye, and he fell from the roof.

Then Skarphedinn went to Grim, and hand in hand they two tried to stamp out the burning beams, but before they had crossed the hall Grim dropped dead, and the roof fell in, and shut Skarphedinn in a corner, so that he could not move.

At daylight a man rode up who had met Kari, and had learned from him that when he had jumped from the roof both Skarphedinn and Grim were still alive, but that was many hours before, and both must long since be dead.

Then Flosi and some of his men drew nearer and climbed up the gable, for the fire had burned low, and only threw out a flame here and there. And as they looked into the hall beneath them, which was a mass of charred and fallen wood, there seemed to rise up from the red ashes a song of triumph, and they held their breath and looked into each other's faces.

'Is it Skarphedinn's song?' asked Glum, 'and is it a token that he is dead? or a sign that he is alive? Let us look for him.'

'That shall not be,' said Flosi quickly. 'Fool that you are, do you not know that even now Kari is gathering together a band to avenge his kinsmen? Therefore let every man take his horse and ride up to the Three-corner Fell, and there we can hide and take counsel how we can escape from our enemies.'

So it was done, and not a whit too soon, for a very great company scattered over the country, seeking Flosi and his Band of Burners — for by this ill name men knew them.

As for Kari himself, he begged Hjallti, Njal's cousin, to go with him to Bergthorasknoll and find Njal's bones and bury them. And, as they went, men joined them, till they numbered nigh on a hundred when they reached Bergthorasknoll.

Kari entered the hall first and led them up to the spot where the bed had stood, and where a great heap of ashes now covered it. The ashes took long to clear away, and underneath was the oxhide, charred and shrivelled. But when the oxhide was pulled away they saw the three bodies fresh and whole, as they had laid them down. Only one finger of the boy was burned, where he had thrust it outside the hide.

When they saw this a great joy fell on the hearts of all, and Hjallti said:

'Never have I seen a dead man with a face as bright as this!' And the other men said likewise.

After that they sought for Skarphedinn, and then found him, fastened by the beam into the corner, and he had driven his axe into the wall of the gable, so that it had to be broken out. And they sought the bones of Grim, and found them lying in the middle of the hall, where he had dropped down dead. And they sought the bones of other men, and found them, and nine bodies in all were carried into the church and buried there.

And that is Burnt Njal's story.

THE LADY OF SOLACE

There was once an emperor who had two things that he loved more than all the world — his daughter and his garden. The finest linen and the richest silks of India or China decked the princess from the moment she was old enough to run alone, and the ships that brought them brought also the fairest flowers and sweetest fruits that grew in distant lands. All the time that he was not presiding over his council, or hearing the petitions of his people, the emperor passed in his garden, watching the flowers open and the fruits ripen, and by-and-by he planted trees and shrubs and made walks and alleys, till altogether the garden was the most beautiful as well as the largest that had ever been seen.

The years passed, and the princess reached the age of fourteen; quite old enough to be married, thought the kings and princes who were looking out for a bride for their sons. The emperor's heart sank when he heard rumours of embassies that were coming to rob him of his daughter, and he shut himself up in his room to try to invent a plan by which he might keep the princess, without giving offence to the powerful monarchs who had asked for her hand.

For a long while he sat with his head on his hands, thinking steadily, but every scheme had some drawback. At length his face brightened and he sprang up from his seat.

'Yes! that will do,' he cried, and went down to attend his council, looking quite a different man from what he had been a few hours before.

The embassies and the princes continued to arrive, and they all got the same answer. 'The emperor was proud of the honour done to himself and his daughter, and would give her in marriage to any man who would pass through the garden and bring him a branch of the tree which stood at the further end.' Nothing could surely be more easy, and every prince in turn as he heard the conditions felt that the fairest damsel on the whole earth was already his wife.

But though each man went gaily in, none ever came out, nor was it ever known what had befallen them. At last so many had entered that fatal gate that it seemed as if there could be no more princes or nobles left, and the emperor began to breathe again at the thought that he would be able after all to keep his daughter.

But one day a knight of great renown, named Tirius, arrived from beyond the seas and knocked at the gate of the castle. Like the others, he was welcomed and feasted, and when the feast was ended he craved that the emperor would grant him the hand of the princess on whatever condition he might choose.

'Right willingly,' answered the emperor; 'there is only one condition I have laid down, and that is an easy one, though for some strange reason no one as yet has been able to fulfil it. You have merely to walk through the garden that you see below, and bring me back a branch from a tree bearing golden fruit, which stands on the opposite side. If fame speaks true, this is child's play to the adventures in which you have borne so noble a part.'

'In good sooth,' said the knight, who saw clearly that there was more in the matter than appeared— 'in good sooth your condition likes me well. Still, as fortune is ever inconstant, and may be tired of dealing me favours, I would first ask as a boon a sight of your fair daughter and leave to hearken to her voice. After that I will delay no longer, but proceed on my quest.'

'I will take you to her myself,' answered the emperor, who thought that he might show this small mercy to a man who was going to his death, and he led his guest down long passages and through lofty halls, till they reached the princess's apartments.

'In five minutes my chamberlain shall come for you, and he shall show you the way to the garden,' said the emperor, 'and meanwhile I bid you farewell;' and, leaving Tirius to enter alone, he went to seek his ministers.

It would be hard to say whether the knight or the princess was most amazed as they stood gazing at each other—he at her beauty and she at his boldness, for never before had any man crossed her threshold. For a moment both were silent; then the knight, remembering how short a time was allowed him, aroused himself from his dream and spoke:

'Gentle damsel, help me now in my need, for I have been drawn hither by love. Full well I know that many have had this adventure before me, and have entered that garden and never returned from it. Without your aid my fate will be such as theirs, and therefore, I pray you, tell me what I should do so that I may win through without harm.'

Now the knight was a goodly man and tall, and perhaps the princess may have bewailed in secret the noble youths who had fallen victims to her father's pleasure. But, however that might be, she smiled and made reply:

'I am ready to marry any man on whom my father wishes to bestow me, and you say you have come hither for love of me. Still, you have asked of me a hard thing, for it beseems not a daughter to betray her father's confidence. Yet, as I am loth that any more fair youths should lose their lives for my sake, I will give you this counsel. You must first pass through a forest, which is the home of a lady who is known to all as the "Lady of Solace." Go to her, and she will give you the help you need to journey safely through the garden.'

The princess had scarcely finished these words when the voice of the chamberlain was heard without, bidding him withdraw, and, glancing gratefully at her, the knight bowed low and took his leave.

In the great hall the chamberlain quitted him, telling him to take his ease and rest till the emperor should return, but instead the knight waited till he was alone and then plunged straight into the forest.

He walked on for a little way till he reached a green space, and there he stopped and cried, 'Where is the Lady of Solace?' Then he sat down on a stone and waited. In a short time he saw coming towards him two ladies, one bearing a basin and the other a cloth.

'We give you greeting, sir,' they said; 'the Lady of Solace has sent us to you, and she bids you first wash your feet in this basin, and then go with us to her palace.' So the knight washed his feet, and dried them in the white cloth, and rose up and went with the ladies to the palace, which was built of blue marble, and the fairest that ever he saw. The Lady of Solace was fair likewise and of a marvellous sweet countenance, and her voice was soft like the voice of a thrush as she asked him what he wanted with her. At that the knight told his errand, and how the princess had bade him come to her, for she alone could help him to win through the enchanted garden.

'I am called the Lady of Solace,' said she, with a smile which seemed made up of all the beautiful things in the world, 'and I give succour to all those who need it. Here is a ball of thread; take it and bind it round the post of the gate of the garden, and hold fast the thread in your hand, unwinding it as you go. For if you lose the clue, you will perish like those before you. And more. A lion dwells in the garden, who will spring out and devour you, as he has devoured the rest. Therefore, arm yourself with armour, and see that the armour be anointed thickly with ointment. When the lion sees you, he will take your arm or your leg into his mouth, and his teeth shall stick fast in the ointment, and when you sunder yourself from him his teeth shall be drawn out, and you shall kill him easily. But during the fight beware lest you let go the clue.'

And after the lion shall come four men, who will set on you and seek to turn you from their path; but beware of them also, and if you are in peril call to me, and I will succour you. And now return to the palace and put on your armour, and so, farewell.'

When the knight heard this he was right glad, and stole back to the palace, where he found that the emperor was still sitting at his council. He sat down in the great hall to await him, but the time seemed very long before his host entered.

'How have you sped?' asked he.

'My lord, now that through your goodness I have seen the princess,' said the knight, 'there can be but one ending to my journey. I go at once in quest of the tree, and I am content whatever fate may befall me.'

'May fortune be with you!' answered the emperor, who never failed to give good wishes to his daughter's suitors, as he felt quite sure that they would be of no use.

So the knight bowed low and left the hall, going straight to the gatekeeper's house, where he had put off his armour on arriving. On pretence of sharpening his sword, he borrowed a pot of ointment from the man, and, unseen by him, rubbed the paste thickly over his armour. After this he looked about to see that no one was watching him, and took the path that led to the garden.

A large iron gate supported by two posts stood at the entrance, and round one of these he firmly bound one end of the thread which the Lady of Solace had given him. Holding the other end in his hand, he advanced for a long while without seeing or hearing any strange thing, till a roar close to him caused him to start. The knight had just time to draw his sword and hold up his shield before the lion was upon him; but, as he had been forewarned, the great beast dashed aside the shield, and fastened his teeth in the arm that held it. The pain was such that the knight leaped backwards, but the lion's teeth were fixed fast in the ointment, and they all came out of his mouth, so that he could bite no more. And when he rushed at his enemy with his claws they stuck also, so that the knight with a blow of his sword was able to kill him with ease.

Mightily he rejoiced at seeing his foe dead before him, and by ill fortune he forgot that, had it not been for the counsel of the Lady of Solace, it was *he* who would have been slain, and not the lion. He swelled with pride and conceit at the ease with which he had won the victory, and never noted that the clue of thread was no longer in his hands.

'Ah, lovely princess, I come to seek my reward,' cried he to himself, and turned his face towards the palace. But a little way on he spied seven trees, very fair to view, all covered with fruit that shone temptingly in the sun. He gathered a cluster that hung just above his head, and when he had eaten that, he thought that it tasted so delicious he really must have another, and another also.

He was still eating when three men passed by, and asked him what he was doing there. The knight was so puffed up that he did not answer them civilly after his manner, but gave them rude words, for which in return he received buffets. In the end, the men dragged him away from the tree and flung him into a ditch that was full of water, and his armour weighed him down, so that he could not get out. Then at last he remembered his clue, and felt for it, but it was not there, and his pride broke down, and he saw that he had brought his ruin on himself. And in despair he lifted up his voice and cried, 'O Lady of Solace, help me, I beseech you, in my great need, for I am nigh dead.' He shut his eyes for very misery, but opened them again in a moment, for a lady stood by him, and she said:

'Did not I tell you that if you lost the clue you could never more find your way out of the garden? I will lift you out of the ditch, but, for the clue, you must seek for it yourself till you find it.' And with that she vanished.

Not that day did the knight find the clue, nor the next, nor the next. Faint and weary was he, but he dared not eat of the fruit that was around him, some hanging from the boughs of trees and some growing on the ground. At length he wandered back to the spot where he had fought with the lion, and there, covered with blood, lay the clue he had so long sought. By its help he was led to the tree with the golden fruit, which stood at the far end of the garden, and plucking one of the boughs he turned to retrace his steps, wondering, now that he held the thread, at the shortness of the way.

'Here is the branch, O Emperor! and now give me the princess,' he said, kneeling and laying the bough down on the steps of the throne. And the emperor could not gainsay him, but bade his officers fetch his daughter, and after they had been married she went with her husband into his own country, where they lived happily till they died.

UNA AND THE LION

Once upon a time there lived a king and queen who had only one child, a little girl, whom they named Una, and they all lived happily at home for many years till Una had grown into a woman.

It seemed as if they were some of the fortunate people to whom nothing ever happens, when suddenly, just as everything appeared going well and peacefully with them, a fearful dragon, larger and more horrible than any dragon which had yet been heard of, arrived one night, seized the king and queen as they were walking in the garden after the heat of the day, and carried them prisoners to a strong castle. Luckily, Una was at that moment sitting among her maidens on the top of a high tower embroidering a kirtle, or she would have shared the same fate.

When the princess learnt what had befallen her parents, she was struck dumb with grief, but she had been taught that no misfortune was ever mended by tears, so she soon dried her eyes, and began to think what was best to do, and to whom she could turn for help. She ran quickly over in her mind the knights who thronged her father's court, but there was not one amongst them to whose hands their rescue could be entrusted. One spent his days in writing pretty verses to the ladies who were about the queen, another passed his time in putting on suits more brilliant than any worn by his friends, a third loved hawking, but did not welcome the rough life and hard living of real warfare; no, she must seek a champion out of her own country if her parents were to be delivered out of the power of the dragon. Then all at once she remembered a certain Red Cross Knight whose fame had spread even to her distant land, and, ordering her white ass to be saddled, she set forth in quest of him.

It were long to tell the adventures Una met with on the way, but at last she found the knight resting after a hard-won fight, and told him her tale.

'Right willingly will I help you, princess,' said he, 'only you must ride with me and guide me to the castle, for I know nothing of the countries that lie beyond the sea;' and Una heard his words with joy, and called softly to her ass, who was cropping the short green grass beside her.

'Let us go forth at once,' she cried gaily, and sprang into her saddle. The knight hastily fastened on his armour, and, placing a blood-red cross upon his breast, swung himself on to his horse's back. And so they rode over the plain, a trusty dwarf following far behind, and a snow-white lamb, held by a golden cord, trotting by Una's side.

After some hours they left the plain and entered a forest, where the trees and bushes grew so thick that no path could they see. At first, in their eagerness to escape the storm which was sweeping up the plain behind them, they hardly took heed where they were going; and besides, the beauty of the flowers and the sweet scent of the fruit caused them to forget the trouble they would have to find the road again. But when the sound of the thunder ceased, and the lightning no longer darted through the leaves, they were startled to perceive they had wandered they knew not whither. No sun could they see to show them which was east and which west, neither was there any man to tell them what they fain would know. At length they stopped, for before them lay a cave stretching far away into the darkness.

'We can rest there this night,' said the Red Cross Knight, leaping to the ground, and handing his spear to the dwarf; 'and first, you, lady, shall remain, here, while I enter and make sure that no fierce or loathsome beasts lurk in the corners.' But Una turned pale as she listened.

'The perils of this place I better know than you,' she answered gravely. 'In this den dwells a vile monster, hated by God and man.' And the voice of the dwarf cried also, 'Fly, fly! this is no place for living men.' They might have spared their warnings; when did youth ever heed them? The knight looked into the cave, and

Forth into the darksome hole he went.
His glistening armour made a little glooming light,
By which he saw the ugly monster plain,
Half like a serpent horribly displayed,
The other half did woman's shape retain.

It was too late to turn back, even had he wished it; but indeed it was the monster who looked round, as if to find a way to flee. Before her stood the knight, his sword drawn, waiting for a fair chance to plunge it into her throat. Escape there was none, and she prepared for battle.

The knight fought valiantly, but never had he met a foe like this. The monster was so large and so scaly that he could not get round her, while his sword glanced, blunted, from off her skin. Blow after blow he struck, but they only served to increase her fury, till, gathering all her strength together, she wound her great tail about his body, pressing him close against her horny bosom.

'Strangle her, else she sure will strangle thee,' cried Una, who had been watching the combat as well as the darkness would let her; and the knight heard, and seized the monster by the throat, till she was forced to let go her hold on him. Then, grasping his sword, he cut her head clean from her body.

Fain would they now leave the dreadful wood which had been the nurse of such an evil creature, and by following a track where the leaves grew less thickly, they at last found themselves on the other side of the plain, just as the sun was sinking to rest. They pushed on fast, hoping to find a shelter for the night, but none could they spy. The plain seemed bare, save for one old man in the guise of a hermit who was approaching them.

Him the Red Cross Knight stopped and asked if he knew of any adventures which might await him in that place. The old man, who was in truth the magician Archimago, the professor of lore which could read the secrets of men's hearts, answered that the hour was late for the undertaking of such things, and bade them rest for the night in his cell hard by. So saying, he led them into a little dell amidst a group of trees, in which stood a chapel and the dwelling of the hermit.

It was but a short space before both knight and lady were sleeping soundly on the beds of fern which the hermit told them he had always at hand for the entertainment of guests. But, for himself, he crept unseen to a little cave inside a rock, and taking out his magic books he sought therein for mighty charms to trouble sleepy minds!

He soon found what he wanted, and repeated some strange words aloud. In an instant there fluttered round him a crowd of little sprites awaiting his bidding, but he motioned all aside except two—one of whom he kept with him and the other he sent on a message to the house of Morpheus, the god of sleep.

'I come from Archimago the wizard,' said the sprite when he reached his journey's end. 'Give me, I pray you, as swiftly as may be, a bad dream, that I may carry it back to him.'

Slowly the god rose up, and, going to his storehouse, where lay dreams of all sorts—dreams to make people happy, dreams to make people miserable, dreams to stir people to good, and dreams to move them to every kind of wickedness—he took from the shelf a small but very black little dream, which the sprite tied round his neck, and hurried to the cave of Archimago.

The wizard took the dream in silence, and, going into the den where the knight was sleeping, laid it softly on his forehead. In a moment his face clouded over; evil thoughts of Una sprang into his mind, till at length, unable to bear any longer the grief of mistrusting her he so loved and honoured, the knight called to the dwarf to bring him his horse, and together they rode away. But when Una woke and found both of her companions departed she wept sorely. Then, mounting her milk-white ass, she set out to follow them.

Meanwhile the Red Cross Knight was wandering he knew not whither, so deep were the wounds in his heart. He rode on with his bridle hanging loosely on his horse's neck, till a bend in the path brought him face to face with a mighty Saracen, bearing on his arm a shield with the words 'Sans foy' written across it. By his side, mounted on a palfrey hung with golden bells, was a lady clad in scarlet robes embroidered with jewels, who chattered merrily as they passed along.

It was she who first perceived the approach of an enemy, and, turning to Sansfoy, bade him begin the attack. He, nothing loth, dashed forward to meet the knight, who had barely time to steady himself to receive the blow, which caused him to reel in his saddle. The blow was indeed so hard that it would have pierced the knight's armour had it not been for the cross upon his breast; which, when the Saracen saw, he cursed the power of the holy emblem, and prepared himself for a fresh attack.

But either the Christian knight was the more skilful swordsman, or the cross lent new strength to his arm, for the fight was not a long one. Only a few strokes had passed between them, when the boastful Sansfoy fell from his horse, and rolled heavily to the ground. The lady hardly waited for the issue of the combat, and galloped off lest she too should be in danger. But the knight did not wage war on ladies, and, calling to the dwarf to bring the Saracen's shield as a trophy, he spurred quickly after her.

He did not take long to come up with her for, in truth, she intended to be overtaken, and turned a woeful countenance to the young knight, who listened, believing, to the false tale she told. Pitying her from his heart, he assured her of his care and protection, and while they are faring through the woods together, let us see what had become of Una.

The maiden was herself wandering distraught, seated on her 'unhastie beast,' when with a fearful roar a lion rushed out from a thicket with eyes glaring and teeth gleaming, seeking to devour his prey. But at the sight of Una's tender beauty he stopped suddenly, and, stooping down, he kissed her feet and licked her hands.

At this kindness on the part of the great creature, Una bent her head and wept grievously. 'He, my lion and my noble lord, how does he find it in his cruel heart to hate her that him loved?' she moaned sadly, and the lion again looked pityingly at her, and at last the maiden checked her sobs and bade her ass go on, the lion walking by her side during the day, and sleeping at her feet by night.

They had travelled far and for many days, through a wilderness untrodden by either man or beast, when at the foot of a mountain they spied a damsel bearing on her shoulder a pot of water. At sight of the lion she flung down the pitcher, and ran to the hut where she dwelt, without once looking behind her. In the cottage sat her blind mother, not knowing what could be the meaning of the shrieks and cries uttered by her daughter, who shut the door quickly after her, and caught trembling hold of her mother's hands.

It was the first lion the girl had ever seen, or she would have known that if he was determined to enter, it was not a wicket-gate that would prevent him. As neither mother nor daughter replied to Una's gentle prayer for a night's lodging, her 'unruly page' put his paw on the little door, which opened with a crash. The maiden then stepped softly over the threshold, begging afresh that she might pass the night in one corner, and receiving no answer—for the women were still too terrified to speak—she curled herself up on the earthen floor with the lion beside her.

About midnight there arrived at the door, which Una had refastened, a thief laden with spoils of churches, and whatever else he had managed to pick up by stealth. To spend the night in thieving was his custom, and hither he brought his spoils, as he thought none would suspect a blind woman and her daughter of harbouring stolen goods.

Many times he called, but the two women were in grievous dread of the lion, and durst not move from the corner where they were crouching; at last the man grew angry, and burst the door asunder, as the lion had done before him. He entered the hut, and straightway beheld the dreadful beast, with glaring eyes and gleaming teeth, as Una had first beheld him. But Kirkrapine (such was his name) had neither beauty nor goodness to still the lion's rage, and in another moment his body was rent in a thousand pieces.

The sun had scarce sent his first beams above the horizon when Una left the hut, mounted on her ass, and, followed by the lion, again began her quest of the Red Cross Knight. But, alas! though she found him not, she met her ancient foe, the magician Archimago, who had taken on himself the form of him whom she sought. Too true and unsuspecting was she, to dream of guile in others, and the welcome she gave him was from her whole heart. In the guise of the knight, Archimago greeted her fondly, and bade her tell him the story of her woes, and how came she to take the lion for her companion. And so they journeyed, the flowers seeming sweeter and the skies brighter to Una, as they went, when suddenly they beheld

One pricking towards them with hasty heat;
Full strongly armed, and on a courser free.

On his shield the words 'Sans loy' could be read, written in letters of blood.

Now, though Archimago had clad himself in the outward shape of the Red Cross Knight, he lacked his courage and his skill in war; and his heart was faint from fear, when the Saracen reined back his horse and prepared for battle. In the shock of the rush the wizard was borne backwards, and the blood from his side dyed the ground.

'The life that from Sansfoy thou tookest, Sansloy shall from thee take,' cried the Paynim, and was unlacing the vizor of the fallen man to deal him his death-stroke when a cry from Una stayed his hand for a moment, though it was not her prayers for mercy that would have kept him from drawing his sword, but the sight of the hoary head beneath the helmet, which startled him.

'Archimago!' he stammered, 'what mishap is this?' And still Archimago lay on the ground stunned, and answered nothing.

For a moment Una gazed in amazement at the strange sight before her, and wondered what was the meaning of these things. Then she turned to fly, but, quick as thought, the Saracen plucked at her robe to stop her.

Now when the lion, her fierce servant, saw that Paynim knight lay hands on his sovereign lady, he sprang on him with gaping jaws, and almost tore the shield from his arm. But the knight leapt swiftly back, and swinging his sword plunged it into the heart of the faithful creature, who rolled over and died amidst the tears of his mistress.

After which the knight set Una on his steed before him and bore her away.

HOW THE RED CROSS KNIGHT SLEW THE DRAGON

While Una was riding through forest and over plains, with her faithful lion for her guard, the knight whom she sought had given himself over into the care of Duessa (for such was the name of Sansfoy's companion), by whom he was led to the gates of a splendid palace. The broad road up to it was worn by the feet of hosts of travellers; but though many peeped through the doors few returned. As the knight stood aside and watched, all manner of strange people passed before him, though none spoke. At length a man, but newly issued from the palace, and bearing a shield with the words 'Sans joy' written across it, stopped suddenly in front of the knight's page, then snatched from his arm a shield like his own, bearing the name 'Sansfoy.' The page, overcome by the quickness of the action, did not resist, but a blow on the helmet from the Red Cross Knight made Sansjoy stagger where he stood.

The fight was fierce, and no one could tell with whom the victory lay till the queen of that place came by, and bade them cease their brawling, for on the morrow they should meet in the lists.

But the battle next day went against the Paynim, in spite of the presence of the queen and the counsel of the false Duessa. Short would have been his shrift had not thick darkness fallen about him, and when the Red Cross Knight cried to him to begin the fray afresh, only silence answered him.

Then the false Duessa, ever wont to take the side of him who wins, hurried up to him, and whispered, as she had whispered to Sansjoy, 'The conquest yours, I yours, the shield and glory yours;' but the knight did not heed her, for his eye was ever bent on the wall of thick darkness which shut in his foe. Indeed, so busy were his thoughts that he never knew that blood was streaming from his wounds, till the queen ordered him to be carried into the palace, and ointments to be laid on his body.

As was her custom, Duessa talked much and loudly of the care she would give him, and of his speedy cure under her hands; but when night fell she stole forth and came to the spot where Sansjoy lay, still covered with the enchanted cloud. Then, in an iron chariot, borrowed from the Queen of Darkness, she drove him down to the underworld, and across the river which divides the kingdom of the living from that of the dead. Here giving him into the hands of the oldest and greatest of physicians, she went her way to the bedside of the Red Cross Knight.

But for all that concerned that knight she might well have stayed in the kingdom of darkness; for in her absence the dwarf, wandering through the palace, had come upon a dungeon full of wretched captives, who filled the air with their wailings.

Filled with fear, the dwarf hastened back to his master and prayed him to flee that place before the sun rose. Which the young knight gladly did, creeping away through a secret postern, though it was hard to find a footing amidst the corpses piled up on all sides, which had come to a bad end by reason of their own folly.

And what had become of Una when she had fallen into the power of Sansloy? Well, trembling she had followed him into the midst of a forest, where, to her wonder, from every bush sprang a host of fauns and people of the wood, and ran towards her. When the Saracen beheld them, he was so distraught with fear that he galloped right away, leaving Una behind him. But she, not knowing what to fear the most, stood shaking with dread, till the wood folk pressed around her, and, kneeling on the ground stroked lovingly her hands and feet. Then she understood that she was safe amongst them, and let them lead her where they would, and smiled at their songs and merry dances. If she could not be with the Red Cross Knight, then it mattered little where she was, and it gave her a feeling of rest and safety to lie hidden among the woods, with a people who would let nothing harmful come near her.

So she stayed with them long, and taught them many things, while they in their turn showed her how to play on their pipes and to dance the prettiest and most graceful of their dances.

Time passed in this wise, when one day it chanced that a noble knight, Satyrane by name, came to seek his kindred among the woodfolk. He wondered greatly to find so lovely a maid among them, and still more to see how eagerly they listened to her teachings, and henceforth he formed part of the throng that sat at her feet when the heat of the day was over.

In this manner Una and the knight Satyrane soon became friends, and at length one day she poured out all her sad tale, and besought his help in her search for the Red Cross Knight. It was not easy to escape from the kind people who always thronged about her, and her heart was sore at the thought of leaving them, but she felt that for her captive parents' sake, as well as for the knight's, she could delay no longer.

Therefore one morning, when the wood folk had gone to hold a feast in the forest, she rode away in company with Satyrane, and issuing from the forest soon reached the open plain. Towards evening they met a weary pilgrim, whose clothes were worn and soiled, and so true a pilgrim did he look, that Una did not know him to be the wizard Archimago. The knight instantly drew rein, and asked what tidings he could impart, and Una begged with faltering voice that he would tell her aught concerning a knight whose armour bore a red cross.

'Alas! dear dame,' answered he slowly, 'these eyes did see that knight, both living and eke dead;' and with that he told her all his story.

When he had finished, it was Satyrane who spoke.

'Where is that Paynim's son, that him of life, and us of joy hath reft?' And the pilgrim made answer that he was hard by, washing his wounds at a fountain.

Satyrane wasted no more words, but went right straight to the fountain, where he found Sansloy, whom he challenged instantly to fight. Sansloy hastily buckled on his armour, and cried that, though he had not slain the Red Cross Knight, he hoped to lay his champion in the dust. Then, both combatants being ready, the battle began.

The sight was too dreadful for Una to bear, and she galloped away, not knowing that her deadliest foe, the wizard Archimago, was following her.

Meanwhile Duessa had left the splendid palace, and was riding over the country in pursuit of the Red Cross Knight, for it was bitter to her to see any escape, who had ever been under her thrall. Her good fortune, which never seemed to forsake her, before long led her to his side, where he lay resting on the banks of a stream, and he greeted her gladly.

The sun was hot, and the water rippling clear over the stones seemed inviting. The knight was tired, and leaned down to drink, never knowing that the stream was enchanted. But in a moment his strength seemed to fail, and his arms grew weak as a child's, though he felt nothing till a horrible bellowing sounded in the wood. At the dreadful sound he started up and looked around for his armour, but before he could reach it a hideous giant was upon him.

The fight did not take long, and in a short while the Red Cross Knight was a prisoner in the hands of the giant, who, accompanied by the false Duessa, carried his captive to a dungeon of his castle. After the door was safely locked and barred, the two then retired into the large hall, where they ate and made merry.

From that day the giant brought forth his choicest treasures with which to deck Duessa. Her robes were purple, and a triple crown of gold was on her head, and, what she liked not so well, he gave her a seven-headed serpent to ride on.

Now the faithful dwarf had watched the fate of his master, and when he saw him borne away senseless by the giant, he took up the armour which had been lain aside in the hour of need, and set out he knew not whither.

He had gone but a little distance when he met Una, who read at a glance the evil tidings he had brought. She fell off her ass in a deadly swoon, and the dwarf, whose heart was nigh as sore, rubbed her temples with water and strove to bring her back to life. But when she heard the tale of all that had befallen the Red Cross Knight since last she had parted from him, she would fain have died, till the thought sprang suddenly into her mind that perhaps she might still rescue him. So with fresh hope she took the road to the giant's castle, but the way was far, and she was woefully tired before even its towers were in sight. Brave though she was, the maiden's courage failed her at last, and she began to weep afresh, when her eyes happened to light upon a good knight riding to meet her. He was clad in armour that shone more than any man's, and well it might, as it had been welded by the great enchanter Merlin. On the crest of his helmet a golden dragon spread his wings: and in the centre of his breast-plate a precious stone shone forth amidst a circle of smaller ones, 'like Hesperus among the lesser lights.'

As he drew near, and saw before him a lady in distress, he reined in his horse, and with gentle words drew from her all her trouble.

'Be of good cheer,' he said, when the tale was ended, 'and take comfort; for never will I forsake you till I have freed your captive knight.'

And, though she knew him not, at his promise Una took heart of grace, and bade the dwarf lead them to the giant's castle.

Conducted by the dwarf and followed by the squire, the knight and lady soon reached the castle. Bidding Una to await him outside, and calling to his squire to come with him, they both walked up to the gates, which were fast shut, though no man was guarding them.

'Blow your horn,' said the knight, and the squire blew a blast. At the sound, the gates flew open, and the giant came foaming from his chamber to see what insolent thief had dared disturb his peace.

And the giant did not come alone. Close after him rode Duessa, 'high mounted on her many-headed beast'; and at this sight the knight raised his shield and eagerly began the attack.

But, horrible though the serpent was, he was not the sole foe that the knight had to fight with. The giant's only weapon was his club, but that was as thick as a man's body, and studded with iron points besides. Luckily for the knight, this was not the first giant to whom he had given battle, and ere the mighty blow could fall he sprang lightly to one side, and the club lay buried so deep in the ground that before the giant could draw it out again, his left arm was smitten off by the knight's sword.

The giant's roars of pain might have been heard in the uttermost parts of the kingdom, and Duessa quickly guided her baleful beast to the help of her wounded friend. But her way was barred by the squire, who, sword in hand, 'stood like a bulwark' between his lord and the serpent. Duessa, full of wrath at being foiled, turned the serpent on him, but not one foot would the squire move till, beside herself with anger, the witch drew out her cup and sprinkled him with the poisonous water. Then the strength went out of his arms and the courage from his heart, and he sank helpless on the ground before the snake, who fain would have trampled the life out of him, and it would have fared ill with him had not the knight rushed swiftly to his rescue, and dealt the snake such a wound that the garments of Duessa were all soaked in blood. She shrieked to the giant that she would be lost if he did not come to her aid, and the giant, whose one arm seemed to have gained the strength of two, struck the knight such a blow on the helmet that he sank heavily on the ground.

The giant raised a shout of joy, but he triumphed too soon. The knight, in falling, caught the covering of his shield upon his spear, and rent it from top to toe. The brilliance that flowed from it burnt into the eyes of the giant, so that he was 'blinded by excess of light,' and sank sightless on the ground. At a fresh cry from Duessa he struggled to his feet, but all in vain. He had no power to hurt nor to defend, and fell back so heavily that the very earth shook beneath him, and was an easy prey for his foe, who smote his head from his body.

Duessa, as we know, never stayed with those with whom the world went ill, and she was stealing away quietly, when once more the squire stopped her.

'You are captive to my lord,' he said, and, holding her firmly, led her back.

Then Una came running full of grateful words, but when she saw Duessa a cloud of fierce wrath passed over her face.

'Beware lest that wicked woman escape,' cried she, 'for she it is who has worked all this ill, and thrown my dearest lord into the dungeon. Oh, hear how piteously he calls to you for aid!'

'I give her into your keeping,' answered the knight, turning to the squire, 'and beware of her wiles, for they are many;' and, leaving the rest behind him, he strode into the castle, meeting no man as he went.

At last there crept forth from one corner an old, old man with a huge bunch of rusty keys hanging from his arm. The knight asked him in gentle speech whence had gone all the people who dwelt in the castle, but he answered only that he could not tell, till the knight waxed impatient, and took the keys from him.

The doors of all the rooms opened easily enough, and inside he found the strangest medley. Everywhere blood lay thick upon the floors, while the walls were covered with cloth of gold and splendid tapestry. No signs were there of any living creature, yet he knew that in some hiding-place in the castle the captive lay concealed.

The knight had come to the last door of all. It was of iron, and no key on the bunch would open it. On one side was a little grating, and through it he called loudly, lest perchance any man might hear his voice.

At that there answered him a hollow empty sound, and for a while he could not make out any words. Then from out the wailing in the darkness something spoke:

'Oh, who is that which brings me happy choice of death? Three moons have waxed and waned since I beheld the face of heaven? Oh, welcome, welcome art thou who hast come to end my weary life!'

The moaning sound of the voice thrilled the brave champion with horror. Putting his shoulder to the iron door, he gave a mighty heave, and the hinges gave way. Nothing could he see, for the darkness was terrible, and his foot, which he stretched cautiously inward, touched no floor. And, besides, the foul smells rushed out, poisoning him with their fumes.

But when he had grown in some measure used to the darkness and the odours, he began to think how he could best deliver the Red Cross Knight from the pit into which he had fallen. To this end he sought through the castle till he found some lengths of rope, which he carried back with him, as he did not know how deep the pit might be. He knotted three or four together and let the rope down, but even when a faint cry from the captive told him that it had reached the bottom, his labours were not ended yet. Twice the knots gave way, by good fortune, before the man was more than a foot or two from the ground, and other pieces of rope had to be fetched. Then, when all was made fast, the prisoner had grown so weak that he could scarce draw himself up; and again the knight feared greatly lest he himself should not have strength to hold fast the rope. But at length his courage and patience prevailed, and the Red Cross Knight, hollow-eyed, and thin as a skeleton, looked once more upon the sun.

His parents might have gazed on him and not known him for their child, but Una's heart leapt when the unknown knight brought him to her.

'Welcome,' she said, 'welcome in weal or woe. Your presence I have lacked for many a day,' and fain would she have heard the tale of his sufferings, had not the knight, who knew that men love not to speak of their sorrows, begged her to tend the captive carefully, so that his forces might come to him again. Further, he bade them remember that they had in their power the woman who had been the cause of all their grief, and the time had come to give sentence on her.

'I cannot slay her, now she is mine to slay,' answered Una, 'but strip her robe of scarlet from off her, and let her go whither she will.'

With her robes and her jewels went all the magic arts that gave her youth and beauty. Instead of the dazzling maiden who had wrought so much havoc in the world, there stood before them an old bald-headed shaking crone, that seemed as ancient as the earth itself. Silently they gazed, then turned away in horror, while Duessa wandered into paths of which she alone knew the ending.

It was not until they had rested themselves awhile in the castle that the stranger knight told who he was and why he came there. He was, he said, Arthur, the ward of Merlin, and had ridden far and long in quest of the Faerie Queen. And having fulfilled his vow to Una, in delivering the Red Cross Knight out of the power of the giant, he bade both farewell, leaving behind him, as a remembrance of their friendship a diamond box containing a precious ointment, which would cure any wound, however deep or poisonous.

So they parted, but not yet was the Red Cross Knight able to face the monstrous dragon who held captive Una's royal parents. For some weeks therefore he rested in the castle till his strength came back, then once more he and Una rode forth side by side.

They had not gone far when they beheld an armed knight galloping fast towards them, and as he went ever glancing over his shoulder as if fearful of some dread thing behind. His matted hair streamed in the wind and the fingers which grasped the reins were like the claws of an eagle. Stranger than all, round his neck was tied a hempen rope. 'He seems to be afraid of himself,' thought the Red Cross Knight as he checked his horse to offer help to the flying man before him.

At first it seemed as if his words fell on dumb ears, but patiently he repeated them over and over again, and at length an answer came from the shaking figure:

'For God's sake, Sir Knight, do not, I pray you, stay me, for look, HE comes, HE comes fast after me;' and as he spoke he urged on his horse afresh. But the Red Cross Knight caught his bridle and bade him fear nothing, as he was safe with him, and to tell him why such awful fear possessed his soul.

At last the stricken man poured forth his tale, and the Red Cross Knight learned that once he was happy and free, like other men, till on an ill-starred day he and a friend had fallen in with a cursed wight who called himself 'Despair,' who had plucked all hope from their breasts, and bade them seek death, the one with a rope, the other with a knife. His friend, whose love had been disdained by a proud lady, fell an easy prey to the persuasions of the giant, and it was the sight of his corpse lying weltering in his blood that drove this man to ride away while yet the rope hung loose. 'O sir,' he added when the sad tale was told—'O sir, be warned by me, and never let yourself stray into his presence! His subtle tongue, like dropping honey, melts into the heart, and ere one be aware, his power is gone and weakness doth remain.'

But the Red Cross Knight made answer that he would never rest till he had seen with his own eyes that baleful being, and begged the stranger, whose name was Trevisan, to guide him hither.

'I will ride back with you, as you ask it of me,' said Sir Trevisan unwillingly, 'but not for all the gold in the world will I stay with you when you reach his cave, for sooner would I die than see his deadly face!'

'Ride on, then, and I will follow,' answered the Red Cross Knight.

The cave lay in the side of a cliff, and was dark and gloomy as a tomb. The only sounds they heard were the hooting of an owl and the wails and howls of wandering ghosts; the only sights were the corpses of men hanging on trees or lying stark upon the ground. Sir Trevisan turned his horse's head and would fain have fled, but the Red Cross Knight stopped him.

'You are safe with me,' he said confidently, and the other, who was ever weak of will, waited.

They entered the cave, and found the doer of all that evil seated on the floor, his eyes as the eyes of a dead man, and his body well nigh as much a skeleton as any of his victims. On the grass beneath him lay a body that was still warm, and in its bleeding wound a rusty knife still stood. The sight stirred the blood in the knight's veins, and he challenged the murderer to fight where he stood.

'Are you distraught, you foolish man,' was all his answer, 'that you should talk in this wild way? It was his own guilt which drove him to his end. He loathed his life, why should he then prolong it? Is it not the part of a friend to free his feet when they stick fast in the mud, and to point to the door that leads to rest, even if some little pain must be suffered in the passage? Is not short pain well borne that brings long ease—sleep after toil, port after stormy seas?'

The Red Cross Knight listened wonderingly. Then he answered:

'The soldier may not cease to watch nor leave his stand until his captain bid.'

But the cursed wight replied boldly, 'The longer life, I wot, the greater sin. The greater sin, the greater punishment. Therefore, I pray you go no further, but lie down and betake you to your rest. A longer life means old age and sickness, and every kind of sorrow. So lay it down while things are yet well with you.'

In spite of Sir Trevisan's warning, the fair-sounding words found an echo in the heart of the Red Cross Knight, as they had done in the hearts of many men before him. The miscreant saw that his courage was wavering, and forthwith he brought forth a store of swords, ropes, poisons, and a brazier of fire, and bade him choose what manner of death he would prefer. The knight gazed at them all, like one who walks in sleep, but touched none of them, and the miscreant, beholding this, chose out a dagger bright and new, and thrust it in his shaking hand. The young man looked at it, his face reddened and then grew pale again, and slowly, as if against his will, he lifted the dagger.

A shriek from Una, who had only just reached the cave, caused him to drop his arm again, and in an instant she had snatched it from his limp fingers, and had flung it on the ground.

'Come away, come away,' she cried, 'let no vain words bewitch you! What have you to do with despair, after all the brave deeds you have done?

Arise, Sir knight, arise and leave this cursed place. Have you forgotten that other work awaits you?'

The voice of Una broke the spell which had possessed him. Once more his eye grew bright and his arm strong. He mounted his horse and rode away by Una's side without ever looking behind him. If he had, he would have seen that the miscreant had placed a rope round his own neck, and hanged himself on a tree. But even so he could not die; the death to which he drove others remained far from him.

The ease with which the Red Cross Knight had been mastered by the wily talk of the gloomy miscreant in the cave showed Una that his mind, if not his body, was still weak from his long imprisonment in the dungeon. She saw that before he could fight the dragon who had carried off her parents he needed yet more repose, and luckily she knew of a house not far off where they would be made welcome for as long as they chose to stay. Hither they fared, and for many weeks the knight's armour was laid away, and the ladies who dwelt in that place gave him all the strength and counsel that they could think of. Then, when at last he had become what he had been of yore, Una bade farewell to her hosts with great thanks, and set out for the royal castle. After three days the walls of a high tower might be seen dimly across the plain.

'It is there that my parents are kept imprisoned by the dragon,' said Una, pointing to it with her hand, 'and I see the watchman watching for good tidings, if haply such there be. Ah, he has waited long!'

As she spoke, a roaring hideous sound was heard that seemed to shake the ground and to fill all the air with terror. Turning their heads, they beheld on their right a huge dragon, lying stretched upon the sunny side of a great hill, himself like a great hill. But no sooner did he see the shining armour of the knight than he roused himself and made ready for battle.

Hastily the Red Cross Knight bade Una withdraw herself to another hill, from which she could see the fight without herself being in danger. Crouching behind a rock, she watched the dreadful beast approaching, half flying and half walking as he went. Run he could not, his size was too vast.

Her heart sank as she looked, for how could mortal man get the better of such a creature!

Besides the brazen scales which thickly covered his body, his wings were like two sails, and at the tip of each huge feather was a many-pronged claw; while his back was hidden with the folds of his tail, which lay doubled in a hundred coils, and in his mouth were three rows of sharp-pointed teeth. Una could look no more; she shut her eyes and waited.

The knight felt that if he was to win the victory at all it must be by means of his lightness of foot, as the monster was so large he could not turn himself about quickly. So, getting a little behind his head, he tried to pierce his neck between the scaly plates, but the spear glanced off harmlessly, and a stroke from the tip of the tail laid both him and his horse on the ground.

They rose again instantly, and returned to the charge, but a second blow met with no better fate. Then the dragon in wrath spread wide his sails and rose heavily above the earth, till, suddenly and swiftly darting down his head, he snatched both horse and man off the ground. But here the knight had the advantage, for with his spear he stung the beast so sore that the monster speedily set his captives again on the earth.

Not giving the dragon time to gather himself up, the knight dealt him a blow under the left wing. With a roar of agony, the beast snapped the spear asunder with his claws, and pulled out the head. At that a sea of blood gushed from the wound which would have turned a water-mill, and in his pain and rage flames of fire gushed from his mouth.

Unwinding his tail from his back, he coiled it like lightning about the legs of the horse, which fell to the ground with his rider. But in an instant the knight was on his feet, and by the mere force of his blows forced his enemy to reel, though the brazen scales were still unpierced. Though his courage was as great as ever, the young man began to lose patience, when of a sudden he noticed that the monster could no longer rise into the air by reason of his wounded wing. That sight gave him heart, and he drew near once more, only to be scorched by the deadly fire from the dragon's jaws. Half blinded and suffocated, he staggered, which the dragon seeing, he dealt the knight such a blow that he fell backwards into a well that lay behind.

'So that is the end of him,' said the dragon to himself; but, if he had only known, it was the beginning, for the well into which the knight had fallen was the well of life, which could cure all hurts and heal all wounds.

All night Una watched at her post, for darkness had come before the knight received his final blow. In the morning, before the sun had risen above the plain, she was looking for the knight, who was lying she knew not where. Her eyes dropping by chance on the well, she was sore amazed to see him rise out of it fairer and mightier than before. With a rush he fell upon the dragon, who had gone to sleep, safe in the knowledge of his victory, and, taking his sword in both hands, he drove right through the brazen scales, and wounded him deep in his skull. In vain did the monster roar and struggle; the blows rained thick and fast, and most of his tail was cut from his body.

Again and again the knight was overthrown, and again and again he rose to his feet, and laid about him as valiantly as ever. But while the fight was still hanging in the balance, the dragon thrust his head forward with wide-open jaws, thinking to swallow his enemy and make an end of him. Quick as thought the knight sprang aside, and, thrusting his sword in the yawning gulf up to the hilt, gave the dragon his death-blow.

Down he fell, fire and smoke gushing from his nostrils—down he fell, and men thought some mighty mountain must have cast up rocks on the earth.

The victor himself trembled, and it was long ere Una dared draw near, dreading lest the direful fiend should stir. But when at last she knew him dead, she came joyfully forth, and, bursting into happy tears, faltered her gratitude for the good he had wrought her.

There is little more to be told of Una and the Red Cross knight.

The watchman on the wall, who had seen the dreadful battle, was the first to tell the king and queen that the dragon was dead and that they were free. Then the king commanded the trumpets to sound and the people to assemble, so that fitting rejoicings might be made at the destruction of their foe.

This being done, a mighty procession came down, headed by the king and queen, to lay laurel boughs at the feet of the victor, and to set a garland of bay on the head of the maiden. Once more Duessa and Archimago sought to prevent the betrothal of the Red Cross Knight and Una by a plot to send the wizard in the guise of a messenger, proclaiming the knight to have been already bound to the daughter of the emperor, but the false tale was easily seen through, and Archimago thrown into a dungeon.

After that the king himself performed the marriage rite, and a solemn feast was held through the land, but the wedded pair were not long left together. A vow the knight had made when he received his spurs to do the Faerie Queen six years of service called him from Una's side, and, sad though the parting might be, both held their word too high ever to break it.

AMYS AND AMYLE

Some time in the Middle Ages there lived in the Duchy of Lombardy, which, as everybody knows, is part of Italy, two knights, who loved each other like brothers. And, what is more to be wondered at, their wives were the best friends in the world. To complete the happiness of the two couples, two little boys were born to them on the same day, and they were given the names of Amys and Amyle.

Now it generally happens that when parents are very anxious for their children to be friends, because they are the same age, or neighbours, or for some equally good reason, the young people make up their minds to hate each other. However, Amys and Amyle did not disappoint their fathers and mothers in this way. From the moment they could walk they were never seen apart; if they ever *did* quarrel no one ever heard of it; and by the time they were twelve years old they had grown so like each other that even their parents could hardly tell the difference between them. Indeed, the likeness between them is supposed to have given rise to the proverb, 'A miss is as good as a mile.'

It was in that year that the duke, their liege lord, bade all his vassals to a great festival to be held in his castle, and many of them took their sons with them, to show them some of the customs of chivalry. Amys and Amyle went with the rest, and endless were the mistakes made about them. The boys themselves, who were merry little fellows, delighted in increasing the confusion, and played so many pranks that the duke declared that they must remain at the court with him, as his life would be too dull without them.

Perhaps the knights thought that their homes would be dull too, but, if so, they did not dare say so; only their wives noticed, as they entered the castle gates, that their heads were bowed, as if some ill had befallen them.

At first the boys felt unhappy and lonely in this strange new world, and clung to each other more closely than ever, but, after a little, they got used to the change, and learned eagerly how to shoot at a mark and tilt at a ring, or to sing sweet love-songs to the sound of a lute.

So the years passed away till Amys and Amyle were eighteen years old, and thought themselves men, and were ready to cross lances with the bravest. The first step they took towards proving to the world that no tie of blood could bind them closer than the love they bore one to another, was to swear the oaths which made them brothers in arms, and obliged them to fight in each other's quarrels, avenge each other's wrongs—even to sacrifice what the other held most dear in the service of his friend. Marriage itself was not more sacred.

All this time the duke had been too busy with his own affairs to have the youths much in his company, though he took care that they had the best chances of learning everything that they ought to know. When, however, he heard that Amys and Amyle had sworn the solemn oaths that made them brothers in arms, he ordered a tournament to be held in their honour, and, when it was over, knighted them on the field. He further declared that henceforth Sir Amys should be his chief butler and Sir Amyle his head steward over his household, thus the steward whom Amyle displaced became their deadly enemy.

Although the young men knew a great deal about hunting, and wrestling, and other such sports, they had no idea what the duties of a butler and a steward might be. But what they *did* know was that they would have to be very careful, for the eyes of the old steward were watching eagerly to report any mistakes to the duke their master. Luckily for them, they were favourites with everyone, and if now and then they forgot their work, or slipped away for a day's hunting, well! the task was done by somebody, and not even the old steward could find out by whom.

Everything seemed going smoothly, and the new-made knights were in danger of being spoilt by the favour of the ladies of the court, when a sudden stop was put to all their pleasures. One day a man-at-arms riding a jaded horse appeared at the palace gateway, and demanded to be led into the presence of the good knight Sir Amyle.

'Oh, my lord,' said he, and knew not that it was Amys before whom he was kneeling, 'it is grievous news that I bear unto you. Your father and mother, that noble knight and his lady, died of a pestilence but seven days agone, and none save you can take their place. Therefore am I sent unto you.'

'*My* father and mother?' cried Amys, staggering back.

'Yes, my lord, yours,' answered the man. 'At least——' he stammered, as Sir Amyle came and stood by his friend, 'I know not if indeed it may be yours. It is long years since I have seen you, and this knight and you have but one face. But it is Sir Amyle with whom I would speak.'

Then Amys laid his hand on his brother's shoulder.

'Be comforted,' he said softly. 'Am I not with thee? and, though I cannot go with thee now, I will follow thee shortly unless thou quickly return to me.'

Early next morning Amyle started with a heavy heart for the home which he had left six years before; but before his departure he had caused to be made two cups of gold, delicately wrought with figures of birds and beasts, such as he and Amys had often chased in the forests and lakes of Lombardy. The cups were no more to be told from each other than were Amys and Amyle themselves, and Amyle placed them in the pockets of his saddle till the moment came for him to part from Sir Amys, who had ridden with him as far as he might. Then, drawing out one of the cups, Amyle placed it in his friend's hands.

'Farewell, my brother,' he said. 'Be true to me as I will be true to you, according to the oath which we sware, that as long as we both shall live nothing and nobody shall stand between me and thee.'

And Sir Amys repeated the words of his oath, then slowly turned his horse's head towards the castle.

Seven days' hard riding brought Sir Amyle back to his native place, and for many months he had much to do in setting aside the pretenders who had sprung up to claim his father's lands. When at last peace was restored and the false traitors had been thrown into prison, a petition on the part of his vassals to take a wife and settle down amongst them, turned his thoughts in other directions.

It was the custom of the country that the ruler of those lands should choose his wife from the most beautiful maidens in the Duchy of Lombardy, no matter what might be their degree. So a herald was sent forth to proclaim that any damsel who wished to fill this high place was to present herself in the courtyard of the palace on the morning following the next new moon, where the chamberlain would receive her. Oh, what a fluttering of hearts there was in the towns and villages, as the herald, with his silver trumpet and his satin coat of red and yellow, covered with figures of strange beasts, passed up and down the streets! How the girls all ran to their mirrors, and turned themselves this way and that to see if there could possibly be a chance for them! Perhaps it was the fault of the headdress they wore that their faces seemed so long and their noses so big, or surely something was wrong with the glass that their cheeks looked so yellow! But even when it was proved beyond a doubt that neither headdress nor mirror was to blame in the matter, there were enough lovely maidens and to spare in the courtyard of the castle on the day following the new moon.

'He is certain to choose *you*,' said one, who in her secret heart thought it was impossible that *she* should be passed over.

'Oh no; fair men's eyes alway rest upon dark women,' answered the girl, whose locks were brighter than the sun, though while she spoke she was really thinking that no one could bear comparison with her. And then all grew silent, for there was heard a blast of trumpets announcing that Sir Amyle was at hand.

The young knight had donned for this occasion a close-fitting coat of silver cloth, while a short blue velvet mantle hung from his shoulders. He walked slowly down the ranks of the maidens, watching each carefully, and noting the way in which she received his gaze. Some looked down and blushed; some looked up and smiled, but one there was who did neither, only stood calm and pale as the young man drew near.

She was a tall girl with dark hair and soft grey eyes, and the chamberlain had doubted long, before he told her father that she might take her stand with the rest. None would have chosen her as Queen of a Tourney, or bidden her preside over a Court of Love, yet there was that in her face which had caused Amyle to pause before her and to hold out his hand.

So they were married, and by the side of his wife Sir Amyle for a while forgot his brother.

Meanwhile Sir Amys dwelt sorrowfully at the court, defending himself as best he might against the wiles of the black-hearted steward, who now received him with smiles and fair words. Nay, he even desired that they should become brothers at arms, but to this Sir Amys replied that, having made oath to one brother at arms, the rules of chivalry did not allow him to take another.

At these words the steward threw off the mask with which he had sought to beguile Sir Amys.

'You will have cause to rue this day,' roared he, nearly choking in his wrath; 'you dog, you white-livered cur!' but Amys only smiled, and bade him do his worst.

By this time the duke's only daughter, Belisante, had reached the age of fifteen, and on her birthday her father proclaimed a great tournament, which was to last for fourteen days. Knights from far and near flocked to break a lance in honour of the fair damsel, but, though many doughty deeds were done, the prize fell to Sir Amys. When he came up to receive the golden circlet from the hands of the duchess—for the duke held his daughter to be of too tender years to be queen of the tourney—Belisante looked earnestly at the knight whose praises had rung in her ears ever since her childhood. It was almost the first time her eyes had beheld him, for she had lived in one of her father's distant castles, and had seldom visited the court.

Now we all know full well that whenever we form to ourselves the picture of a man or woman of whom great things are said, woeful is in general the disappointment. But even in that assembly Sir Amys was taller and stronger and fairer to look upon than the rest.

'He shall be my knight,' said Belisante to herself, never dreaming that any man alive could pass her by. But Sir Amys' thoughts dwelt not upon women, and he hardly so much as marked her where she sat.

This slight was more than the spoiled damsel could bear. She fell sick with love and anger, and for many days lay in bed, pondering how she should win the love of Sir Amys.

A full week went by, and still she had never had speech of him—nor had even so much as caught sight of him as he followed her father to the chase. But one morning her lady brought her word—for indeed she had guessed something of her mistress's heart—that Sir Amys had so wearied himself in pursuit of a boar the previous evening that he had let his lord ride forth alone. So Belisante bade her maiden bring her kirtle of green silk, and clasp it with her golden belt set with precious stones, and place a veil of shining white upon her hair; then seeking her mother they went down into the garden together.

It was not long before her quick-glancing eyes beheld Sir Amys lying under a tree by the side of a stream, but in her guile she took no heed of him, but turned away and entered a little wood.

'I can sleep now,' she said, stretching herself on a bank of soft moss. 'Listen to the birds, how sweetly they sing! Methinks I hear the voice of the nightingale, for the trees make such darkness that he knows not night from day.'

'Let us leave her,' answered her mother, and signing to her ladies they all returned to the castle.

For a moment Belisante lay still, feigning to sleep; then she raised herself on her arm and looked about her. Nothing was to be seen save the green darkness about her, nothing was to be heard save the songs of the birds. Softly she rose to her feet, and stole out of the wood to the orchard where Sir Amys was resting, thinking, though she guessed it not, of his brother in arms Amyle.

He sprang to his feet in surprise as Belisante the Fair drew near him; but she begged him to sit beside her, and told him how that she had been sick of love, and besought him of his grace not to withhold this good gift from her. Sir Amys hearkened to her words, not knowing if he had heard aright, but, calling his wits to his aid, he answered that she was the daughter of a great prince while he was only the son of a poor knight, and that marriage between them might never be. This speech so wrought upon Belisante that she broke out in such tears and entreaties that Sir Amys, to gain time to ponder what best to do, replied that if in eight days her mind was still set on him, he would ask her hand in marriage.

By ill-luck for both the knight and the maiden, the steward, who had been seeking a chance of doing Sir Amys an ill turn, had seen Belisante leave the wood and go in search of Sir Amys. Creeping stealthily up to them, he hid himself behind a clump of bushes and heard all that was said. Cunningly he made his plan, and on the eighth day he waylaid the duke and told him that Sir Amys was about to repay all the kindness shown him by a secret marriage with the duke's daughter.

Sir Amys was keeping guard that day in the hall of the palace, when, sword in hand, his liege lord stood before him charging him with beguiling his daughter. In another moment Amys would have fallen dead, but behind him was a little room, and into this he stepped, shutting the door, so that the sword stuck in the hard wood as it came against it. This mischance somewhat cooled the duke's anger, and, bidding Sir Amys come out and speak with him, he again accused him of having sought to steal away his daughter, whom he wished to betrothe to the emperor's son.

Sir Amys was in sore straits. If he could have borne the penalty alone, he would have suffered gladly whatever sentence the duke might have passed on him; but this could not be. So, to save Belisante from her father's wrath, he swore a great oath that there was no truth in that tale, and, flinging down his glove, offered to fight any man whom the duke should appoint, and prove his innocence on his body. Then the king bade his steward pick up Sir Amys' glove, and fixed a morning, fourteen days hence, when the two should meet in single combat.

Still it was not enough that Sir Amys and the steward should agree to fight; it was needful also that sureties should be found, and such was the steward's power at court that all men feared to come forward on behalf of Sir Amys. The young man would have fared badly, and indeed would at once have been thrown into prison, had not both Belisante and her mother offered themselves as sureties for his presence when the day arrived.

But not all the wiles of the fair Belisante could chase the gloom from the face of Sir Amys. He never forgot that he had sworn a false oath, and it was to no purpose that Belisante reminded him of all the ill deeds done by the steward to him and others. 'This time,' he said sadly, 'I have the wrong and *he* the right, therefore I am afraid to fight,' and no other answer could she wring from him.

Way out of the tangle there seemed none. Fight Sir Amys could not, with the weight of a false oath on his soul, yet to run away were to confess all, and leave Belisante to bear her father's anger alone. Turn his thoughts which side he would, escape seemed barred, till the image of Sir Amyle flashed across him. 'Fool, why had he not remembered him earlier? Luckily there was yet time, and he could ride with full speed to his brother's castle, and bid him return to take the battle on himself.' With a gladder face than he had known for long, he sought out the duchess and her daughter, and told them his plan.

Before the sun rose Sir Amys was in the saddle, and so busy was he with all that had befallen him that he pushed on and never drew rein till his horse dropped dead under him from sheer weariness. As there was no town or house where he might find another, he was forced to proceed on foot. But by-and-by he too fell from lack of sleep, and when Sir Amyle was returning home through the forest after a day's hunting, he discovered his brother stretched across the path in the shade of a tree.

Joy at meeting gave new life to Sir Amys, and, sitting up, he told his friend all his woes, and how he dare not fight with a false oath on his conscience.

'Oh! that is easily to be managed,' cried Sir Amyle, with a great laugh. 'Go home to my castle,' said he, 'and tell my wife that you have sent the horse to Sir Amys, at court, as you heard he had sore need of one. None will know you from me, no more than they did of old, and, as to my wife, it was but now I told her that business called me to the most distant parts of my lands, so this very night you can bid her farewell.'

Sir Amys did as his brother bade him, and Sir Amyle hastened with all speed to the duke's palace.

He was only just in time. The hour for the fight had come, and the steward had entered the lists, and, looking round in triumph, proclaimed to all whom it might concern that his adversary knew himself to be a traitor to his lord, and had fled. Therefore, according to all the rules of chivalry, a fire should be made, and his sureties burned before all the people.

At these dreadful words, the hearts of the king and his wife and daughter trembled within them. For the steward had spoken truly, and the order for the execution must be given. It was in vain that the men worked right slowly; linger as they might, the pile was ready at last, and with one despairing glance round, the duchess and her daughter were bravely walking up to it, when Sir Amyle hastily pushed his way to the duke and demanded that the captives should be instantly set free. Then, followed by the duchess and Belisante, he entered the palace to gird himself with the armour of Sir Amys.

When his helmet and sword were buckled on him, he prayed them to leave him, as he would fain be alone for a short space before he mounted his horse. So the two ladies embraced him and left him, wishing him God-speed. As the door closed upon them, Sir Amyle held up his sword and muttered a prayer before it.

'Come weal or woe, I will help my brother,' he said softly; then mounting his horse he rode into the lists, and, kneeling, took the oath that he was guiltless of wrong and would prove his innocence on the body of his foe.

The fight lasted but a short time; the steward's sword was keen, and he knew how to use it, and it was not long before he had given Sir Amyle a sharp thrust through the shoulder, and the young knight reeled in his saddle. The steward uttered a cry of fierce joy, and raised his arm to deal a second blow, when Sir Amyle suddenly spurred his horse to one side and pierced his enemy to the heart. Then, all bleeding as he was, the false Amys cut off the head of the traitor, and gave it to the duke, proving to him and to all the court that the right had conquered. But hardly had he done so when, faint from loss of blood, he fell senseless on the ground, and was carried into the palace, where the duke's best leeches were called in to attend him. In a few days the fever left him, and he was able to receive a visit from the duke himself.

'O Amys, my friend, how I have misjudged you!' cried the duke, falling on his knees weeping; 'but I will let my people know that you were always true, and you shall marry my daughter as soon as you can stand upon your feet, and I will hold a feast, and proclaim you heir to my duchy.'

And the wounded man gave him thanks and grace, but sent off a messenger in all haste to Sir Amys, bidding him be by a spring in the forest, nine days hence, which message Sir Amys obeyed, wondering what had passed. Then the two knights changed their clothes once more, and Sir Amyle returned to his wife and Sir Amys to his bride, and they lived happily to the end of their lives.

THE TALE OF THE CID

In the year 1025, when Canute the Dane was sitting on the throne of England, there was born in the ancient Spanish city of Burgos a baby, to whom was given the name of Rodrigo Diaz de Bivar. He came of noble blood on both sides of the House, and his forefathers had borne some of the highest offices of the land, and from his childhood the boy had been taught that it was his duty never to fall one whit behind them in courage and in honour. As he grew older, he burned more and more for a chance to show the metal of which he was made, and longed to join the companies of knights that were ever going forth to fight the Arabs, who for nearly four hundred years had reigned over the fairest provinces of Spain. But to all his prayers, his father, Don Diego Lainez, turned a deaf ear.

'Wait, wait, my son!' he would say; 'the little shoot must first grow into a tree. Go now and practise that sword-thrust in which you failed yesterday.'

It was when he was sixteen that the longed-for opportunity came.

Don Diego Lainez, now old and weak, had gone to do his homage to King Fernando, who had managed to unite the small kingdoms of Northern Spain under his banner. Some dispute arose between him and the powerful count, Don Lozano Gomez, probably as to which had the right to pass first into the presence of their king, and in the presence of the whole court Don Lozano spoke words of deadly insult to the old man, and even gave him a buffet on the cheek. The courtiers all cried shame, and Don Diego's hand clutched the pommel of his sword, but his rage had deprived him of the little strength that remained, and he was powerless to draw it. At this the count laughed scornfully, and, bowing mockingly to the king, who held it best that men should settle their own quarrels, rode away to his castle. Then, without another word, Don Diego turned and mounted his horse and set out homewards.

A broken man and older by ten years was he when he entered his hall, but many days passed before any could guess what had wrought this change in him. All night he lay awake staring into the darkness, and when food was brought him it was carried away untasted, and his wife whispered to her ladies, 'If we rouse him not he will surely die! Would that I knew what has stricken him like this?'

Fifteen days went by in this manner, and none thought to see him leave his bed again, when one morning he strode into the hall with some of the fire of his former years, and called his sons to him. One by one he signed to each to draw near, and taking their soft hands in his palms, pressed so hard that the boys cried to him to loosen his grasp, or they would die of the pain. But when he came to Rodrigo, he heard no prayers of mercy from *him*, only threats and hot words uttered with blazing eyes and cheeks burning with anger. And the old man wept for joy, and cried:

'Thou art indeed my true son; your rage calms me, your fury heals me. It is you who will redeem my honour, which I held lost.' And then he told the youth the tale of what had passed at court.

'Take my blessing,' were his last words, 'and take this sword also, which shall deal the count his death-blow. After that, you shall do greater deeds still.'

Young though he was, Rodrigo had heard enough of war to know Lozano Gomez would not prove an easy prey; but, easy or not, he meant to fight him. So, vowing to his sword that should he ever bring dishonour on the weapon that had done his House good service, he would sheathe it in his breast, he mounted his horse and rode to meet his foe.

'Is it a knightly or a brave deed, think you, to smite an old man who cannot defend himself?' asked he. 'But when you dealt that blow you may have thought that his sons were yet in their cradles, and that there was none to avenge him. Well, traitor, you are wrong. *I* am his son, and his honour is mine, so look to yourself, lest I take your head home with me.'

And Gomez laughed to hear him, and bade him cease crowing like a young cock, but a furious onslaught from Rodrigo cut his words short, and hardly did he escape being unhorsed. Before he had steadied himself in the saddle Rodrigo had charged again, and this time his enemy was borne to the ground.

'So may all dastards die!' cried the victor, as he cut off his head.

Don Diego Lainez was sitting at the table in his great hall, the tears rolling down his cheeks as the shameful scene of his dishonour rose up before him. Suddenly a clatter of hoofs was heard in the courtyard, and the doors swung open. The men-at-arms gathered round the board rose to their feet as Rodrigo entered, carrying the head of Count Gomez by the long front lock. Taking Don Diego by the arm, he shook him roughly:

'Open your eyes wide, my father, and raise your head, and let your heart be merry, for I have cut down the poisonous weed; I have stamped out the plague-spot; the robe of your honour is stainless as of yore.'

For a moment the old man kept silence, and then he looked up, his face shining.

'Son of my heart,' he said, 'it is enough. From henceforth the seat of honour is yours, and you shall take my place as the head of my House.'

From that day the young knights vied with each other in gaining leave to ride in the train of Rodrigo Diaz, or 'the Cid' as he was afterwards called, and to this name was later added the proud title of 'Campeador.' Three hundred youths in splendid attire followed him to the court of Fernando, when he went in his turn to do the king homage, and stood by his side as he challenged anyone of the blood of Count Lozano to fight and avenge his death; but no one came. Then his father and his noble company left their horses to kiss the hand of the king, but Rodrigo remained in his saddle.

'Get down, get down, Rodrigo!' cried his father, fearing lest the king should resent his rudeness. 'Swear fealty to thy lord, and kiss his hand, as a loyal subject should do.'

Now, ever since he had fought with Count Gomez, Rodrigo had felt himself to be a man, and, more than that, to be much greater than other men, and he was not pleased to be scolded by his father in the presence of so many people. Still, he was wise enough to know that it would do him no good in the eyes of the nobles gathered round, to disobey his father, and slowly he got down from his horse to do homage with the rest. But so clumsy was he that, as he knelt, his sword nearly fell out of its sheath, and the king, thinking Rodrigo meant to kill him, started back, exclaiming:

'Away, away! you devil! If you have the form of a man, your deeds are those of a lion.'

'It is base to kiss the hand of such a craven,' answered Rodrigo in anger, 'and I hold that my father has heaped disgrace on his family by humbling himself in such a fashion!' And so saying, he rode away, with his followers behind him.

A few centuries later a man might have lost his head for such words, but in those days people were accustomed to speak their minds even to kings, and little harm came of it. Six weeks later, Rodrigo had forgotten all about it, and, what was more to the purpose, so had the king, at any rate he pretended to do so, and when Don Diego sent his son to do his business with Fernando, who was at Burgos, the young man went willingly. The morning after he reached the city he was dining in the hall of the palace with the king and his nobles, when word was brought to the royal table that Ximena, the daughter of Count Gomez, and her train stood at the gates, and demanded an audience of the king. Fernando rose from his seat, and, signing to his nobles to follow him, he went to meet Ximena.

A figure of woe was she, clothed all in black, even her face hidden by a black veil. Throwing herself on her knees, she implored that justice might be done on the murderer of her father, for not till then would the stain be wiped out which had killed her mother and was killing her. 'He rides to and fro under my lattice,' said she, 'and the hawk on his wrist slays my doves, and my mantle is sprinkled with their blood. If you do not do me right, O king, you are not fit to reign, or to call yourself a knight.'

Thus spake Ximena, and the king sat silent and pondered her words. 'I cannot punish Don Rodrigo, either by imprisonment or death,' he said to himself, 'for my nobles would not suffer it; I must find some other way to satisfy Ximena.' Then turning to her, he bade her go home, and added that no damsel should have cause to complain that wrong had been done them at his hands.

Then Ximena rode away, and by-and-by Rodrigo departed also.

Six months later King Fernando was seated in the great hall of his palace of Burgos, dispensing justice to high and low, when there entered once more Ximena, followed by thirty esquires and pages.

'I come, though I know it is in vain,' she cried, when she had made her way to the foot of the throne. 'Five times I have appeared to demand my rights, and no longer will I be put off with empty words. No king are you, who are swayed this way and that by every man that passes, and dare not even avenge your friends, for fear of what may come of it.'

'Not so,' answered the king; 'but is there no other way by which your quarrel may be appeased? Has Rodrigo on his side suffered no insult? You have heard of the fame he has lately won, when he took captive the five Moorish kings who broke suddenly into the land and ravaged it with fire and sword. And to prove that it was fame and not gold he wanted he set them all free, with only a promise of homage from them. Ah, if there were but a few more like him, Spain would soon be rid of the Moors. Happy is the woman he shall choose for his wife; she will live all her days in safety and in honour.'

Then the king paused, and watched to see how Ximena took his words.

She was silent for some moments, but the king could not see her face, as she had pulled her veil over it. Suddenly she raised her head, and cast the veil back over her shoulders.

'It is true, O king, what you speak, and I will forego my vengeance. Nay, I think my father himself would have it so. Give me Don Rodrigo for my husband; all my days I will be a loyal wife to him, and his honour shall be mine.'

Perhaps the king was not so surprised as some of his courtiers as they listened to Ximena's request. If he smiled, his beard was thick enough to hide it, and he answered gravely:

'You say well, my daughter, and I will to-day send a messenger bidding Don Rodrigo meet me at Palencia, and I will give him lands and riches, so that in wealth as in birth he may be equal to you.'

When the messengers reached Don Rodrigo,

with the offer of Ximena's hand, his heart was glad, and, calling his friends to dress themselves in their most splendid cloaks and brightest armour, he rode at their head towards the city of Palencia. Ximena with her train was already in the royal palace, and in the presence of the king the two plighted their troth. But Rodrigo swore by the cross on his sword that the marriage rite should not be fulfilled till he had beaten five foes in the field, and, leaving Ximena under the care of his mother, he bade her farewell, and set forth to accomplish his vow.

However, he was not destined to be absent very long, for in those days enemies were not far to seek, and in less than two months the wedding preparations began. His brothers took pride in arraying him themselves, and buttoning on the doublet of black satin which his father had worn in many of his battles, while over this he wore a jacket of stout leather and a loose cloak lined with plush.

At the last he girded on his sword Tizona, the Dread of the World, then, surrounded by his friends and his family, the bridegroom walked to the court, where the king, the bishop, and all the nobles were awaiting him.

Soon the noise of trumpets was heard, and there entered Ximena dressed in a robe of fine white cloth, brought from London across the seas, with a border of silver embroidered on it. On her head was a close hood of the same stuff, and high shoes of red leather were on her feet. Round her neck was a necklace made of eight round medals, with a little figure of St. Michael hanging from them.

Don Rodrigo went forward to lift Ximena from her horse, and kissed her, whispering as he did so:

'It is true, O my lady, that I killed your father, but I did it in fair fight, as man to man. And in his stead you shall have a husband that will care for you and protect you to the end of your life.'

Now, although Don Rodrigo was married, he did not stay at home much more than he had done in other days, and his sword was ever unsheathed in the service of his king. He was the champion chosen by Fernando to meet in single combat Martino Gonzalez, the stoutest knight in Spain, and decide a quarrel between Castile and Aragon. The victory lay with Rodrigo, and no sooner was the duel over than he rode off to fight the Moors in the North of Spain. At length the patience of Ximena was worn out, and she wrote a letter to Fernando in which she told him plainly all that was in her mind.

'What was the use,' she asked, 'of her marrying Rodrigo if the king kept him for ever engaged in his service, and away from her?' She had no father, and might as well have no husband, and she implored his master to think upon her loneliness, and to let Rodrigo return to her side.

But the king would make no promises, and by-and-by Ximena had a little girl to comfort her, to whom Fernando stood godfather.

It seems strange that after these great deeds King Fernando never thought of making Don Rodrigo a knight, but so it was. Not till the long siege of the city of Coimbra was ended, and the Moorish mosque turned into a Christian church, was the order of knighthood conferred on Don Rodrigo in return for the mighty works that he had done. But Don Rodrigo knew well that his sword-thrusts would have availed him nothing had it not been for the aid of a Greek bishop who dreamed when at the shrine of St. James that the gates of the city would only fall when a successor of the Apostle should appear before them. So the bishop arose and clad himself in armour and rode into the Christian hosts, and as he drew near, the walls fell down like Jericho of old, and the army entered in triumph.

After this the Cid, as men now called him, from a Moorish word which meant a man of great valour and fame, went home for a short space to see his wife and his little daughter, who by this time was seven years old and had never beheld her father. Rest was sweet to Don Rodrigo, but before it could grow irksome to him he was summoned to court by the death of Fernando, who left all his children under the wardship of the Cid. Unluckily, the old man's will had not been a wise one, and bitter quarrels soon raged between the new king Sancho and his brothers and sisters. In vain Don Rodrigo tried to heal the feuds, but war soon broke out, and by his oath of allegiance he was forced, sorely against his wish, to fight under the king's banner. By his aid Sancho despoiled his two brothers and one of his sisters of the lands which were theirs by right, but when the king demanded that he should go as envoy and bid the princess Doña Urraca yield up her town of Zamora in exchange for much gold, the Cid prayed him to send someone else, for he could not take arms against the princess whom he had known when they were children together. His words, however, were useless. The king would listen to nothing, and the Cid rode forth to Zamora with a heavy heart. Silently he bore the reproaches of Doña Urraca, and returned in five days to tell Fernando that the citizens of Zamora had sworn in his presence, that the city would never be given up till they all lay dead upon her walls. This answer so infuriated Don Sancho that he falsely accused the Cid of having put the words into the mouths of his enemies, and bade him begone out of the kingdom.

But a man like the Cid could not lightly be dismissed, and very soon the king was forced to humble himself, and send messengers to beg his forgiveness. The Campeador was too generous to bear malice, and rode joyfully back, to find Sancho besieging Zamora. And an ill day it was for the king when he resolved to wrest his sister's possessions from her; for one of her citizens, spurred by love to his lady, gained admittance into the royal camp and offered to betray the city. A councillor of the princess, the old Arias Gonzalo, cried to the king from the walls to lend no ear unto the man's words, for he was a traitor; but Dolfos had a wily tongue, and easily persuaded Sancho to come with him to see the small door across the trench by which the army might enter. They were hardly outside the camp when Dolfos struck him between the shoulders with his spear, and the king rolled in his death agony on the ground. The sight was seen by Don Rodrigo, who had watched eagerly and anxiously the movements of Dolfos, and now sprang towards the traitor with his drawn sword. But Dolfos was too quick for him, and the postern was flung open by some of the men of Zamora, before the Cid could get across the trench.

'Oh, fool was I not to have fastened on my spurs, and then I should have caught him!' cried Don Rodrigo shaking with rage, as he turned sadly back to stand by the bedside of his dying master, waiting for the vengeance which the future would bring.

Now directly she heard that King Sancho was dead, Doña Urraca, his sister, the lady of Zamora, sent the tidings to her brother, Don Alfonso, in exile at Toledo.

'We have been sent to summon you, King Alfonso,' said the messengers when they found him, falling on their knees as they spoke. 'Don Sancho was foully stabbed by Bellido el Dolfos, and the men of Castile and Leon call on you to take his place. Don Rodrigo only hangs back, and swears he will never take the oath of fealty till you have proved that you had no part in the murder of your brother.'

Don Alfonso felt glad at their words. He had received nothing but ill at the hands of his brother, and he hurried to place himself at the head of the army of Castile. But the Arab ruler was not willing to let him go, and many days passed before he was able to escape at night, climbing silently with a few followers down the walls of Toledo; then, turning the shoes on the feet of their horses, so that the track should point south instead of north, they made the best of their way to Zamora.

The nobles received the king with joy, and, kneeling to kiss his hand, vowed to be true to him. The Cid alone held aloof.

'You are heir to the throne, Don Alfonso,' said he, 'but before I bend the knee to you I demand that you and twelve of your vassals shall swear that you are innocent, in deed or in word, of the blood of your brother.'

'I will swear it,' answered Alfonso, 'when and where you please, and twelve men of Leon shall swear it likewise.'

'You shall swear to me in the holy cathedral of Santa Gadea in Burgos,' said the Cid; and thither they all rode silently and solemnly, while Don Rodrigo, standing at the altar, held out the crucifix to the kneeling king. But though the oath was taken freely, both by Alfonso and his vassals, deep in the heart of the Cid lay a doubt of his truth.

'You shall swear it thrice,' he said, and Alfonso, devoured as he was with rage, knew the Cid's power too well to disobey, though his face grew pale with wrath.

'You shall answer for this,' he cried as he rose to his feet, and from that day the king never ceased to seek for an excuse to compass Don Rodrigo's banishment. At last he found one.

The Moorish king of Toledo laid a complaint against the Cid that, in spite of his alliance with Alfonso of Castile, his lands had been ravaged and his people made captive. Well Alfonso knew that it was the Moors themselves who had broken faith with him, and had wasted the Spanish territories which lay along their borders, but he eagerly snatched at the plea, and bade the Cid go, an exile, from Castile, while his possessions were declared forfeit.

With every insult heaped on him that the king could invent, the Cid left the city and rode to his castle of Bivar, only to find that his enemies had been before him and had stripped it bare, while his wife and children had sought refuge in the convent of San Pedro de Cardeña.

It was on his way thither that the Cid in his dire distress did the one mean deed recorded of him, which he never ceased to bewail during his life, and afterwards on his deathbed. He had reckoned on finding money for his needs at Bivar, and there was none, and he knew not what to do. In this strait he invited two rich Jews to his tent under the walls of Burgos, and, pointing to two large chests which stood on the ground, he told the Jews that they were filled with silver plate, and begged that they would take them, and give him a thousand crowns in exchange. The Jews, used though they were to being cheated and despoiled by Christians, yet trusted to the honour of the Cid, and counted out the money. Then, placing the coffers on the backs of two stout mules, they returned with them into Burgos, first promising that they would not open them till a year had passed. At the time appointed they lifted the lid, and, behold, the coffers were full of sand!'

But except in this matter, for which his repentance was bitter, the Cid never ceased in his exile to be true to his knighthood, and in all the wars which he and his followers made on the Moors he always sent part of the spoils to Alfonso. At length the king found that he could not do without him. Young knights there were in plenty, but neither in battle nor in the council chamber could they vie with Don Rodrigo; so after many years, when the Cid had captured strong cities and great towns from the Moors, Alfonso sent messengers to say that he was willing to pardon him. And the Cid vowed anew to serve him, but his heart was heavy for the death of his only son in the siege of Consuegra.

From time to time the king's jealousy broke out afresh, and more than once Don Rodrigo was banished, but in the end the Cid always returned to Castile, for in truth, as we have said, the land prospered but little in his absence. After conquering the Moors in Valencia and elsewhere, his fame and wealth grew greater than ever, and two of the proudest nobles in Castile, the counts of Carrion, prayed Alfonso to use his rights as liege lord, and to grant them the Cid's daughters in marriage. Now, the proposal pleased Don Rodrigo but little, and his wife even less. He knew something of the two young men who wished to be his sons-in-law, and he felt that it was his wealth, and not his daughters, that was wooed. Besides, he liked not the boastfulness of the two brothers, and feared that beneath their proud and haughty ways the hearts of cowards might be hidden. But outwardly all was fair-seeming, and when the king in a meeting on the banks of the Tagus bade the Cid consider well the matter, Don Rodrigo could only reply that, in his view, his daughters were as yet too young to be wedded, but that they and all that belonged to him were in the hands of the king, to be dealt with as he thought best. To which the king answered that he knew the maidens to be wise beyond their years, and, summoning the counts of Carrion to his presence, he informed them that he had resolved to grant their desire, and bade them kneel and kiss the Cid's hand, which they did with joy. So the next day they all rode back to Valencia, and the Cid made a feast for fifteen days, and the marriage rite was performed by the Bishop Geronymo, mighty in battle.

It was not long after the wedding that the counts showed of what metal they were made, and that the Cid had read them truly. One evening they and Don Bermudo, nephew of the Cid, were sitting laughing and jesting in the hall of the castle, when a cry arose from without, 'Beware of the lion; he has broken from his den'; and in an instant the huge beast had sprung through the door. Don Bermudo sat still, waiting to see what the lion would do, but Don Diego, the elder count, took refuge in a closet, while Don Fernan, his brother, hid himself under the bed on which the Cid was stretched sleeping. The noise awoke Don Rodrigo, who sprang up, when the lion at once lay down on the ground and began to lick his feet. The Cid stooped and stroked its head, then calling to the beast to follow, he led it back to its den, which it entered quietly, for it knew its master well.

'Where are my sons-in-law?' asked he as he entered. 'Methought I heard their voices but a moment agone.'

'Here,' cried one of his nephews, and 'here' cried another, and the counts were dragged forth, their fine clothes disordered and their faces pale with fear.

The Cid looked at them silently, till they grew red with shame and anger.

'Are these your wedding garments?' said he at last. 'Truly I should scarce have guessed it'; and he passed on, leaving hate and a longing for revenge in the young men's hearts.

The matter of the lion did not dwell long in the mind of the Cid, for news was speedily brought him that the Moorish king of Morocco was advancing with an army to besiege the fair city of Valencia. He quickly gathered together a host large enough to give battle in the plain outside the walls, but while mounting his horse Babieca he counselled his sons-in-law to remain in safety behind the walls of the town. This they would gladly have done, but dared not set at naught the mocking eyes of the knights around them, so, clad in shining armour, they rode forth with the rest. Hardly had the fight begun, when a Moor attacked the younger brother, who turned and fled. Another instant and he would have sunk to the ground, pierced by the enemy's lance, when Don Bermudo suddenly appeared, and engaged the Moor in deadly combat. After a hard struggle the infidel was overborne and slain, and the victor turned to Don Fernan Gonzalez:

'Take his horse and his armour,' he said, 'and tell the Cid it was you who killed him; I will not gainsay you.' And, as cowards are generally liars also, Don Fernan gladly snatched at the crown of glory that belonged to another.

Don Bermudo was rewarded for his generous deed when he saw the joy of the Cid. Perhaps he had condemned them wrongly, thought Don Rodrigo, and that the souls of men were at last awaking in them. So he praised them for their valour, and if there were those present who could have told a different tale, they held their peace.

But whether they were, perforce, following the Cid in the field, or basking in the wealth and pleasures of Valencia, the counts of Carrion never forgot or forgave the scorn they had read in the eyes of the Cid on the day when they had hidden from the lion. Together they plotted to take vengeance on them, and it was a vengeance as mean as their souls.

One morning they entered the great hall of Valencia, where the Cid was sitting, and prayed him to give them their wives, and let them depart forthwith to their lands. Their words were fair, yet the Cid felt troubled; why, he knew not.

'I gave you my daughters to wife, at my king's bidding,' answered he at last, 'and I cannot withhold them from you if indeed you desire to take them unto your own lands. But see that they are treated as beseemes them; if not, woe to you.'

And the counts of Carrion, with treason in their hearts, promised that all honour should await their brides.

Eight days hence, the procession passed out of the city gates, and the Cid went first, with Doña Elvira on his right hand, and Doña Sol on his left. For the space of a league he rode, and then he reined up his horse. Calling his nephew Don Ordoño to his side, he bade him follow unperceived, and bring back news of what befell his daughters.

And so they parted.

For many miles the procession went slowly on, and was received with kindness and hospitality by the great Moslem lords through whose country the road lay, a kindness repaid whenever possible by theft and cruelty by the counts of Carrion. Then, when they had reached a wood which was neither in the lordship of the Cid nor of the Moors, they felt that the time for which they had so long waited was come. Ordering the guards and attendants to ride forward to the Castle of Carrion and prepare for their reception, the counts scarcely delayed until they were out of their sight before they dragged their wives from their mules, and stripped their bodies bare. Next, seizing them by their hair, they flung them to the ground, and dug their spurs into them till their bodies were covered with blood.

'Farewell, beautiful damsels,' they cried mockingly, bowing low, 'you were never fit mates for the counts of Carrion, and, besides, it was needful to avenge the affront that the Cid your father put on us in the matter of the fierce beast who would have slain us.' And, stooping low from their horses, the base knights rode away.

From a distant hill Don Ordoño had seen and heard all that had passed, and he now came forth to help and comfort his cousins. 'Take heart,' he said, 'I will bring you your lost garments, and if you have lost your husbands, who deserve nothing better than the fate of traitors, remember that you have yet a father, without a peer throughout the world.'

None can tell the wrath of the Cid when his daughters came home. Little he said, for he was ever a man of few words, but he sent forthwith messengers to the king, telling him of the base deeds of the counts of Carrion, and begging for leave to plead his cause before the Parliament at Toledo. This permission Alfonso granted gladly, and bade the counts of Carrion to be present also and answer the Cid.

Many days they waited ere Don Rodrigo, accompanied by his wife and daughters, and followed by a train of nobles, rode through the gates. The king was sitting surrounded by the Cortes or Parliament, but he desired that the Cid should be brought to him at once, and then commanded him to set forth his wrongs.

'It is you, O king, and not I, who gave my daughters in marriage to these base men, therefore it is you, and not I, who must answer for this. I ask you that you will force them to restore my swords Colada and Tizona that I girded on them when they bore my children from Valencia.' And the hearts of the counts were glad when they heard his words, and they hasted to place the gold-pommelled swords in the hands of the Cid.

Next, Don Rodrigo demanded that the dowries of his daughters should be given back to him, and this also the king adjudged to be his right. Last, he set forth the treatment his daughters had suffered from the counts of Carrion, and challenged them and also their uncle, who had ever given them evil counsel, to fight with three of his knights that day.

Before the combat could take place a sound as of armed men was heard in the courtyard, and in rode two youths covered with golden armour and tall plumed helmets, and one was Don Ramiro of Navarre, and the other Don Sancho of Aragon.

'It has reached our ears,' said they, 'that the marriages between the counts of Carrion and the daughters of the Cid are about to be set aside, and we have come to pray that the ladies may be given to us to wife.'

And the king answered: 'If it pleases the Cid, it pleases me also, but the Cortes here present must grant its consent.'

So the Cid kissed the hand of the king in token of the honour done him, and the Cortes cried with one voice that the man who allied himself with Don Rodrigo de Bivar was honoured above all. Therefore, the weddings were celebrated without delay, the counts of Carrion having been pronounced outlaws and their former marriages null and void.

This matter being settled, the king directed that there should be no more delay in arranging the fight between the champions of the Cid and the counts of Carrion, which at the request of the counts was to be held three weeks later in their own castle. Don Rodrigo himself did not mean to fight. His honour was, he knew, safe in the hands of Don Bermudo and his other nephews, and he rode blithely home to Valencia. But Alfonso declared that he would be present to see that the combat was fairly fought, and it was well that he went, for the counts, thinking themselves safe on their own lands, had planned treachery. However, the king, mistrusting them, made a proclamation that in case of false dealing the traitor should be slain upon the field, and his possessions be forfeit. Baulked in this direction, the counts then entreated the king to forbid their foes to use the swords Tizona and Colada which they had been forced to give up, but Alfonso answered that it was now too late to make conditions, and they must get to the fight with stout hearts. This they could not do, for they had not got them, but, finding there was no help for it, they mounted their horses and put their lances in rest.

Between such adversaries the combat lasted but a short while. Fernan Gonzalez was soon unhorsed by Don Bermudo; Don Diego and his uncle confessed themselves vanquished. Their lands were declared forfeit by the judges, though their lives were granted them; but the tale of their cowardice spread far and wide, and none would speak to them or have dealings with them.

Thus was the Cid avenged.

For five years the Cid lived on in Valencia wearied of wars, and turning his thoughts to repenting him of his sins, and chief among them the wrong he had done many years before to the two Jews of Burgos. His strength grew daily less, till at length he could rise from his bed no more, neither could he eat food. While he lay in this manner, tidings were brought him that the Moors were preparing to besiege Valencia. This news roused the dying man, and for a moment it seemed as if he might be well again. Clearly he gave his orders how best to resist the attack, and bade his followers fight under the banner of Bishop Geronymo. 'As for me,' he said, 'you shall take my body and fill it with sweet spices, and shall set me once more on Babieca, and place Tizona in my hand. With cords shall you fasten me to the saddle, and so you shall lead me forth to my last fight with the Moors. Ximena my wife will care for Babieca, and when he is dead she will bury him where no Moorish dogs may root up his grave. And let no women be hired to make mourning for me. I want no tears to be shed over me but the tears of Ximena my wife. But for the Christians in this city, well know I that they are too few men to conquer the Moors, therefore let them prepare their goods, and steal forth by night, and take refuge in Castile. So farewell to you all, and pray that God may have mercy on my soul.'

Thus the Cid died, and all was done as he had said, and the king put rich garments on him, and set Tizona in his hand, and seated him in a carved chair by the altar of San Pedro de Cardeña.

THE KNIGHT OF THE SORROWFUL COUNTENANCE

Everybody knows that in the old times, when Arthur was king or Charles the Great emperor, no gentleman ever rested content until he had received the honour of knighthood. When once he was made a knight, he left his home and the court, and rode off in search of adventures, seeking to help people in distress who had no one else to help them.

After a while, however, the knights grew selfish and lazy. They liked better to hunt the deer through the forest than wicked robbers who had carried off beautiful ladies. 'It was the king's business,' they said, 'to take care of his subjects, not theirs,' so they dwelt in their own castles, and many of them became great lords almost as powerful as the king himself.

But though the knights no longer went in search of noble adventures, as knights of earlier days had been wont to do, there were plenty of books in which they could read if they chose of the wonderful deeds of their forefathers. Lancelot and Roland, Bernardo del Carpio, the Cid, Amadis de Gaule, and many more, were as well known to them as their own brothers, and if we will only take the trouble they may be known to us too.

Now, several hundreds of years after Lancelot and Roland and all the rest had been laid in their graves, a baby belonging to the family of Quixada was born in that part of Spain called La Mancha. We are not told anything of his boyhood, or even of his manhood till he reached the age of fifty, but we know that he was poor; that he lived with a housekeeper and a niece to take care of him, and that he passed all his days in company with these old books until the courts and forests which were the scenes of the adventures of those knights of bygone years were more real to him than any of his own doings.

'I wish all those books could be burned,' said the noble gentleman's housekeeper one day to his niece. 'My poor master's wits are surely going, for he never understands one word you say to him.

Indeed, if you speak, he hardly seems to see you, much less to hear you!'

What the housekeeper said was true. The things that belonged to her master's every-day life vanished completely bit by bit. If his niece related to him some scrap of news which a neighbour had run in to tell her, he would answer her with a story of the giant Morgante, who alone among his ill-bred race had manners that befitted a Spanish knight. If the housekeeper lamented that the flour in her storehouse would not last out the winter, he turned a deaf ear to all her complaints, and declared that he would give her and his niece into the bargain for the pleasure of bestowing one kick on Ganelon the traitor.

At last one day things came to a climax. When the hour of dinner came round, Don Quixada was nowhere to be found. His niece sought him in his bedroom, in the little tower where his books were kept, and even in the stable, where lay the old horse who had served him for more years than one could count. He was in none of these; but just as she was leaving the stable a strange noise seemed to come from over the girl's head, and on looking up she beheld her uncle rubbing a rusty sword that had lain there long before anybody could remember, while by his side were a steel cap and other pieces of armour.

From that moment Don Quixada became deaf and blind to the things of this world. He was in despair because the steel cap was not a proper helmet, but only a morion without a vizor to let down. Perhaps a smith might have made him what he wanted, but the Don was too proud to ask him, and, getting some cardboard, cut and painted it like a vizor, and then fastened it to the morion. Nothing could look—at a little distance—more like the helmet the Cid might have worn, but Don Quixada knew well that no knight ever went forth in search of adventures without first proving the goodness of his armour, so, fixing the helmet against the wall, he made a slash at it with his sword. He only dealt two strokes, whereas his enemy might give him twenty, but those two swept clean through the vizor, and destroyed in three minutes a whole week's work. So there was nothing for it but to begin over again, and this time the Don took the precaution of lining the vizor with iron.

'It looks beautiful,' he cried when it was finished; but he took care not to try his blade upon it.

His next act was to go into the stable and rub down his horse's coat, and to give it a feed of corn, vainly hoping that in a few days its ribs might become less plainly visible.

'It is not right,' he said to himself, one morning, as he stood watching the animal that was greedily eating out of its manger—'it is not right that a knight's good horse should go forth without a name. Even the heathen Alexander bestowed a high-sounding title on his own steed; and so, likewise, did those Christian warriors, Roland and the Cid!' But, try as he might, no name would come to him except such as were unworthy of the horse and his rider, and for four nights and days he pondered the question.

Suddenly, at the moment he had least expected it, when he was eating the plain broth his housekeeper had set before him, the inspiration came.

'Rozinante!' he cried triumphantly, laying down his spoon—'Rozinante! Neither the Cid's horse nor Roland's bore a finer name than that!'

This weighty matter being settled, the Don now began to think of himself, and, not being satisfied with the name his fathers had handed down to him, resolved to take one that was more noble, and better suited to a knight who was destined to do deeds that would keep him alive in the memory of men. For eight days he took heed of nothing save this one thing, and on the ninth he found what he had sought.

'The world shall know me as Don Quixote,' he said; 'and as the noble Amadis himself was not content to bear this sole title, but added to it the name of his own country, so I, in like manner, will add the name of mine, and henceforth will appear to all, as the good knight Don Quixote de la Mancha!'

Now Don Quixote de la Mancha had read far too many books about the customs of chivalry not to be aware that every knight worshipped some lady of whose beauty he boasted upon all occasions and whose token he wore upon his helmet in battle. It was not very easy for Don Quixote to find such a lady, for all his life long, the company which he met in his books had been dearer to him than that which he could have had outside his home.

'A knight without a liege lady is a tree without fruit, a body without soul,' he thought. 'Of what use will it be if I meet with some giant such as always crosses the path of a wandering knight, and disarm him in our first encounter, unless I have a lady at whose feet he can kneel?' So without losing more time he began to search the neighbouring villages for such a damsel, whose token he might wear, and at length found one with enough beauty for him to fall in love with, whose humble name of Aldonza he changed for that of Dulcinea del Toboso.

The sun had hardly risen on the following morning when Don Quixote laced on his helmet, braced on his shield, took his lance in hand, and mounted Rozinante.

Never during his fifty years had he felt his heart so light, and he rode forth into the wide plain, expecting to find a giant or a distressed lady behind every bush. But his joy was short-lived, for suddenly it came to his mind that in the days of chivalry it never was known that any man went in quest of adventures without being first made a knight, and that no such good fortune had happened to him. This thought was so terrible that he reeled in his saddle, and was near turning the head of Rozinante towards his own stable; but Don Quixote was a man of good courage, and in a short while he remembered on how many knights Sir Lancelot had conferred the honour of knighthood, and he determined to claim his spurs from the first that he managed to conquer in fight. Till then, he must, as soon as might be, make his armour white, in token that as yet he had had no adventures. In this manner he took heart again.

All that day he rode, without either bite or sup, and, of the two, Rozinante fared the better, for he at least found a tuft of coarse grass to eat. At nightfall a light as big as a faint star was seen gleaming in the distance, and both master and horse plucked up courage once more. They hastened towards it, and discovered that the light came from a small inn, which Don Quixote's fancy instantly changed into a castle with four towers and pinnacles of shining silver, surrounded by a moat. He paused a moment, expecting a dwarf to appear on the battlements and announce by the blasts of his trumpet that a knight was approaching, but, as no dwarf could be seen, he dismounted at the door, where he was received with courtesy by the landlord or the governor of the castle, as Don Quixote took him to be.

At the sight of this strange figure, which looked as if it had gone to sleep a thousand years ago, and had only just woke up again, the landlord had as much ado to keep from laughter as the muleteers and some women who were standing before the door. But being a civil man, and somewhat puzzled, he held the stirrup for Don Quixote to alight, offering to give him everything that would make him comfortable except a bed, which was not to be had. The Don made little of this, as became a good knight, and bade the landlord look well after Rozinante, for no better horse would ever stand in his stable. The man, who had seen many beasts in his day, did not rate him quite so highly, but said nothing, and after placing the horse in the stable returned to the house to see after the master.

As it happened, it was easier to provide for the wants of Rozinante than for those of Don Quixote, for the muleteers had eaten up everything in the kitchen, and nothing was left save a little dried fish and black bread. Don Quixote, however, was quite content; indeed, he imagined it the most splendid supper in the world, and when he had finished he fell on his knees before the landlord.

'Never will I rise again, noble sir,' said he, 'until you grant my prayer, which shall be an occasion of glory to you and of gain to all men.'

The landlord, not being used to such conduct on the part of his guests, tried to lift Don Quixote on to his feet, but the knight vowed that he would not move till his prayer was granted.

'The gift I would ask of you,' continued the Don, now rising to his feet, 'is that to-night I may watch my arms in the chapel of your castle, and at sunrise I shall kneel before you to be made a knight. Then I shall bid you farewell, and set forth on my journey through the world, righting wrongs and helping the oppressed, after the manner of the knights of old.'

'I am honoured indeed,' replied the landlord, who by this time saw very clearly that the poor gentleman was weak in his wits, and had a mind to divert himself. 'As a youth, I myself wandered through the land, and my name, the champion of all who needed it, was known to every court in Spain, till a deadly thrust in my side, from a false knight, forced me to lay down my arms, and to return to this my castle, giving shelter and welcome to any knights that ask it. But as to the chapel, it is but a week since it was made level with the ground, being but a poor place, and in no way worthy of the service of noble knights; but keep your watch in the courtyard of my castle, as your books will have told you that others have done in case of need. Afterwards, I will admit you into the Order of Chivalry, but before you take up your vigil tell me, I pray you, what money you have brought with you?'

This question surprised the Don very much.

'I have brought none,' he answered presently, 'for never did I hear that either Roland or Percival or any of the great knight-errants whose example I fain would follow, carried any money with them.'

'That is because they thought it no more needful to say that they carried money or clean shirts than that they carried a sword or a box of ointment to cure the wounds of themselves or their foes, in case no maiden or enchanter with a flask of water was on the spot,' replied the landlord; and he spoke so long and so earnestly on the subject that the Don promised never again to start on a quest without money and a box of ointment, besides at least three clean shirts.

It was now high time for his watch to begin, and the landlord led the way to a great yard at the side of the inn. Here the Don took his arms, and piled them on a trough of stone that stood near a well. Then bearing his lance he walked up and down beside his trough.

For an hour or two he paced the yard, watched, though he knew it not, by many eyes from the inn windows, which, with the aid of a bright moon, could see all that happened as clearly as if it were day. At length a muleteer who had a long journey before him drove up his team to the trough, which was fed by the neighbouring well, and in order to let his cattle drink, stretched out his arms to remove the sword and helmet which lay there. The Don perceived his aim, and cried in a voice of thunder:

'What man are you, ignorant of the laws of chivalry, who dares to touch the arms of the bravest knight who ever wore a sword? Take heed lest you lay a finger upon them, for if you do your life shall pay the forfeit.'

It might have been as well for the muleteer if he had listened, and had led his cattle to water elsewhere, but, looking at the Don's tall lean figure and his own stout fists, he only laughed rudely, and, seizing both sword and helmet, threw them across the yard. The Don paused a moment, wondering if he saw aright; then raising his eyes to heaven he exclaimed:

'O Lady Dulcinea, peerless in thy beauty, help me to avenge this insult that has been put upon me'; and, lifting high his lance, he brought it down with such a force on the head of the man that he fell to the ground without a word, and the Don began his walk afresh.

He had not been pacing the yard above half an hour when another man, not knowing what had befallen his friend, drove his beasts up to the trough, and was stooping to move the Don's arms, so that the cattle could get at the water, when a mighty blow fell on *his* head, splitting it nearly into pieces.

At this noise the people from the inn ran out, and seeing the two muleteers stretched wounded on the ground picked up stones wherewith to stone the knight. The Don, however, fronted them with such courage that they did not dare to venture near him, and the landlord, making use of their fears, called on them to leave him alone, for that he was a madman, and the law would not touch him, even though he should kill them all. Then, wishing to be done with the business and with his guest, he made excuses for the rude fellows, who had only got what they deserved, and said that, as there was no chapel to his castle, he could dub him knight where he stood, for, the watch of arms having been completed, all that was needful was a slap on the neck with a palm of the hand and the touch of the sword on the shoulder.

So Don Quixada was turned into Don Quixote de la Mancha, and, mounting Rozinante, he left the inn, and with a joyful heart started to seek his first adventure.

THE ADVENTURE OF THE TWO ARMIES WHO TURNED OUT TO BE FLOCKS OF SHEEP

The first adventure of the new knight did not turn out at all to his liking, nor answered his expectations, for in all the books of chivalry which he had read, never had he heard of a good knight being sorely wounded by a mere pack of common fellows, as happened to himself shortly after leaving the inn; though indeed he comforted his soul by thinking that, had not Rozinante stumbled over a stone and fallen, it would have fared ill with his foes.

He lay upon the ground for some time, aching in every bone, and repeating in a weak voice some lines out of his favourite romance of the 'Marquis of Mantua,' when a labourer from his own village came by and went to see if the man stretched on his back across the road was dead or only wounded.

'What ails you, master?' asked he; but as the vizor over the Don's face prevented his answer being understood, the labourer pulled it off with some trouble, and then stood, staring with surprise.

'Master Quixada!' cried he, wiping off the blood as he spoke, 'what villain has served you like this?' but, as Don Quixote only replied to his questions with long stories of the heroes of romance, the man gave it up, and after gathering up the stray bits of armour, and even the broken lance, helped the Don on to his own ass and took Rozinante by the bridle.

In this manner Don Quixote returned home.

When the knight dismounted and entered the house he found his housekeeper and niece filled with dismay, and bewailing his loss to the priest and the barber, who were wont to spend many an hour in company with the Don, listening to the strange tales that were always on his tongue. The joy with which they heard his well-known knock, in the middle of their discourses, was somewhat spoilt when they saw the condition he was in, and he stopped them quickly when they flew to embrace him.

'Let no one touch me,' cried he, 'for by the falling of my horse I am sore wounded. Carry me to bed, and summon the wise woman Urganda to heal me with her enchanted water.'

'Oh, never fear, your worship, we can cure you without her,' answered the housekeeper; 'and right glad we are to see you back, wounded or not.'

So between them all they bore him up the narrow stairs and laid him on his bed. And when he was undressed they sought his wounds, but found none, only a black bruise so they told him.

'Is it so?' he answered. 'Then the deeds that I did were yet more valorous than I thought. It was while I was fighting with ten giants, the biggest and strongest who ever gave battle to any Christian knight, that Rozinante fell, and I with him.'

'Oh! so there are giants in the dance now,' whispered the priest to the barber. 'I will not close my eyes this night till the books which have brought this evil are safely in the fire.' And, so saying, they left Don Quixote to sleep.

He was still sleeping next morning, when the priest came to ask for the keys of the little room where Don Quixote kept the old books he so much loved. They were handed to him with joy by the girl, who held books to be the enemy of all mankind, and when they all four entered they found more than a hundred volumes large and small, which was a great number for so poor a gentleman. One by one the priest examined them, and condemned them to the flames, unless by chance there was any doubt about their wickedness; that is, unless they had been written by a friend of the priest. In these cases, after the barber had been consulted, the books escaped the doom of the rest.

For fifteen days Don Quixote stayed at home and seemed content to stay there, passing the evenings in talk with the priest and the barber. Nothing was needed, he said, to put right the wrongs of the world, save a new order of knighthood, of which he had set the example. After much of this talk he suddenly remembered that a knight ever had a squire riding behind him, and that before he rode forth on his next quest he must needs provide himself with such an one. This was almost as hard a matter as finding a liege lady, but at length he bethought him of a poor peasant living in the same village, who possessed a wife and children, and not much else. This man he sent for, and promised him such great things and such noble rewards that Sancho Panza, for such was his name, readily agreed to serve him. 'Who knows,' said Don Quixote, 'what island I may conquer, and it would then fall to you to be the governor, or if you disdain the island, and would prefer to follow my fortune, I can make you Count at least! But, remember, my business admits of no delay, and next week we go forth to seek adventures. Meanwhile, I will give you money wherewith to provide all that is needful for our journeying, and take heed that you bring wallets with you.'

'Worshipful knight,' answered Sancho Panza, 'I will do all that you bid me, but, by your leave, I will bring my ass also, for she is a good ass, and never did I walk when a beast was at hand.'

'I know not,' replied Don Quixote, 'if any knight was ever yet followed by a squire mounted on an ass's back. Yet, bring the beast, for it will doubtless not be long before I meet some discourteous knight, whom I will speedily overcome, and his horse shall be yours.'

When all was ready, Sancho Panza bade his wife and children farewell, and, joining his master, they rode for some hours across a wide plain without seeing anything which would enable them to prove their valour. At length Don Quixote reined up Rozinante with a jerk, and turning to his squire he said:

'Fortune is on our side, friend Sancho. Look there, what huge giants are standing in a row! thirty of them at the least! It is a glorious chance for a new-made knight to give battle to these giants, and to rid the country of this wretched horde.'

'What giants?' asked Sancho, staring about him. 'I see none.'

'Those drawn up over there,' replied the Don. 'Never did I behold such arms! Those nearest us must be two miles long.'

'Go not within reach of them, good master,' answered Sancho anxiously, 'for they are no giants, but windmills, and what you take for arms are the sails, by which the wind turns the mill-stones.'

'How little do you know, friend Sancho, of these sorts of adventures!' replied Don Quixote. 'I tell you, those are no windmills, but giants. Know, however, that I will have no man with me who shivers with fear at the sight of a foe, so if you are afraid you had better fall to praying, and I will fight them alone.'

And with that he put spurs to Rozinante and galloped towards the windmills, heedless of the shouts of Sancho Panza, which indeed he never heard. Bending his body and holding his lance in rest, like all the pictures of knights when charging, he rushed on, crying as he went, 'Do not fly from me, cowards that you are! It is but a single knight with whom you must do battle!' And, calling on the Lady Dulcinea to come to his aid, he thrust his lance through the sail of the nearest windmill, which happened to be turned by a sharp gust of wind. The sail struck Rozinante so violently on the side that he and his master rolled over together, while the lance broke into small pieces.

When Sancho Panza saw what had befallen the Don—though indeed it was no more than he had expected—he rode up hastily to give him help. Both man and horse were half stunned with the blow; but, though Don Quixote's body was bruised, his spirit was unconquered, and to Sancho's complaint that no one could have doubted that the windmills were giants save those who had other windmills in their brains, he only answered:

'Be silent, my friend, and do not talk of things of which you know nothing. For of this I am sure, that the enchanter Friston, who robbed me of my books, has changed these knights into windmills to rob me of my glory also. But in the end, his black arts will have little power against my keen blade!'

'I pray that it may be so,' said Sancho, as he still held the stirrup for his master, when he struggled, not without pain, to mount Rozinante.

'Sit straighter in your saddle,' went on the worthy man; 'you lean too much on one side, but that doubtless comes from the fall you have had.'

'You speak truly,' replied Don Quixote; 'and if I do not complain of my hurt, it is because it was never heard that any knight complained of a wound, however sore!'

'If that is so, I am thankful that I am only a squire,' answered Sancho; 'for this I can say, that I shall cry as loud as I please for any pain, however little it may be—unless squires are forbidden to cry out as well as knights-errant.'

At this Don Quixote laughed, in spite of his hurts, and bade him complain whenever he pleased, for squires might lawfully do what was forbidden to knighthood. And with that the conversation ended, as Sancho declared it was their hour for dinner.

Towards three o'clock they returned to the road, which Don Quixote had left on catching sight of the windmills. But before entering it the knight thought well to give a warning to his squire.

'I would have you know, brother Sancho,' said he, 'that in whatsoever danger you may see me you shall stand aside, and never seek to defend me, unless those who set on me should come of base forefathers, and not be people of gentle birth. For if those who attack me are knights, it is forbidden by the laws of chivalry that a knight be attacked by any man that has himself not received the honour of knighthood.'

'Your lordship shall be obeyed in all that you say,' answered Sancho, 'and the more readily that I am a man of peace, and like not brawls. But, see, who are these that approach us?'

The question was natural, for the procession advancing along the road was a strange one, even at that day. First came two monks of the Order of St. Benedict, mounted on mules so large that Don Quixote, with some reason, took them to be dromedaries. The better to conceal their faces they had masks, and carried parasols. After them came a coach which had for a guard four or five mounted men and two muleteers, and inside the coach was seated a lady on her way to join her husband in the city of Seville. In reality the monks were strangers to her, and had nothing to do with her party, but this Don Quixote did not know, and, being ever on the watch to give help to any who needed it, he said:

'Either my eyes deceive me, or this is the most wonderful adventure that ever fell to the lot of a knight. For those black shapeless monsters that you see yonder are magicians carrying off some princess, and I must undo this wrong with all the strength I have.'

'Look you, master,' answered Sancho hastily, 'if you take up with this adventure, you will fare worse than you did with the windmills. Those are no magicians but monks of St. Benedict, while the others are travellers, journeying for business or pleasure. Think, I pray you, lest it be a snare of the Evil One.'

'I have often told you, Sancho, that, being what you are, you can know nothing of adventures,' replied Don Quixote; 'but what I have said, I do, as you will see'; and as he spoke he planted himself in the middle of the road, and awaited the approach of the friars.

As soon as they drew near enough for his voice to reach their ears, Don Quixote cried loudly:

'Fiends and scum of all the wicked, set free on this instant the captive princess whom you hold imprisoned in that coach, or else prepare for death, which is the just punishment of all your crimes.'

The monks reined in their mules and stared at Don Quixote, whose figure, to say truth, was no less startling than his words. At first they were very angry, then gentler counsels prevailed, and they answered:

'Fair sir, we are neither fiends nor scum, but only two friars of St. Benedict, who are riding peacefully along the king's highway, and know nothing of any captive princess.'

'Miscreants that you are, do you think I am a man to be deceived by false speeches?' cried the Don, now beside himself with fury, and, dashing with his lance in rest at the friar next him, he would indeed have given him his last shrift had not the monk slipped cleverly from the other side of his saddle, so that the lance passed over his head. His companion, fearing that like treatment was in store for him, galloped away with all his might.

As for the squire, directly he saw the man fall to the ground he ran up and began to strip off his clothes, till he was stopped in this proceeding by a blow on his head from one of the attendants of the two monks. The friar, left to himself, jumped on his mule, and rode off pale and trembling to rejoin his companion, while Don Quixote busied himself with conversing with the lady in the coach, and assuring her of his protection.

It were long indeed to tell of the many battles delivered by Don Quixote, who troubled himself little about the sore wounds he received on his own body as long as he could give aid to those in distress. What grieved him far more than mere sword-thrusts or bruises was the loss of his helmet.

But, come what might, his spirit was never daunted, though he could not deny that, as Sancho Panza truly said, never had they gained any battle, unless they counted one which was doubtful, and even at that the knight had come off the poorer by half an ear and half a helmet.

'From the first day we set out,' went on the good squire, 'until this moment, we have received nothing but blows and more blows, beatings and more beatings, over and above the tossing I once got in a blanket. And you tell me that the fellows who maltreat me so are enchanted, and would not feel my blows if I had a chance of returning them. In truth, my eyes are too dull to see where lies the pleasure of conquering one's foes, of which your worship is always telling me.'

'Ah, Sancho, that is just what grieves me,' answered Don Quixote sadly; 'but henceforth I will seek to gird myself always with a sword that shall be enchanted in such a manner that it will defend me from any spells they may try to throw over me. Maybe that Fortune will send me that of Amadis, one of the keenest blades in the world, and the best sword that ever knight had. But look, do you see that cloud of dust rising out there? That tells us that a large army, made up of men and nations without number, are marching towards us.'

'By that way of reckoning,' answered the squire, 'another army must be advancing to meet them, for behind us the cloud is just as thick.'

Filled with joy at the thought of fighting two armies, Don Quixote turned to look, and his heart beat high. The dust was so thick that neither he nor Sancho could perceive that the clouds of dust were caused by two immense flocks of sheep. To the mind of the knight they *could* be nothing but vast armies, and this he declared so positively that at length Sancho Panza came to believe it also. The squire, however, looked on the fact with very different feelings to his master, and asked anxiously:

'Noble sir, what are we to do?'

'What *can* we do,' replied the knight, 'except fly to the help of those who need it? For you must know, friend Sancho, that the army in front of us is led by the Emperor Alifanfaron, while the other, which is marching to meet him, is Pentapolin of the Uplifted Arm, so called because he rides into battle with his right arm bare.'

'And what is their quarrel?' asked Sancho.

'Alifanfaron is a Moslem, yet desires to marry the daughter of Pentapolin,' replied Don Quixote, 'but her father will not give her to him till he ceases to be an unbeliever.'

'By my beard,' cried Sancho, 'if I see this Pentapolin driven back I will strike a blow for him with all my might.'

'And you will do well,' replied Don Quixote, 'for in such battles it is not necessary to be a knight.'

'But what shall I do with my ass?' inquired the squire anxiously, 'for I suppose that until this day no man has ever yet ridden into combat on an ass.'

'Let him loose,' said Don Quixote, 'and think no more of him, for after we have vanquished our enemies we shall have such choice of horses that I may light upon one even better than Rozinante! But let us stand on yonder little hill, for I would fain describe to you the names and arms of the noble knights that are approaching.'

For a long while he spoke, telling his squire of the countries from which those leaders of the armies had come. And truly it was wonderful to listen to him, seeing that they were all children of his own brain. From time to time Sancho Panza stared hard at the dust, trying to see as much as his master, and at last he cried:

'If there is a knight or a giant there, they must be enchanted like the rest; for, look as I may, I cannot see them.'

'How can you speak such words?' answered Don Quixote reproachfully. 'Do you not hear the horses neighing, the drums beating, the trumpets sounding?'

'No, I hear nothing of all that,' replied Sancho stoutly; 'all *I* hear is the bleating of sheep and of ewes.' And as he spoke the dust was lifted by the wind, and he saw the two flocks in front of them.

'It is the deadly fear which has overtaken you,' answered Don Quixote, 'which has clouded your eyes and ears, and made everything seem different from what it is. If you are afraid, stand aside then, for my arm alone carries victory with it'; and, so saying, he touched Rozinante with his spurs, and with his lance in rest galloped down the hill, unheeding the cries of Sancho, who shrieked out that it was only a flock of sheep that he saw, and that there were neither giants nor knights to fight with.

He might have spared his voice, for Don Quixote, if he heard him, which is doubtful, rode on without turning his head, shouting defiance at the Moslem leader, and spearing the sheep which could not get out of his way, as if they were indeed the soldiers he took them for.

When the shepherds had recovered from this unexpected onslaught, they shouted with all their might to Don Quixote to leave off spearing their sheep, but, as he paid no heed to their warnings, they took out the slings they carried with them, and whirling them round their heads let fly large stones. Don Quixote, however, cared no more for the stones than he had done for the cries, and galloped up and down wildly, calling as he went:

'Proud Alifanfaron, where can I find you? I, a solitary knight, challenge you to meet me in single combat, that I may avenge the wrongs that you have done to the noble Pentapolin!' Doubtless the knight would have said still more had not a stone hit him on his side at that very moment, breaking two of his ribs. At first he thought he was dead, but, recollecting the balsam which he kept in his wallet, he drank a draught of it, although it was only intended to be laid on the outside of wounds and bruises.

He was still in the act of swallowing it when another missile struck him full on the face, and knocked out some of his teeth. He reeled in his saddle from the blow, and then fell heavily to the ground.

The shepherds, frightened at what they had done, ran up to look at him, and seeing him lying there senseless, drove quickly off the rest of their flock, leaving the seven that Don Quixote had speared stretched beside him.

Directly the shepherds had departed, Sancho Panza came down to look after his master, and finding him bruised and bleeding, but not stunned, he fell to reproaching him for his folly. But the knight only answered that if the enemies around him seemed to bear the likeness of sheep, it was only because they had been enchanted, and that their fellows now marching along the road would soon regain their proper shape, and become straight men and tall again.

Then, with Sancho's help, he mounted Rozinante, and the two rode slowly along the road, hoping that they might shortly discover an inn, where they could get food and rest.

THE ADVENTURE OF THE BOBBING LIGHTS

Both Rozinante and his master had fared so ill at the hands of the shepherds that they journeyed but slowly, and darkness fell without their having reached an inn, or even caught sight of one. This grieved sorely both knight and squire, for not only did all Don Quixote's bones ache from the stoning he had undergone, but somehow or other their wallets had been also lost, and it was many hours since they had broken their fast.

In this plight they travelled, man and beast hanging their heads with fatigue, when they saw on the road, coming towards them, a great multitude of lights, bobbing up and down, as if all the stars of heaven were shifting their places. Neither Don Quixote nor Sancho felt much at their ease at this strange spectacle, and both pulled up their beasts, and waited trembling. Even Don Quixote feared he knew not what, and the hair stood up on his head, in spite of his valour, as he said to Sancho:

'There lies before me, Sancho, a great and perilous adventure, and one in which I must bear a stout heart.'

'It seems to be an adventure of phantoms,' whispered Sancho fearfully, 'which never was to my liking.'

'Whatever phantoms they be,' answered the knight, 'they shall not touch a hair of your head,' replied Don Quixote soothingly. 'If they mocked at you in the inn, it was for reason that I could not leap the fence. But here, where the ground is open, I can lay about me as I will.'

'And what if they bewitch you, as they did that other time?' asked the squire. 'How much will the open ground profit you then'?

'Trust to me,' replied Don Quixote, 'for my experience is greater than yours'; and Sancho said no more.

They stood a little on one side watching the lights approaching, and soon they saw a host of men clad in white riding along the road. The squire's teeth chattered at the sight of them, and his terror increased when he was able to make out that the moving stars were flaming torches which men in white shirts carried in their hands, and that behind them followed a litter draped in black. After the litter came six other men dressed in black and mounted on mules. And Sancho had no doubt that he saw before him shadows from the next world.

Though Don Quixote's heart quailed for a moment at the strangeness of the vision, he soon recalled his valour. In an instant his fancy had changed the litter into a bier, and the occupant into a knight who had been done to death by foul means, and whom he was bound in honour to avenge. So he moved forward to the middle of the road, and cried in a loud voice:

'Proud knights, whoever you may be, stand and give me account of yourselves, and tell me who it is that lies in that bier. For either you have done an ill deed to some man, or else a wrong has been done to you.'

'Pardon me, fair sir,' answered the foremost of the white-shirted men, 'but we are in haste, and the inn is far. We have no time for parleying.'

This reply only confirmed Don Quixote's worst suspicions.

'Stop, or you are a dead man,' cried he in tones of thunder. 'Tell me who you are and whither you are going, or else I will fight you all'; and with that he seized the mule by the bridle. The mule, not being used to such rough treatment, reared herself up on her hind legs, so that her rider slipped off her back. At this sight one of the other men ran to his aid, calling the knight all the ill names he could think of, which so inflamed the anger of Don Quixote that he laid about him with his spear on every side. Even Rozinante seemed to have gotten a new spirit as well as a new body, for he turned him about so nimbly that soon the plain was covered with flying white men, still holding the bobbing torches. The mourners who rode behind did not escape so easily, for their long skirts and cloaks hindered them from moving, and Don Quixote struck and beat them just as he would, till they took him to be a giant or enchanter rather than a man.

Sancho, as was his custom, bore no part in the fray, but stood by and said to himself: 'Had ever any man such a master!'

When Don Quixote's rage was somewhat abated, he paused and gazed about him. Then, seeing a burning torch lying on the ground, and a figure near it, he went up, and perceived by the light that it was the man whom he had first attacked.

'Yield, or I will slay you!' he shouted, and the man answered grimly:

'I seem to have "yielded" as much as can be required of me, as my leg is broken. If you are indeed a Christian knight, I pray you of your nobility to spare my life, as I am a member of the Holy Church.'

'Who brought you here, then?' asked Don Quixote.

'Who? My ill fortune,' replied he. 'I and the eleven priests who have fled with the torches set forth as escort to the body of the gentleman that lies in the litter, bearing it to its tomb in the city of Segovia, where he was born.'

'And who killed him?' said Don Quixote, who never imagined that any man could die naturally.

'He died by reason of a most pestilent fever,'

answered the wounded man.

'Then,' replied Don Quixote, 'I am delivered from the duty of avenging his death, which would otherwise have fallen to me. For in case you are ignorant, I would have you know that I am the knight Don Quixote de la Mancha, and it is my place to wander through the world, helping those that suffer wrongs and punishing those who inflict them.'

'As to helping those who suffer wrongs,' replied the churchman, 'for my part I can see nothing but that it is you and no other who have inflicted the wrong upon me. For whereas I was whole before, you have given me a thrust which has broken my leg, and I shall remain injured for ever.'

'You and your friends the priests,' answered Don Quixote, in no wise abashed by this remark, 'have wrought the evil yourselves by coming in such wise, and by night, that no man could think but that you were ill creatures from another world.'

'Then, if you repent you of the wrong that you have done me,' said the man, 'I pray you, worshipful knight, to deliver my leg from the bondage of this ass, who has my leg fastened between the stirrup and the saddle.'

The kind heart of Don Quixote was shocked at his thoughtlessness, and he answered quickly:

'You should have told me of your pain before, or I might have talked on till to-morrow'; and he called to Sancho Panza, who was busily robbing the mule that carried the provisions. Hearing his master's voice, Sancho left off with an ill grace, and, placing the bag of food on his own donkey, went to see what his master wanted.

Between them both they set the mule on its feet, and the man on its saddle. Don Quixote then put the torch in his hand and bade him ride after his companions, and not to forget to ask their pardon in his name for the wrong he had unconsciously done them.

'And,' added the squire, 'if your friends should ask the name of this gentleman, who now craves their forgiveness, tell them that it is the famous Don Quixote, the Knight of the Sorrowful Countenance!'

THE HELMET OF MAMBRINO

The morning after the last adventure Don Quixote and his squire were riding along the road, when the knight saw in front of him a man on horseback, with something on his head which looked as if it were made of gold.

'If my eyes do not deceive me,' he said, turning to Sancho Panza, 'here comes one who wears on his head the helmet of Mambrino.'

'If I had your worship's leave to speak,' answered Sancho, who was by this time beginning to learn a little wisdom, 'I could give many reasons to show that you are mistaken.'

'How *can* I be mistaken?' cried Don Quixote angrily. 'Do not you see for yourself that a knight is coming towards us, mounted on a grey horse and with a golden helmet on his head?'

'All that *I* can see,' replied the squire, 'is that the man is mounted on a grey donkey like my own, and he has on his head something that glitters.'

'What you see,' answered Don Quixote solemnly, 'is the helmet of Mambrino. Go, stand aside and let *me* deal with him, for without even speaking to him I will get possession of his helmet, for which my soul has always longed.'

Truth to tell, the real story of the helmet, for so Don Quixote took it to be, was very simple. A rich man who lived in a village only a few miles away had sent for the nearest barber to shave and bleed him. The man started, taking with him a brass basin, which he was accustomed to use, and, as a shower of rain soon came on, he put the basin on his head to save his hat, which was a new one. The ass, as Sancho Panza rightly said, was very like his own.

The good man was jogging comfortably along, thinking what he would like for supper, when suddenly he saw Don Quixote galloping towards him, head bent and lance in rest. As he drew near he cried loudly:

'Defend yourself, or give me up the helmet, to which you have no right.'

The barber was so taken by surprise that for a moment he did nothing; then he had only just time to escape the lance thrust by sliding off his ass and running so swiftly over the plain that even the wind could scarcely overtake him. In his flight the basin fell from his head, to the great pleasure of Don Quixote, who bade his squire bring it to him.

'The Unbeliever who wore this helmet first must have had indeed a large head,' cried he, turning it over in his hands, seeking the vizor; 'yet, even so, half of it is wanting.'

At this Sancho began to laugh, and his master asked him what he found to divert him so much.

'I cannot but laugh when I think how large was the head of the Unbeliever,' replied Sancho gravely, knowing that the knight did not love the mirth of other men. 'But, to my mind, the helmet looks exactly like a barber's basin.'

'Listen to me,' answered Don Quixote, 'and I will tell you what has happened. By a strange accident this famous helmet must have fallen to the lot of someone who did not know the value of his prize. But, seeing it was pure gold, he melted half of it for his own uses, and the rest he made into a barber's basin. Be sure that in the first village where I can meet with a skilled workman I will have it restored to its own shape again, and meanwhile I will wear it as it is, for half a helmet is better than none.'

'And what,' inquired Sancho, 'shall we do with the grey horse that looks so like an ass? The beast is a good beast.'

'Leave the ass or horse, whichever it pleases you to call it,' replied the Don, 'for no knight ever takes the steed of his foe, unless it is won in fair fight. And perchance, when we have ridden out of sight, its master will come back and seek for it.'

Sancho, however, was not overmuch pleased by this speech.

'Truly the laws of chivalry are strict,' he grumbled, 'if they will not let a man change one donkey for another! And is it forbidden to change the pack-saddle also?'

'Of that I am in doubt,' replied Don Quixote; 'and until I have certain information on this point, if your need is great, you may take what you need.'

Sancho hardly expected such good fortune to befall him, and stripping the ass of his harness he speedily put it upon his own beast, and then laid out the dinner he had stolen from the sumpter mule for himself and his master.

Not long after this event, as Don Quixote and his squire were riding along the road, discoursing as they went of matters of chivalry, they saw approaching them from a distance a dozen men or more, with iron chains round their necks, stringing them together like beads on a rosary, and bearing iron fetters on their hands. By their side were two men on horseback carrying firelocks, and two on foot with swords and spears.

'Look!' cried Sancho Panza, 'here come a gang of slaves, sent to the galleys by the king.'

'What is that you say—*sent*?' asked Don Quixote. 'Can any king *send* his subjects where they have no mind to go?'

'They are men who have been guilty of many crimes,' replied the squire, 'and to punish them they are being led by force to the galleys.'

'They go,' inquired Don Quixote, 'by force and not willingly?'

'You speak truly,' answered Sancho Panza.

'Then if that is so,' said the knight, 'it is my duty to set them free.'

'But think a moment, your worship,' cried Sancho, terrified at the consequences of this new idea; 'they are bad men, and deserve punishment for the crimes they have committed.'

Don Quixote was silent. In fact, he had heard

nothing of what his squire had said. Instead he rode up to the galley-slaves, who by this time were quite near, and politely begged one of the soldiers who had charge of them to tell him of his courtesy where these people were going, and why they were chained in such a manner.

The guard, who had never read any of the romances of chivalry, and was quite ignorant of the speech of knights, answered roughly that they were felons going to the galleys, and that was all that mattered to anybody. But Don Quixote was not to be put aside like this.

'By your leave,' he said, 'I would speak with them, and ask of every man the reason of his misfortune.'

Now this civility of the knight made the soldiers feel ashamed of their own rudeness, so one of them replied more gently than before:

'We have here set down the crimes of every man singly, but if your worship pleases you may inquire of the prisoners yourself. And be sure you will hear all about their tricks, and more too, for it is a mighty pleasure to them to tell their tales.'

The soldier spoke truly; and wonderful were the stories which Don Quixote listened to and believed, until the knight, smitten by compassion, turned to the guards and implored them to set free the poor fellows, whose sins would be punished elsewhere.

'I ask you to do this as a favour,' he ended, 'for I would willingly owe you this grace. But, if you deny me, my arm and my sword will teach you to do it by force.'

'That is a merry jest indeed,' cried the soldier. 'So we are to let go the king's prisoners just because you tell us to do it. You had better mind your own business, fair sir, and set that pot straight on your head, and do not waste your time in looking for five feet in a cat.'

Don Quixote was so furious at the man's words that he felled him to the earth with a blow from his sword, while for a moment the other guards stood mute from surprise. Then seizing their weapons they rushed at Don Quixote, who sat firm in his saddle as became a knight, awaiting their onslaught. But for all his valour it would have gone hard with him had not the attention of the soldiers been hastily called off by the galley-slaves, who were taking advantage of the tumult to break their fetters. The chief among them had snatched the sword and firelock of the man whom Don Quixote had overthrown, and by merely pointing it at the other guards he so frightened them that they fled in all directions, followed by a shower of stones from the rest of the captives.

'Let us depart from here,' whispered Sancho Panza, knowing better than his master in what a sorry plight they might presently find themselves. 'If we once reach those hills, none can overtake us.'

'It is well,' replied the knight; 'but first I must settle this matter,' and, calling together the prisoners, he bade them go with all speed and present themselves before the Lady Dulcinea del Toboso, and say that they had come by the command of the Knight of the Sorrowful Countenance, and further to relate the doughty deeds by which they had been set free.

At this the convicts only laughed, and replied that if they were to fulfil his desires and travel together in a body they would soon be taken captive by their enemies, and would be no better off than before, but that in gratitude for his services they would be willing to pray for him, which they could do at their leisure.

This discourse enraged Don Quixote nearly as much as the words of the guard had done, and he answered the fellow in terms so abusive that the convict's patience, which was never very great, gave way altogether, and he and his comrades, picking up what stones lay about, flung them with such hearty goodwill at the knight and Rozinante, that at length they knocked him right out of the saddle. The man then dragged the basin from his head, and after dealing him some mighty blows with it dashed it to the ground, where it broke in pieces. They next took the coat which he wore over his armour, and stripped the squire of all but his shirt. Having done this, they went their ways, fearing lest they might be overtaken.

HOW DON QUIXOTE WAS ENCHANTED WHILE GUARDING THE CASTLE

In the course of their adventures Don Quixote and his squire found themselves at the door of an inn which they had already visited, where they met with many friends. The hours were passed in pleasant discourse, and in the telling and reading of strange stories; the company parted at night well satisfied with their entertainment.

Don Quixote, however, did not share in these joys, for he was sorely cast down by reason of wounds he had received a few days previously in seeking to right a wrong. So, leaving the remainder of the guests to each other's society, he threw himself on the bed that had been made for him, and soon fell fast asleep.

The guests below had forgotten all about him, so absorbed were they in the interest of a tale of woeful ending, when the voice of Sancho Panza burst upon their ears.

'Hasten! hasten! good sirs; hasten and help my master in the hardest battle I have ever seen him fight. By my faith, he has dealt such a blow to the giant that his head he has cut clean off.'

'What is that you say?' asked the priest, who was reading out the tale. 'Are you out of your senses, Sancho?' But his question was lost in a furious noise from above, in which Don Quixote might be heard crying:

'Rogue, thief, villain! I have you fast, and little will your sword avail you'; then followed loud blows against the wall.

'Quick, quick! don't stand there listening, but fly to the aid of my master. Though, indeed, by this time there can be little need, for the giant must be dead already, and will trouble the world no more. For I saw his blood spurt and run all over the floor, and his head is cut off and fallen to one side.'

'As I am alive,' exclaimed the innkeeper, 'I fear that Don Quixote has been fighting with one of the wine-skins that I put to hang near the bed, and it is wine not blood that is spilt on the ground.' And he ran into the room, followed by the rest, to see what had really happened.

They all stopped short at the sight of Don Quixote, who did, in truth, present a most strange figure. The only garments he had on were a shirt and a little red cap; his legs were bare, and round his left arm was rolled the bed covering, while in the right he held a sword, with which he was cutting and thrusting at everything about him, uttering cries all the while, as if in truth he were engaged in deadly combat with a giant. Yet his eyes were tight shut, and it was clear to all that he was fast asleep; but in his dream he had slashed at so many of the skins that the whole room was full of wine. When the innkeeper perceived this, the loss of his wine so enraged him that he in his turn flew at the knight, and struck him such hard blows with his fists that, had not the priest and another man pulled him off, the war with the giant would soon have ended.

Still, curious to say, it was not until a pannikin of cold water had been poured over him by the barber that Don Quixote awoke, and even then he did not understand what he had been doing, and why he stood there in such a dress.

Now the priest had caught hold of Don Quixote's hands, so that he should not beat those who were pouring the water over him, and the knight, having only partly come to his senses, took him for the princess, for whose sake he had made war on the giant.

'Fair and gracious lady,' he said, falling on his knees, 'may your life henceforth be freed from the terror of this ill-born creature!'

'Well, did I not speak truly?' asked Sancho Panza proudly. 'Has not my master properly salted the giant? I have got my earldom safe at last.' For Sancho never ceased to believe in the knight's promises.

Everyone was driven to laugh at the strange foolery of both master and man, except the innkeeper, whose mind was still sore at the loss of his wine-skins. The priest and the barber first busied themselves in getting Don Quixote, now quite worn out with his adventure, safely into bed, and then went to administer the best consolation they could to the poor man.

Many days passed before Don Quixote was well enough to leave the inn, but at length he seemed to be cured of the fatigue he had undergone during his previous adventures, and had bidden his squire get all things ready for his departure. Maritornes, the servant at the inn, and the innkeeper's daughter, having overheard the plans of Don Quixote, resolved that he should not leave them before they had played him some merry tricks.

That night, when everyone else had gone to bed, and Don Quixote, armed, and mounted on Rozinante, was keeping guard in front of the inn, the two girls crept up to a loft. Nowhere in the inn was there such a thing as a proper window, but in the loft was a hole through which the knight could be seen, leaning on his lance uttering deep sighs and broken words about the Lady Dulcinea.

The innkeeper's daughter, falling in with his humour, advanced to the hole, and invited him to draw a little nearer. Nothing more was needed than for Don Quixote to imagine that the damsel was sick of love for him, and he told her straightway that any service he could do her short of proclaiming her his liege lady she might command. Upon this, Maritornes informed him that her mistress would be content were she permitted to kiss his hand, which Don Quixote answered might be done without wrong to the Lady Dulcinea. So, without more ado, he passed it through the hole, when it was instantly seized by Maritornes, who slipped a noose of rope over his wrist, and tied the other end of it tightly to the door of the loft.

After that they both ran off, overflowing with laughter, leaving the knight to reproach them for their ill-usage.

There the poor knight remained, mounted on Rozinante, his arm in the hole and his hand fastened to the door, fearing lest Rozinante should move and he should be left hanging. But in this he did wrong to his horse, who was happy enough to stand still.

Then Don Quixote, seeing himself bound, instead of seeking to unloose himself as many others would have tried to do, sat quietly in his saddle, and dreamed dreams of the enchantment which had befallen him. And thus he stayed till the day dawned.

His dreams were rudely broken into when there drew up at the inn door four men well armed and mounted. As no one answered their knock, they repeated it more loudly, when Don Quixote cried to them:

'Knights or squires, or whoever you may be, it is not for you to knock at the gates of this castle; for sure, any man might tell that those within are asleep, or else it is their custom not to open until the sun touches the whole floor. You must wait until it is broad day, and then it will be seen whether you can be admitted within the gates.'

'What sort of castle is this, which receives no guests without such ceremonies?' mocked one of the men. 'If you are the innkeeper, bid your servants open to us without delay. We are neither knights nor squires, but honest travellers, who need corn for our horses, and that without delay.'

'Have I the air of an innkeeper?' asked Don Quixote loftily.

'I do not know of what you have the air,' answered the man, 'but this I *do* know, and that is that you are jesting when you call this inn a castle.'

'But it *is* a castle,' replied Don Quixote, 'and one of the finest in the whole country! And within are those who carry crowns on their heads and sceptres in their hands.'

'It may well be that inside are players with crowns and sceptres both,' answered the traveller, 'for in so small an inn no real kings and their trains would find a place'; and, being weary of talking, he knocked at the door with more violence than before.

Meanwhile, one of the horses had drawn near to Rozinante, wondering what the strange creature could be, of a form like unto his own, but to all outward seeming formed of wood. Rozinante, cheered by the presence of one of his own kind, moved his body a little, which caused Don Quixote to slip from his saddle, and to remain hanging by his arm, though his feet almost touched the ground. The pain of thus being suspended from his arm was so great that, knight though he was, he shrieked in agony, till the people in the inn ran to the doors to see what was the matter.

Maritornes alone, fearing punishment, slipped round another way, and unfastened the cord which bound Don Quixote, who dropped to the ground as the travellers came up, and in answer to their questions mounted Rozinante, and, after riding round the field, reined up suddenly in front of them, crying:

'Whoever shall proclaim that I have suffered enchantment I give him the lie, and challenge him to meet me in single combat.'

But instead of answering his defiance the guests merely stood and stared at him, till the innkeeper whispered that he was a noble gentleman, a little touched in his wits, so they took no further notice of his words. This so enraged Don Quixote that he was only withheld from fighting them all by remembering that nowhere in the records of chivalry was it lawful to undertake a second adventure before the first had drawn to a good end.

Meanwhile a new strife had begun in the inn, for two of the travellers who had lodged there during the night were found trying to leave the inn without paying their reckoning. But it happened that the landlord detected their purpose and held them fast, upon which the two fellows set on him with blows, till his daughter ran to Don Quixote and implored his help.

'Beautiful damsel,' replied the knight slowly, 'just now I cannot listen to your prayer, for the laws of chivalry forbid my engaging in a fresh adventure. But tell your father to keep his assailants at bay, while I ride to the Princess Micomicona, in whose service I already am, and ask her leave to aid him in his trouble.'

'And long before your return,' cried Maritornes, 'my poor master will be in another world'; but Don Quixote, not heeding her, turned his back, and, falling on his knees before a lady present, begged that she would grant him permission to rescue the lord of the castle.

This being given, the knight braced on his shield and drew his sword, and hastened to the inn door, where the two men were still beating the landlord. But the moment he reached the combatants he stopped and drew back, in spite of the entreaties of Maritornes and of the innkeeper's wife.

'It has come into my mind,' he said, 'that it is not lawful for me to give battle to any except belted knights. Now there are no knights here, and the task belongs to my squire Sancho, who I will bid to undertake it in my stead.'

So the fight still raged, till at length the men's arms grew tired, which, Don Quixote seeing, he persuaded them to make peace, and the two guests to pay the sum which they rightly owed the landlord.

DON QUIXOTE'S HOME-COMING

By this time the company of friends who had been passing their days so pleasantly at the inn, were called away by other business, but, not liking to leave Don Quixote to himself, they contrived a plan by which the priest and barber were to carry him home, where they hoped his wits might come back to him.

So they set about making secretly a large cage of poles, having the sides latticed, so that Don Quixote should receive both air and light, and this cage was to be placed on a bullock-cart which happened to be going in the same direction. The rest of the company put on masks and disguised themselves in various manners, so that the knight might not know them again.

These preparations being finished, they stole softly into his room at the dead of night and tied his hands and feet firmly together. He woke with a start, and, seeing the array of strange figures about him, took them to be the phantoms which hovered about the enchanted castle, and believed without doubt that he himself was enchanted likewise, for he could neither move nor fight.

This reasoning pleased the priest greatly, as in

just such a manner he had reckoned that the knight would behave. Sancho alone had been left in the garments that he commonly wore, and he was not deceived by the ghosts who passed before him. But he looked on and said nothing till he should see how the matter turned out.

When all was ready, Don Quixote was picked up and carried to the cage, where they laid him at full length, but taking good care to nail the door, so that it could not be opened. Then a voice was heard from behind to utter a prophecy, which Don Quixote understood to mean that he was setting forth on his wedding journey, and that he was to be bound in marriage to the Lady Dulcinea del Toboso, whose name he had always upheld in battle.

The knight responded joyfully to the words he heard, beseeching the mighty enchanter in whose power he was not to leave him in his prison till these glorious promises had been fulfilled, and appealing to Sancho never to part from him either in good or ill fortune. Sancho bowed in answer and kissed his master's hand; then the ghosts took up the cage and placed it on a waggon.

Don Quixote beguiled the way after his usual fashion, recalling the stories of enchantments he had read, yet never finding a knight who had been enchanted after his fashion.

'No knight that ever *I* heard,' said he, 'was drawn by such heavy and sluggish animals. Strange it is indeed to be carried to adventures in an ox-cart, instead of flying through the air on a griffin or a cloud! Yet, mayhap, the new chivalry, of which I am the first knight, may have new ways'; and with that he contented himself, and discoursed to Sancho about the ghosts, while Rozinante and the ass were saddled. Then Sancho mounted his ass and took Rozinante's rein, the priest meanwhile giving the troopers a few pence a day to ride by the ox-cart as far as Don Quixote's native village.

After allowing Don Quixote to bid farewell to the good people gathered at the inn door, the priest, still masked, gave the signal to the driver, and the cart drawn by the oxen started at a foot's pace. The troopers rode on each side to guard it, and behind them came Sancho riding on his ass, leading Rozinante, while the priest and the barber, mounted on a pair of fine mules, brought up the rear.

They journeyed in silence for some time, till the driver of the ox-cart, who was a lazy fellow, called a halt as he himself wished to rest, and the grass was rich and green for the oxen. Soon they were joined by a company of well-dressed men on horseback, who stopped in surprise on seeing such a strange sight as that of a man in a cage. The leader of the party, who made himself known to them as a canon of Toledo, entered into conversation with the captive knight. Don Quixote informed him that he was enchanted by reason of envy of his glorious deeds, which was denied by Sancho Panza, who declared that when he was at liberty his master ate, drank, and slept like other people, and if no one hindered him would talk more than thirty lawyers.

The canon and his friends rode on with the priest for some distance, as he desired greatly to hear the tale of Don Quixote's adventures, for never before had he met with such a strange man. In the heat of the day they again rested in a shady spot, and here, at the petition of the squire, Don Quixote was unloosed from his bonds and set at liberty.

For a while he was content to pass the hours of his journey in hearing and telling of matters of chivalry, rejoicing to find himself once more on the back of Rozinante. But unfortunately the sight of a procession of men in white approaching him stirred up all his anger, for, as was his custom, he instantly divined that they were assembled for some unlawful purpose, though in sooth they were a body of penitents praying that rain might fall upon their thirsty land. He dashed up to battle, followed by Sancho on foot, who arrived just at the moment that his master fell to the ground stunned by a tremendous blow. The penitents who formed the procession, seeing so many men running up, received them with fists and candlesticks, but when one of them cast his eyes on the priest who was journeying with Don Quixote he found that he had known him formerly, and begged him to tell what all this might mean.

By the time the story was told Don Quixote's wits began to return to him, and he called to Sancho to put him back into the cage, as he had been nigh dead, and could not hold himself on Rozinante.

'With all my heart,' answered Sancho, thankful that the adventure had ended no worse; 'and if these gentlemen will do us the honour to go with us, we will return home and there make plans for adventures that will bring us more profit and glory.'

The villagers were all gathered together in the great square, when at the end of six days a cage containing a man passed through their midst. The people pressed close to see who the captive might be, and when they saw it was Don Quixote, they sent a boy to tell his housekeeper and his niece that the knight had come back looking pale and lean from his wanderings.

Loud were the cries raised by the good women when they saw him in so sorry a plight, and they undressed him and put him to bed with what speed they were able.

'Keep him there as long as you may,' said the priest who had brought him; but it is whispered that this period of rest and repose did not last, and that soon Don Quixote might have been seen again mounted on Rozinante and seeking adventures.

THE MEETING OF HUON AND OBERON, KING OF THE FAIRIES

In the days of the emperor Charles the Great there lived two young men named Huon and Gerard, sons of the duke of Bordeaux and heirs of his lands. Now by all the rules of chivalry they were bound to hasten to Paris as soon as their father died and do homage to the emperor as their liege lord; but, like many other youths, they were careless of their duties, and put off the long and tedious journey from day to day.

This conduct was particularly foolish, because there was present at the emperor's court the famous earl Amaury, who, rich though he was, coveted the estates of the duke of Bordeaux, and whispered in the ear of his master that the young men were rebels and traitors. By this time Charles was old, and his mind, as well as his body, had waxed feeble; the crown was too heavy for him, and he was thinking of resigning it to his son Charlot. So Amaury cunningly represented to him that he must summon the young men to his court without delay, and then himself plotted with Charlot to waylay and kill them. But, though they made their plans with great care, fortune was on the side of Huon and Gerard, for they defended themselves so bravely that, though they were taken by surprise, Gerard only received a slight wound, while Charlot was slain by Huon.

When Amaury returned to Paris with these dreadful tidings, the emperor was beside himself with anger, and ordered Amaury to fight a duel with Huon, who was the elder of the two, and bid him take heed not to spare him. As Huon was young and slight, and Amaury one of the strongest men at the court, neither the emperor nor the earl ever had a moment's doubt with whom the victory would lie; but if Amaury was more powerful, Huon was quicker on his feet, and before long he had stretched his enemy dead upon the ground.

The emperor was watching the fight from a window of his palace, and his anger at the triumph of Huon was so great that it very near killed him. Still, as the duel had been fairly fought, he dared not punish Huon, and he was forced to content himself with sending him on a mission to the king of Babylon, knowing well the perils which would beset him on the way.

The small vessel in which Huon sailed for Jerusalem met with so many dangers that oftentimes the young duke thought that he would be dead long before he had touched the shores of Palestine. Thrice they were attacked by pirates, who were hardly beaten off; twice such terrible storms arose that they were almost driven on the rocks, and once they had much ado to avoid being drawn into a whirlpool. But somehow or other they escaped everything, and Huon was safely landed on the holy soil with his uncle Garyn and a few followers.

He was at first so thankful to be on dry land again that he felt as if his journey was already over, but he soon found that the worst part was yet to come. Leaving Jerusalem behind them, the little band entered a desert, dreary and boundless as far as they could see. Hunger and thirst they suffered, and death felt very near them, when at last they reached a tiny hut, before which an old man was sitting. At the sight of Huon, thin and wasted as he had grown, the old man broke into sobs, crying that his face was like unto the face of the duke of Bordeaux, whom he had known when he was young.

'Thirty years have I dwelt in these deserts,' said he, 'and never have my eyes lighted on the face of a Christian man.'

Then Huon answered that he was indeed the son of the duke of Bordeaux whom he had known in his youth, and while they rested each man told his tale.

'It is indeed good fortune that guided you here,' said Gerames when Huon had ended his story, 'for without me and my counsel never would you have reached the kingdom of Babylon. There are two roads which lead to that great city; one will take you forty days, and the other fifteen days, but if you will be ruled by me you will travel by the longer.'

'And wherefore?' asked Huon, whose body was still sore from the hardships he had suffered, and whose ears had been tickled with the tidings of the soft couches and lovely gardens of Babylon the Great.

'The short way leads through a wood which is the home of fairies and other strange creatures,' answered Gerames, 'and in it dwells Oberon, the king of them all, in stature no higher than a child of three years old, but with a face more beautiful than any worn by mortal man. His voice is softer and his words more sweet than we are wont to use; but beware of listening to them, for should you speak to him one word, you will fall into his power for ever. But if you hold your peace think not to escape that way, for he will be so wroth with you that he will cause all manner of tempests to spring up, and a great and black river to rise before you. Fear not to pass this river, black and swift though it be, for it is but a fantasy, and will not even wet the feet of your horse. And now that I have told you the ills that lie in that wood, I pray you hearken to my counsel, and ride by the way that is longer.'

Huon paused before he answered. In sooth, Gerames' words had not awakened dread in his soul. Instead, he desired greatly to meet that dwarf, and to try whose will should prove strongest. So he answered that it would ill become a knight, and the son of his father, to shun a meeting with anyone, be he man or fairy, and it might be well for him to take the short road, for many adventures might befall him by the longer.

'Sir,' said Gerames, 'be it as you will; whichever way you take I will go with you.'

Then Huon and Gerames rode at the rear of their company, and entered the wood where Oberon, king of the Fairies, abode. For two days they had neither food nor drink, and Huon repented him of his journey and wished that he had hearkened to Gerames, as perchance the other road might have been easier.

'Let us all alight and seek for food,' said he; but at that moment, Oberon, richly dressed, and covered with precious stones, appeared before them. A magic bow was in his hand, whose arrows never failed to hit the beast he aimed at, while round his neck was slung a horn. Now this horn was unlike any other in the whole world, for one blast of it could cure a man's sickness, even if he was nigh to death, or make him feel satisfied if he lacked meat, or joyful though he was poor, or summon whomsoever he wanted, if he was distant a hundred days' journey.

Seeing the doleful plight of the little company, Oberon blew the third blast, and, behold! Huon and his companions began to sing and dance, as if good fortune had come to them.

'Ah, what strange thing has come to pass!' cried the young knight. 'But now I was like to fall from my horse from hunger, but in an instant I am filled and wish for nothing.'

'Sir,' said Gerames, 'it is Oberon who has wrought this; but do not suffer yourself to be drawn into speech with him, or you will rue it.'

'Have no fears for me,' answered Huon, 'I will be steadfast.'

He held his head very high when Oberon the dwarf came up, and begged the knight to speak to him; but Huon only leaped on his horse and signed to his men to do likewise. At that the dwarf waxed angry, and bade a tempest arise, and with it came such a rain and hail that they were sore affrighted. Many times Gerames prayed them to take courage, for these were devices of the fairy king, and would not really hurt them, and as long as they spoke no words they would be safe.

'Have no doubt of me,' answered Huon.

For a while they lost sight of the dwarf, and Huon vainly hoped that they had beaten him off, and that they were rid of him. But in a little time they reached a bridge which spanned a great river, and on the bridge was Oberon himself. Fain would they have slipped past him, but the bridge was narrow, and Oberon stood in the middle. Once more he spoke soft words to Huon, and offered to do him service, but Huon held his peace. Again Oberon was angered sorely, and blew a blast which hindered the company from riding onwards, while four hundred knights of his own came galloping up.

'Slay these men at once,' he cried, shaking with wrath, but their leader implored him to spare them for a space.

'It will be time enough to kill them if they still keep silence,' said he; and Oberon agreed that he would give them yet another chance, and Huon and his companions rode hastily onwards.

'We have left him full five miles behind us,' said Huon, drawing rein; 'and now that he is not here to trouble us I will say that never in my life did I see so fair a creature. Nor do I think he can do us any ill. If he should come again, I fain would speak to him, and I pray you, Gerames, not to be displeased with me thereat.'

Gerames' heart was heavy at these words, but he knew well the wilfulness of young men, and he answered nothing. For fifteen days they rode on, and Gerames began to hope that Oberon had given up their pursuit, when suddenly he again appeared.

'Noble sir,' he said to Huon, 'have you resolved in good sooth not to speak to me? I know all your past life, and the task set you by the emperor, and without my help never will you come to the end of that business. Therefore, be warned by me, and go no further.'

'You are welcome, sir,' answered Huon at last, and Oberon laughed for very joy.

'Never did you give a greeting so profitable as this one,' he said, and they rode on together.

HOW OBERON SAVED HUON

Oberon was so rejoiced that Huon had at last made friends with him, that he did everything that he could think of to give pleasure to the knight and his friends.

'There is nothing in the world that I cannot have by wishing for it,' said he, 'and all I possess is yours. And to prove that my words are not vain I will set before you the richest feast that ever you ate. After you have finished, you shall go whithersoever you will.'

So they ate and drank to their hearts' content, but, before they departed, Oberon bade one of his fairy knights to bring him his golden cup, which he showed to Huon.

'Behold,' he said, 'this cup is empty, and will so

remain, if any man who has done a deadly sin should seek to drink of it. But he who has led a goodly life, the moment that he takes it in his hands it will become full of wine. Make proof of it yourself, and if you are found worthy the cup shall be yours.'

'Alas, sir,' answered Huon, 'I fear very greatly that I have sinned too deeply for that cup to have any virtue for me, but yet I have repented, and desire from henceforth to wrong no one.' Then he lifted the cup, and the wine brimmed over.

Oberon was right glad when he saw this sight, and gave the cup into his keeping.

'As long as you are true and faithful, you shall never lack drink in it,' said he, 'but if you do falsely to any man, it will lose all its virtue and my help will go from you also. I have likewise another gift for you: take this horn of ivory, and when you are in great straits, and will blow it, however far I may be, I will come to you, and will bring with me a great company to lend you aid. But beware, as you set store by my friendship and by your life, that you do not blow the horn lightly.'

'I give you great thanks for your kindness, and will hearken to your words,' said Huon; 'and now, I pray, let me depart hence to do the emperor's bidding.'

So the knight and the fairy king took leave of each other, and they fared on their way, and in the evening they sat and rested in a green meadow, and ate and drank of the food that Oberon had given them. Now Huon was uplifted by the gifts the king had given him, and thought that he himself must be in some way better than other men, to be singled out for such honour, and, as young men will, he began to boast and talk idly, making pretence that he doubted the magic qualities of the horn and the cup, so that he might prove them at once before his company.

'It was a fair adventure for me when I spoke to Oberon,' said he, 'and that I did not listen to the counsel of Gerames. When I fulfil my mission and return unto the court of the emperor, I will present him with the cup, the like of which he has not got in all his treasury. But as for the horn, how do I know if Oberon spoke the truth concerning it?'

'Oh, sir, be not rash, I entreat you!' cried Gerames, 'for he charged you straitly not to blow the horn save in your direst need.'

'Ay, surely,' answered Huon, 'but for all that I will try what power it has,' and, raising it to his mouth, he blew a loud blast.

At that all the company rose up, and sang and danced joyfully, and Garyn, Huon's uncle, begged him to blow the horn once more.

Oberon heard it, though he was full many miles away.

'What man is so bold as to seek to do him ill whom I love best in all the world?' said Oberon. 'I wish myself and a hundred good men in his company'; and in an instant Huon and his friends beheld the horses' skins flashing in the bushes. Then Huon's soul smote him, and he bowed his head before Oberon, saying:

'Sir, I have done ill; tell me quickly if death must be my punishment?'

'Where are those that would work you evil?' asked Oberon sternly; but in spite of his wrath Huon took heart of grace, and, confessing his folly, prayed for pardon, which Oberon granted him for very pity, knowing, he said, that Huon would have much to suffer, some things through the wicked ways of others, but more from his own pride and self-will. Then, bidding the young man farewell afresh, the fairy king rode back to the wood.

All befell just as the fairy king had foretold. Giants and mortals alike barred his way; small would have been his chance of ever reaching Babylon had not Oberon himself watched over him, and sent him help when he knew it not. Only one thing he asked of Huon in return—to keep himself from ill-doing and lies, so that he might be worthy to drink from the golden cup.

And thus it came to pass that after many perils Huon knocked at the first of the four gates of the city.

No sound was heard in answer to his knock, so he seized the great bell that hung there, and rang it loudly. At this a porter opened a little lattice, and asked what great lord it might be who demanded admittance in so rude a fashion, to which Huon answered hotly that he was an envoy from the emperor Charles, and that if the porter refused him entrance he would have to answer for it to his own master.

At that the porter said that if the stranger was an infidel like themselves, the gates should be thrown open at once, but that, should he allow any Christian to enter, he would pay for it with his head.

'But I am as much a Saracen as yourself,' said Huon, who only thought of getting into Babylon and paid no heed to the lie he was telling, or to the dishonour of his words. Then the gates were opened wide, and he entered.

It was not till he was crossing the bridge which stood before the second gate that the wickedness of what he had done came upon him, and then he felt ashamed, and sorry, and frightened altogether. And how should he pass through the other three gates without again denying his faith and steeping himself in dishonour? He was about to turn back in despair, when he remembered the two good gifts of a giant whom he had overcome—a suit of armour which no sword could pierce, and a ring which would throw open all doors. So he showed the ring to the porters that guarded all the other three doors, and soon found himself in the garden of the palace.

Even the groves of palms, and the trees of delicious fruits, could not make him forget the lie he had uttered. Indeed, if he had wished to do so, he could not, for presently he came to a fountain beside which was written that no traitor should drink thereof on pain of being destroyed by the serpent that dwelt therein. At this Huon suddenly felt himself forsaken of all, and he sat down and wept bitterly.

'O noble King Oberon, listen to me once more,' he cried, and tremblingly blew his horn.

'I help no liars,' said the fairy king when the blast echoed through the forest, and, though Huon could not hear his answer, the silence soon told him what it was.

'If he slays me, at least it will be soon over,' he thought to himself, and, putting forth all his strength, he blew a fresh blast.

This time it was so loud that it reached the ears of the lord of Babylon, who was sitting at a feast in the Hall of Moonbeams. And he rose up, together with his nobles and their squires and their wives and daughters, and every one in the palace from the least to the greatest, and began to dance and sing. They sang and danced as long as the horn kept on blowing, and when it had ceased the ruler of Babylon called to his lords and bade them follow him into the garden, as of a surety some great enchanter must have strayed therein.

'Seek him and bring him to me, wherever I be,' commanded the emir; but the gardens were so large, and it took so long to find Huon, that the emir went back into the palace and laid himself down on a pile of soft cushions at the end of the hall.

By his side on a great carved chair was the king of a neighbouring country, who arrived hither only a few days before to beg for the hand of the emir's fair daughter, the princess Esclaramonde, who was said to be the loveliest maiden in the whole world. To be sure, it was whispered among the courtiers that the princess did not look on him with a favourable eye, when she had watched his arrival from behind her lattice, and that more than once she had protested that she was too ill to leave her room when sent for by her father; but of course, if marriage was resolved upon, it would have to be.

Huon had heard talk of these things between his guards when they were marching through the gardens that were almost as big as a town, and up the long flight of marble steps that led to the palace. He said nothing; perhaps by this time he had learnt a little wisdom, but he knew who the man was whose dress was so rich and his air so proud, and before anyone even saw him lift his arm the king's head was rolling in the dust.

For a moment all remained still, too astonished to speak. Then the emir recovered his wits, and ordered Huon to be carried off to a dungeon, and not to be let go or the guards lives would be forfeit. But quick as thought Huon held out his hand with the ring on it.

'Do you know this?' he said, and the king started back at the sight of it, and cried to the soldiers to let the prisoner go, for in that place he might do whatsoever he would. At this permission Huon turned to where the princess Esclaramonde was sitting by her father, and kissed her thrice.

The emir was not altogether pleased at this fashion of Huon's, but he said nothing, and in a moment the knight told him how the emperor had sent him to pray the emir to become a Christian, otherwise he should proceed against him with a mighty host.

The emir laughed in scorn as he listened to Huon's vain boast.

'Fifteen envoys has he despatched on a like errand,' answered he, 'and all fifteen have I hanged. Right willingly should you make the sixteenth but for the ring which you wear. Tell me, I pray you, whence you got it?'

But when Huon confessed that it had been given him by the giant, the emir waxed more wroth than before, and ordered his guards to seize him and cast him into prison, which in the end they did, though he resisted them well by reason of the harness that was on him.

For a long space Huon lingered in that dark prison, and sad indeed would have been his lot had it not been for the secret visits of the princess Esclaramonde, who, the better to preserve his life, assured her father of his death.

At length, when the emir was sore beset by the army of the giant Agrapart, she deemed it a favourable time to betray to her father that Huon was still alive in his prison, and was ready to do battle with the giant if, as was usual in that country, the princess's hand should be given to the victor. Both the emir and the giant agreed that their quarrel should stand or fall by single combat, and so the fight began.

Huon felt in his heart that there was more at stake than even the hand of the princess. He stood forth as the champion of Christendom amidst a host of pagans, and it behoved him to strike with all his strength. In the end the victory was his, and the giant Agrapart was overcome, but his life was spared on condition that he would serve the emir faithfully all his days, which solemn oath he took gladly. After that, Huon drew out the cup the fairy king had given him, and, having made the sign of the cross over it, it was filled with wine, and he drank of it. For he had long since repented of the lie he had told, and was clean again. Then the emir tried to drink also, but no wine would come.

'You must forsake your false gods, and be a Christian such as I am,' said Huon, 'and if you like not fair words you shall see how an armed host pleases you;' but, as was natural, the ruler of Babylon was not the man to be moved by such persuasions. He angrily bade Huon cease, and to speak to him no more on the matter or all the hosts of Charlemagne himself should not avail to save his head.

'You will repent you too late,' said Huon, and blew his horn.

At first the emir and his courtiers began to dance and sing wildly, they knew not wherefore, while in the wood far away Oberon heard the sound. 'Huon, my friend, has great need of me,' he thought to himself, 'and his ill-doings have been punished enough, so I will pardon him, for there is not in all the world so noble a man. Therefore I wish myself at his side, with a thousand men behind me.' And in another moment, no man could tell how, Oberon and his men were within the walls of Babylon. The guards of the palace fell before them on every hand, till at last they reached the emir himself.

'He is yours to spare or to slay,' said Oberon, and once more the knight gave the Paynim his choice.

'Be a Christian or you die,' said Huon, and the emir made answer:

'I will never forsake my own.' They were the last words he spoke, for his head rolled upon the floor. After that Huon cut off the emir's beard and pulled out four of his teeth, and hid them in the beard of his old friend Gerames, who had lately returned to Babylon.

'Now I must leave you,' said Oberon, when these things were over. 'See that in all ways you behave yourself as a good and true knight should do, and have no share in ill-doings. I bid you take ship and carry the princess Esclaramonde, your bride, into France, and guard her from all ills on the way. And if you do not that which I bid you, great evil shall happen unto you.'

But, alas! no sooner was the ship out of sight of land than the good counsels of Oberon faded out of Huon's mind, and he fell into many sins. The cup would not fill with wine, and Oberon was deaf to the blast of the horn. Then an awful tempest arose; the ship struck on a rock and was rent in pieces, and all were drowned save Huon and the princess, who were washed on an island. But even here they were not safe, for Huon was bound and tortured, and left under a tree, while Esclaramonde was carried away by the pirates who were dwellers on the isle.

Meanwhile, the knowledge of Huon's plight had reached Oberon, and, angry though he was, he began to think how best to send help to him, when a monster of the sea, called Mallebron, who had before given him aid on his journey to Babylon, begged to be allowed to deliver him once more.

'It pleases me well,' answered Oberon, 'that this caitiff Huon should suffer pain for the evil that he has wrought, but if you love him so much that for his sake you shall endure to wear the shape of a fish for twenty years longer I will grant you your wish on two conditions. Carry him away from the island and place him on the mainland, only never more let mine eyes light on him. Be careful also to bring back to me my golden cup, my horn, and my fairy armour, for it is long since he has shown himself unworthy of them.'

So Mallebron swam straightway to the island, and, finding Huon fast bound, as Oberon had said, he loosed him, and he stood on his feet. But when Huon heard the message of Oberon he was sore angered, and, forgetting his own misdeeds, complained bitterly of Oberon's hardness of heart in commanding that the gifts he had given him should be yielded up again. But, wail as he might, he could not move Mallebron, who bade him farewell, and departed with Oberon's treasures.

It were long to tell of Huon's adventures after he had left the island. At one time he took service with a minstrel and was his varlet. At another time he was forced to play chess for the hand of a king's daughter, but refused to marry her when he had won the game. Unknowingly, he once fought with Gerames, and only found out who he was in the course of the battle. He afterwards entered the city with him, and visited Esclaramonde, who was a captive in the palace, and right glad were they to meet. After that he and some French knights who had joined him were besieged in the castle by the Paynims, and were rescued by a French ship, which carried Huon and Esclaramonde and all the company on their way to Wana, together with much treasure which they had found in the castle.

But, happy though Huon felt on the road home again, he heard with wrath that Gerard, his brother, had persuaded the emperor that by now Huon must be dead, and that *he* was rightful heir to the duchy. It was so long since any tidings had been received of Huon—for none had fared that way—that some thought Gerard spoke reasonably, and upheld his suit, which in the end was granted by Charles. And no sooner was the new duke invested with the lands than he began to oppress all his subjects, till the duchess his mother died of grief at the misery of her people.

'He shall pay me for that,' muttered Huon grimly.

There was one thing, however, that could not be delayed a moment more than was needed, and this was the marriage between Huon and Esclaramonde, for the princess had promised to become a Christian and to receive baptism at the hands of the pope. So they bade the captain put into the port nearest to Rome, and, taking horse, rode thither as fast as they might.

The pope was seated on his throne with his threefold crown on his head, holding counsel with his cardinals, when Huon and his company entered the hall two by two, and saluted humbly. At the sight of Huon leading Esclaramonde by the hand, the pope, who had once visited the court of the duke of Bordeaux, and remembered the face of Huon, rose up to greet him, kissed him on both cheeks, and bade him tell his adventures, and how he had fared.

'Ill enough, good sir, and these others also,' answered Huon; 'but I have by grace won through it all, and I have brought the daughter of the great emir of the Paynims, whom I desire you should make my wife, after she has been baptized by your hands.'

'Huon,' said the pope, 'all this pleases me right well to do, and it is my will that you tarry with me here this night.'

So they tarried; and the next day the wedding feast was held, and there were great rejoicings in the pope's palace. And early the next morning, Huon and his wife and his friends took ship for Bordeaux.

But not yet were Huon's trials ended. Gerard, his brother, had no mind to give up his lands and honours lightly, and many were the plots that he laid against Huon. Indeed, he not only contrived to throw the new-comers into prison, but prevailed on the emperor to journey himself to Bordeaux, to the intent that Huon should be put to death, which would have happened had it not been for the timely help of Oberon.

It was thus it came about.

The fairy king was seated at dinner in his palace in the wood, when the knowledge came to him that the emperor Charles had taken an oath to hang Huon ere he slept, and at the thought thereof he broke into weeping.

'I have sore punished the sins he has committed,' said he, 'and great has been my wrath. But now it is time that I help him, or he will be gone from me. So I wish my table and all that is on it near to the emperor's table, only about two feet higher. And I will that on my table be set my cup and horn and armour. And I wish that with me shall go a hundred thousand men, such as I am wont to have in battle.'

Great was the marvel of the emperor when this table appeared beside him, and he took it for an enchantment of duke Names; but Huon and Gerames and Esclaramonde, who were present at the feast with fetters on their wrists, knew that Oberon had come to their deliverance.

Soon the clank of swords was heard throughout the streets, and you could not see the stones for the armed men who stood on them.

'See that none leave the gates,' said Oberon, 'and when you hear the blast of my ivory horn, come to me in the palace, and slay everyone you shall meet on the way'; and so saying he entered the hall, and many of his lords with him. Their dresses were the richest that had ever been seen, and on their necks they wore collars of precious stones. As the king passed by Charles, he knocked against him, so that his hat fell upon the ground.

'Who is this dwarf who so rudely has shouldered me?' asked the emperor, 'and whence comes he? I will see what he will do, for, small as he is, he is the fairest creature that ever I saw.'

Leaving the emperor behind him, the fairy king came to the spot where Huon and the captives were standing, and he wished that the fetters might fall off their feet, and that they might be free men. Then silently he led them before Charles, and caused them to sit down at his own table, and bade the lords of the court drink out of the magic cup after Huon and Esclaramonde and Gerames had drunk out of it. But only for duke Names would the wine bubble up.

Afterwards Oberon ordered Gerard to confess his sins and his plots that he had plotted, which out of very shame he was constrained to do, and then Oberon prayed the emperor to command Gerard and those who had helped him to work ill to be hanged on the gallows which had been reared for Huon, and this was done also; and the emperor Charles and Huon, duke of Bordeaux, made reconciliation together.

'Come to me in my city of Mommur four years from now, Huon,' said Oberon, 'and I will give you my realm and my dignity, for I know in truth I shall not long abide in this world. But beware, as you love your life, that you fail not to be with me at the day I have appointed, else I shall cause you to die an ill-death.'

When he heard, Huon stooped down and kissed his feet, and said:

'Sir, for this great boon I thank you.'

HAVELOK AND GOLDBOROUGH

Once upon a time there lived in England a king called Athelwold, who ruled the land so well that everyone was rich and happy: or, if they were not, it was their own fault. His people all loved him dearly, and would do anything for him, and when he went to war there was no sovereign that could count on a larger following of stout brave men. He was quite a youth when he came to the throne, and at first all sorts of traitors and robbers from other countries took refuge in his kingdom, but Athelwold sought them out so carefully and punished them so severely that they soon betook themselves and their crimes elsewhere.

Now one thing grieved the king sorely. He had no son to sit on his throne after he was dead, to protect the poor and put down the lawless. And how was his little daughter, who was not yet fourteen, to keep order, or to uphold the laws?

'If she were a woman grown, it might be different,' he thought to himself, 'for Goldborough sees clearly and acts promptly. But as yet she has little knowledge, and her ways are those of a child. And full well I know that my death is nigh at hand, and there is none to watch over her.'

Long the king pondered in his mind what he could best do for his daughter's safety and the welfare of his people, and in the end he sent messengers with letters to all his earls and barons from Roxborough to Dover, bidding them come to his castle of Winchester as swiftly as they might, for he could no more mount his horse, neither could he swallow meat or pasties.

Sadly his vassals received the summons, for each loved him as his own father, and not one lurked behind. The king gave them a glad welcome, but they could not forbear shedding tears when they saw his weakness and heard his feeble voice. Athelwold let them have their way a little while, and then he said:

'I am dying, as you see, and I have sent for you hither, to ask you all to tell me which of you will best guard my daughter when I am dead, till she has come to years when she can guard herself.'

And they answered as one man:

'Earl Godrich of Cornwall.'

Then the king bade the priest bring the holy vessels, and earl Godrich swore on them that he would be faithful and true in peace and in war to Goldborough; and, further, that he would seek out a man who was better and fairer and stronger than all others to be her husband, so that the land might have peace, as in the days of Athelwold.

After the earl had sworn to fulfil what the king required of him, Athelwold made his will, and gave England into the keeping of Godrich. This done, he lay back in his bed, and that same morning he died in the arms of his daughter.

But bad indeed was the choice which king Athelwold's vassals had made when they proclaimed earl Godrich as the fittest guardian for the young princess. In the beginning, indeed, while Goldborough was still a child, everything went smoothly. The earl appointed justices and sheriffs to carry out the laws, and, though he took more heed to gather riches for himself than to protect his people, yet on the whole he governed well.

Thus six years passed away, and Goldborough was twenty years old. She had lived far away from the castle of Winchester, and had never seen her guardian since the day that her father had been buried, and, for his part, he had hardly remembered her, he was so busy making laws and amassing treasures. Still, other people recollected Goldborough, if he did not, and one Eastertide, when the princess's twentieth birthday was at hand, an old pilgrim chanced to stop at Winchester on his way to Canterbury. He had but lately passed through the town where Goldborough was living, and had many tales to tell of her fair and gracious ways.

Godrich let him talk, but his face was gloomy and he answered nought. But, though his tongue was silent, his heart was base and his thoughts were evil.

'Have I toiled all these years for nothing?' he said to himself, 'and shall England be ruled by a fool, a maiden? I have a son, a full fair knave; he shall have England and be king.'

So Goldborough was brought from her woods and gardens, and shut up in the castle of Dover, where none might visit her. And no company had she but her foster-sister, and an old woman who had been her nurse.

At the time when Athelwold ruled England there reigned in Denmark a king called Birkabeyn, who had three children, two girls named Swanborough and Helfled and a boy called Havelok. Birkabeyn was strong and healthy, and thought to live many years, when a wound in battle proved his death-blow. Like Goldborough, the children were all young, and he was forced to choose someone to protect them till they were of full age. The man on whom Birkabeyn's choice fell was his own close friend, who had served him all his life, and who, he thought, loved his children well. And so perhaps the earl would have done had not such power been given into his hands, but this he was not proof against. No sooner had the king died than he caused the three children to be cast into prison, where he murdered the two girls himself.

At the dreadful fate of his sisters, Havelok, who was the youngest, fell on his knees and implored the wicked earl to spare him.

'If it is Denmark you want, it shall be yours,' cried the boy, 'and never will I seek to take it from you. Nay, give me a ship, and to-day I will leave the country for ever.'

Even the earl's heart was for a moment softened by the child's tears and prayers, and at first he thought that he would let him go, as it would be many years before he would be old enough to be an enemy. But then he remembered that, if Havelok died unwedded, he and his sons would be heirs to the crown, for he was the king's cousin. However, he pretended to grant the child's prayer, and bade him follow him down to the shore, where dwelt an old fisherman. Havelok wandered down to the water, and wondered which of the ships drawn up on the beach he should set sail in, and where he would go. He was still terrified at the death of sisters, and shook with fear as long as their murderer was in sight.

Meanwhile the earl was speaking to the fisherman, who stood at the door of his cottage, which was built just out of reach of the waves.

'Grim,' he said, 'to-day you are my thrall, but to-morrow you shall be a free man if you will do my bidding. Take the boy that stands there, and throw him into the sea, that he drown. Fear nothing: the penalty will be mine, not yours.'

'Your bidding shall be done,' answered the fisherman, 'though the deed is but little to my liking.'

'So be it,' said the earl, and went home to hold counsel with his family how best to take possession of the crown.

Grim took down a cord from a hook in the roof, and went out to the child, who screamed with terror as he drew near, but there was no one to help him, and Grim thrust a cloth in his mouth to stifle his cries, while he bound his hands behind his back with a cord. When this was done, he put the boy in a black bag, and carried him to his wife, who flung him on the floor, where he lay for many hours, thinking every moment that he would be thrown down a well or stabbed by a dagger.

At midnight, when all was still, and the men in the ships were sleeping soundly, Grim arose, and told his wife to kindle a fire and to light a candle.

'Why, there is a light in the room already,' said she, 'and it seems to come from the farthest corner, and to shine as brightly as if it were the sun itself'; and with that she sprang out of bed and ran over the floor, calling to Grim to follow her.

And in truth it was as she had said, for round the bag which held the boy a brilliant light was shining.

'If we touch him we shall rue it all our lives,' she whispered to her husband; then, stooping, she cut the knots which held the bag, and drew out Havelok, who was well-nigh dead with fright and suffocation. Next she stripped him of his clothes, and on his shoulder she found the mark of a tiny cross, from which the light came.

'He is born to be king,' said Grim softly, 'and surely it is he and no other who is the son of Birkabeyn, and who some day shall come to his own. It is easy to see that he will grow into a man, tall and strong, who shall come back from over the sea where I shall send him, and avenge himself on the traitor.' Then Grim fell on his knees before Havelok and prayed his forgiveness.

'You shall stay here awhile,' he said, 'till I can fit out a ship, and in it we will all set sail, you, and I, and my wife and my three sons, but it must be done in secret, lest the earl should come to know of it.'

So they gave Havelok bread to eat and milk to drink, and laid him in a bed in a dark corner, where no man could see him, and the next day Grim set out for the traitor's castle to ask for the reward that had been promised him.

'Your bidding is done, and I have come to claim my freedom,' said Grim when he stood in the presence of the traitor. But the earl made answer:

'Who is there to know what lies betwixt us? Go home, and be my thrall, as you have ever been.'

Full of rage though he was, Grim dared say no more, lest his head should pay forfeit; but the earl's words had filled him with fear, and he hastened to get ready a ship and to fill it during the night with food enough to last them for three weeks. By that time, he thought, they would reach the shores of England.

When all was finished, Grim and his wife, his three sons and two daughters and little Havelok, stole away very early one morning before the sun was up, and set sail southwards. A north wind soon sprang up and drove him, in ten days, to the mouth of a great river called the Humber. Here he steered his ship on to the beach, and then they all got out and set up a tent, till they could look about for a little and see what best to do.

It was a wild place where they landed, and for many miles there was not even a hut to be seen, but Grim liked it well, and he built houses for himself and his family, and by-and-by more people came thither also, and a town was built and was called Grimsby, after Grim. But that happened afterwards.

Fish were plentiful at the mouth of the river—lampreys and sturgeon and turbot and great cod—and Grim and his sons were good fishers, both with net and line, and Havelok soon learned to fish too, and was as happy as any boy could be. Sometimes he stayed at home with the women while the others carried fish round the country in baskets.

Twelve years passed in this manner, during which Grim had prospered greatly, but he began to get old, and the long journeys with heavy panniers on his back tried him sorely. This Havelok perceived, and one day he spoke:

'I am a man grown, and shall I sit at home idle mending nets while my father travels over the whole country-side carrying weights too heavy for him to bear? Not so! To-morrow I go forth, and my father shall take his seat by the fire, and shall mend the nets.'

Whatever Havelok said he did, and early the next morning he took the panniers on his shoulders, and started for the houses where Grim was wont to sell his fish. But soon, none could tell why, a bad time came, and there was no corn in the land, and no fish in the sea. And Grim felt pity in his heart for Havelok, who was young and strong, and needed more meat than other men. So one day Grim spoke:

'Havelok, dear son, you have come upon evil days, and must stay with us no longer. Go to the city of Lincoln. It is a rich town, and there you may find work for all you need. But, woe is me! no clothes can I give you, save this old sail, which the women shall fashion into doublet and hose for you.'

The sail was soon cut and fashioned by Grim's wife and daughters, but there was nothing to make into shoes, and Havelok walked into Lincoln barefoot, and he fasted from meat for two or three days; at length the earl's cook took him into his service as porter, and his chief duty was to carry the earl's fish into the castle. But the cook had many porters besides Havelok, and when the cry of 'barmen' was heard they all tried one to outdo the other in obtaining the pot in which lay the hot fish. However, Havelok was taller and stronger than the rest, and generally was able to thrust the others on one side.

Besides bearing the cauldron of fish, Havelok had many things to do. He had to fill a huge tub in the kitchen with water, and to cut wood for the fire, and to do anything the cook told him. And, whatever happened, he was full of mirth, and would jest and play with the children who ran about the back of the castle.

At last his clothes, which had been fashioned out of the old sail, fell into holes, and the cook, out of pity and liking, bought him some new ones, and when he put them on there was no man, be he who he might, that was fairer to see. Then folk began to notice that he was taller than any man in the castle, and that he was very strong. Very soon a chance came to him to prove his strength.

Godrich the earl—or the king, as he called himself—now held his court at Lincoln, and summoned a parliament to be held there to settle the affairs of the nation. They came in great companies, and everyone had a following, and so many were they that they were forced to dwell in tents outside the city walls. It was not long before they fell to wrestling and such sports.

For a while Havelok looked on, and bided his time. He took no part in the wrestling, though there was not a champion on the ground that he could not easily have overcome.

When they were tired of throwing each other, someone proposed that they should put the stone, and a large smooth piece of rock was chosen. Man after man came forward, but hardly one could raise it from the ground, far less cast it any distance from him. At this moment the cook strolled up and saw his scullion standing there.

'It is your turn,' he said to Havelok; 'show them what you can do, for the honour of Lincoln,' and Havelok obeyed him. He lifted the mighty stone to the height of his shoulder, and sent it spinning through the air.

'Measure the cast,' said the cook proudly; and when it was measured it was found to be twelve feet beyond the cast of any other man.

Little was talked of that day but the wonderful throw of the young scullion, and soon it reached the ears of the knights at court, and in time, Godrich himself. As he listened to the tale, there flashed across his memory the words of the dying Athelwold: 'Find out the man who is better and fairer and stronger than any man in the world, and give him to be husband to my daughter.' Was there any man living stronger than this Havelok? and could he himself be ill-spoken of if he should carry out Athelwold's dying wish? So thought Godrich; but far back in his heart he knew that once Goldborough was wedded to a scullion there would be small chance of her becoming queen.

Next morning a knight mounted on a big bay horse, and attended by two men-at-arms, might have been seen riding southwards through the fair county of Lincoln, and in twenty days' time he returned, bringing with him the princess. Godrich greeted her with tokens of great joy, and told her that, as her father had bidden him, he had found at last the fairest and strongest man in the world, and he should be her husband.

Goldborough listened quietly to his words, and when he had ended she looked at him.

'Let him be as strong and fair as he may,' she said, 'but if he is not a king or a king's son he is no husband for me.'

At this Godrich waxed wrath, and his whole body trembled with anger.

'Your father bade me swear to him when he was dying that you should marry the strongest man in the world, and none other,' cried he, 'and, by the Rood, it is he you seek to disobey, and not me. The man who is to be your husband is the servant of my cook, and to-morrow we will have the wedding.'

The heart of Goldborough was filled with horror when she heard the fate that was in store for her, and she fell weeping on her knees before the earl to implore him the rather to let her enter a convent; but Godrich answered her nothing, and strode out of the hall.

The bells were ringing next day when Havelok woke, and before he was dressed a message came ordering him to go at once to the earl's presence. He wondered for what cause he was wanted, for never yet had he had speech of the earl, and still more surprised was he to find Godrich clad in his most splendid robes, as if for a festival. But if Havelok was astonished at all this, he was nearly struck dumb by the words which he heard.

'Master, will you take a wife?' and the young man gazed at him in silence; for why should the ruler of all England take heed whether his scullion was wedded or not?

'Will you take a wife?' asked Godrich again, in tones of impatience; then Havelok found his voice.

'No, by heaven I will not,' he cried; 'what should I do with a wife? I could neither feed, nor clothe, nor shoe her! For myself, I should have no clothes either, had it not been for the bounty of your cook.'

In his rage Godrich seized a thick staff and laid it across his scullion's shoulder.

'Promise me that you will wed her within an hour, or I will hang you on the nearest tree,' he cried; and Havelok, who had no liking for death, consented.

His purpose thus gained with Havelok, the earl now summoned Goldborough, whom he threatened to burn if she withstood him. All night the princess had wept and pondered how to escape so dreadful a doom, but at last she took comfort in the thought that in accepting this husband, however lowly born he might be, she would be fulfilling her father's wishes. So as soon as Godrich gave her a chance to speak she said she would resist him no longer.

Then Godrich for the first time in six years felt that he was indeed King of England.

'You are a wise maiden,' cried he, his face glowing with joy; 'and, to show you how well I love you, I will give you much gold, and you shall have an archbishop to bless your marriage.' And so it was done.

Both Havelok and his wife felt that they could

stay in Lincoln no longer, and the next day they bought two horses and set forth for Grimsby. To Havelok's great grief he found that the fisherman had died just before, after a few days' illness, but his sons and daughters gave them a glad greeting, and bade them stay in their house, promising that they themselves would be their servants.

Weary with travel, Havelok soon went to bed, but Goldborough knelt praying before the window, when suddenly a bright light filled the room. She turned to see what it might be, and beheld it issuing from a cross on Havelok's shoulder. While she gazed wondering, she heard a voice saying, 'Goldborough, let sorrow depart from you, for your husband is no scullion, but the son of a king, and he shall rule over England and Denmark.' At that her heart grew light again, and she kissed Havelok and woke him, and told him what the voice had said.

'Let us sail at once,' added she, 'for who knows when Godrich the traitor may change his mind? And bid the sons of Grim sail with us.'

Goldborough's counsel seemed good to Havelok, and he rose in haste and sought Grim's sons, whom he found setting forth to fish. He begged them to wait, and to listen to his story, which Grim had always hidden from them, and when they heard it, they said that they would go with him, and help him to slay the murderer of his sisters and the robber of his crown.

'You shall be rich men the day he dies,' vowed Havelok; and the boat was made ready for sea.

A fair wind blew them to Denmark, and Havelok left his wife with his three foster-brothers, and betook himself to the house of Ubbe the earl, whom his father had loved dearly. He said no word as to his birth, but asked him leave to trade on his lands, offering a ring as earnest-money.

Ubbe looked at the ring, and then at the young man who gave it.

'You look fitter to do a knight's work than to buy and sell,' he said, and Havelok answered:

'That will come, fair sir, but I must first go softly. Meanwhile I have left my wife Goldborough under the care of her foster-brothers, and can tarry here no longer.'

'Bring her hither,' said Ubbe, 'and dwell with her in this castle, and if no man has dubbed you knight I will take that upon me.'

And so it was done, and the heart of Goldborough rejoiced, for by this time she loved her husband dearly.

That same midnight Ubbe was wakened by a great light, which seemed to fill the castle. He rose from his bed, and went from room to room, and all were bright as day, though he could not tell why. Then he came to the room where Havelok and Goldborough lay asleep, and out of Havelok's mouth came a flame like that of a hundred and ninety-seven candles. And on his shoulder was the cross of kingship, and that was shining too.

When Ubbe saw that, he knew that Havelok was indeed the son of Birkabeyn, his friend, and the rightful king of Denmark; and, waking the sleeping man, he bade him sit up and receive his homage. After that he sent for his lords, and commanded that they should swear fealty to their king. And when the lords had sworn, Ubbe summoned the people, and told them, what many had known before, that the earl had betrayed his trust, and that now he should pay forfeit of his wickedness.

Blithe were Havelok and Goldborough that day as they moved amidst the groups of men who shared in the sports which the people of Denmark ever loved, and once more Havelok cast the stone further than any one there could throw it. His first act, after he had been proclaimed king, was to make Grim's three faithful sons barons with fair lands. Then he bid them go and seek the earl, and bring him back with them.

This was not done without a hard fight, for the earl and his men defended themselves stoutly; but at length he was bound and placed upon an old horse and carried before Havelok, who was waiting in the castle with his lords about him.

'What judgment will ye pass on him, fair lords?' asked the king.

'That he may be hanged as beseems a murderer and a traitor, and that his head be planted over the chief gate of the town as a warning to all,' they said with one voice, and this was done also.

For a while Havelok stayed in Denmark to see to the affairs of the kingdom, and then, leaving Ubbe to rule, he set sail for England with Goldborough his wife, and a large army, in many ships with high carved prows. Once again he landed at the mouth of the Humber, and his first act was to found a church in memory of Grim. Next, he placed his army in order of battle, and awaited the attack of his enemy. Godrich the earl had heard that he had come, and had hastily collected a great host, with which he marched upon Lincoln. The attack was begun by the English, and fierce was the fight. Many were killed, both of English and Danes. At last, just as the English were being beaten slowly back, Havelok and Godrich came face to face with each other. Bitterly the earl then rued the day when he had married Goldborough to the strongest man in the world, scullion though he were! Many times Havelok might have slain him, but such was not his purpose, and, taking a cord from his waist, he bound the traitor's arms, and bade one of his knights ride and fetch Goldborough, whom he had left under a guard at a little distance.

When she drew near, Havelok commanded that a flag of truce should be waved, so that the fighting might cease. Then, taking his wife by the hand, he led her forward, and told her story to them all, and how Godrich the earl had wronged her. And the English fell on their faces and did obeisance, and vowed to serve her faithfully all the days of their lives.

'And what is the law of England respecting a traitor?' asked Havelok, when Goldborough had been proclaimed queen with trumpets and shouting.

'That he be laid on an ass and burned at the stake,' cried they. And this was done also.

After this, Havelok gave his two foster-sisters in marriage to great lords, and made the cook to whom he had owed his good fortune earl of Cornwall in place of the wicked Godrich. He left Ubbe to rule in Denmark, while he and Goldborough remained in England, but every two years he sailed across the sea to be sure that all went well in the country of his birth.

And for sixty years Havelok and Goldborough lived happily together and had many children, and wherever Havelok went, Goldborough went too.

CUPID AND PSYCHE

Once upon a time there lived a king who had three daughters. The two elder girls were very fair, and many were their suitors, but the youngest was so beautiful that it was whispered in the city that the goddess Aphrodite was not her equal in loveliness, and as she walked through the streets men touched their foreheads, and bowed low to the ground, as if Aphrodite herself had passed by.

Now it was not long since the shepherd Paris had given the goddess the golden apple, in token that neither on the earth nor even on Olympus was a woman to be found as fair as she. And when she heard of the honours paid to Psyche, she rose up in her wrath and sent a winged messenger for Cupid, her son.

'Come with me,' she said, when Cupid appeared before her, 'I have somewhat to show you'; and without further speech the two flew through the air together, till they reached the palace where Psyche was sleeping.

'That is the maiden to whom men pay the homage due to me alone,' she whispered, while her grey eyes darted gleams like fire. 'I have brought you hither that you may avenge me by pricking her with an arrow that will fill her heart with love for one of the basest of mortals. And now I must depart in haste, for Oceanos awaits me.'

Aphrodite vanished, but Cupid remained where

he was, gazing on the sleeping maiden and confessing in his heart that those who paid her the honours due to his mother were not much to blame.

'Never will I do you such wrong,' he murmured, 'as to mate you with some base wretch, who has no thought beyond the wine-cup. From me and my darts you are safe. But am I safe from yours?' Then, fearing to stay any longer, lest his mother should wax wroth with him, he also took his way to the palace of Oceanos.

If Aphrodite had not been a goddess, and had known a little more about the hearts of men, she might not have envied Psyche so bitterly; for, though all men bowed down before her and worshipped her beauty, each felt that she was too far above him to woo for his bride. So that, while her sisters had homes and children of their own, Psyche remained unasked and unsought in her father's palace.

At length the king grew frightened as months and years slipped by, and Psyche was past the age when Greek maidens left the hearth where they had grown into girlhood. He summoned some wise men to give him counsel, but they shook their heads, and bade him consult the oracle of his fathers. It was a three days' journey to his shrine, and then no man knew when the oracle would speak, so the king took with him sheep and oxen, and skins of wine for himself and his followers.

Ten days later he returned to the city with bowed head and white face. The queen, with anxious heart, had been watching his arrival from the roof of the palace, and awaited him at the door of the women's apartments.

'What has happened?' she said, as she greeted him; but he drew her on one side, where none might hear them.

'The oracle has spoken,' answered he, 'and decrees that Psyche shall be left upon a barren rock till a hideous monster shall come and devour her. And it is for this that men have paid her honours which were the portion only of the gods! Far better had she been born with the hair of Medusa and the hump of Hephæstos.'

At these dreadful tidings the queen and her maidens broke into weeping, and when the news spread through the city no sounds but those of wailing were heard. Only the voice of Psyche was silent among them. She moved about as one that was sleeping, and indeed she felt as if the boat, with its grim ferryman, had already borne her across the Styx. So the days passed on, and one evening a white-clad priest arrived from the shrine to bid the king tarry no longer.

That night a sad procession left the gates of the city, and in the midst was Psyche, clad in garments of black, and led by her father, while her mother followed weeping behind. Singers wailed out a dirge, which was scarcely heard above the sobs of the mourners, and the torches burned dimly and soon went out.

The sun was rising when they reached the bare rock on top of a high mountain where the oracle had directed that Psyche should be left to perish. She made no sign when her father and mother took her in their arms for the last time, and, though they cried bitterly, she never shed a tear. What was the use? It was the will of the gods, and so it had to be!

Not daring to look back, the king and queen took their way home to their desolate palace, and Psyche leaned against the rock trembling with fear lest every moment the monster should appear in sight. She was very tired, for the road to the mountain had been long and stony, and she was likewise exhausted by her grief, so that slowly a deep sleep crept over her, and for a while her sorrows were forgotten.

While she thus slumbered, Cupid, unknown to herself, had been watching over her, and at his bidding Zephyr approached and played round her garments and among her hair. Then, lifting her gently up, he carried her down the mountain side, and laid her upon a bed of lilies in the valley.

While she slept, pleasant dreams floated through her mind, and her terrors and grief were forgotten. She awoke feeling happy, though she could not have told why, for she was in a strange place and alone. In the distance, through some trees, the spray of a fountain glimmered white, and she rose and walked slowly towards it. By the fountain was a palace, finer by far than the one in which Psyche had lived, for that was built of stone, while this was all of ivory and gold. Vast it was, and full of precious things, as Psyche saw for herself when, filled with wonder mixed with a little fear, she stepped across the threshold.

'This palace is as large as a city,' the maiden

said aloud, as she passed from room to room without coming to an end of the marvels; 'but how strange to find that there is no one here to enjoy these treasures, or to guard them!' She started, as out of the silence a voice answered her:

'The palace with all it contains is yours, lady. Therefore, bathe yourself, if you will, or rest your limbs upon silken cushions, till the feast is prepared, and we your handmaids clothe you in fine raiment. You have only to command, and we obey you.'

By this time all fear had departed from Psyche, and with gladness she bathed herself and slept. When she opened her eyes she beheld in front of her a table covered with dishes of every kind, and with wines of purple and amber hues. As before, she could see no one, though she heard the sound of voices, and when she had finished, and lay back on her cushions, unseen fingers struck a lyre, and sang the songs that she loved.

So the hours flew by, and the sun was sinking, when suddenly a veil of golden tissue was placed on her head, and at the same time a voice that she had not heard spoke thus:

'Dip your hands in this sacred water'; and Psyche obeyed, and, as her fingers sank into the basin she felt a light touch, as if other fingers were there also.

'Break this cake and eat half,' said the voice again; and Psyche did so, and she saw that the rest of the cake vanished bit by bit, as if someone else were eating it also.

'Now you are my wife, Psyche,' whispered the voice softly; 'but take heed to what I say, if you would not bring ruin on yourself, and cause me to leave you for ever. Your sisters, I well know, will soon seek you out, for they think they love you, though their love is of the kind that quickly turns to hate. Even now they are with your parents weeping over your fate, but a few days hence they will go to the rock, hoping to gather tidings of your last moments. It may chance that at last they may wander to this enchanted place, but as you value your happiness and your life do not answer their questions, or lift your eyes towards them.'

Psyche promised she would do her unseen husband's bidding, and the weeks slipped swiftly by, but one morning she felt suddenly lonely and broke into wailing that she might never look on her sisters' faces again, or even tell them that she was alive. All the long bright hours she sat in her palace weeping, and when darkness fell, and she heard her husband's voice, she put out her arms and drew him to her.

'What is it?' he asked gently, and she felt soft fingers stroking her hair.

Then Psyche poured out all her woe. How could she be happy, even in this lovely place, when her sisters were grieving for her loss? If she might only see them once, if she might only tell them that she was safe, then she would ask for nothing more. If not—why, it was a pity the monster had not devoured her.

There was a silence after Psyche had poured forth her entreaties, and then the bridegroom spoke, but his voice seemed somehow changed from what it had been before.

'You shall do as you wish,' he said, 'though I fear that ill will come of it. Send for your sisters if you please, and give them anything that the palace contains. But once again let me beseech you to answer nothing to their questions, or we shall be parted for ever.'

'Never, never, shall that be,' cried Psyche, embracing her husband with delight. And, whoever and whatever you may be, I would not give you up, even for the god Cupid. I will tell them nothing, but bid, I pray you, Zephyr, your servant, to carry them hither to-morrow, as he carried me.'

Next morning Zephyr found the two sisters seated on the rock, tearing their hair and beating their breasts with sorrow. 'Psyche! Psyche,' they cried, and the mountains echoed 'Psyche! Psyche,' but no other sound answered them. Suddenly they felt themselves gently lifted from the earth, and wafted through the air to the door of the palace, where stood Psyche herself.

'Psyche! Psyche!' they cried again, but this time with joy and wonder, and for a while they forgot everything else in the world. Then Psyche bade them tell her of her father and mother, and how the days had passed since she had left them, and she pictured to herself their gladness when they heard how different had been her fate from that which the oracle had foretold.

After her sisters had made known to her

everything they had to tell, Psyche invited them to see the palace, and, calling to the voices, ordered them to prepare baths with sweet-smelling spices, and to set forth a banquet for her guests. At these tokens of riches and splendour, envy began to arise in their hearts, and curiosity also. They looked at each other, and the glances of their eyes promised no good to Psyche.

'But where is your husband?' asked the eldest. 'Are we not to see him also?'

'Yes,' said the other, 'you have not even told us what he is like, and our mother will assuredly wish to know that.'

Their questions recalled to Psyche's mind the danger against which she had been warned, and she answered hastily:

'Oh, he is young and very handsome—the handsomest man in all the world, I think. But he spends much of his time in hunting, and has now gone far into the mountains to chase the boar. It was thus that, feeling myself lonely, I sent a messenger for you. And now, come and choose what you will out of the treasure-chamber, for the hour of your departure draws nigh!'

The sight of gold and precious stones heaped up in the treasure-chamber only made the sisters more jealous than before; but their jealousy did not prevent their carrying off the most splendid necklaces they could find before Psyche summoned Zephyr to bear them unseen back to their own homes.

'Why has Fortune treated her so differently from us?' cried the eldest, before they were out of sight of the palace. 'Why should *she* have boundless riches, and be married to a man who is young and handsome, and own slaves who fly through the air as if they were birds? Far indeed are the days when she sat in our father's house, and no suitor came to woo! But, though she was lonely and forlorn enough in the city, here she is treated as if she were a goddess, while I am linked to a husband whose head is bald, and whose back is a hump!'

'My plight is worse than yours,' groaned the other sister, 'for I have to spend my time nursing a man who is always ill and rarely suffers me to leave his side. But do not let us flatter her pride by telling our father and mother of the honours Fate has heaped on her. Rather let us consider how best to humble her and bring her low.'

Meanwhile night had fallen, and Psyche's husband came to her side.

'Did you take heed to my warnings,' asked he, 'and refuse to answer the questions of your sisters?'

'Oh yes,' cried Psyche; 'I told them nothing that they wished to know. I said that you were young and handsome, and gave me the most beautiful things in the world, but that they could not see you to-day, for you were hunting in the mountains.'

'So far it is well, then,' sighed he; 'but remember that even at this moment they are plotting how they may destroy you, by filling your heart with their own evil curiosity, so that one day you may ask to see my face. But recollect, the moment you do this I vanish for ever.'

'Ah, you do not trust me,' sobbed Psyche; 'yet I have shown you that I can be silent! Let me prove it again by suffering Zephyr to bring my sisters once more, and then never, never will I crave another boon from you.'

For long her husband refused to grant her what she asked, but at last, wearied by her tears and prayers, he told her that this once she might bid Zephyr bring her sisters to her. Eagerly they ran through the garden into the palace, and greeted Psyche with warm embraces and gentle words, while she on her part did everything she could think of to give them pleasure. As before, she bade them choose whatever they most desired, and when they had returned from the treasure-chamber and were eating fruit under the trees by the fountain the elder sister spoke:

'How it grieves me to see you the victim of such deceit, and how I long to be able to ward off the danger!'

'What do you mean by such words?' asked Psyche, turning pale. 'No one is deceiving me, and no goddess could be happier than I.'

'Ah! you do not know—I dare not tell you,' gasped the other in broken accents. 'Sister, you try; I cannot shape the words.'

'It is hard, but my duty demands it of me,' said the second sister. It is—oh, how shall I tell it?—your husband is not such as you think, but a huge serpent whose neck swells with venom, and whose tongue darts poison. The men who work in the fields have watched him swimming across the river as darkness falls, at the moment that he goes to seek you!'

Their groans and sobs, no less than their words, convinced Psyche, who fell straightway into the pit they had digged for her.

'It is true,' she said with a trembling voice, 'that never yet have I beheld my husband's face, and that many times he has warned me that the moment my eyes light upon him he will abandon me for ever. His words were always sweet and gentle, and his touch hardly resembles the skin of a serpent. It is not easy to believe; but yet, if you know, I pray you, of your love for me, to come to my aid in this deadly peril.'

'Ah, hapless one, it is for that we are here,' answered the elder; 'and this is what you must do. This very night, fill a lamp full of oil, and cover it with a dark cloth, so that not a ray of light can be seen; then take a sharp knife and hide it in your bosom. After the serpent is sound asleep, steal softly across the room, and snatch the cloth from the lamp, so that you may see where to strike home, for if he should wake before you have cut off his head your life will be forfeit.'

Having said this, they both hurriedly embraced their sister, and were wafted home on the wings of Zephyr.

Left alone, Psyche flung herself on the ground, and for many hours lay trying to subdue her misery. At one moment she thought that she could not do it—that her sisters might be wrong after all. But her faith in them was strong, and as night approached she rose up to do their bidding.

So well did she feign happiness that her husband heard no change in her voice as she bade him welcome, and, having travelled far that day, he soon laid himself down on the couch and fell sound asleep. Then Psyche seized the lamp and snatched off the covering, but by its light she saw stretched on the cushions, not a huge and hideous serpent, but the most beautiful of all the gods, Cupid himself.

At this sight her knees knocked together with surprise, and she gave a step backwards, and the lamp, trembling in her hand, let fall a drop of burning oil on Cupid's shoulder. He sprang to his feet, and with one reproachful look he turned, and would have flown away had not Psyche grasped his leg, and was borne up with him into the air, till at length her strength gave way and she fell to the ground, where for some time she remained unconscious.

When her senses came back, she was so miserable that she sought eternal forgetfulness in a neighbouring stream, but the river, in pity, carried her gently along and placed her on a bank of flowers. Finding that even the river would have none of her, she rose up, and resolved to wander night and day through the world till she should find her husband.

The first spot at which she halted was a temple on the top of a high mountain, where, to her surprise, she saw blades of wheat, ears of barley, sheaves of oats, scythes and ploughs, all scattered about in wild confusion. Never before had she seen such disorder about a temple, and, stooping down, she began to separate one thing from another and to place them in heaps.

While she was busy with this, a voice cried to her from afar:

'Unhappy girl, my heart bleeds for you! Yet even while you are pursued by the wrath of Aphrodite, you can labour in my service. May you find some day the rest that you deserve! But now, quit this temple, lest you draw down on me the anger of the goddess.'

With despair in her soul, Psyche wandered from one place to another, not knowing and not caring whither her feet might lead her. At length she was tracked and seized by one of Aphrodite's attendants, who dragged her by the hair into the presence of the goddess herself. Here she was beaten and scourged, both by whips and by cruel words, and, when every kind of suffering had been heaped on her, Aphrodite took a number of bags containing wheat, barley, millet, and many other seeds, and, tumbling them all into one heap, bade her separate and place them each in its own bag by the evening.

Psyche stood staring where Aphrodite had left her, not even trying to begin a task that she knew to be hopeless.

She would certainly be killed, thought she, but, after all, death would be welcome; and she laid her weary body on the floor and sought sleep. At that moment a tiny ant, which had been passing through the storehouse on his way to the fields, and saw her terrible straits, went and fetched all his brothers, and bade them take pity on the damsel, and do the work that had been given to her.

By sunset every grain was sorted and placed in its own bag, but Psyche waited with trembling the return of Aphrodite, as she felt that nothing she could do would content her.

And so it happened, when Aphrodite entered, and thirsting for vengeance, cried with glee, 'Well, where are my seeds?' Psyche pointed silently to the row of bags against the wall, each with its mouth open, so that at the first glance it could be seen what kind of seed it contained. The goddess grew white with rage, and screamed loudly, 'Wretched creature, it is not your hands that have done this! you will not escape my anger so easily'; and, tossing her a piece of bread, went away, locking the door behind her.

Next morning the goddess bade one of her slaves bring Psyche before her.

'In yonder grove,' she said, on the banks of a river, feed sheep whose wool is soft as silk and as bright as gold. Before night I shall expect you to return with as much of this wool as will make me a robe. And I do not think that you will find any one to perform your task this time!'

So Psyche went towards the river, which looked so clear and cool that she stepped down to the brink, meaning to lay herself to rest in its waters. But a reed sang to her, and its song said:

'O Psyche, do my bidding and fear nothing! Hide yourself till evening, for the sheep are driven mad by the heat of the sun, and rush wildly through the bushes and thickets. But when the air grows fresh they sink exhausted to sleep, and you can gather all the wool you want from the branches.'

Then Psyche thanked the reed for its counsel and brought the wool safely back to the goddess; but she was received as before with scornful looks and words, and ordered to go to the top of a lofty mountain and fill a crystal urn from a fountain of black water which spouted from between walls of smooth rock. And Psyche went willingly, thinking that this time surely she must die.

But an eagle which was hovering over this dark and awful place came to her aid, and taking the urn from her he bore it in his beak to the fountain, which was guarded by two horrible dragons. It needed all his strength and skill to pass by them, and indeed it was only when he told them that Aphrodite needed it to give fresh lustre to her beauty that they ceased to snap at him with their long fangs.

Joyfully the eagle bore back the urn to Psyche, who carried it back carefully in her breast. But Aphrodite was still unsatisfied. Again and again she found new errands for Psyche, and hoped that each one might lead her to her death, though every time birds or beasts had pity on her.

If Cupid had only known his mother's wicked schemes, he would have contrived to stop them and to deliver Psyche. But the wound on his shoulder where the burning oil had fallen took long to heal, and for some time he was in ignorance of all that Psyche was suffering. At last, however, the pain ceased, and his first thought was to visit Psyche, who, nearly fainting with joy at the sound of his voice, poured forth all that had happened since that dreadful night which had destroyed her happiness.

'Your punishment has been sore,' said he, 'and I have no power to save you from the task my mother has set you. But while you fulfil this I will fly to Olympus, and beseech the gods to grant you forgiveness, and, more, a place among the immortals.'

And so the envy and malice of Aphrodite and the wicked sisters were brought to nought, and Psyche left the earth, to sit enthroned on Olympus.

SIR BEVIS THE STRONG

Many hundreds of years ago there lived in the South of England an earl of Southampton, whose name was Guy. He spent most of his life in defending his country from all sorts of invaders who sailed from beyond the seas, and it was not until he was getting old that he had time to think of a wife. Then he made a very foolish choice, for he asked in marriage the daughter of the king of Scotland, who had already plighted her troth to the young and handsome Sir Murdour.

But though Sir Murdour was brother to the emperor, the Scottish king preferred to wed the princess to the stout earl of Southampton, whom he had known of old, and his word was law to all his court. So the bride journeyed with a great following to the south of England, where the marriage took place, and the next year a baby was born that was called Bevis.

Now, though her husband was good and kind, and gave her the most beautiful dresses and horse-trappings in the whole kingdom, the princess hated him with a deadly hatred, just because he was not Sir Murdour. And when her son Bevis was seven years old she determined to seek the help of her old lover, and entice the earl to his death.

To this end she made use of her charms and beauty to gain over to her side some of her husband's most trusted lords, and when this was done she chose out a faithful messenger to ride north to Sir Murdour.

'Bid him,' she said, 'to come without fail on the first of May to the great forest that lies by the sea. Thither will I take care that my lord shall fare, with but a small company, and—the rest Sir Murdour can grasp. Only, I should like to see a bleeding head, in proof that all has gone as I wish.'

Sir Murdour did not delay when he heard this message, but called together a troop of armed knights, and set sail with them for the forest on the water over against Southampton. They landed late one night, and Sir Murdour bade his foster-brother go secretly to the palace, and let the countess know that he was close at hand. After that he posted his men in deep dells and behind trees, and awaited his enemy.

The sun was scarcely up before the countess roused her husband, who was sleeping heavily after a day's hunting.

'Awake,' she cried, shaking his shoulder, 'I am feeling like unto death, and I have dreamed that this day I shall surely die if I eat not of the flesh of a wild boar of the forest.'

At these woeful tidings the earl sprang from his bed, and in a short while he was riding with a pack of hounds and a few attendants towards the part of the forest where the wild boars were most plentiful. The dogs were soon racing down a track, having scented a boar, and the earl was preparing to follow when Sir Murdour and his men leapt out from their hiding-places and suddenly surrounded him.

'I am here at your lady's bidding,' said the knight; 'she has begged me to send her your head, and I mean to do it.'

The earl's face grew pale at these dreadful words. He did not fear any man alive, but the thought of his wife's baseness took the strength from his arm and the courage from his heart. Still, for the honour of his name and knighthood, it behoved him to fight his best, though his only weapon was a boar spear. The battle lasted long, but at length the earl's horse was killed under him, and he fell to the ground. In another moment Sir Murdour struck his head from his shoulders, and, placing it on a spear, he ordered his squire to bear it to the castle.

Bevis, who was standing on the battlements, saw this terrible sight, and seeking out his mother he vowed vengeance against the murderer. Though he was only seven years old, his strength was so great that the countess felt that her life would not be safe if once he discovered the truth, so she ordered his uncle Saber to take the boy to some distant place and there to slay him. Saber did not dare to disobey. He took Bevis with him to a small hut near the forest, and, killing a pig, sprinkled the child's garments with the blood and sent them to his mother. Afterwards he dressed Bevis in the clothes of a peasant, and, putting a stout staff in his hands, set him to watch a flock of sheep.

The boy did what he was told without a word, but the sheep wandered far that day, and by-and-by he found himself in sight of his father's castle.

Then a sudden fury filled his soul, and, leaving the sheep to go whither they would, he ran swiftly down the hill, and never stopped till he reached the castle gate. Here the porter, to whom the countess had given much gold, tried to stop him, but Bevis only knocked him down with his cudgel, and on into the hall he went, and there he beheld his mother and Sir Murdour feasting at the high table.

'Traitors and murderers!' cried he, and lifting his staff, he dealt three fierce blows at the head of Sir Murdour, which felled him to the ground, where he lay unconscious. Then the boy turned and walked out of the hall, none daring to stop him.

He told his uncle what had happened, but Saber was never ready of counsel, and before he had time to think what was best the countess entered the hut attended by two knights, whom she ordered to seize Bevis, and sell him as a slave to any captain in the port of Southampton who might be sailing that night for the lands of the Infidel.

The captain of the ship was a kind man and took a liking to the boy whose fate was so hard, and when a fair wind blew them into the harbour of Heathenesse he bade the child bear him company to the palace. The king, whose name was Ermyn, thought he had never seen any boy of his age so tall and beautiful, and asked him many things as to his past life. These Bevis answered with so much truth and spirit that Ermyn was persuaded that he would grow into a man much above the common, and declared that he would make him heir to his throne and wed him in due course to his daughter Josyan, if he would only give up Christianity and become a convert to the faith of Heathenesse. But this Bevis swore he would never do.

The good captain feared greatly that the king might be angered by Bevis's refusal, but instead Ermyn seemed to think that the boy, who would not break his vows lightly, was fain to turn out a true and loyal man. So he smiled, and told Bevis that he would make him his chamberlain, and when he was of age to be a knight, he should be his banneret.

Eight years passed by, spent by Bevis in learning all the feats with the sword and spear for which the knights of Heathenesse had long been famous. His life was smooth and pleasant, and it was only when he had counted fifteen summers that he had his first adventure.

It was Christmas Day, and Bevis was riding with a large company of Paynim knights through the great plain that surrounded the city. The talk ran upon the many lion chases they had held in that very place, when suddenly one of the knights who had journeyed both to Rome and Jerusalem turned to Bevis, who happened to be next him, and asked if he knew what day it was.

'No,' answered Bevis; 'why should I? Is it different from any other day?' and the knight laughed and told him he was but a poor Christian. This angered Bevis, who said that, as he had lived among heathens since he was seven years old, it was not likely he should have learnt anything about his faith, but that in defence of it he was ready to tilt with the knights one after the other and hoped that in so good a cause he might prevail.

'Listen to the crowing of this young cock' cried one of the party, highly wroth at the answer of Bevis; and indeed so furious were they that they set upon him at once and dealt him many wounds before the boy was able to defend himself. Then he snatched a sword from the man nearest him, and laid about him so hardly that in a short time they were all stretched dead upon the ground, while their horses galloped back to their stalls. Bevis himself, suffering great pain, went quietly back to his room in the palace and waited to see what would come next.

When king Ermyn heard the news, and how so many of his best knights had been put to death by his page, he was beside himself with fury, and gave orders that Bevis should be instantly beheaded. But Josyan, his daughter, pleaded so hard for the young page that the king agreed to hear his story, and when he had heard it he not only forgave the youth, but told Josyan, who was skilled in leechcraft, to heal his wounds. And in a little while Bevis was raised to higher favour than ever by slaying a boar which had carried away and eaten several children on the outskirts of the city.

By this time the fame of the princess's beauty had spread far and wide, and the king of Damascus sent an embassy to the court of king Ermyn, praying that she should be given him to wife.

'But,' added he, 'in case you do not well

consider my suit, I would have you know that I will gather together a great army, and lay waste your land with fire and sword. So think well before you refuse me.'

King Ermyn was little used to language of this sort, and for all answer collected twenty thousand men, whom he commanded to be in readiness. Next, at the request of his daughter, he dubbed Bevis a knight, and the princess herself clad him in a richly inlaid helmet, and buckled on him the good sword Morglay. As a parting gift she bestowed on him a swift white horse called Arundel, and very proud was Bevis as he rode away at the head of the army beside the commander.

It were too long to tell of all the deeds wrought by Sir Bevis during the fight with the king of Damascus, whose standard-bearer, the giant Radyson, he slew at the very outset of the battle. In the end, and owing in a great measure to the valour of the young knight, the Damascenes owned themselves beaten, and their king remained a captive in the hands of Sir Bevis.

'I will spare your life on one condition only,' said the victor, 'and that is that you shall swear fealty on my sword to king Ermyn, and acknowledge yourself to be his vassal.'

The king's heart was sore when he heard what was demanded of him, for never before had he been vanquished in war. Still, he saw that there was no help for it, and he took the oath that Bevis required of him, after which he was suffered to depart into his own country.

King Ermyn could not do enough honour to Sir Bevis when he came back to the palace, and, as was the custom, he bade his daughter rid him of his heavy armour, to put on him gorgeous robes, and to wait on him when he sat down to table. Sir Bevis was half glad and half ashamed to receive these services at the hands of the princess, but Josyan heard her father's orders right willingly, and led him away to fulfil them at once.

The first thing she did was to order her slaves to prepare a bath for him, and to make it soft with all manner of sweet-smelling spices. Then she summoned him to her chamber, where she had prepared food and wine, and, like a wise woman, spoke nothing till he had eaten and drunk as much as he would. When he had satisfied his hunger, he flung himself to rest on a pile of cushions, and Josyan seated herself near him. Taking one of his hands in hers, she said softly:

'Oh, Bevis, little do you know what I have suffered these many months from the love I bear you! Indeed, so grievous have been my pains that I marvel that I am alive this day. But if you return not my love, of a surety I am a dead woman.'

Now Bevis had long loved the princess in secret; but his heart was proud, and, besides, he feared to seem that he had betrayed the king's trust. So he answered:

'Fair Josyan, I thank you for your gentle words, but it would ill become me to take advantage of them. There is no prince in all the world, be he who he may, who would not crown you queen, and hold himself honoured. For me, I am but a poor knight, and one from a strange land, to whom your father has shown more favour than I deserve. It is not thus I should repay his kindness.'

These words struck a chill through Josyan. All her life she had never known what it was to be denied anything she asked for, and she fell to weeping.

'I would sooner have you, poor as you are, than the greatest king alive,' sobbed she; but when Bevis sat still and kept silence her grief turned to wrath.

'Am I, who might reign over any of the kingdoms of the earth, to be flouted by you, a mere churl? Out of my chamber this instant, and betake yourself to working in the fields, for they are fitter setting for one of your birth than a lady's bower!'

'Damsel,' said Bevis, 'you wrong me. No churl am I, but the son of an earl, and a knight withal. And now farewell, for I shall depart into my own country.'

For a short time Josyan's anger held sway in her heart, and even the death of Bevis would hardly have moved her, but when she heard that Bevis was actually preparing to leave the city her pride broke down, and she sent a messenger to implore his forgiveness. But she had to learn that Bevis was no less proud than she, and he dismissed the messenger with a ring that the king had given him, merely saying that he had already bid good-bye to the princess Josyan.

Then Josyan saw that if she would keep Bevis at

her side she must humble herself to the dust, so she went herself to the chamber of Bevis, and implored him to forget her hasty words, and not to forsake her. Nay, she would even promise to give up her own faith and to become a Christian.

At this proof of her devotion, Sir Bevis's resolve gave way, and he told her that he had loved her always, but feared that her father would never accept him as a son-in-law. Josyan made light of this obstacle, and declared that her father would never refuse her anything she had set her heart upon; but Bevis was not so hopeful, and soon events proved that he was right.

Two knights whom Bevis had rescued from captivity and had brought to the palace overheard the vows exchanged between him and Josyan, and her offer of being baptized. Hating and envying the good fortune of Bevis, they sought out the king, and told him that his daughter was about to give up the faith of Mahomet, and to fly from the country with a Christian knight.

These tidings were grievous to king Ermyn. He could not forgive his daughter, and yet, after all the deeds he had done, the people of the city would not suffer Bevis to be punished. What was he to do? The more he thought of it the more bewildered he felt; and all the while the two traitors stood patiently by, knowing well what was passing through the king's mind.

At length he turned, as they were sure he would, and asked their counsel, which was quite ready.

'Let your Majesty write a letter to King Bradmond, as from liege lord to vassal, and let Sir Bevis be the bearer of it, and bid the king put the knight to instant death.' So said the traitors, and, though the device was neither new nor honourable, it would serve. Bevis was summoned to the king's presence, and listened carefully to all he was told. Joyful was he at being chosen for this mission, which he thought betokened special favour, though his spirits were somewhat damped by the assurance that he must leave his sword Morglay and Arundel, his swift horse, behind him.

'It were an insult to the king to approach him on a war-horse, and brandishing the sword that has slain so many of his men,' said Ermyn. 'You shall ride the ambling palfrey on which I make my progress through the city; and, as for weapons, you will have no need of them.' So Arundel remained quietly in his stable, while Bevis unwillingly jogged along at the slow pace of the palfrey. But in one thing he disobeyed king Ermyn, for under his tunic was hidden a short sword.

On the way he fell in with a pilgrim, whose offer to share his dinner Bevis accepted gladly. They soon began to tell each other their adventures, and, to his surprise, Bevis found that the pilgrim was his own cousin, the son of his uncle Saber, and that he had come so far with no other purpose than to seek out the young knight and to inform him of all that had happened during the years that had passed since his father's death.

The vassals of the old earl, said the pilgrim, had been so ground down by the wicked Sir Murdour and his wife, that they had risen up as one man, and, headed by Saber, had defended the Isle of Wight against the usurper. But it was greatly to be desired that the young earl should return home as fast as possible, and attack Murdour in his castle of Southampton, and for this reason had he set forth to seek him.

Bevis's heart and his blood waxed hot with the listening, but he did not wish that the pilgrim should learn just then who he was, so he answered that the young earl was his friend and brother, and that on his part he would promise speedy help to the faithful vassals fighting in his cause. With this they parted, and Bevis pursued his way to Damascus.

On entering the gates of the city he found himself in the midst of a large crowd, who were making ready a sacrifice to a wooden idol, which was carried in a golden car. This roused the wrath of the young man, and, forcing his way through the multitude, he seized the idol and flung it into the mud, calling loudly on the people to go and help their god, since he could not help them. In an instant a thousand arms were raised against the stranger who had dared to insult the majesty of their idol, and, though Bevis drew his short sword and defended himself bravely, he could not have held out against such numbers had not the palace gates been close behind. Still fighting, Bevis entered the gates, and drawing the letter from his tunic ordered the guards to take him at once into the presence of the king.

Bradmond read the letter with joy, as he felt that his enemy was delivered into his hands, and the tidings of the attack on the idol hardened his heart still more. Without further delay he bade the guards take Bevis and carry him off to a deep dungeon under the palace where lived two huge dragons, who would be fain to eat him forthwith.

'And I do this,' said Bradmond, 'not to avenge my own wrongs, but to perform my oath of duty unto my sovereign lord king Ermyn. For this is the service he requires of me, in the letter that you yourself have brought.'

Ropes were tied under Bevis's arms, and he was lowered down, down, down, till he could see nothing but four fiery eyes which glared furiously up at him. Soon after his hands knocked against something hard and rough, which moved under his touch. At the same moment his feet touched the bottom, and he found himself standing in a large cave with a feeble ray of light coming from the far end. By this he dimly perceived two horrible dragons, but for a moment they were still, and did not move to attack him.

Bevis made use of the short time allowed him to feel about if perchance he could find some weapon with which to defend himself instead of the short sword which had been taken from him, and he came upon a stout staff, thrown into one corner, and by the aid of this he held those two monsters at bay for a whole night and day. By this time the dragons, who had been weakened by a slothful life and the flesh of many prisoners, were too weak to resist any longer, and fell an easy prey to the strong arm of Bevis.

Of course it was not long before the men who had charge of the dungeon discovered that the dragons were dead, but they were so filled with admiration of Bevis's courage that they kept his counsel, and let down into his prison daily a good portion of wheat cake, so that he managed to keep himself alive. Bradmond the king very soon forgot all about him, so that the soldiers did as they pleased.

Thus some years passed away.

At the end of that time one of the gaolers died, and the other was sent to a distant city. The two men who took their places knew nothing of Bevis, save that he was a captive in the dungeon, and that as long as he was alive it was part of their duty to feed him every day. 'Let us murder him,' said one man to another; 'it is small use to feed a man in a dungeon who is forgotten by himself and all the world'; so one of them fastened a ladder of ropes to the side and climbed down it, in the hope of finding an easy victim lying on the ground. Instead there was a man as strong as ten other men, who leapt swiftly aside to avoid the blow of his sword, and struck him dead to the ground with a blow of his fist. The other gaoler, hearing no noise from below, crept down the ladder to see what had taken place; but as soon as he was on the floor of the dungeon Bevis gave a mighty spring which snapped the chain that had bound him to the rock, and thrust him through with the sword he had taken from his fellow. Then, when, as far as he could reckon, the night was nearly gone, he climbed up the ladder, and stood once more a free man.

At the first gleam of dawn, Sir Bevis stole out to the stables, where the king's horses were being groomed. Peeping through a hole, he discovered a room hung round with suits of armour, and, getting in through the roof, he took down a coat of mail, a helmet, and a shield, while he chose out a good sword from a pile standing in a corner. Then entering the stable, he cut off the heads of several of the men, while the rest fled out of reach of the strange being with the long hair and strong arm. When they were all gone Bevis brought out the best horse in the stable, and rode out across the drawbridge into the world again.

Of course, directly he was missed, king Ermyn sent his best knights in pursuit of him, but in one way or another Sir Bevis got the better of them all, and made his way to Jerusalem, where, for the first time since he was seven years old, he entered a Christian church. But so anxious was he to hear some tidings of Josyan, that he remained only a short time in the city, and soon rode on again along the road to her father's court.

On the way he met with a young knight who had once been his squire, and who told him a sad tale. Josyan, he said, had been asked in marriage by the most powerful and fierce of all the kings of Heathenesse, but she steadily refused to wed any man who was not a Christian like herself. This so enraged her father that he gave leave to her suitor to do with her as he would; so king Inor, for so was he named, carried her off to his own kingdom, and shut her up in a tower till she should come to a better mind, and be ready to return to her old faith.

'In her tower she is still,' continued the knight; 'but if you would have speech with her it is first needful to persuade the king to go on some distant mission. And first you must put on a disguise, for at any moment those may come by who knew you well at the royal palace.'

This advice Bevis followed; he hid himself with his friend behind a clump of bushes till a pilgrim passed on the way to Jerusalem. The young knight then left his hiding-place, and prayed the pilgrim for the sake of charity and a dole of money to be given in alms that he would exchange clothes with Sir Bevis. To this the pilgrim readily agreed, and soon Bevis was arrayed in a long mantle, carrying a staff in his hand.

'Now go and stand about the door of the palace, and when the king comes from hunting he will see you, and will ask you where you come from, and what news is stirring in the world. And you must say to him that you have lately journeyed from Syria, from the kingdom of his brother, and that the land has been overrun by strange armies, and that the country is in a great strait. When he hears that he will of a surety hasten to his aid, and then you will be able to escape with Josyan without danger of losing your head.'

Now Inor the king had placed Josyan under the charge of Boniface, the chamberlain, who had been long in the service of her father, and in order the better to help her had pretended to approve of the evil way in which she was treated. Directly he heard of the plot he began to play his part towards its fulfilment, and in the evening of the day on which the king had departed he managed to give the steward, who had been left to rule the city, such a powerful sleeping draught that he did not wake for twenty-four hours. Meanwhile Sir Bevis chose out the best suit of armour in the king's armoury and the fastest horse in his stable; and when night fell Josyan stole softly down from her tower, and, mounting Arundel, whom she had brought with her from her old home, rode out of the gates by the side of Bevis. Boniface followed close after them. He did not dare to stay behind, as he knew that his head was forfeit.

But as things happened he might as well have remained where he was, for the very next day, when Bevis was hunting, two lions came up to the cave where Josyan and her chamberlain lay concealed. Without an instant's pause they devoured Boniface and his horse, which was tethered outside, though Josyan's beauty so overawed them that they bent their heads humbly in her presence.

The next adventure that befell Sir Bevis was a battle with a giant thirty feet high, who had been sent by the steward to catch the two runaways. During the fight he was sore wounded, and in the end owned Bevis to be his master, and begged to be allowed to take service with him. Sir Bevis agreed, though somewhat doubtfully, but soon found reason to rejoice in his new page, for by his help he was able to turn some Saracens out of a ship which bore them all with a fair wind to the city of Cologne.

Here he found his uncle, the bishop; who was brother to his father and to Sir Saber, and, leaving Josyan in safety under his care, he set sail with a hundred knights for Southampton. Before landing he sent one of his most trusty squires for tidings as to how fared Sir Murdour, and received for answer that the quarrel still raged betwixt him and Sir Saber. Then Bevis went on shore with all his knights, and bade one of them tell Sir Murdour that they had sailed from France in quest of service, and that if he so willed they would fight under his banner, but, if not, they would offer themselves to his foe.

Sir Murdour was overjoyed at the sight of the strangers, and asked the name of their leader.

'Sir Jarrard,' said Bevis, who did not wish to make himself known, and inquired further what were the causes of the war with Sir Saber, and how long it had lasted. To this Sir Murdour made reply that Sir Saber had been seeking for many years past to wrest from him the heritage which was his by purchase from the spendthrift heir Bevis, who had afterwards quitted the country, but that with the help of the strangers an end would speedily be put to the quarrel.

While Bevis stood listening to Sir Murdour, his fingers unconsciously crept to the handle of his sword, but he forced back his wrath and answered that, had they brought their horses with them, the dispute might have been settled that very night. Still, much might be done if Sir Murdour would give them a ship in which to sail to the Isle of Wight, and would provide them with horses.

Sir Murdour did not need to be asked twice; he

gave to Sir Bevis his finest horses and his best armour, and before many hours Bevis was standing on the Isle of Wight by the side of his uncle Saber.

'Take yonder fishing-boat,' said he to one of his knights, 'and return to Southampton and enter the castle. Then tell Sir Murdour that the man to whom he has given his arms and his horses is no knight of France, but Sir Bevis earl of Southampton, who has come to take vengeance for the death of his father.'

The battle which decided the strife was fought upon the island, and never for a moment did Bevis lose sight of his enemy. In vain did Murdour ride from one part of the field to the other; Bevis was always there, though it was long before he was close enough to thrust at him. At last he managed to hurl him to the ground, but Murdour's followers pressed hard on him, and Bevis could not, by his own self, take him captive.

'To me! To me!' he cried at last, and Ascapard strode up, cleaving the heads of all that stood in his way.

'What shall be done with him?' asked he, picking up the fallen knight and holding him tightly.

'Put him in the cauldron that is boiling outside the camp,' said Bevis. 'For that is the death for traitors.'

So Sir Bevis got his own again, and he sent to Cologne for Josyan, and was wedded to her by his uncle the bishop in his good town of Southampton.

OGIER THE DANE

Long, long ago, a baby lay asleep in a cot in a palace. It was a royal baby, therefore it was never left alone for a moment, but always had two or three ladies watching it, by day and by night, so that no serpent should crawl into its cradle and bite it, nor any evil beast run off with it, as sometimes happened in other countries.

But one evening, after a very hot day, all the ladies in waiting felt strangely drowsy, and, though they tried their best to keep awake, one by one they gradually dropped off to sleep in the high carved chairs on which they sat. Then a gentle rustle might have been heard outside on the staircase, and when the door opened a brilliant light streamed in, though the ladies slept too soundly to be awakened by it. Wrapped round by the light were six fairies, more beautiful than any fairies that ever were seen, who glided noiselessly to the cradle of the baby.

'How fair he is!' whispered one; 'the true son of a king.'

'And how strong he is!' answered another; 'look at his arms and legs,' and the whole six bent forward and looked at him.

'The world shall ring with his fame,' said the first, whose name was Gloriande, 'and I will give him the best gift I have. He shall never fear death, and no word of shame shall ever touch him.'

Then the second fairy leaned forward and lifted the baby out of his cradle. She was tall, and on her head was a ruby crown, while a plate of gold covered her breast.

'Through all your life,' she murmured, 'wherever war and strife may be, you shall be found in the midst of it, even as your forefathers.'

'Yes,' said a third; 'but my gift is better than hers, for you shall never be worsted in any fight, and every one shall add to your honour.'

'And though you are the first of knights,' exclaimed the fourth, 'you shall win fame for your courtesy and gentlehood, no less than for your valour.'

'The hearts of all women shall turn to you, and they shall love you,' said the fifth, who was clad in a robe of transparent green; 'but beware how you give them back their love, for this love of mortals needs proving'; and with that she slipped away from the cradle.

The sixth fairy looked silently at the child for a few moments, though her thoughts seemed to be with something far away.

At length she spoke, and these were her words:

'When you are weary of travel and of strife and have won all the glory and honour that may fall to men, then you shall come to me in my palace of Avallon, and rest in the joys of fairyland with Morgane le Fay.'

After that the light began to fade, and the six fairies vanished none could tell how or whither.

By-and-by the baby's attendants woke up, and never knew that during their sleep the child's fate had been fixed as surely as if he had been bitten by a serpent or carried off by a wolf. Everything *seemed* the same as it had done before, and so they took it for granted that it *was*.

Time passed on, and Ogier, for that was the name they gave him, was ten years old. He was tall and strong and could send his arrows farther than most boys many years older. He could handle a spear too, and his thrusts went straight at the mark; while he could sing a song, or touch the lute as delicately as a maiden. His father was proud of him, and it went sore with him when Charlemagne the emperor, who had had a bitter quarrel with the king of Denmark, demanded that Ogier should be sent as a hostage to his court of Paris.

For four years the boy lived happily in Paris, daily making new friends, and learning to be a skilled swordsman; but at the end of that time the Danish king sank some of Charlemagne's ships, and the emperor vowed that Ogier should pay for his father's deed. His life was spared, but the youth was banished to St. Omer, a little town on the coast. Here he spent some years, which would have been dull and very wearisome but for the kindness of the governor, who not only allowed him to fish and hunt on receiving his word that he would not try to escape, but gave him his daughter, the fair Belissande, as his companion, and even consented to a marriage between them. For, kind though he was, he did not forget that the captive youth was after all heir to the Danish throne.

Ogier would have been quite content to stay where he was, when suddenly the emperor summoned him to come to Paris and take part in a war which had broken out between him and the Saracens, who had landed in Italy. Unwilling though he was, of course Ogier was forced to obey, and he speedily won such fame that in a little while Charlemagne declared that from henceforth he should have in battle the place of honour on the right hand of the emperor himself. This favour so excited the jealousy of Charlot, the emperor's son, that he laid many snares for Ogier's life, but, owing to the gift of the fairy Gloriande, the young man contrived to escape them all.

On his return to France with the army, after the war was over and the Saracens had been beaten, he found two pieces of news awaiting him. One was that his father was dead, and that he was king of Denmark, and the other was that during his absence a son had been born to him.

Taking leave of the emperor, he chose the swiftest horse he could find in the stables and rode straight to St. Omer. The boy was by this time three years old, and promised to be tall and strong like his father. Already he could mount a pony and use a tiny bow and arrows that had been made for him, and even could tell the names of some of the battles his father had won.

But Ogier could not tarry long in the castle of St. Omer. Taking his wife and son with him, he set out at once for Denmark, and spent several years in the kingdom making laws and teaching his people many things that he had learnt in his travels.

After ten years, however, he became weary of this peaceful life, and, after Belissande died, he felt he could bear it no longer. So, leaving the crown to his uncle, he returned to France with his son and fought once more by the side of Charlemagne. This was the life he loved, and it seemed as if it might have gone on for ever had it not been for the prince Charlot, who, unhappily, only grew more quarrelsome and foolish the older he got.

Charlot was one day playing chess with the son of Ogier, and, as he was hasty and impatient, the game went against him. Like many others, he had never learned how to take a beating like a man, and, raising his hand, he struck the youth a blow on the temple which killed him. Charlemagne, grieved though he really was, refused to punish Charlot, and after saying bitter words Ogier left Paris, and took service with the king of Lombardy, but was soon captured, while asleep, by Archbishop Turpin.

By this time Charlemagne had felt the loss of Ogier so greatly, and had besides suffered so much from further ill-doings on the part of his son, that he lent a ready ear to Ogier's offer of reconciliation, provided he were allowed to avenge himself on the murderer. But just as Ogier was about to strike off Charlot's head, and rid the world of a man who never did any good in it, he was stopped by a mysterious voice which bade him to spare the son of Charlemagne. So Charlot was left to work more mischief throughout the land.

A second time a crown fell to Ogier in right of his wife, the princess Claria of England, who had been delivered by Ogier out of the hands of the Saracens. But the princess died not many months after, and the fetters of the throne were no more to Ogier's taste in England than in Denmark. So he assembled all his barons, and bade them choose themselves a king from among them. This done, he set sail across the sea for the life of adventure that he loved.

For some time Ogier fought in Palestine, where he gained great fame, for no army and no city could stand before him. But his heart always turned to France, and directly peace was made he said farewell to his companions and took ship for Marseilles. At first the breeze was fair, but when they had made half the voyage a tempest arose and the vessel was driven on a rock, while all the crew except Ogier himself were drowned. This happened early in the morning, but as soon as darkness fell and Ogier was fearing that he might die of hunger, as no living thing could be seen on the island, he suddenly beheld facing him a castle of adamant. He rubbed his eyes and gazed at it in amazement, thinking it was a vision, for he knew not that this castle was enchanted, and, though unseen by day, shone by night from light of its own. However, he did not hesitate at the strangeness of his adventure, but taking his sword in his teeth he swam ashore, and mounted the flight of steps that led to the open door.

Rich and beautiful things lay scattered everywhere, but not a sign was there of any one to enjoy them. Room after room was empty, and Ogier was fast losing hope and wondering whether he was to die of starvation in the midst of all this splendour. He had searched every chamber of the castle except one which lay before him at the end of a long gallery. He would go into that too, but if it should prove as barren as the rest then his case was indeed perilous.

With a beating heart he drew back the bolts and lifted the latch of the great carved door. Before him a long table was spread with fruits and food of the rarest sort, while in a large chair at the further end a horse was seated enjoying a huge pasty. At the sight of Ogier he rose politely and bowed, after which he presented him with a golden bowl full of water and returned to his chair.

During his travels Ogier had beheld many strange things, but never before had a horse been his host, and he was so startled that, hungry though he was, he hardly touched the food which the horse heaped on his plate, expecting every moment that a magician might appear or the whole castle crumble away.

Quiet though Ogier was, the horse, who had been taught manners in the court of the sultan of Babylon himself, took no notice of his guest's behaviour but finished his own supper, which was a very hearty one. When it was done he rose again, bowed a second time to Ogier, who had risen also, and, signing with his fore hoof towards a curtain on one side of the hall, passed through, followed by his guest. In the centre of a magnificent chamber stood a soft bed, at which Ogier gazed longingly. The horse saw the direction of his eyes, and with another bow he withdrew.

In the morning Ogier awoke early and passed through the door into a meadow bright with flowers. He looked round him, and saw a group of ladies sitting under a tree plucking fruit from its branches, and filling golden cups from a clear stream that ran at their feet. Not having eaten since his scanty supper of the night before, he approached the ladies, one of whom arose and spoke to him, saying:

'Welcome, Ogier of Denmark! I have waited for

you long. A hundred years have passed since I stood by your cradle—a hundred years of war and of fighting. But you have tired of them at last and have come back to me! And now you shall rest in the palace of Avallon. I am Morgane le Fay.'

She held out her hand, and Ogier placed his within it, and thus they entered the castle. Then she went to her closet and drew a casket from it, and from the casket she took a ring, which she slipped on Ogier's finger. Afterwards she placed on his head a wreath of golden laurels intertwined with bays, and his white hair became once more like sunshine, and the wrinkles faded from his brow. And with the wrinkles faded also the recollection of the battles he had fought, and of Charlemagne himself, and even of Belissande, whom he had loved so well. Soft sounds of singing floated through the palace, and fairies trailing flowers glided in and out in the dance. While Ogier stood entranced and dumb, there entered King Arthur, to whom spoke Morgane le Fay:

'Draw near, Arthur, my lord and brother, come and salute the flower of chivalry, the boast of the court of France, he in whom courtesy, loyalty, and all virtue are united.'

And Arthur drew near, and they embraced each other.

Two hundred years passed as a single day, till one morning when Ogier was lying on a bank listening to the birds which sang like no birds which mortal ears have ever heard, he took for an instant the crown from off his head. In a moment the memories of his old life flashed across him, and, starting up, he sought Morgane le Fay, and bade her give him his sword, for he was going to fight for fair France again. In vain the fairy besought him not to forsake her, but he would hear nothing, and she was fain to do as he wished. So by her magic she conjured up a little boat which bore Ogier to Marseilles, whence he hastened to the war, which was being carried on in Normandy.

Great was the surprise of the warriors and ladies of the court at the sight of the new-comer, whose face was as young and fresh as their own, but whose arms and whose speech were of a time long gone by. At first some were inclined to try him with jests, but they speedily found that, strange though his manners might seem, it were wiser to accept them. Indeed, it was not long before Ogier's presence had caused itself to be so felt throughout the camp that he was given command of an army that was about to march against the enemy who were invading France and utterly routed them. In gratitude the king begged him to counsel him in all things, and in a few months some of Ogier's strength and wisdom had passed into the people.

Now night and day Ogier wore the ring which Morgane le Fay had placed on his finger, and as long as it was there no youth about the court was fairer and more splendid than he. The gift with which he had been endowed in his cradle had lost none of its power, and as he passed through the crowd, towering full a head over other men, the hearts of the ladies went out towards him. *He* could not help it, and *they* could not help it. It had been so ordained by the fairy. Even age could not preserve them; nay, it seemed to render them an easier prey.

Amongst the noble ladies whose pulses beat faster at the sight of Ogier's golden hair was the Countess of Senlis. Old was she, and withered of face, but she had never ceased to think that she was young, and she mistook the kindliness and courtesy of Ogier's manner for the love that man bears to woman.

One morning, in crossing the garden to attend upon her mistress the queen, the countess came upon Ogier lying asleep under the trees. She stopped and looked upon him tenderly; then her eyes fell upon the ring on his finger, whose stone, of a strange green hue, was graven with devices.

'If I could see them close, perchance I might guess who he is and whence he came,' said she to herself, and, stooping, she drew lightly the ring from his hand, not knowing that the queen had crept up and stood behind her. But what an awful change came over him all at once! His limbs grew shrivelled, his hair white, his eyes so shrunken that they seemed hardly more than points; but when the queen turned with horror to ask her lady what it meant, the change in her was hardly less wondrous, for, though the old countess was ignorant of it, fifty years had been swept from her, and she was straight and winsome as of yore.

They were still standing, dumb with surprise, when Ogier awoke and glanced about him with feeble, uncertain gaze. Catching sight of the ring, which the countess was still holding, he stretched his shaking hand towards it. The action was more than the queen could bear.

'Give it back to him,' she said; and, unwilling though she was to part with such a treasure, the countess was forced to obey.

Tremblingly Ogier restored the ring to its place, and in an instant his youth and beauty returned to him.

Soon after this the king of France died, and when the time of mourning was over the queen made known to Ogier that she wished to take him for her second husband. Gentle was she and fair, and easy it was for Ogier to love her, and his heart beat high at the thought of sitting on the throne where Charlemagne had once sat. The people rejoiced greatly when they heard of the marriage, for with Ogier for their king they were safe, they thought, from invaders.

The wedding day had come, and scarce a man or woman in Paris had closed their eyes the night before. Magnificent indeed would the procession be that was to end in the new cathedral; gorgeous would be the trappings of the horses, dazzling the dresses of the ladies that would ride, some in litters and some on horses, through the streets that bordered the river. Early was the queen astir, to be tired by her maidens, and if Ogier's slumbers lasted longer—well, it was not the first time that he had been crowned a king.

At length he was awakened by the sound of a voice calling his name:

'Ogier, Ogier!' and at the sound the present was forgotten, and the past rushed back. 'Ogier, Ogier!' whispered the voice again, and, looking, he saw standing by his bed not the queen, but Morgane le Fay.

'Rise quickly,' she said, 'and put on your wedding garments. Clothe yourself in the mantle Charlemagne wore, and the crown that was placed upon his brow. Set on your feet his shoes of gold, and let me see you once as France would have seen you.'

He did her bidding, and she gazed at him awhile, then slowly drawing nigh she lifted the crown from his hair, and in its stead she put on him the wreath of laurel which brought peace and forgetfulness.

'Now come with me,' she said, holding out her hand, and together they left the palace unseen, and entered a barge that was waiting in the river, and in the sunrise they sailed away to the castle of Avallon.

HOW THE ASS BECAME A MAN AGAIN

Once upon a time there lived a young man who would do nothing from morning till night but amuse himself. His parents were dead and had left him plenty of money, but this was fast vanishing, and his friends shook their heads sadly, for when the money was gone they did not see where more was to come from. It was not that Apuleius (for that was the name of the youth) was stupid. He might have been a good soldier, or a scholar, or a worker in gold, if so it had pleased him, but from a child he had refused to do anything useful, and roamed about the city all day long in search of adventures. The only kind of learning to which he paid any heed was magic, and when he was in the house he would spend hours poring over great books of spells.

Fond though he was of sorcery, he was too lazy to leave the town and its pleasures—the chariot-racing, the theatre, and the wrestling, and to travel in search of the wizards who were renowned for their skill in the art. However, the time came when, very unwillingly, he was forced to take a journey into Thessaly, to see to the proper working of some silver mines in which he had a share, and Thessaly, as everybody knows, is the home of all magic. So when Apuleius arrived at the town of Hypata, where dwelt the man Milo, overseer of his mines, he was prepared to believe that all he saw was enchanted.

Now, if Thessaly is the country of magic, it is also the country of robbers, and Apuleius soon noticed that everybody he met was in fear of them. Indeed, they made this fear the excuse for all sorts of mean and foolish ways. For instance, Milo, who loved money and could not bear to spend a farthing, refused to have any seats in his house that could be removed, and in consequence there was nothing to sit upon except two marble chairs fixed to the wall. As there was only room in these for one person, the wife of Milo had to retire to her own chamber when the young man entered.

'It was no use,' explained Milo, 'in laying out money on moveable seats, with robbers about. They would be sure to hear of it and to break into the house.'

Unlike his guest, Milo was always occupied in adding to his wealth in one form or another. Sometimes he sent down a train of mules to the sea, and bought merchandise which the ships had carried from Babylon or Egypt, to sell it again at a high price. Then he dealt in sheep and cattle, and when he thought he might do so with safety made false returns of the silver that was dug up from the mines, and kept the difference for himself. But most often he lent large sums at high interest to the young men of the neighbourhood, and so cunning was he that, whoever else might be ruined, Milo managed to make large profits.

Apuleius knew very well that his steward was in his way as great a robber as any in Thessaly, but, as usual, he found it too much trouble to look into the matter. So he laughed and jested with the miser, and next morning went out to the public baths and then took a stroll through the city. It was full of statues of the famous men to whom Hypata had given birth; but as Apuleius had made up his mind that nothing in Thessaly *could* be what it seemed, he supposed that they were living people who had fallen under enchantment, and that the oxen whom he met driven through the streets had once been men and women.

One evening he was returning as usual from a walk when he saw from afar three figures before Milo's house, who he at once guessed were trying to force an entrance. 'Here is an adventure at last,' thought he, and, keeping in the shadow, he stole softly up behind them, and drawing his short sword he stabbed each one to the heart. Then, without waiting to see what more would befall, he left them where they were and entered the house by a door at the back.

He said nothing of what had happened to Milo his host, but the next day, before he had left his bed, a summons was brought him by one of the slaves to appear before the court at noon on a charge of murder. As has been seen, Apuleius was a brave man and did not fear to face three times his number, but his heart quailed at the thought of a public trial. Still, he was wise enough to know that there was no help for it, and at the hour appointed he was in his place.

The first witnesses against him were two women with black veils covering them from head to foot. At the sound of the herald's trumpet, one of the two stepped forward and accused him of compassing the death of her husband. When she had ended her plaint the herald blew another blast, and another veiled woman came forward and charged him with her son's murder. Then the herald inquired if there was not yet a third victim, but was answered that his wound was slight, and that he was able to roam through the city.

After the witnesses had been called, the judge pronounced sentence. Apuleius the murderer was condemned to death, but he must first of all be tortured, so that he might reveal the names of the men who had abetted him. By order of the court, horrible instruments were brought forward which chilled the blood of Apuleius in his veins. But to his surprise, when he looked round to see if none would be his friend, he noticed that every one, from the judge to the herald, was shaking with laughter. His amazement was increased when with a trembling voice one of the women demanded that the bodies should be produced, so that the judge might be induced to feel more pity and to order more tortures. The judge assented to this, and two bodies were carried into court shrouded in wrappings, and the order was given that Apuleius himself should remove the wrappings.

The face of the young man grew white as he

heard the words of the judge, for even a hardened criminal cares but little to touch the corpse of a man whom he has murdered. But he dared not disobey, and walked slowly to the place where the dead bodies lay. He shrank for a moment as he took the cloth in his hand, but his guards were behind him, and calling up all his courage he withdrew it. A shout of laughter pealed out behind him, and to his amazement he saw that his victims of the previous night had been three huge leather bottles and not men at all!

As soon as Apuleius found out the trick that had been played on him he was no less amused than the rest, but in the midst of his mirth a sudden thought struck him.

'How was it you managed to make them alive?' asked he, 'for alive they were, and battering themselves against the door of the house.'

'Oh, that is simple enough when one has a sorceress for a mistress,' answered a damsel, who was standing by. 'She burned the hairs of some goats and wove spells over them, so that the animals to whom the hairs and skins had once belonged became endowed with life and tried to enter their former dwelling.'

'They may well say that Thessaly is the home of wonders,' cried the young man. 'But do you think that your mistress would let me see her at work? I would pay her well—and you also,' he added.

'It might be managed perhaps, without her knowledge,' answered Fotis, for such was the girl's name; 'but you must hold yourself in readiness after nightfall, for I cannot tell what evening she may choose to cast off her own shape.'

Apuleius promised readily that he would not stir out after sunset, and the damsel went her way.

That very evening, Hesperus had scarcely risen from his bed when Fotis knocked at the door of the house.

'Come hither, and quickly,' she said; and without stopping to question her Apuleius hastened by her side to the dwelling of the witch Pamphile. Entering softly, they crept along a dark passage, where they could peep through a crack in the wall and see Pamphile at work. She was in the act of rubbing her body with essences from a long row of bottles which stood in a cupboard in the wall, chanting to herself spells as she did so.

Slowly, feathers began to sprout from her head to her feet. Her arms vanished, her nails became claws, her eyes grew round and her nose hooked, and a little brown owl flew out of the window.

'Well, are you satisfied?' asked Fotis; but Apuleius shook his head.

'Not yet,' he answered. 'I want to know how she transforms herself into a woman again.'

'That is quite easy, you may be sure,' replied Fotis. 'My mistress never runs any risks. A cup of water from a spring, with some laurel leaves and anise floating in it, is all that she needs. I have seen her do it a thousand times.'

'Turn me into a nightingale, then, and I will give you five hundred sesterces,' cried Apuleius eagerly; and Fotis, tempted by the thought of so much money, agreed to do what he wished.

But either Fotis was not so skilful as she thought herself, or in her hurry she neglected to observe that the bird bottles were all on one shelf, and the beast bottles on another, for when she had rubbed the ointment over the young man's chest something fearful happened. Instead of his arms disappearing, they stretched downwards; his back became bent, his face long and narrow, while a browny-grey fur covered his body. Apuleius had been changed, not into a nightingale, but into an ass!

A loud scream broke from Fotis when she saw what she had done, and Apuleius, glancing at a polished mirror from Corinth which hung on the walls, beheld with horror the fate that had overtaken him.

'Quick, quick! fetch the water, and I will seek for the laurels and anise,' he cried. 'I do not want to be an ass at all; my arms and back are aching already, and if I am not swiftly restored to my own shape I shall not be able to overthrow the champion in the wrestling match to-morrow.'

So Fotis ran out to draw the water from the spring, while Apuleius opened some boxes with his teeth, and soon found the anise and laurels. But alas! Fotis had deceived herself. The charm which was meant for a bird would not work with a beast, and, what was worse, when Apuleius tried to speak to her and beg her to try something else, he found he could only bray!

In despair the girl took down the book of spells,

and began to turn over the pages; while the ass, who was still a man in all but his outward form, glanced eagerly down them also. At length he gave a loud bray of satisfaction, and rubbed his nose on a part of the long scroll.

'Of course, I remember now,' cried Fotis with delight. 'What a comfort that nothing more is needed to restore you to your proper shape than a handful of rose leaves!'

The mind of Apuleius was now quite easy, but his spirits fell again when Fotis reminded him that he could no longer expect to be received by his friends, but must lie in the stable of Milo, with his own horse, and be tended, if he was tended at all, by his own servant.

'However, it will not be for long,' she added consolingly. 'In the corner of the stable is a little shrine to the goddess of horses, and every day fresh roses are placed before it. Before the sun sets to-morrow you will be yourself again.'

Slowly and shyly Apuleius slunk along lonely paths till he came to the stable of Milo. The door was open, but, as he entered, his horse, who was fastened with a sliding cord, kicked wildly at him, and caught him right on the shoulder. But before the horse could deal another blow Apuleius had sprung hastily on one side, and had hidden himself in a dark corner, where he slept soundly.

The moon was shining brightly when he awoke, and looking round he saw, as Fotis had told him, the shrine of Hippone, with a branch of sweet-smelling pink roses lying before it. It was rather high up, he thought, but, when he reared himself on his hind legs, he would surely be tall enough to reach it. So up he got, and trod softly over the straw, till he drew near the shrine, when with a violent effort he threw up his forelegs into the air. Yes! it was all right, his nose was quite near the roses; but just as he opened his mouth his balance gave way, and his front feet came heavily on the floor.

The noise brought the man, who was sleeping in another part of the stable.

'Oh, I see what you are at, you ugly beast,' cried he; 'would you eat roses that I put there for the goddess? I don't know who may be your master, or how you got here, but I will take care that you do no more mischief.' So saying, he struck the ass several times with his fists, and then, putting a rope round his neck, tied him up in another part of the stable.

Now it happened that an hour or two later some of the most desperate robbers in all Thessaly broke into the house of Milo, and, unheard by anyone, took all the bags of money that the miser had concealed under some loose stones in his cellar. It was clear that they could not carry away such heavy plunder without risk of the crime being discovered, but they managed to get it quietly as far as the stable, where they gave the horse some apples to put it in a good temper, while they thrust a turnip into the mouth of Apuleius, who did not like it at all. Then they led out both the animals, and placed the sacks of money on their backs, after which they all set out for the robbers' cave in the side of the mountain. As this, however, was some distance off, it took them many hours to reach it, and on the way they passed through a large deserted garden, where rose bushes of all sorts grew like weeds. The pulse of Apuleius bounded at the sight, and he had already stretched out his nose towards them, when he suddenly remembered that if he should turn into a man in his present company he would probably be murdered by the robbers. With a great effort, he left the roses alone, and tramped steadily on his way.

It were long indeed to tell the adventures of Apuleius and the number of masters whom he served. After some time he was captured by a soldier, and by him sold to two brothers, one a cook and the other a maker of pastry, who were attached to the service of a rich man who lived in the country. This man did not allow any of his slaves to dwell in his house, except those who attended on him personally, and these two brothers lived in a tent on the other side of the garden, and the ass was given to them to send to and fro with savoury dishes in his panniers.

The cook and his brother were both careful men, and always had a great store of pastry and sweet things on their shelves, so that none might be lacking if their lord should command them. When they had done their work they placed water and food for their donkey in a little shed which opened on to the tent, then, fastening the door so that no one could enter, they went out to enjoy the evening air.

On their return, it struck them that the tent

looked unusually bare, and at length they perceived that this was because every morsel of pastry and sweets on the shelves had disappeared, and nothing was left of them, not so much as a crumb. There was no room for a thief to hide, so the two brothers supposed that, impossible though it seemed, he must not only have got *in* but *out* by the door, and, as their master might send for a tray of cakes at any moment, there was no help for it but to make a fresh supply. And so they did, and it took them more than half the night to do it.

The next evening the same thing happened again; and the next, and the next, and the next.

Then, by accident, the cook went into the shed where the ass lay, and discovered a heap of corn and hay that reached nearly to the roof.

'Ah, you rascal!' he exclaimed, bursting out laughing as he spoke. 'So it is you who have cost us our sleep! Well, well, I dare say I should have done the same myself, for cakes and sweets are certainly nicer than corn and hay.' And the donkey brayed in answer, and winked an eye at him, and, more amused than before, the man went away to tell his brother.

Of course it was not long before the story reached the ears of their master, who instantly sent to buy the donkey, and bade one of his servants, who had a taste for such things, teach him fresh tricks. This the man was ready enough to do, for the fame of this wonderful creature soon spread far and wide, and the citizens of the town thronged the doors of his stable. And while the servant reaped much gold by making the ass display his accomplishments, the master gained many friends among the people, and was soon made chief ruler.

For five years Apuleius stayed in the house of Thyasus, and ate as many sweet cakes as he chose; and if he wanted more than were given him he wandered down to the tent of his old masters, and swept the shelves bare as of yore. At the end of the five years Thyasus proclaimed that a great feast would be held in his garden, after which plays would be acted, and in one of them his donkey should appear.

Now, though Apuleius loved eating and drinking, he was not at all fond of doing tricks in public, and as the day drew near he grew more and more resolved that he would take no part in the entertainment. So one warm moonlight night he stole out of his stable, and galloped as fast as he could for ten miles, when he reached the sea. He was hot and tired with his long run, and the sea looked cool and pleasant.

'It is years since I have had a bath,' thought he, 'or wetted anything but my feet. I will take one now; it will make me feel like a man again'; and into the water he went, and splashed about with joy, which would much have surprised anyone who had seen him, for asses do not in general care about washing.

When he came back to dry land once more, he shook himself all over, and held his head first on one side and then on the other, so that the water might run out of his long ears. After that he felt quite comfortable, and lay down to sleep under a tree.

He was awakened some hours later by the sound of voices singing a hymn, and, raising his head, he saw a vast crowd of people trooping down to the shore to hold the festival of their goddess, and in their midst walked the high priest crowned with a wreath of roses.

At this sight hope was born afresh in the heart of Apuleius. It was long indeed since he had beheld any roses, for Thyasus fancied they made him ill, and would not suffer anyone to grow them in the city. So he drew near to the priest as he passed by, and gazed at him so wistfully that, moved by some sudden impulse, the pontiff lifted the wreath from his head, and held it out to him, while the people drew on one side, feeling that something was happening which they did not understand.

Scarcely had Apuleius swallowed one of the roses, when the ass's skin fell from him, his back straightened itself, and his face once more became fair and rosy. Then he turned and joined in the hymn, and there was not a man among them all with a sweeter voice or more thankful spirit than that of Apuleius.

GUY OF WARWICK

Everyone knows about the famous knight Sir Guy, the slayer of the great Dun Cow which had laid waste the whole county of Warwick. But besides slaying the cow, he did many other noble deeds of which you may like to hear, so we had better begin at the beginning and learn who Sir Guy really was.

The father of Guy, Segard the Wise, was one of the most trusty councillors of the powerful earl of Warwick and Oxford, who was feared as well as loved by all, as a man who would suffer no wrong through the lands which he governed.

Now the earl had long noted the beauty and strength of Segard's young son, and had enrolled him amongst his pages and taught him all manner of knightly exercises. He even was versed in the art of chess-playing, and thus whiled away many a wet and gloomy day for his master, and for his daughter the fair Felice, learned in astronomy, geometry, and music, and in all else that professors from the schools of Toulouse and Spain could teach a maiden.

It happened one Pentecost that the earl of Warwick ordered a great feast, followed by a tourney, to be held in the open space near the castle, and tents to be set up for dancing and players on the lute and harp. At these tourneys it was the custom of every knight to choose out his lady and to wear her token or colours on his helmet, as Sir Lancelot did the red sleeve of Elaine, and oftentimes, when Pentecost and the sports were over, marriages would be blessed by the priest.

At this feast of Pentecost in particular, Guy stood behind the chair of his master the earl, as was his duty, when he was bidden by the chamberlain of the castle to hasten to the chamber of the Lady Felice, and to attend upon her and her maidens, as it was not thought seemly for them to be present at the great feast.

Although, as we have said, the page had more than once been called upon to amuse the young damsel with a bout of chess, she had ever been strictly guarded by her nurse and never suffered to exchange a word with the youth whose place was so much below hers. On this evening, however, with none to hinder her, she chattered and laughed and teased her ladies, till Guy's heart was stolen from him and he quite forgot the duties he was sent to fulfil, and when he left her presence he sought his room, staggering like one blind.

Young though he was, Guy knew—none better—how wide was the gulf that lay between him and the daughter of his liege lord. If the earl, in spite of all his favour, was but to know of the passion that had so suddenly been born in him, instant death would be the portion of the over-bold youth. But, well though he knew this, Guy cared little, and vowed to himself that, come what might, as soon as the feast was over he would open his heart to Felice, and abide by her answer.

It was not easy to get a chance of speaking to her, so surrounded was she by all the princes and noble knights who had taken part in the tourney; but, as everything comes to him who waits, he one day found her sitting alone in the garden, and at once poured forth all his love and hopes.

'Are you mad to think that *I* should marry *you*?' was all she said, and Guy turned away so full of unhappiness that he grew sick with misery. The news of his illness much distressed his master, who bade all his most learned leeches go and heal his best-beloved page, but, as he answered nothing to all they asked him, they returned and told the earl that the young man had not many days to live.

But, as some of our neighbours say, 'What shall be, shall be'; and that very night Felice dreamed that an angel appeared to her and chided her for her pride, and bade her return a soft answer if Guy again told her of his love. She arose from her bed full of doubts and fears, and hurried to a rose bower in her own garden, where, dismissing her ladies, she tried to set her mind in order and find out what she really felt.

Felice was not very successful, because when she began to look into her heart there was one little door which always kept bursting open, though as often as it did so her pride shut it and bolted it again. She became so tired of telling herself that it was impossible that the daughter of a powerful noble could ever wed the simple son of a knight, that she was about to call to her maidens to cheer her with their songs and stories, when a hand pushed aside the roses and Guy himself stood before her.

'Will my love ever be in vain?' he asked, gasping painfully as he spoke and steadying himself by the walls of the arbour. 'It is for the last time that I ask it; but if you deny me, my life is done, and I die, I die!' And indeed it seemed as if he were already dead, for he sank in a swoon at Felice's feet.

Her screams brought one of her maidens running to her. 'Grammercy, my lady, and is your heart of stone,' cried the damsel, 'that it can see the fairest knight in the world lying here, and not break into pieces at his misery? Would that it were *I* whom he loved! I would never say him nay.'

'Would it *were* you, and then I should no more be plagued of him,' answered Felice; but her voice was softer than her words, and she even helped her maiden to bring the young man out of his swoon. 'He is restored now,' she said to her damsel, who curtseyed and withdrew from the bower; then, turning to Guy, she added, half smiling:

'It seems that in my father's court no man knows the proverb, "Faint heart never won fair lady." Yet it is old, and a good one. *My* hand will only be the prize of a knight who has proved himself better than other men. If *you* can be that knight—well, you will have your chance with the rest.'

The soul of the youth leaped into his eyes as he listened; for he knew that this was much for the proud Felice to say. But he only bowed low, and with new life in his blood he left the castle. In a few days he was as strong as ever he had been, and straightway sought the earl, whom he implored to bestow on him the honour of knighthood.

'Right gladly will I do so, my page,' answered Rohand, and gave orders that he would hold a solemn ceremony, when Guy and twenty other youths should be dubbed knights.

Like many young men, Sir Guy thought that his first step on the road was also to be his last, and instantly sought the presence of Felice, whom he expected to find in the same softened mood as he had left her. But the lady only laughed his eagerness to scorn.

'Think you that the name of knight is so rare that its ownership places you high above all men?' asked she. 'In what, I pray you tell me, does it put you above the rest who were dubbed by my father with you to-day? No troth of mine shall you have until your name is known from Warwick to Cathay.'

And Sir Guy confessed his folly and presumption, and went heavily unto the house of Segard.

'O my father,' he began before he had let the tapestry fall behind him, 'I would fain cross the seas and seek adventures.'

'Truly this is somewhat sudden, my fair young knight,' answered Sir Segard, with a mocking gleam in his eyes, for Guy's father had not been as blind as fathers are wont to be.

'Other knights do so,' replied Guy, drawing figures on the floor with the point of his sword. 'And I would not that I were behind them.'

'You shall go, my son,' said Segard, 'and I will give you as companions the well-tried knights Sir Thorold and Sir Leroy, and Héraud, whom I have proved in many wars. Besides these, you shall have men-at-arms with you, and such money as you may need.'

Before many days had passed, Sir Guy and his friends had sailed across the high seas, and had made their way to the noble city of Rouen. Amidst all that was strange and new to him, there was yet much that was familiar to his eyes, for there were certain signs which betokened a tournament, and on questioning the host of the inn he learned all that he desired. Next morning a tourney was to be held by order of the emperor and the prize should be a white horse, a milk-white falcon, and two white greyhounds, and, if he wished it, the hand of the princess Whiterose, the emperor's daughter.

Though he had not been made a knight a month ago, Sir Guy knew full well the customs of chivalry, and presented a palfrey, scarcely less beautiful than the one promised as a prize, to the teller of these happy tidings. Then he put on his armour and rode forth to the place of the tourney.

In the field over against Rouen was gathered the flower of Western chivalry. The emperor had sent his son, and in his train came many valiant knights, among them Otho duke of Pavia, hereafter to be Sir Guy's most bitter enemy. The fights were long and sore, but one by one the keenest swordsmen rolled in the dust, and the prize was at length adjudged to the youngest knight there present.

Full courteously he told all who might wish to hear that he might not wed Whiterose, the princess, for his faith was already plighted to another across the sea. And to Felice and to her father he sent the falcon and horse and greyhounds as tokens of his valour. After that he and his friends journeyed to many lands, fighting tournaments when there were any tournaments to fight, till the whole of Christendom rang with the name of Sir Guy.

'Surely I have proved my worth,' he said, when a whole year had gone by. 'Let us go home'; and home they went.

Joyful was the welcome bestowed on him by every one he met—joyful, that is, from all but Felice.

'Yes, you have done well,' she said, when he knelt before her, offering some of the prizes he had won. 'It is truly spoken among men that there are not twelve knights living as valorous as you. But that is not good enough for me. It matters not that you are "one of the best"; my husband must be "the best of all."'

In vain Sir Guy pleaded that with her for his wife his strength would be doubled, and his renown also.

'If you cannot conquer all men for my sake *now*, you will never do it after,' she answered; and Sir Guy, seeing his words were useless, went out to do her bidding.

The wrath of his father and mother was great when their son came to tell them he was going to seek a fresh quest, but, though his heart was sore rent with their tears, he only embraced them tenderly, and departed quickly, lest he should make some promise he might not keep.

For long he found no knight whose skill and strength were equal to his own, and he was beginning to hope that the day was drawing nigh that should see him stand without a peer, when, in a tourney near the city of Benevento, his foe thrust his lance deep into his shoulder, and for many days Sir Guy lay almost senseless on his bed.

Now Otho duke of Pavia had neither forgotten nor forgiven his overthrow by the young knight at Rouen, more than a year agone, and he resolved to have his revenge while his enemy was still weak from loss of blood. So he hid some men behind some bushes, which Sir Guy would needs pass while riding along the road to the north, 'and *then*,' thought he, 'I will cast him into prison, there to await my pleasure.'

But though his plans were well laid, the fight went against him, and in the end Sir Guy, nearly fainting with weariness and loss of blood, was again the victor, and Otho's best knight, Sir Guichard of Lombardy, owed his life to the swiftness of his horse. His victory, however, was to Sir Guy as sad as many defeats, for his constant companions lay dead before him.

'Ah, Felice, this is your doing,' said he.

Long were it to tell of the deeds done by the noble knight Sir Guy; of the tourneys that he won, of the cities that he conquered—even at the game of chess he managed to be victorious! Of course many men were sorely jealous of him and his renown, and wove plots for his ruin, but somehow or other he contrived to escape them all.

By this time Sir Guy had grown to love wandering and fighting so well that he had well-nigh forgotten who had sent him from his native land, and why he was not dwelling in his father's castle. Indeed, so wholly had the image of Felice faded from his memory, that when Ernis emperor of Constantinople, under whose banner he was serving, offered him the hand of his only daughter and half of his dominions, Sir Guy at once accepted his gifts.

The sight of the wedding-ring brought him back to his allegiance. He no longer loved Felice it is true, and he *did* love a younger and gentler maiden. But he must abide by the oath he had sworn, though it were to his own undoing.

His grief at the loss of the princess Lorette sent Sir Guy to his bed for many days, but as soon as the fever left him he felt that he could stay at court no longer, and began to make plans to seek other adventures in company with his friend Héraud and a lion which he had saved from the claws of a dragon.

Since that day this lion had never quitted his side, except at his master's bidding, and he always slept on the floor by his master's bed. The emperor and all his courtiers were fond of the great beast, who moved among them as freely as a kitten, but

Sir Morgadour, the chief steward of the emperor of the West, who was visiting the court, had ever been Sir Guy's mortal enemy, and one evening, thinking himself unseen, gave the lion a mortal wound as he was sleeping quietly in the garden. He had just strength enough to drag himself to Sir Guy's feet, where he died, and a damsel who had marked the cruel deed proclaimed loudly that it was done by Sir Morgadour. In an instant Sir Guy's dagger was buried in his breast; but when he grew calmer he remembered that his presence at court might bring injury upon Ernis, as the emperor of the West would certainly seize the occasion to avenge the death of his steward. So the next day he left the city, and slowly turned his face towards England.

It was some months before he arrived there, so many adventures did he meet with on the way. But directly he landed he hastened to York to throw himself at the feet of Athelstan the king.

'Ah, welcome indeed, fair son,' cried he; 'the fame of your prowess has reached us these many years past, and we have just received the news that a fearful and horrible dragon, with wings on his feet and claws on his ears, is laying waste our county of Northumberland. He is as black as any coal, and as rough as any foal, and every man who has gone out to meet him has been done to death ere he has struck a blow. Go, therefore, with all speed and deliver us from this monster, for of dragons you have slain many, and perchance this one is no more evil than the rest.'

The adventure was one after Sir Guy's own heart, and that very day he rode northwards; but even *his* well-proved courage failed somewhat at the sight of the dragon, ten times uglier and more loathsome than any he had ever beheld. The creature roared hideously as he drew near, and stood up at his full length, till he seemed almost to stretch as far as Warwick. 'Verily,' thought Sir Guy to himself, 'the fight of old with the great Dun Cow was as the slaying of a puppy in comparison with this!'

The dragon was covered thickly with scales all over his body, his stomach as well as his back. They were polished and shiny and hard as iron, and so closely planted that no sword could get in between them.

'No use to strike there,' muttered Sir Guy, 'a thrust down his throat is my only chance.'

But if Sir Guy knew this, the dragon knew it much better, and, though the knight managed to jump aside and avoid the swoops of his long neck and the sudden darting of his sharp claws, he had not even tried to strike a blow himself for fear lest his sword should break in two against that shining horny surface. This was not the kind of warfare to which the dragon was accustomed, and he began to grow angry, as anyone might have seen by the lashings of his tail and the jets of smoke and flame that poured out of his nostrils. Sir Guy felt that his chance would soon come, and waited patiently, keeping his eye for ever fixed on the dragon's mouth.

At length the monster gave a sudden spring forward, and if Sir Guy had not been watching he could scarcely have leaped out of the way. The failure to reach his prey enraged the dragon more than ever, and, opening his mouth, he gave a roar which the king heard on his throne at York. He opened his mouth; but he never shut it again, for Guy's sword was buried in it. The death struggles were short; and then Sir Guy cut off the head and bore it to the king.

After this, his first thought was for his parents, who, he found, had died many years agone, and having said a prayer over their graves, and put his affairs in order, he hurried off to Warwick to see Felice, and tell her that he had fulfilled the commands she had given him long years ago, when he was but a boy. He also told her of the ladies of high degree whose hands he had won in fair fight—won—and rejected. 'All of them I forsook for thee, Felice,' he said.

He had kept his word; but he had left his heart in Constantinople. Perhaps Felice did not know this, or perhaps she did not set much store by hearts, and cared more for the renown that Sir Guy had won throughout Christendom. Anyhow, she received him gladly and graciously, and so did her father, and the marriage was celebrated with great pomp, and for a space Sir Guy remained at home, and after a time a son was born to him.

But at the day of his son's birth Sir Guy was far away. In the quiet and idleness of the castle he began to think, and his conscience pricked him sore, that all the years of his life he had done ill to many a man

And slain many a man with his hand,
Burnt and destroyed many a land.

And all was for woman's love,
And not for God's sake above.

'The end should be different from the beginning,' he said, and forthwith he put on the dress of a pilgrim, and took ship for the Holy Land, carrying with him a gold ring, given him by Felice.

Once more he came back, an old man now, summoned by Athelstan, to deliver the city of Winchester out of the hands of the Danes, who were besieging it. Once more he returned to Warwick, and, unseen, watched Felice training her son in all the duties of knighthood, and once more he spoke with her, when, dying in his hermitage, he sent her the ring by his page, and prayed her to come and give him burial.

HOW BRADAMANTE CONQUERED THE WIZARD

Many of you will remember reading of the death of Roland, fighting against the Infidels in the Pass of Roncesvalles. Well, there is another book called 'Roland the Wrathful,' or in Italian (in which it was written), 'Orlando Furioso,' telling of the adventures of the great Paladin when he was a young man, and those of his friends. It is of one of these stories about a lady named Bradamante that you are going to hear now.

From childhood, Bradamante had loved all feats of arms, and her chiefest joy was to mount the most fiery horses in her father's stable. She grew up very tall and strong, as well as fair to see, and soon put on man's armour, and began to take her part in tournaments, and it was rare indeed that she failed to carry off the prize. In truth, it was not long before her skill was said to be equal to that of Roland's cousin, the renowned Rinaldo.

Of course so wise and beautiful a maiden had no lack of wooers, but Bradamante listened to none, save only to the brave Roger, who had quitted the Moorish court to seek adventures in the lands of Charlemagne the emperor. But she kept silence as to her love, and was content to wait till such time as Roger should think fit to claim her as his bride.

Suddenly the tidings came to her that Roger had vanished from among men, no one knew whither. As was her wont, Bradamante heard, and said nothing, but the next morning she sharpened her sword, and looked to the fastenings of her helmet, and rode off to seek him if perchance some ill had befallen him.

In this quest she met with some adventures of her own, but of these we have no time to tell. Bradamante, we may be sure, did not linger over them, but pushed on till she crossed a mountain, and reached a valley watered by a stream and shaded by large trees.

On the bank lay a young man with his head buried in his hands and seemingly in a state of deepest misery. He had flung his horse's bridle over the branch of a beech, and on the same bough he had hung his shield and sword. His looks and posture were so forlorn that Bradamante was moved to pity, and he himself was nothing loth to confess his woes, pretending the while to take her for a man, though he knew well she was a maiden. He was journeying, such was his tale, to the court of Charlemagne with a company of spearmen to aid the emperor in the war he was waging with the Moorish king of Spain. In the company was riding a damsel whom the knight had but lately freed from the power of a dragon. The beauty of this damsel had fired his heart, and as soon as the Infidel was crushed he hoped to wed her. But as they rode along by the side of a rapid river a winged horse guided by a man in black was seen hovering in the air above the troop. Swifter than lightning he swooped down upon the maiden; the rider bent low and snatched her off her palfrey, and was out of sight in the heavens almost before he knew that she was gone.

'Since that day,' continued he, 'I have sought her through forests and over mountains, wherever I heard that a wizard's den was to be found. But each time it was a false hope that lured me on, and now my horse is spent and not another step can he go, though at length I know that hidden among yonder rocks is my captive maiden.'

'If it is there she lies, I will free her,' cried Bradamante; but the knight shook his head more grievously than before.

'I have visited that dark and dreadful place,' he said, 'which indeed I think seems more like the valley of death than aught on this fair and lovely earth. Amidst black and pathless precipices stands a rock, and on its top is a castle whose walls are of steel. It was built, so I have since learned, by a magician, and none can capture it.'

'But did you see no man who would take pity on you, and tell you what to do?' asked Bradamante.

'As I lingered, unable to tear myself away from that loathly prison, there appeared a dwarf guiding two knights whose faces I had often seen upon the battlefield and at court. One was Gradasso king of Sericane, the other and more valiant was the young Roger.'

'And what did they there?' asked Bradamante, casting down her eyes.

'They had come to fight the wizard who dwells in the castle, so said the dwarf,' replied the knight, 'and I told them my sad tale, and they answered in knightly fashion, that as long as their lives should last they would fight for the freedom of my lady. Little need have I to tell how my bosom was rent as I stood aside waiting for the combat to begin.

'Each good knight was eager that the first blow might fall to him, but it was Gradasso who seized the horn and blew a blast which rang through the castle.

'In a moment there shot into the sky the winged horse bearing his master, clad as before in black armour. He hovered for a little space so high that even the eagle could scarcely have followed him, then darted straight downwards, and Gradasso felt a spear-thrust in his side. The knight struck sharply back, but his sword cleft the empty air, for the horse was already far out of reach. Roger ran to staunch the blood and bind up the wound, never thinking of what might befall himself. But, in truth, how could mortal men fight with a wizard who had studied all the magic of the East, and had a winged horse to help him? His movements were so swift that they knew not where to smite, and both Gradasso and Roger were covered with wounds and bruises, while their enemy had never once been touched.

'Their strength as well as their courage began to fail in the stress of this strange warfare. The blows they dealt grew ever wilder and more feeble, when from off his shield which hung upon his arm the wizard drew a silken covering, and held the shield towards them as a mirror. As I looked and wondered, behold the knights fell upon their faces, and I also, and when next I opened my eyes I was alone upon the mountain.'

'And Roger?' said Bradamante.

'Roger and Gradasso had doubtless been carried by the wizard to the dark cells of the prison, where my fair lady lies,' answered the knight, and he again dropped his head upon his hands.

Now the knight was count Pinabello, the false son of a false race, and woe betide the man or maid who trusted him. But this Bradamante knew not, and thinking that the end of her quest was come cried joyfully:

'Oh, take me to the castle, sir knight, with all the speed you may, and I shall be beholden to you for ever!'

'If you so desire it I will lead you there,' answered the knight; 'but remember that I have warned you that the danger is great! When you have climbed those walls of steel, you will find yourself a prisoner like the rest.'

'I care nothing for that,' said Bradamante.

So they set forth, but it was not by the road to the castle that Pinabello led the maiden. Wrapped in his gloom begotten of treachery and hate, he wandered from the path into a wood, where the trees grew so thickly that the sky was scarcely visible. Then a dark thought entered his mind. 'She shall trouble me no more,' he murmured as he went; and aloud, 'The night is at hand, and ere it comes it were well that we found a shelter. Rest, I pray you, here a short while, and I will climb that hill and see if, as I expect, there is a tower not far off where we can lie. To-morrow we will proceed on our way.'

'Let me go with you,' answered Bradamante, 'lest you should never find *me* again, or *I* the wizard's castle,' and, so saying, she guided her horse after his.

Thus they rode for some way, when Pinabello, who was in front, espied among the rocks a deep cavern with sides so steep and smooth that no mortal could have climbed them. He jumped off his horse and peered to the bottom, but no bottom could he see. Then his heart leaped at the thought that now, once and for all, he would be rid of Bradamante.

'Ah, good knight, you did well to follow me,' turning to greet her, as her horse came panting up the steep hill.

'A damsel lies imprisoned in that dark place, and it is foretold that only a knight with a white mantle and a white plume in his helm can deliver her. Now I think that you must be that knight, and if you have the courage to go down into that cavern as I went, you will get speech of her, as I did.'

'I will go right willingly,' answered Bradamante, and looked about her for some means of descending into the cavern. Near the mouth was a stout oak, and Bradamante cut off a branch with her sword and plunged it down the mouth of the cave. She gave Pinabello one end to hold fast, and lowered herself carefully into the darkness.

'Can you jump?' asked the count suddenly, with a laugh, and, giving the bough a push, it fell with Bradamante into the pit.

But the traitor triumphed without a cause. In the swift passage down the cave the branch struck the bottom first, and, though it broke in pieces, Bradamante was saved from being dashed against the floor, where she lay for a while bruised and shaken.

When she became used to the darkness, she stood up and looked around her. 'There may be some way out, after all,' thought she, noting that the cave was less gloomy than she had fancied, and felt round the walls with her hands. On one side there seemed to be a passage, and going cautiously down it she found that it ended in a sort of church, with a lamp hanging over the altar.

At this moment there opened a little gate, and through it came a lady, bare-footed, with streaming hair.

'O Bradamante,' she said, 'long have I awaited you, for Merlin, who lies here, prophesied before he entered this living tomb that ages hence you would find your way hither. He bade me come from a far-distant land, and be with you at the hour when his spirit, though dead, should tell of the glories of the race that will spring from you and Roger.'

'I am not worthy of such honour,' answered Bradamante, casting down her eyes, though her heart beat with joy at the thought that though she and Roger might be parted now, yet in the end they would be united. 'Let my lord speak, and I will hearken to him.'

At that a voice rose from the sepulchre where Merlin had lain buried for many hundreds of years.

'Since it is decreed that you shall be the wife of Roger, take courage, and follow the path that leads you to him. Let nothing turn you aside, and suffer no adventure to ensnare you till you have overthrown the wizard who holds him captive.'

The voice ceased, and Melissa, the kind magician who went through the world seeking to set wrongs right, showed from a book the glories that would attend the children of Bradamante.

'To-morrow at dawn,' she said when she had finished and put away the magic scroll—'to-morrow at dawn I myself will lead you to the wizard's castle. Till then it would be well for you to seek of the wisdom of Merlin guidance to overcome the dangers bestrewing your path.'

Next morning Melissa and Bradamante rode out from the cavern by a secret way, and passed over rushing rivers, and climbed high precipices, and as they went Melissa held discourse with Bradamante how best to set Roger free.

'No man, however brave, could withstand the wizard, who has his magic mirror as well as his flying horse to aid him. If you would reach Roger, you must first get possession of the ring stolen from Angelica by Agramante, the African king, and given by him to Brunello, who is riding only a few miles in front of us. In the presence of this ring all charms and sorceries lose their power; but, take heed, for to outwit Brunello is no easy task.'

'It is good fortune indeed that Brunello should be so near us,' answered Bradamante joyfully; 'but how shall I know him from other men?'

'He is of low stature, and covered with black hair,' replied Melissa; 'his nose lies flat upon his face, and his skin is yellow, as the skin of those who come from the far lands beyond Scythia. You must fall to talking with him upon magic and enchantments, but beware lest he guess who you are or what your business, and lead him on till he offer himself your guide to the wizard's castle. As you go, strike him dead, before he has time to spy into your heart, and, above all, before he can slip the ring into his mouth. Once he does that, you lose Roger for ever.'

Having thus said, Melissa bade Bradamante farewell, and they parted with tears and promises of speedy meeting. Forthwith Bradamante entered an inn hard by, where Brunello was already seated, and if she at once marked him amongst other men he no less knew her, for many a time he had seen her at jousts and tourneys.

Thus, both feigning, they fell into talk, and held discourse upon the castle and the knights who lay imprisoned therein. 'Many an adventure as perilous have I dared,' at length said Bradamante, 'and never have I failed to trample under foot my foe. So, if our worthy host will but give me a guide, I myself will challenge this wizard to deadly combat.'

But Brunello would suffer no man to be her guide save himself, and together they climbed the mountain till they stood at the foot of the castle. 'Look at those walls of steel that crown the precipice,' began Brunello; but before he could say more a strong girdle was passed round his arms, which were fastened tightly to his side; and in spite of his cries and struggles Bradamante drew the ring off his finger and placed it on her own, though kill him she would not.

Then she seized the horn which hung from a cord, and, blowing a loud blast, waited calmly for the magician to answer.

Out he came on his flying steed, bearing on his left arm his silken-covered shield, while he uttered spells that had laid low many a knight and lady. Bradamante heard them all, and was no whit the worse for the blackest of them.

Furious at his defeat, the wizard snatched the cover from the shield, and Bradamante, knowing full well what was wont to follow, sank heavily on the ground. At this the wizard covered his shield once more, and guided his steed swiftly to where the maiden lay. After that, unclasping a chain from his body, he bent down to find her. It was then that she lifted her ringed hand, and there stood before her an old man with white hair and a face scarred with sorrow.

'Kill me, I pray you, gentle lady,' cried he; 'yet know before I die that my love to Roger has been the cause of these heavy woes to so many gallant knights and fair damsels. I am that Atlantes who watched over him in childhood, and as he grew to manhood he was ever the first in all deeds of chivalry. So reckless was he, that many a time it needed all my magic to bring him back to life when seemingly he lay dead. At length, to keep him from harm, I built this castle, and filled it with all that was beautiful, and, as you know, with knights and ladies to be his companions. When everything was ready I captured Roger himself.'

'Now, take my horse and shield, and throw open wide the castle doors—do what you will, but leave me only Roger.'

The heart of Bradamante was not wont to be deaf to the sorrows of others, but this time it seemed turned to stone.

'Your horse and shield I have won for myself,' she said; 'and have you lived so long in the world without learning that it is idle to war against fate? It is fate which has given you into my hands, and it is useless to strive against it. Therefore, lead the way to the gate, and I will follow.'

They climbed in silence the long flight of steps leading to the castle; then Atlantes stooped and raised a stone on which was graven strange and magic signs. Beneath the stone was a row of pots filled with undying flames, and on these the wizard let the stone fall. In a moment there was a sound as if all the rocks on the earth were rent, the castle vanished into the air, and with it Atlantes.

Instead, a troop of knights and ladies stood before Bradamante, who saw and heard none save only Roger.

THE RING OF BRADAMANTE

When Bradamante had freed Roger and his companions from the enchanted castle, she thought that henceforth they would never more be parted. But she forgot that she had to deal with a wizard, and that wizards are not easily outwitted.

On a little plain beneath the mountain the winged horse was grazing, and when the knights and ladies came gaily down the path Bradamante left the rest and went up to take it by the bridle. Atlantes, however, had laid other plans, and had thrown a spell over the horse, so that directly Bradamante was close to it the creature moved away to a little distance. At this the knights, thinking to help her, gave chase, but the horse led them up and down the mountain, over rocks and through streams, till one by one they dropped behind, and in front there remained only Roger.

As it had been taught by Atlantes, the horse stood still, while Roger, with a cry of delight, seized the bridle and jumped upon its back. With a bound it sprang into the air, and, though Roger tried to guide it downwards to the earth, it was all in vain, for so the enchanter had willed it. Below stood Bradamante gazing up; her joy turned quickly to despair, and when the traces of Roger had vanished she rode sadly away, taking with her the horse Roger had left behind.

Meanwhile Roger was flying through the air swifter than an arrow or the lightning. Since he could not make the horse swerve an hair's breadth to the right or left, he ceased his useless efforts, and let himself be carried this way or that. Suddenly he felt that, instead of going forward they were gradually dropping down, down, down; and soon the horse stopped on a lovely island.

Where the island might be Roger did not know, nor could he tell how long he had been on his journey thither. In truth, he was content to feel himself on solid ground once more, and to smell sweet flowers and eat delicious fruits, for how could he guess that this also was devised by Atlantes—that these sights and sounds might lull his senses, and keep him safe from war? Atlantes was a great wizard and wise beyond most, but he had never learned that it was a better thing to die in battle than to live only for pleasure.

On reaching the ground Roger was careful to hold fast the bridle, having no mind that the horse should fly up into the air and leave him helpless on the island. Then, looking round, he saw a strong myrtle, and he tied the reins tightly to it, so that he himself could roam about as he would.

At length he grew tired of wandering and returned to the place where he had left his horse, which he found champing and struggling to shake itself free. As he drew near a voice cried in melancholy tones:

'If, as I think, you are a knight, and bound by the rules of chivalry, release me, I pray you, from this monster, who only adds to the pains which I myself endure.'

Startled at the sound, Roger looked around, but nought could he see save the myrtle to which the horse was fastened.

'I crave your pardon,' answered he, 'for having unwittingly done you wrong; but tell me who you are, and what has caused your present plight?'

'I am Astolfo, peer of France,' replied the tree, 'and I was enchanted by the fairy Alcina, who thus rids herself of her friends and her servants when they have ceased to please her. Even this island is not hers by right, but was stolen from her sister Logistilla, who is as wise and kind as Alcina is wicked. But so beautiful is Alcina, that none can withstand her if once she looks on them, therefore fly while you may and ask counsel of Logistilla if there is aught that you would know.'

'Oh, tell me, good tree, how I can escape without crossing the path of the cruel Alcina?' cried Roger.

'There *is* a way,' answered the tree, 'but it is rough to the feet, and beset by fierce and ill-tongued men, placed there by the fairy. He who would quit Alcina's isle needs open eyes and deaf ears.'

'I will have both,' said Roger.

But, alas! he boasted overmuch, as young men are wont to do. He was indeed in no wise affrighted at the strange shapes that met him and sought to bar his progress. Some had heads of apes and feet of goats; some rode eagles or bestrode cranes; while the captain of all was mounted on a tortoise. They swarmed on him like a crowd of flies, and Roger was so sore bested that he gave no thought to his magic shield, which perchance might have saved him.

For into the *mêlée* came two maidens of such wondrous beauty that Roger dropped his lance and stood without defence to gaze his fill. Two snow-white unicorns bore them from the city gates, and, at their coming, the noisy rabble vanished as if they had never been. Then the ladies stretched out their hands, and prayed the knight to follow them into the city.

'We have need of your brave heart and mighty arm,' they said, 'to vanquish a giantess who guards a bridge which none can pass'; and well they knew that, if Roger was to be ensnared by them, it must be by slow degrees, for not all at once would he drop into the idle life of the dwellers on the island.

So, nothing loth, Roger gladly did their behest, and went forth to meet the giantess.

The fight did not last long, and soon the monstrous creature lay stretched on the ground at Roger's feet; but her life was spared at the request of the damsels, and at their bidding he followed them over the bridge and up a hill. On the top was a large meadow full of flowers, in which maidens were playing at ball or singing sweet songs on the lute, while others were dancing.

In their midst was a damsel so fair that the rest, even the guides of Roger, looked swarthy beside her, and she came forth from among them, and held out her hand for him to kiss.

Vain it were to seek to tell Alcina's charms, but even as his eyes fell on her Roger felt that everything said by Astolfo in her despite was false. Even Bradamante was forgotten, as if she had never lived at all; yet for this Roger was hardly to blame, for how should he stand against Alcina's magic!

It was here that Melissa, clad in the form of Atlantes, found him after many months had gone by, during which Bradamante had sought him vainly. At last fate brought Melissa again across her path, and from her the forsaken damsel learnt who it was that kept him from her.

'Be comforted,' said Melissa, when she beheld Bradamante's tears. 'You yourself have the ring which can free him from those evil spells, and bring him back to your side. So lend it me, I pray, and by to-morrow's dawn I will be with him.'

Roger was lying on a bed of soft moss, when Atlantes, for so he took her to be, stood before him.

He lifted his head lazily, and smiled, but the face of his old master was grave as he said sternly:

'And is it *you*, Roger, whom I find thus, your hair curled and scented, your neck circled with jewelled chains? Was it for this you passed your boyhood in waging war against fierce beasts, fearing neither hunger nor thirst as you tracked them to their lair? But, as I loved you once, I will give you a chance to shake off this shameful life, and to become once more worthy of Bradamante. Take this ring, and when next Alcina comes this way mark well the change that is wrought in the queen of this fair land.'

With shame and repentance burning at his heart, Roger slowly drew the ring upon his finger; and by its virtue he beheld not Atlantes but Melissa.

'Yes, it is I,' she said, 'and it is Bradamante who sent me hither, to save you by means of the ring which she took from the hand of Brunello. It will break the strongest spells that wizard ever wove, and open wide the eyes that have been longest blinded.'

With that she vanished, and Roger rose and followed the path which led to the palace.

On the marble steps he saw, as he went, a troop of ladies standing. Their clothes were rich and made of shining stuffs, and well became their golden hair or curly raven locks; but who was she in their midst whose form was unknown to him? Her back was bowed with age, and scarce a hair remained upon her head, while all her skin was shrivelled and yellow. Roger gazed in horror, expecting, as he looked, the lean body to crumble into dust before him. Yet something, what he knew not, seemed not wholly strange in that pale and shrunken figure—something that, in spite of all, spoke to him of Alcina. A thrill of horror ran through him, but he remembered in time the counsel of Melissa, and, trembling though he was, he greeted her with fair words.

Dreading lest he should again fall under the fairy's enchantments, Roger never parted from the ring, and kept guard over himself, lest perchance Alcina should guess what was passing within him.

To gain possession of his armour, long laid aside, he feigned a wish to prove if his life of idleness had unfitted him to bear the weight of it, or if his chest had grown too broad for the clasps of his breast-plate to meet. Then, laughing still, he strolled carelessly to the stables, calling back as he went that perhaps his horse might have become as fat and lazy as himself. But when he reached the stables he passed by the winged steed which had borne him to the island, for he bethought himself once more of Melissa's words: 'Beware of the hippogryph,' she had said, 'you will never wed Bradamante if you mount that.' So he left the great creature flapping its wings with longing to soar once more into the sky, and led out a strong black horse. Vaulting on his back, he touched him with his spurs, and dashed through the guards at the gate before Alcina knew that her captive had won his freedom.

When the fairy found that the knight did not return, she sent a messenger for tidings of him, and so great was her wrath when she learned that he had passed the gate, and was far on the road to her sister, the good Logistilla, that she ordered all the guards to be put to death. Then she commanded her ships to be got ready, and put to sea herself, thinking by that means she might bring him back. But all was vain, and at last she was forced to believe that Roger had shaken off her yoke for ever.

THE FULFILLING OF THE PROPHECY

For a long while Bradamante waited quietly in Marseilles, thinking that every day Roger would come to her, but as time passed and he gave no sign she grew heart-sick and impatient. Some evil must surely have befallen him, she whispered to herself, yet where to seek him she did not know.

At length one morning, when hope had almost left her, the enchantress Melissa stood by her side and smiled at her.

'Have no fear for Roger,' said Melissa; 'he is safe, and counts the hours to your meeting. But once more he has been taken captive by Atlantes, who ensnared him by putting on your form and face, and entering his palace, whither Roger followed eagerly. Never look so cast down, Bradamante, but listen to my counsel and abide by it, and all will be well.'

Then Bradamante sprang up, grasping tightly her sword and shield.

'Whatever you tell me to do, I will do it,' cried she; and Melissa went on:

'This time Atlantes will change his shape for that of Roger, that you also may fall a victim to his wiles. Beware lest you be deceived, or instead of saving Roger you will find yourself also a prisoner in the castle. Harden your heart, and slay him as he stands before you, and Roger shall be free for evermore.'

So spoke Melissa not once, but many times, before they drew near the castle, where she bade farewell to Bradamante, dreading that the wizard should see her and take fright. The maiden rode on till she reached an open space, where two fierce giants were pressing Roger sore and well-nigh overcoming him. In a moment all the words of Melissa were forgotten, or rather she deemed that jealousy or revenge had prompted her words. And, as these thoughts ran swiftly through her, a cry for help sounded in her ears. Slay Roger? Melissa must have indeed been mad when she gave her this counsel, and, spurring her horse, she galloped after the wounded knight, who, pursued by his foes, was riding at full speed to the castle.

When they were all four inside the courtyard, the gate swung to and Bradamante was a prisoner.

Now it was written in the magic book carried by Astolfo, the knight who had been changed by Alcina into a myrtle tree and restored by Melissa, that if a stone on the threshold were raised, the whole palace would vanish into smoke as the other castle had done before. Though he knew it not, Melissa stood by his side as he rode through the wood, many weeks after Bradamante had entered the castle, and whispered to him that the time had come to prove the truth of the prophecy. First blowing a blast with the horn which affrighted all that dwelt within the walls, with a mighty heave he raised the magic stone. In an instant the earth rocked, and he was thrown flat upon the ground, while with a roar the castle crumbled into dust. The knights and ladies imprisoned therein ran forth in fear, and it was not until the ill-fated place was left far behind that they stopped to look about them.

It was then that Roger and Bradamante beheld each other once more, and in the joy of meeting forgot the pains they had endured since they had parted. But one promise Bradamante asked of Roger before she would be his wife. 'I cannot wed an infidel,' said she. 'You must become a Christian first.'

'Right willingly,' answered Roger, and it was agreed between them that they should set out at once for a fair abbey, so that the rite might be delayed no longer.

Thus they talked; but not yet were they to be united. On their way a distressed damsel met them on the road imploring help, which both knight and lady readily granted. But, alas! in seeking to give the aid prayed of them they strayed unwittingly down various roads, and it was long before fortune again brought them together. For hardly had Roger brought to an end his adventure than he learned that his liege lord, Agramante king of Africa, was hard pressed by Charlemagne the emperor, and needed his vassal to fight by his side. So Roger turned his face to the west, first bidding his squire ride back to Bradamante and tell her that, once the war was finished, nothing further should delay his baptism.

The war went ill with Agramante, and many a time Roger was sore wounded and like to die. Far away, in the house of her father among the mountains, tales came now and then to Bradamante of Roger's doings in the fight. Bitterly her soul chafed at not being by his side to help and tend him; but, if she could not fight against him, far less could she fight in the ranks of the infidels. Thus, weary at heart, she waited and sat still, or wandered about the forests, hoping to meet someone who could bring her tidings of Roger.

For long no one came through the thick dark woods, and Bradamante was almost sick with despair, when a Gascon knight rode by.

'Are you from the war, brave sir?' asked she, springing up from the bank where she had cast herself, and going eagerly to meet him. 'Are you from the war, and have you news from one Roger?'

'Alas! madam,' he answered, 'but a month since he was sore wounded in fight with one Mandricado, and has since lain in his bed, tended by the lady Marfisa, who wears a breast-plate as easily as she does a woman's gown. Had it not been for her skill, Roger would long have been buried, and when he is able to bear arms again doubtless he will offer his hand to the damsel in marriage. At least, so say all in camp. But the sun is low and time presses. I must begone.'

He went on his way, and when he was out of sight Bradamante turned and loosed her horse from the tree to which she had tied him and rode back to the castle. Without a word she mounted the stairs to the tower where she dwelt, and, throwing herself on her bed, gave vent to the torrents of jealousy which possessed her soul. Then, rising up, she bade her maidens weave her with all speed a sad-coloured mantle, and when it was ready she took the lance of gold belonging to Astolfo, which had (though she knew it not) the gift of unhorsing every warrior whom it touched, and, going to the courtyard, led out and saddled her horse.

Alone, without even a squire to help her, Bradamante began her journey to Arles, where the army of Agramante lay encamped. On the road thither she met with many an adventure, but by the aid of the golden lance always bore down her foe. After one of these fights she fell in with the Lady Flordelice, who was herself riding to Arles in the hope of gaining news of her husband, now a prisoner in the hands of the Moors. By her Bradamante sent a message challenging Roger to come forth to meet her in single combat.

'And if he asks my name say it is unknown to you,' she added, 'but that the stranger knight had bidden you take this horse, and prayed that he might bestride it in battle.'

Flordelice was careful to fulfil the trust laid upon her, and no sooner was she within the gates of Arles than she sought out Roger and delivered him the message and the horse. The young man, perplexed at the defiance of the nameless knight, sought counsel of his father, who bade him accept the challenge and prepare for battle without delay. While he was making ready other knights were not slow to seize the chance of giving the haughty Christian a lesson, and went out to fight in the plain beyond the walls. But a single touch of the magic lance was enough to unhorse them all, and one by one Bradamante sent them to their lord.

'Tell him I await a better man than you,' said she.

'And what is his name?' asked Ferrau of Spain when he rode before her, having craved permission to try his strength against the stranger.

'Roger,' answered she, and, as her vizor was raised, Ferrau could not but see the red that flushed her face, though he feigned to notice nothing.

'He shall come to you,' replied Ferrau, 'but first you must cross swords with me,' and, spurring his horse, he rode to share the fate of the rest.

Right glad was Roger to hear that the peerless knight Ferrau had been borne down like those who had gone before him, and that it was he and no other whom the victor wished to fight. But the courtiers of King Agramante now thronged around Ferrau, asking if perchance he had seen the face of his foe, and knew it for having beheld it elsewhere.

'Yes, I saw it,' said Ferrau, 'and it bore something of the semblance of Rinaldo. But since we know that it cannot be, and that the young Ricardo has neither the strength nor the skill to unhorse so many well-proved knights, it can be none other than their sister Bradamante. Truly she is mightier even than Rinaldo or her cousin Roland the Wrathful.'

At that Roger started, and his cheeks reddened even as those of Bradamante had done. He stood silent and awkward under the eyes of the whole court, for he feared to meet Bradamante and to read in her face that during the long months of his absence her love had given place to anger.

While Roger waited, uncertain whether to accept or refuse the challenge of Bradamante, Marfisa buckled on her coat of mail, and rode out in his stead to meet the foe. Bradamante felt in her heart who the knight was with the plume of blue and shining golden corselet, and hate burned in her soul as fiercely as in the breast of the other.

Thrice the magic lance stretched Marfisa on the ground, and thrice she rose and sought to avenge herself by a sword-thrust. At this point a body of knights, with Roger in their midst, arrived upon the field, while a band of pagan warriors approached from the opposite side. Blows were soon struck, and Bradamante, caring nothing for her own life, galloped wildly about seeking to catch sight of Roger.

The silver eagle on a blue shield was hard to find, but Bradamante found it at last, and crying, 'Traitor, defend yourself!' dashed wildly at him. Yet, in spite of herself, the arm which had been strong before was strangely weak now, and Roger could, with one thrust, have borne her off her horse, but instead his lance remained in air; she might slay him if so she chose; she had the right, but every hair of her head was safe from him.

So the day that began so badly ended happily for them all. Roger renewed his vow and became a Christian, but once more declared that by all the laws of honour and chivalry he could not desert Agramante in his dire straits. Fate again divided him from Bradamante, and sent him to join the army of Agramante, which had been worsted in many battles. The king had broken a truce with Charlemagne, and was trying to collect men and ships in Africa, and Roger felt that he was bound in honour to go to his aid. He put off in a small barque, but a violent tempest drove them up and down all night, and cast Roger at dawn upon a barren shore. But, so exhausted was he by his fight with the waves, that even yet he must have died from hunger and cold had not a hermit who dwelt in a cave close by come to his help. Here Roger rested till his strength came back to him, and before he bade farewell to the hermit he had been baptized a Christian.

No sooner was Roger healed from the hurts given him by the winds and waves, than he watched eagerly for a passing boat that might take him back to France. He waited and watched for long, but at length a ship put into the island, having on board both Rinaldo and Roland. Right welcome did they make Roger, whom both knew to be the flower of infidel chivalry, and when they heard that, Agramante being slain in battle, Roger was free to swear fealty to the emperor, and had besides been baptized a Christian, Rinaldo at once promised him the hand of his sister Bradamante.

And now it may well be thought that the time had come for the prophecy of Melissa to be fulfilled, and for Roger and Bradamante to receive the marriage blessing. But their happiness was to be delayed still further, for the old duke Aymon declared that he had chosen a husband for his daughter in the son of Constantine, emperor of the East, and not all the tears and prayers of Bradamante and Rinaldo would move him one whit. By the help of her brother, Bradamante contrived once more to see Roger, who bade her take heart, as he would himself go to Constantinople and fight the upstart prince and dethrone his father, then he would seize the crown for himself, and Bradamante should be empress after all. At these words Bradamante plucked up her courage and they embraced and parted.

After Roger had set forth the days hung heavily at duke Aymon's court, till one night, as Bradamante was lying awake, wondering if the vision of Melissa would ever come to pass, she saw suddenly a way out of her distresses. So the next morning she rose early, and fastening on her armour, left her father's castle for Charlemagne's camp. Craving speedy audience of the emperor, she besought him as a boon that he would order proclamation to be made that no man should be given her for husband till he had first overcome her in battle. To this Charlemagne consented, although duke Aymon, who had followed his daughter, prayed the emperor to refuse her this grace, and the old man, waxing very wroth at his defeat, shut up the damsel in a strong tower between Perpignan and Carcassonne.

While these things were taking place at home, Roger had reached the shores of Constantinople, and learned that the emperor of the East was engaged in a fight with the Bulgars, and that his army was encamped in a field near Belgrade. Thither Roger rode with all the speed he might, and finding that the king of the Bulgars had just been slain by the hand of Leo, son of Constantine, he offered to be the leader of the army, and soon put the Greeks to flight. Indeed, such were his mighty deeds, that Leo himself, rival (though he knew it not) of Roger, could not fail to wonder at them. When the battle was over, the Bulgarian army begged him to be their king, so sure were they that victory would follow his banner; but he declined, for the secret reason that he purposed to follow the prince, and slay him in single combat.

But instead of killing each other these two brave knights ended in becoming friends and brothers, for Leo delivered Roger from prison, where he had unjustly been thrown by the sister of Constantine, and they both journeyed together to France, to enter the lists for the hand of Bradamante.

Although they travelled with all the speed they might, they only arrived at the appointed place outside Paris on the day of the combat, when Bradamante was arming herself for the struggle. The prince knew well by this time that it was hopeless for him to think of winning for himself the love that had so long been given to another, and he prayed Roger to do him the grace to wear his arms and to bear his name in the tourney. It cost Roger somewhat to lay aside the arms and the name that had stood him for many a year in such good stead, but he owed the prince too much to say him nay, although to bid farewell to Bradamante when he had won the prize in fair fight would be bitter indeed.

With a double-headed eagle on Leo's crimson shield, and Leo's velvet surcoat over his coat of mail, Roger did obeisance to the emperor and then walked into the lists. He had chosen to give battle on foot, since Bradamante was riding his horse Frontino.

All day long the combat lasted, and, as Bradamante had been unable to bear down her foe, she was proclaimed vanquished. But of what value was the victory to him, seeing that he had gained the reward for another? So, hastily stripping off the armour belonging to the Greek prince, he left the tent unseen, and, catching sight of Frontino grazing quietly among some trees, sprang quickly on his back and plunged into the forest.

'Let death come soon,' he said to himself, 'since life is worthless.'

Meanwhile the court in Paris rang with the name of Leo the prince, and duke Aymon informed his daughter that the marriage feast need no longer be postponed. But to this Bradamante turned a deaf ear.

'I will wed none but Roger,' she cried, and though her parents taunted her with her broken vow, and threatened her with the wrath of the emperor, she would give no other answer.

'I can always die,' she thought to herself.

The court was all confusion and perplexity; the emperor loved Bradamante, but he did not wish to offend either her powerful father or the still more powerful Constantine. The test had been proposed by Bradamante herself, and how could he give permission that she should break her plighted word?

It was Melissa who once more set this tangle straight. She appeared to Leo, who was standing idly at his tent door, and told him that Roger was dying in the depths of the forest. The prince, who had grieved sorely for the loss of his friend, heard eagerly her tale, and consented gladly to go with her to seek him.

The Roger whom they found at last was very different from the Roger who had entered the lists but three days agone. His face was pale, his hair was damp, his clothes hung loosely on his body. Leo's heart smote him as he gazed, and, sinking on his knees beside Roger, he pulled his hands gently down from his face.

It was not long before he had drawn out from the young knight the secret which Roger had hidden so carefully when he had thought that honour and gratitude demanded it. Leo listened in amaze and took shame to himself that he had never guessed it sooner.

'Oh, Roger,' he cried, when at length the tale was ended, 'sooner would I give up a thousand Bradamantes and all I possess in the world than lose a friend so noble and generous as you. So rise quickly and let us hasten back to where Bradamante awaits us.'

And so the prophecy was fulfilled in the end, and everyone was made happy. Yes, even duke Aymon and his wife Beatrice; for before the wedding rejoicings were begun an embassy arrived from the Bulgarian people, begging leave from the emperor Charlemagne to offer their crown to his vassal Roger. And nobody grudged Roger and Bradamante their happiness, for they had waited so long for it, and worked so hard for it.

THE KNIGHT OF THE SUN

Once upon a time two little boys were born, and the elder had on his breast the image of a sun, which shone so brightly that the ladies who were waiting on his mother, the princess Briane, were forced to shut their dazzled eyes. On the breast of the younger one lay a pink rose, and it was hard to believe that the flower had not been newly flung there, so fresh was its colour and so vivid its green.

So the elder baby was called in after years 'the Knight of the Sun'; while his little brother was known as Rosiclair.

Now it happened that their mother, the princess Briane, had been secretly married to Trebatius, emperor of Constantinople, who had courted her under the name of prince Theodoart. Soon after their marriage her husband, while riding through the forest, had been astonished at the sight of a magnificent chariot which dashed furiously along the road, and, as it passed, he felt sure that his wife, the princess Briane, was seated inside. Without losing a moment, he turned his horse instantly round, and followed the chariot, but, spur his steed as he might, it was impossible to overtake it. However, he rode on as fast as the thick creepers and fallen trees would let him in the direction in which the chariot had disappeared, and at last he left the forest behind him and entered a beautiful meadow.

Here the emperor paused in surprise, for in front of him stood the greatest and finest castle he had ever seen, which would have held thirty thousand men with ease. At each corner was a large tower, while a wide moat of clear water would have kept a large army at bay. Happily for the emperor's curiosity, the drawbridge was at the moment let down, so he knocked at the door, which straightway opened to him, and boldly entered the castle.

He looked around the magnificent hall to see some traces of his wife, but, instead, a powerful odour stole gradually over his senses. At the same instant a golden curtain was drawn aside, and a lady whose beauty dazzled his eyes glided up to him and laid her hand on his shoulder.

'You belong to me now,' she said, as she led him away; and twenty years went by before the emperor again left the castle.

Meanwhile the little boys were carried away in the night by one of the mother's ladies, whose name was Clandestrie, and taken to her sister's house, where they lived freely and happily for some years till they were old enough to be brought to the convent where the princess Briane still remained, and taught the duties of pages. Rosiclair was always good and quiet, but his brother gave his teachers a great deal of trouble, though that did not prevent their loving him dearly. He was so tall and strong and high-spirited, that it was difficult to remember he was only a child after all, and the moment he was left alone he was always seeking some adventure.

One day, while Rosiclair was learning from his mother to play on the lute, the Knight of the Sun—for so they called him—had gone with his nurse to the banks of the broad river, and was amusing himself with scrambling in and out of a boat that lay moored to the side. There were no mirrors in the convent, and the boy jumped hastily back with dismay when he saw some one dressed like himself looking at him from out of the water.

He grew red with rage and struck out with his fist, and the arm in the water struck out too. Then the prince sprang forward, but, as he did so, he began to perceive that it was nothing but his own image that was looking at him and imitating his movements. 'How could I be such a baby!' he said to himself, and turned to leave the boat, when, to his dismay, he found that the rope had got loose and he was gently floating down the stream.

At this sight his courage began to fail him; he called loudly to his nurse, who had been talking to some friends and had not noticed the child's danger. At his cries she rushed into the river a little lower down, hoping to catch the boat as it danced by, but the current swept her off her feet, and she would certainly have been drowned had not a wood-cutter, who had watched her from above, held out a long stick which she was able to reach.

Very soon the little boat was a mere speck in the distance, and, now that there was nothing to be done, the boy took heart again and thought of all he would have to tell Rosiclair when he came back—for come back he would some day, he was sure of that.

By-and-by the grass and the trees, and even the big mountains, vanished, and all around him was the blue sea, with not even a sail to look at. How long he remained in that boat he never knew, but one day, just before sunrise, when the air is clearest and you can see farthest, he was roused from his sleep by a shout. At first he took it for part of his dream and did not move; then the shout came again, and he jumped up and waved his hand, for sailing towards him was a large vessel. At the prow stood a man in a beautiful purple tunic edged with gold. This was Florian prince of Persia.

Oh, how glad the little boy was to be amongst friends again, and how hungrily he ate the food they put before him! When he was quite rested, they brought him a child about the same age, whom they had picked up from a wreck a few days before; and then the ship's head was turned towards Babylon.

It took them a long while to get there, but at last they entered the great river which flowed past the gates of the city, and the sultan, hearing of their approach, came down from his palace to greet them. He had lived as a youth at the court of prince Florian's father, and was delighted to meet his old friend once more. As for the boys, he took a fancy to them at once, and kept them in his palace till many years had gone by and they were almost men.

When the Knight of the Sun was about sixteen he was taller than any one in all Babylon, for he took after his father, the emperor Trebatius, who was fully eight feet high. The youth was also very strong, and was afraid of nothing and nobody, and in many ways was different from his companions, especially in liking to ride and hunt alone instead of with a troop of merry young men. His friends were all fond of him, but rather afraid of him, as people often are of those who are quicker than themselves.

One morning the sultan arranged a great hunting expedition, which was to take place in some huge forests a few miles from Babylon. The sun was hot, and the sultan was old, so he soon gave up the chase, and returned to join the princess and her maidens, who were lying under the shady trees, with a stream rippling by to make them think they were cool.

Suddenly, without any warning, a band of giants sprang upon them from behind a rock, and, seizing the sultan and the ladies, bound them rapidly with silken cords. Their shrieks brought a few knights who were within earshot to their aid, but these were soon overpowered by the strength of the giants, except one, who managed to make his escape, and plunged deep into the forest.

He was flying along, half mad with terror, when a voice cried out:

'Sir knight, look well to it, or you will lose your spurs in your unseemly haste.'

'Fair youth,' replied the knight, 'do not, I pray you, waste the moments in idle talk; for the sultan and the princess have but now been attacked by an army of giants, and are being borne captive to some unknown land.' But before his tale was ended the youth was riding fast down the path along which the knight had come.

He was just in time: the tallest and strongest giant had laid hold of the sultan, bound and helpless as he was, and was carrying him off to a huge coal-black horse that was picketed to a tree close by. A blow on his helmet forced him to drop his burden, and he turned rapidly on his assailant.

'Bah! a boy!' he cried disdainfully; but the 'boy' struck him another swinging stroke, which almost cleft his shield. Then the giant drew out his great double-edged battle-axe, but the champion sprang aside, and the axe crashed harmlessly on a rock, while a well-aimed throw from the javelin pierced the joints of the giant's harness, and he fell heavily to the ground.

'It is an earthquake,' whispered the people of Babylon, as the houses shook and the swords rattled.

After this the giant's followers, who, big though they were, had no mind to face such a fighter, fled into the forest, and were seen no more.

The first thing to be done was of course to cut the cords which had been carefully wound round the arms and legs of the prisoners, who, seizing the champion's hands, shed tears and kisses over them. As to the sultan, he was well-nigh speechless from gratitude, but when he was able to speak he begged the youth to ask for some boon that he could grant, even if it were the half of his kingdom.

'That I will tell you to-morrow,' said he.

By this time the evening had come, and the chariots and the horses were made ready, and the company returned to the palace in Babylon, though neither the princess nor her ladies felt very safe till they were within the gates of the city.

Early next day the sultan sent the grand vizier to bid the youth await him in the great hall, that he might declare in presence of all the court what guerdon should be given him for saving his master's life.

And a right noble company was gathered together, for the victor was well loved of all, and every man expected that he would ask the hand of the princess.

All stood up and bowed low as the sultan swept down between them clothed in his royal robes, and wearing his golden crown on his head; for he wished the goodly assemblage to know how priceless a service the young man had done him. Nay, he too thought, like his people, that there was only one boon that the youth could fitly crave.

When he was seated on his throne, he signed to the chevalier to draw near.

'And what is the reward that I shall give you?' he asked with a smile as the young man knelt before him.

'O mighty sultan, grant me this, that with the sword which slew your enemy you will make me a knight'; then he paused and grew red, as a cloud came over the sultan's brow.

'By all the rules of chivalry — —' But the sultan's words were drowned by a tumult in the hall, and pushing her way between the crowds came a richly clad maiden, closely pursued by a huge black king.

'Save me!' she cried, looking wildly on the company of knights that stood round. 'I am the daughter of as mighty a monarch as you, and was carried off from my father's island by this black man whom you see before you. One grace he has given me, that for the space of a year I may wander where I will, seeking a knight to be my champion. But, despite their mighty names, not one has ever managed to pierce his armour.'

And again she looked on the knights, but not a man stirred from his place.

Then the chevalier rose to his feet and spoke out boldly.

'Make *me* a knight, O sultan, and *I* will fight this man who is feared by all the world! Oh, I know what you would say, that I am yet too young to bear the weight which has sometimes proved too heavy for many a goodly knight. But, if my years are few, my deeds have proved that I am no whit behind the doughtiest knight of your court. So grant me my boon or this day I will leave you for ever.'

'Be it so,' answered the sultan at last, 'though I would rather have given you the half of my kingdom or the hand of my daughter. But watch this night beside your arms in the temple, and to-morrow you shall be admitted into the order of chivalry.'

Now the sultan had a brother named Lyrgander, who was wise in every kind of enchantment, and, though he was at this time in a far country, he learned by means of his arts what strange things were happening at the court of Babylon. Without losing a moment he went to the room where his treasures were kept, and opened a large chest, from which he took two suits of armour. One, which was all white, he meant for the chevalier, and the other was for his friend Claberinde. Then he poured a few drops of a yellow liquid into a glass and drank it, wishing, as he did so, that he was in Babylon. Before the glass fell from his hand he found himself there. Very early after the youth had ended his watch, Lyrgander came to him and girded on him the suit of white armour. Led by Lyrgander, and followed by all the knights and nobles of the court, the chevalier entered the presence-chamber, where the sultan was sitting on his throne awaiting him. Once again the youth knelt, and the sultan, drawing the magic sword from its sheath, struck him three times lightly on the head with it. Afterwards, the sultan put back the sword in the scabbard and buckled it on the side of the kneeling youth.

Then, stooping down, he lowered the vizor, and said slowly and solemnly:

'I dub you knight, and arm you knight. May the high gods have you in their care!'

'Amen!' said the chevalier, and he rose from his knees and went out to the place where the lists had been prepared. And the court sat round to watch the fight, while in the midst of them all, her eyes fixed on her champion, was the captive princess, who was resolved to kill herself with her own hands rather than fall into the power of the black king.

The Knight of the Sun had chosen the best horse in the sultan's stables, and was waiting in his place till the signal should be given.

At the other end, the black king bestrode a huge black horse, and the moment he caught sight of his foe poured out a stream of abuse, which only ceased when the sound of the trumpets drowned his voice.

'I have never been conquered by mortal man,' said he, 'and shall yon wretched beardless boy, who should now be sitting with his mother's maidens, the child who but an hour ago was dubbed a knight by special grace of the sultan, have strength to do what the hardiest knights have failed in doing? By the eyes of my fathers! he will make fine food for the vultures before the sun sets.'

And the young knight heard, and the blood flew to his cheeks under his vizor, and his fingers closed more tightly on his sword.

With the first blast of the trumpets he spurred his horse, and his onslaught was so fierce that the giant reeled in his saddle.

'They have tricked me,' he said to himself, as he righted himself again. 'That blow was never given by the boy I saw; they have put someone else in his place. The battle will be harder than I thought, but the end is sure'; and he reined his horse back for a second rush.

The hours passed by, and the sun grew high in the heavens, but the flashing of swords never ceased, and the watchers of the fight could hardly breathe. Once the chevalier was thrown right on to his horse's neck, and was forced to cling to it lest he should fall to the ground. Once again—and here a murmur of terror could be heard in the crowd—a blow on his head rendered him sick and dizzy, and the charger carried him three times round the lists while he sat grasping the bridle, unconscious where he was and what he was doing. But after all, the swift rush through the air brought back his senses, and, by the time the black king was expecting that one more thrust would gain him the day, the knight spurred his horse quickly to one side, and, taking his adversary unawares, swept him dead from his saddle.

Then at last the silence was broken, and a roar of triumph and relief burst from the crowd.

Slowly the young man turned and rode along the lists, pausing before the lady Radimere as she sat by the sultan.

'You are free, princess,' he said, as he lifted his vizor; and with those words he disappeared in the crowd, before anyone had time to stop him.

It was whispered, perhaps truly, that the princess Radimere would fain have made him her husband, and have given him lordship over her island; but all we know for certain is that she returned there alone, and soon after married the son of a neighbouring king.

HOW THE KNIGHT OF THE SUN RESCUED HIS FATHER

When once the youth had been made a knight by the sultan of Babylon, and had slain the black king, he set off by himself in quest of other adventures, desiring greatly to see the world. For the next few years the young man wandered from court to court, fighting giants and delivering enchanted damsels, till at last his feet led him to a kingdom where Rosiclair his brother happened to be.

Now Rosiclair was scarcely a whit behind the Knight of the Sun in manly deeds, and not long before had done such good service to the king of England that Olive, the king's daughter, had, at her father's bidding, clasped a collar of gold around his neck, and held out to him a crown studded with jewels. Rosiclair bent gladly to receive the collar, and then taking the crown from the hands of the princess he placed it on her head.

'Lady, I am evermore your knight,' said he.

This tale and many others had come to the ears of the Knight of the Sun, and he longed to see his brother again, and to break a lance with him in good fellowship, but some time had yet to pass before they met, and then it fell out in this wise. After the combat in the lists in London, where Rosiclair had cut off the arms of the giant Candramarte, the giant's daughter had brought him by her wiles to the island in which lay her father's castle.

No sooner had he stepped on shore than the damsel pushed off, crying as she did so to her brothers and their knights to avenge the giant's wounds. In a moment all the little island was alive with men, whirling lances or swords or axes above their heads, and all pressing forward to the spot where Rosiclair awaited them. Luckily he had time to place himself with the sea at his back, so that he could not be attacked from behind, and, covering himself with his shield, stood ready.

Never was there such a dreadful fight, and Rosiclair seemed to have a hundred arms, and to be able to strike fifty ways at once. He hardly knew himself what he did, so great was the stress of battle, but hour by hour the ground slowly reddened round him, and there looked to his dimming eyes to be fewer men in front. But by this time his strength was fast failing him, and he felt he could not hold out much longer. A mighty blow from an axe made him reel, and well-nigh fall; another such, and he would be rolling on the sand among the dead men lying at his feet. Suddenly the upraised axe flew from the hand of the giant in front, and with a cry that echoed through the island he fell backwards on the shore.

Rosiclair was still too hard beset to turn and see from whom help had come, but he took fresh courage and his sword no longer hit so wildly as before. The other sword was even stronger and surer than his own, and soon the few men who were left alive ran off and took refuge within the gates of the castle.

Then the two knights looked at each other.

'Who are you, and whence do you come?' asked Rosiclair. 'I owe you my life this day.'

'I am called the Knight of the Sun,' replied the other; 'this shining star upon my breast has given me my name. And I come from wandering over the seas in a little boat that just holds me and my horse. I descried you from afar, and hastened to your help. Of a truth, it is the noblest fight that ever I saw.'

Now, when Rosiclair had seen the emblem of the sun on the new knight's breast he wondered if this might indeed be his brother. But being warned by his mother not to hold converse with strangers concerning private matters, he began to tell of the fight with Candramarte in the lists of London, when a cry from the sea caused them both to turn. On the prow of a boat stood the giant's daughter, pointing with her forefinger at the bodies which lay upon the shore.

'O cruel and bloody wolves,' she called, 'the ocean will give me the pity which I have been denied both by heaven and earth. And the god of storms will avenge me.' With that she jumped into the sea, but, instead of sinking, was held up by the waves. This the Knight of the Sun beheld, and, forgetting the evil she had done, jumped into his boat, and pushed off to her aid before Rosiclair had time to get in after him. However, the Knight of the Sun was never able either to reach the damsel or to return to his brother, for a furious wind sprang up, which drove him before it, in some direction that he did not know.

In his hurry to reach the side of Rosiclair, the Knight of the Sun had forgotten to place his oars in the bottom of the boat, but just left them loose in their holes, so that they had floated away; now he had no means of directing his course, but was forced to go wherever the waves took him. For many days he drifted past the shores of strange countries and saw from afar the gleam of white cities, but though he fain would have landed, he could not, but was bound to remain where his adventure carried him. At length, to the joy of his heart, the boat stopped of its own accord on the beach of a beautiful island, and the young man once more felt soft grass under his feet, and heard the sound of trickling streams. Close by was a forest, and from between the bushes peeped the heads of little goats and tiny deer, all gazing with wonder at the stranger. From the look of the place it was plain that seldom indeed did man come to disturb their lives, and the Knight of the Sun felt he must go further inland if he wished to meet with any adventures. So, breaking through the creepers which hung from tree to tree, he struggled on bravely, and at last the trees grew less thickly, and he came out upon a wide open space in front of a big castle.

This castle was quite different from any he had seen, either in Babylon or in the other countries he had visited. It seemed to be made of nothing but towers, and every tower had a steep pointed roof, so high that you would have thought it reached up to heaven itself. In the tower nearest him was a door of shining steel, and on top of a row of steps above it was a column, from which hung a horn of ivory edged with gold. Under the horn some words were cut deep into the column, and mounting the steps the knight read:

'This is the castle of the peerless Lindarasse,

whose door will never open save to him who blows the horn. Yet let him beware who seeks to blow it, for if the door *should* open he will find it is guarded by fierce and cruel porters, and his life will pay for his rash curiosity.'

The Knight of the Sun laughed out at the thought that any such threats could stop his going wherever he pleased, and, seizing the horn, blew so powerful a blast that the sound rang through the whole island. In an instant the gates of steel burst open, and between them stood a giant with an iron club in one hand, and in the other a chain which was fastened round the neck of a serpent. Now in all the world there was no serpent more horrible than this, for it did not wriggle along the ground as serpents generally do, but advanced erect, its head higher than a man seated on a horse, while it trailed besides a tail ten feet behind it. At the sight of the young man it lashed its tail so violently that the earth trembled as if with an earthquake, while its forky tongue darted in and out with a deafening hissing noise.

The few knights who had dared to blow the horn had been so frightened at this terrible creature that they had stood as if frozen, and thus the giant killed them with his club without any trouble. He, of course, expected this knight to behave like the rest, but to his surprise the young man remained quietly where he was. Then the giant dropped the chain and the snake began to mount the steps, opening its mouth wide enough to swallow a man and showing its long and yellow fangs. The Knight of the Sun swung his sword in the air and let it fall on the serpent's neck with a force that seemed as if it must have severed its head from its body; but to his amazement the weapon bounded back as if it had been made of wood, though the snake was for the moment half stunned and was unable to throw itself on its prey. However, in another moment it had reared itself high and was preparing to fling itself forward, when the knight leaped behind the column and from its shelter struck again at the serpent's head. This time the horrible creature sank to the ground, though the sword glanced off harmlessly without penetrating its skin; but it became more angry than before, and glided rapidly towards the column, hoping to seize his enemy in his gaping jaws. The giant meanwhile stood planted, club in hand, at the bottom of the steps, ready to receive the young man when the serpent should have done with him.

It was not long before this happened. The Knight of the Sun was so intent watching the movements of the head of his horrible foe, that he forgot everything else till a violent blow from the serpent's tail cast him to the ground and sent him rolling down the steps to the place where the giant stood. Before he could raise himself, the iron staff had split his helmet in pieces, and, as it seemed, his skull with it. Luckily for him, the giant felt sure he must be dead, and thus the knight was enabled to lie still for some minutes till his senses and his strength came back to him, and, springing to his feet, he snatched his sword from its sheath and sent half of the giant's body flying one way and half the other. But before he was able to rejoice at having slain one foe the serpent was upon him for a second time. The knight had proved that the sword was useless against it, so seizing the club of the dead giant he struck such a blow that its head fell in pieces.

Then he took the ivory horn, and entered the door of the first tower. As soon as the Knight of the Sun reached the second tower, he found it was shut by a door of steel, just as the first had been. He sounded a blast on his horn, and the door flew open with a grating and horrible noise, which might have filled the heart of the bravest with terror, and another giant stepped forth, no less horrible to look upon than his brother, with a club in one hand and a huge chained lion in the other. The great beast was larger than any bull that ever was seen, and each of its nails was as long as the foot of a man. Directly its chain was loosed, the lion reared itself up and sprang upon the knight, who awaited it as calmly as if it had been only a sheep. But after the fight with the serpent the attack of the lion seemed quite easy to parry, and, without pausing till they came together, the young man turned nimbly aside and felled him to the earth with the iron staff. After that he turned to meet the giant.

This time the battle was soon over, for the giant, like many very big people, was heavy and clumsy, and the Knight of the Sun stepped past his dead body to the third gate, which flew open at the blast of his horn. Behind it stood a fresh giant taller than the last, and all covered with thick wiry hair, that looked as if it would resist the keenest sword-blade which had ever been forged in Damascus. The young knight felt much more afraid of him than of the two tigers which he held on a chain, and which showed their teeth and snarled wickedly. But before long the knight had stretched them both on the ground, and summoned all his strength for the struggle with the giant.

This was much harder than any he had fought yet. The wiry hair turned the edge of his sword, and he felt he might almost as well try to cut through a fence of iron. Besides, in spite of his great height, this giant was much quicker of eye and of hand than the last, and several times the young champion was brought to his knees, though he rose again before his enemy could deal him a second blow. At length the Knight of the Sun noticed a place on the giant's neck where the hair seemed less thick than on the rest of his body, and, dropping his sword, he seized his dagger and drove it home.

Thus, step by step, fighting giants and beasts every inch of the way, the Knight of the Sun at last reached the hall of the castle, where the emperor Trebatius sat by the side of the fair Lindarasse. The spells she had woven round him were so strong, that for years he had not only never been outside the castle walls, but had ceased to wish to see the world again. But, powerful though Lindarasse might be, the Knight of the Sun did not fear to meet her, as before he had left Babylon the wise Lyrgander had given him a ring, which preserved him from all enchantments.

At the entrance of the young man the fair Lindarasse looked up; she knew who he was and why he had come.

'What is the matter, Wonder of the World?' asked the emperor Trebatius, raising his head from her lap, where it had been resting.

'I am a dead woman, my good lord,' answered she, 'unless you will slay me that knight who has forced his way into my castle.'

These words filled the emperor with fury, and the spirit awoke within him from its long sleep.

'I will teach him manners,' he said grimly, and stalked proudly to the gallery where his arms had hung for many a day.

Meanwhile the fair Lindarasse, who, in spite of her haughty bearing, bore a sinking heart, tried both by threats and soft words to persuade the Knight of the Sun to leave the castle.

'Not till the emperor goes with me!' he answered steadily. 'You took him from his wife, and if you will not give him back to her I will take him.'

And Lindarasse ground her teeth, and held her peace for a few moments. Then she broke into tears and sobs, thinking to move him by these means; but this method fared no better than the other.

Thus were they standing when the emperor entered the hall, armed *cap-à-pie*.

Now the knight knew that Trebatius's skill in fight had grown rusty from want of use, and that as long as he remained inside the castle the spells which the fair Lindarasse had woven round him would weaken his arm and confuse his head. So the youth refrained from striking, and with his shield and sword defended himself the while from the blows which the emperor dealt in all directions—for his hand no longer followed his eye. And all the while the Knight of the Sun stepped gently backwards, drawing Trebatius with him till, after twenty years, the emperor stood outside the walls, and the enchantment fell from him like a cloak. Then with a rush the remembrance of his wife, the princess Briane, came back to him, and in that very moment, though he knew it not, the fair Lindarasse fell dead in the place where he had left her. For, evil as she was, she had loved him truly, and felt that he had gone from her for ever.

So Trebatius was set free by his son, and became a man once more. And the two journeyed back towards Hungary, to the monastery where the princess Briane still lived. But on the road an adventure claimed the Knight of the Sun, so that the emperor alone stood before his wife, whose heart was almost broken with joy at the sight of him.

As for their two sons, the Knight of the Sun and his brother Rosiclair, who was also known as the Knight of Love, no such deeds had been wrought as were done by them since the days of Lancelot and the Round Table.

Made in the USA
San Bernardino, CA
29 June 2019